Tommy's Last Gift

By
Keith J McIntosh

Paperback: 978-1-7381273-1-3

Hardcover: 978-1-7381273-3-7

Ebook: 978-1-7381273-2-0

Book Cover by Robert Belland

1st edition 2024

FOREWORD.

For those few, incredible people who are actually following these *forewords* and *to my readers* sections may recall in Oberon's Calling I mentioned the next book was going to be a cosmic horror novel. Well, obviously that didn't happen. I have the book all plotted out and ready to go, but then a song got stuck in my head. From that song, came an idea that grew into a story and it kept growing inside my head until I had to write this book just to clear my mind.

Sorry.

At the end, this story has become very special to me. Like my other books, I put a lot of myself into the main characters, but more than that, this book is also set in rural Manitoba. Around an area that is very special to me as I consider it to be my second home. My wife grew up in that area, and most of her family is still there. It's a quiet, unassuming place, but it is blessed with a serene beauty that calms the soul. I pray I did that place, and those wonderful people, justice with this humble story.

Also, be sure to connect with me on social media. I'd love to hear from you.

ACKNOWLEDGEMENTS

I would like to express my deepest thanks to my wife for her continued support in this endeavor. She has unwittingly become my chief editor, and sacrifices a lot of her time to ensure I put out a good product. She is slowly making me a better writer.

As with my other books, I'd like to thank Robert Belland for not only his incredible books covers, but also for his advice and friendship over the years.

A big thanks goes out to my first fan, who has been promoted to Beta Reader, Kathy Carter. I am grateful for her honesty and her support. If she's excited about a project, I know I'm on the right track.

Lastly, I would like to thank my Manitoba family. They unabashedly took a quiet, city kid and adopted him into their family. I would like this humble story to be a thank you for all the wonderful memories they have given me.

This is dedicated to all my family in my second home.

To the Fouillards, the Wottons, the Cadieuxs, the Talbots, and the Souchuks.

PROLOGUE

Tommy

Prison wasn't so bad. It was mostly the routine that bothered the new guys. The early mornings were the hardest. The hour-long wait staring at the closed cell door while they prepared breakfast was unbearable. It was usually disappointing, but it came with fresh grapefruit sections.

After that, the scheduled work crews went off to their morning shifts doing their various jobs. Tommy was fortunate enough to get on with the custodial staff. He spent his mornings quietly cleaning bathrooms and scrubbing floors. He didn't mind the work. His meager pay went into his commissary account, which he could use to purchase *luxury* items for his cell, or maybe a tasty treat to eat alone in his bed.

In the afternoons, most inmates went back to work for the extra scratch but Tommy used the afternoons for *personal development courses*. He had a group therapy session he attended for an hour with a bunch of other violent offenders, and then he sat for an hour in a desk that was too small for his frame and tried to pay attention during his accounting class. Three times a week he met with a therapist for a forty-five-minute session that cut into the hour-long *free time* he had in his cell before dinner was served. The evening was his block's scheduled outside time, assuming the weather was nice enough. Tommy avoided people in the yard. He was friendly enough to the other inmates, but he wasn't looking for friends. He just wanted to do his time and get out.

He was six months into his seven-year sentence.

Tommy Brooks didn't mind the routine. It was the isolation that made him want to claw at his skin.

While Tommy was in Stony Mountain Institution, working on personal development and paying his supposed debt to society, the outside world spun out of control. Spinning out of *his* control, which seemed worse somehow. Tommy would never admit to being the glue that held shit together in any situation. His talents lay more in the breaking side of things, but at least he was there. At least he could help when needed. In here, he was a non-entity. He existed, but he couldn't affect anything beyond the concrete walls and barbed wire fences.

Like a ghost.

His therapist said the isolation from the outside world would be hard for him. She said he had a *classic Guardian Personality*, whatever that meant. As much as Tommy loved to have his whole life's experience summed up into a cute three-word term, he couldn't deny that he always thought of himself as somebody's guardian.

At first, it was his little brother, it was natural to slide into that role. Comfortable even. Then Rebecca Lemoine came into his life, and Tommy couldn't think of a better life than being by her side. Protecting her. Not that she needed it, at the time. She was fierce, confident.

That was before Clive Adler got to her though.

Nobody blamed Tommy for what he did to that son-of-a-bitch, but nobody, not even Tommy, could deny what he had done. He pleaded no contest to the manslaughter gift the Crown was offering and threw himself on the mercy of the court, which amounted to seven years in a medium security prison. He probably would have gotten a lighter sentence, being a first-time offender, but the judge saw the crime scene photos. He saw with his own eyes what Tommy did to that asshole with his bare hands.

It was pretty damning stuff.

Now, Becky was out there somewhere in the world languishing, and there was nothing he could do about it. Hell, he didn't even know what he could do to ease her demons even if he was on the outside, but he would be with her. He could hold her, and wipe away the tears when they came. He loved Becky with all his heart, and nothing Clive Adler did could ever change that. If he was on the outside, he could show Becky that.

But he wasn't.

He was stuck here for the foreseeable future. It was enough to make Tommy want to punch the walls until his knuckles bled. Instead, he waited on his bed patiently for the guard to come for him. Normally, he would be in the yard, probably talking shit with some of the other inmates he was friendly with, but today was special.

Today was visiting day.

"Okay, my lucky ones." The guard's voice exploded down the hall. Tommy looked to the wrist-watch on the side of the steel sink. *Right on time.* The staff at Stony Mountain prided themselves on keeping to their schedules. "Thank you for your patience," he said with light-hearted sarcasm. "Your time has arrived. All your family members, loved ones, and friends are filing into the visiting room where they eagerly await your arrival. Please do not fuck with their expectations of a happy reunion by breaking the rules or pissing me off in any way. Those of you on my block who are scheduled to, may exit their cells and be checked off my list. Those who are not visiting today will remain in their cells until the Lucky Ones have filed out."

Tommy rose off his bed and walked out of his cell when the block's cell doors opened. A bookish-looking guard with a clipboard walked down the row, checking the awaiting inmate's numbers against the list clipped to his board. There were about a dozen of them standing outside their cells waiting to be checked off. Nobody caused a problem, or even made a sound. Visits from loved ones were special times, and nobody wanted to fuck with that. Messing up a guy's visit could result in dire consequences later on. When the bookish guard finished, he walked back to the head of the line where the Block Boss stood like a valiant king and nodded to him once.

"Alright, ladies, you know the drill. Single file to the visiting room, no pushing or any bullshit like that, and have a wonderful visit." The large, greying guard at the head of the line who directed them even sounded like he meant it.

Tommy and the other *Lucky Ones* followed the bookish guard obediently as he led them toward the exit out of the cell block. Each inmate passed by the large, imposing guard who personally wished each inmate a good visit. Tommy was the only inmate the Block Boss didn't have to look down on in order to meet his eyes. Tommy grinned fractionally and nodded towards the man as he slowly walked by.

"Have a good visit," The Boss said softly.

He came from cattle farmers. Well, maybe that wasn't exactly true. His little brother, Emmett, he came from cattle farmers. Tommy still remembered the time before the farm. He was young, before the age when memories started to form solidly inside the mind. Their father was at the height of his fighting career when Emmett came into the picture. Tommy still remembered the large house they had in Scarborough, a suburb of Toronto. He could still recall the faint funk of the gym his father trained at. His father would take Tommy there on some occasions to watch him train for his next fight.

Then one day, it all ended.

Years later, Tommy learned of the assault charge and how it changed everything in his father's life. The contracts stopped coming in, but the bills didn't. Decisions had to be made, and that was when his father walked away from the fighting game forever. He was never the same after.

Emmett didn't know about any of that. He only knew the life they had on that small farm. Emmett only knew that money was tight, chores had to be done, and their father had the tendency to be an angry drunk.

Tommy had plans to change all that. His father, as dejected with the fighting game as he was, still trained Tommy and Emmett. He still made sure the Brooks boys could look after themselves. With Emmett's condition, school was difficult and some of the other kids just wanted to make it more difficult for him.

You are Emmett's shield, son, his father had said to him after taking him aside one day. *He needs you.*

It took a few scraps, but the nice thing about small towns is that word travels fast. It didn't take long for the other kids at their school to learn that Emmett Brooks was officially off-limits.

He had his life all mapped out. He would get into MMA fighting, like his father before him. He had talent. Tommy knew that. He would earn enough for Emmett to go to a good university, maybe even the University of Toronto. He was good enough. Emmett was the smartest person Tommy had ever known. His condition kept it from everyone, but Tommy knew if he could just get Emmett out of St. Lazare and into a place where he wasn't hampered by his condition, there would be nothing Emmett couldn't do with his life.

After that, Tommy would etch out a life for himself and Becky with whatever fight he had left in him. He hoped it would be enough for them to live a quiet life together where they could raise their children in peace.

Then Clive Adler came into their lives.

The Lucky Ones were buzzed through two separate doors, and walked a series of long hallways before they were finally buzzed through the door that led into the visiting area. The visiting area itself was nicely decorated with warm colors and featured many pictures and posters that emphasized togetherness and the importance of family values. They shared the wall with some informational posters that helped visitors cope with the different aspects of having incarcerated loved ones. The space had a dozen or so cream-colored steel tables that were bolted to the floor. Each table had four rounded seats welded into place around it.

The other inmates ahead of him immediately started filtering themselves towards their respective tables. Tommy saw Emmett immediately as he entered the space.

He's getting big, Tommy thought to himself as he witnessed his younger brother rise off his seat and rush towards him. The two brothers crossed the space between them and met with a fierce embrace.

"Hey little bro," Tommy said warmly into his brother's ear because his hands were currently occupied. Emmett responded by whistling quietly into his ear.

Emmett was born without vocal chords but that never stopped him from developing a plethora of little sounds to try and communicate. It was amazing what he could convey with only whistles and clicks. The other kids, when Tommy wasn't around, would call him R-two. After R-two-D-two, the little droid from the Star Wars franchise that communicated in a similar manner. Emmett hated that name, but he lived with it.

He had to.

Tommy let the embrace come to its natural conclusion, and when it did, he gently pushed his brother away to free up his hands to really talk.

You look good. Bigger. Are you finally gaining weight? Tommy quietly signed while smiling. He then reached out and gave Emmett's biceps and shoulders a quick squeeze.

Emmett could hear just fine, but over the years, sign language just became their special way of communicating that no one else was privy to. Their secret language.

A little, Emmett shyly grinned and signed quickly.

Are you still training?

To that, Emmett first motioned towards their tables and the pair shuffled to their seats before continuing. Tommy couldn't help but notice the large manilla envelope in the center of the table when he took his seat.

When I can, Emmett started to sign, and by the look on his face, Tommy figured there was more coming. *Dad won't train me anymore. He said he doesn't want another Brooks going to prison.* Emmett raised his eyebrow at him.

Tommy just sighed deeply.

I'm sorry about that. Tommy signed slowly, using the soft, gentle motions to try and convey his remorsefulness. Emmett was having none of it, he just stared Tommy down until he was finished.

I had to quit Karate too.

What?! Tommy switched to a sharper motion to convey his surprise. *Why*?

Emmett had been taking Karate for the last five years. Much to the amusement of their father, but it was the only thing Emmett really took an interest in. Emmett didn't care for most sports. He confessed once to Tommy that his condition made him feel like he was always the weakest link in the team. With his inability to speak, he was isolated even though he was on a team.

In the beginning, it had been Tommy who was tasked with driving Emmett two towns over to Russell for the lessons. It was a forty-minute drive. Tommy would usually spend the hour Emmett was in his class at the lounge at The Russell Inn. That's where he met Becky.

Garry said I made some of the parents uncomfortable. Emmett stopped to make the air quotes in front of him before he signed the last word. *He said I should take a break for a year or so to let things blow over.*

Tommy could only squeeze his fist together on the table as his brother signed.

Makes sense, he thought to himself with disdain. *They don't want the little brother of a convicted killer teaching their precious little babies Karate.*

Tommy forced himself to take a breath, his therapist warned him about this. The guilt. The weight that came with knowing his actions had affected the people he loved in ways he couldn't even fathom as he was beating the life out of Clive Adler.

The feeling came with an added sting because Tommy knew that even if he was given the chance, with full knowledge of the repercussions of the act, he still would have killed Clive Adler. It felt predestined, as if Tommy were only playing his part in a cosmic drama. God knew when Clive Adler touched Becky in that way, his life was over. Tommy was just the instrument of that divine retribution.

I'm sorry about that too. Tommy signed slowly.

He wasn't a goddamn hero. His inability to see another way around the problem of Clive Adler was a character defect of his. His therapist showed him that. Some long dormant notion of protecting his loved ones had spurred him on, but he forgot about the consequences. This wasn't a movie. This was real life. He couldn't walk into a bar and beat a man to death in front of a whole crowd of people and expect to get away with it. Now, he was in here, cut off from the people he loved when they needed him the most. *That* was the real punishment.

Then there's this. Emmett signed sharply and tapped the manilla envelop.

Did you sign it?

Did I sign it?! Emmett signed using quick, jagged motions. *What the hell is it? Who the hell is Isabelle Lemoine?*

Tommy took a deep breath. *Here we go,* he thought to himself as he steeled himself for this next part.

My daughter. Tommy used slow, smooth motions to sign the impossible words.Emmett clicked his tongue three times as he swayed away from the table like the news hit him like a physical blow. He looked around the room with wild eyes, like he was searching for his next words on the walls.

Since when?! Emmett signed quickly which made it difficult to understand his hand motions. It was the sign language equivalent of slurring his words.

Since April twenty first. Tommy continued to sign slowly, trying desperately to bring the tone of the conversation down.

It was mid-summer. Isabelle would be just over four months old by now. It had taken him that long to get the paperwork together and get them sent away to his brother. *Did you tell Mom and Dad?*

You told me not to.

Did you tell Mom and Dad? Tommy signed again, giving his brother a hard look.

No. Tommy sighed deeply and eased his expression before his brother continued. *Nobody has seen Becky since you were sentenced. How is it nobody knows about this?*

She moved to Toronto to live with her aunt. Tommy signed and watched as his brother nodded thoughtfully. He understood. *She's going to live there until I get released. She doesn't want people to know.* There was a pause between the brothers and Tommy used the time to think of the last time he'd seen Becky.

In the courtroom, as the bailiff took him away from everyone he had known, he looked back and locked eyes with Becky. He saw the desperate way she was looking at him, like the world was taking away her last good thing.

She looked like she was breaking apart on the inside.

How do you know she's yours? Emmett signed after a moment. He was always good at math.

I know.

How do you know? Did Becky do one of those tests? To figure out if you're the father? Emmett signed sharply and in rapid succession.

Emmett, Tommy signed slowly as Emmett continued. *Please.*

Because it might not be your baby. Emmett then loudly tapped the envelope on the table with his finger. *This is for guardianship. This means I'm legally responsible for this Isabelle person, who may or may not even be yours. What if Becky comes around looking for child support? I can't afford that. Shit! I can barely afford to take care of myself. Where would I even get the money for something like that?* Tommy remained still and clenched his fists together while Emmett continued. *What we should do is sue the Adlers for this. If somebody has to pay for this, it should be-*

Wham!

Tommy's fists slammed the steel tabletop, the noise echoing through the room. All other conversations ended.

"Goddamnit Emmett!" Tommy's voice boomed a second later. In his periphery, Tommy could see the guard at the edges of the room take a single step forward.

"Hey!" a guard behind him barked. "Settle down, or you *will* be removed!"

"Sorry," Tommy said lightheartedly as he raised his hands in muted surrender. Tommy turned and addressed the room that had fallen silent after his outburst. "Sorry." Tommy switched gears and settled his heated gaze back onto his little brother. Tommy signed like he was cutting the air in front of him. *You will never say that again.*

But-, Emmett began but Tommy just halted his hands with a snap of his finger.

If you love me, Emmett, you will never question whether Isabelle is my daughter ever again. I say she is my daughter, so she is. That's all there is to it. Becky is going to be well taken care of at her aunt's place. You might not even hear from her. But if you do, Tommy paused and lowered his brow towards his brother. *I expect you to help her with whatever she needs, to the best of your ability.* To that, Emmett just huffed a bit and looked away. Tommy reached out and squeezed his hand in an effort to bring his brother back into the conversation. When Emmett looked back, Tommy gave him an empathetic look. *Look, I'm sorry about this. About all of it. This wasn't part of the plan. I fucked it all up. Everything.*

Why did you have to kill him?

You didn't see how he left Becky. After I saw her, looking like that, I knew he was going to die and I was going to be the one who did it. Look, that's not important. I did what I did. Now, I'm here. I need you to know that I'm sorry for leaving you on your own. This is a setback, for sure. But we can still make the plan work.

How? Emmett signed sharply, demanding an explanation. *You're a convicted felon now. You're fighting days are over.*

But yours are not.

I'll be twenty-five by the time you get out of here, Emmett signed with a disappointed look on his face. Tommy just shook his head.

No. I'm getting out early. When Tommy finished Emmett gave him a skeptical look. *Really. I signed up for group therapy, I'm taking some accounting courses, and I'm even seeing a therapist. Look, I'm going to be doing anything and everything I can to get myself released from this shithole early. Until then, I need to know the people I love are taken care of.* Tommy nodded towards the envelope. *All of them.*

Shouldn't Mom or Dad sign this?

No. Tommy shook his head and signed sharply. *They have enough to deal with. They don't need this.* Emmett clicked his tongue in protest.

I don't need this. I have enough problems being the mute brother of a murderer in a small town where there's only a handful of people I can talk to.

Tommy looked down at his shoes and breathed deeply a couple times before he looked to his brother again. *This is going over like a lead balloon,* Tommy thought to himself as he gave his brother a defeated look.

So, you won't sign it? He couldn't afford to beat around the bush anymore. He needed to know if Emmett was going to sign it or if he was going to have to think of something else to cover this particular loose end.

I never said that. Emmett signed quickly and gave him an exasperated expression. *I just...*Emmett paused, searching for the words. *I just don't think I'm the right guy for this sort of thing.* Tommy just smiled warmly.

I can't think of a better person.

I can think of at least three, and I'm not even trying. Emmett then let out a big sigh and crossed his arms. That was the signal he was done talking. Tommy signed nothing further. There was nothing else to say. Before a full minute had passed, Emmett huffed again and reached down and slid the envelope towards him. *Fine. Here.*

You'll sign it. Tommy motioned excitedly.

I signed it in the parking lot. I didn't drive four hours just to bust your balls.

Thank you, Tommy signed warmly and then pulled the envelope over to his side of the table. *This means a lot to me.*

With that business concluded Tommy was quick to steer the conversation to simpler topics. Mostly he just inquired about people they both knew back home. It was just gossip really. It felt natural to do and it took them away from the ugly business of the last year. It was nice to focus on something other than how he and Clive Adler had ruined everything.

When their time was up, a polite chime rang throughout the room that signaled to its occupants that their visit had come to an end. Tommy and Emmett both rose from their seats and moved in for a tight embrace. When they parted, Emmett was the first to sign.

I love you, brother.

I love you too, Tommy was quick to sign back before he fell in with the other inmates. On his way out of the room, Tommy looked back and saw that his brother was still standing in the same place. *He* is *getting bigger,* Tommy thought affectionately and then waved good-bye to his brother.

I love you, Emmett signed again before Tommy and the other inmates were hustled out of the room.

It would be the last time Tommy ever saw his brother alive.

CHAPTER 1

Emmett

Emmett awoke to the sound of the house phone ringing loudly in the kitchen.

It instantly put him in a bad mood.

He was disappointed to find that he had fallen asleep on the couch. He hoped that in his drunken stupor last night he had made it to the bedroom. Instead, hungover, he hissed as the ringing persisted and forced himself upright on the worn sofa. He reached out and quickly checked his phone.

No calls or texts.

That meant Meredith was on-duty this morning. Susie would have tried his cell first before calling the house.

Fuck!

Emmett rose from the tired sofa and tripped over King, his middle-aged German Shepherd, who just groaned loudly and shifted his position on the floor where he was sleeping. He took two hurried steps towards the kitchen before his weary eyes fell on the two urns inside the large china cabinet in the dining room.

It all started with you, brother, Emmett thought with a strange mixture of remorse and disdain as he walked up the two steps from the living room into the dining room.

His foot caught on the last step and Emmett pitched forward into the large dining room table where his family used to eat their dinners. But that was a long time ago. Now, the table just housed various items Emmett had yet to find a home for. His large frame crashed hard into the table, rattling everything on top of it.

Goddammit! Emmett cursed silently as he rebounded off the table and carried on towards the kitchen, furiously rubbing the spot on his thigh that struck the table.

He stumbled through the archway into the kitchen and ignored the peeling wallpaper as he passed. Emmett rubbed his face to steel himself before he reached down and pressed the green button on the Telex machine. It was a compact device that looked like a small laptop that allowed Emmett to talk on the phone.

"Hello," the sterile computerized male voice said over the speaker.

"Emmett?" He instantly recognized the voice and sighed. "It's Meredith down at Peaceful Hills. Listen, Emmett, I'm sorry for calling you so early." This was usually how Meredith started these calls. Emmett waited patiently for the rest. He looked out the east-facing window of the kitchen and saw the light blues of the early morning on the horizon. "It's your father. He's acting up again." Emmett didn't wait for the rest, he bent down and started typing on the keyboard.

"I'll be right there," the sterile voice repeated his words over the line.

"Oh, that's wonderful news, thank you. When you get here, there's a few things we're going to have to discuss." There was a slight pause before she dropped the hammer. "Again."

"I understand. I'm on my way." Emmett hit the disconnect button before Meredith had a chance to say anything else. He imagined she would have plenty to say once he got there.

Wham!

Emmett softly punched the top of the small table in front of the refrigerator where he ate his meals. The sound broke the house's calm and shook the tiny table, but thankfully it didn't break. Emmett had a bad habit of unintentionally breaking things in these moments.

Emmett took a breath to compose himself.

Well, I guess I better face the day and take whatever shit is going to be poured on me, Emmett thought bitterly. He moved to the window, looked over the empty yard, and planned his day. He briefly contemplated making himself a coffee. God knows he could use the caffeine to clear his head. Then he thought of his father and the poor staff at the nursing home and decided he better get over there as quickly as possible. *Not a great start.*

Emmett snapped his fingers twice and heard King quickly jump into action in the other room. Seconds later the big dog came bounding to his side, where he nuzzled up against Emmett's leg. He looked down at the dog his mother had brought home as a puppy a few years after Tommy died in prison.

"This place could use a little life," she had said at the time.

He reached down and scratched King behind the ear, just the way he liked him to, and patted him soundly on the dog's beefy shoulder.

Let's go, Emmett signed to the dog before he moved towards the front door of the small farm house.

He took his insulated denim coat off the hook on the wall that already had two other jackets on it. All the other hooks on the wall still had the coats and jackets that had collected there over the years. He suspected he wouldn't have to dig down too far before he found a coat that belonged to Tommy. He quickly slipped on his work boots without bothering with the laces and grabbed his Blue Jays hat from the shelf above the hooks before he exited the house into the crisp morning air. He didn't worry about locking the house up, people didn't drop by unexpectedly like they used to.

He and King hopped into Emmett's dated Chev pickup. King jumped into his usual seat on the passenger side where he circled the seat twice before he plopped himself down. Emmett fired up the engine and sprayed tiny rocks out the back-end as he accelerated down the lane towards the gravel road. The pickup fishtailed slightly after the turn onto the road as Emmett struggled to keep the vehicle in the center of it. He didn't even slow down at the stop sign at the intersection, just pulled on the wheel and let the truck explode onto the highway. The trip to Russell normally took forty minutes but Emmett had managed to shorten the time down to an even half hour by pushing past the speeding limit by about thirty kilometers. He's done this run a few times now. The police usually didn't watch the roads this early in the morning. If they did, he was banking it would be Calvin who was on-duty. He would recognize the truck, just like he would understand why Emmett might be speeding towards Russell at such an ungodly hour.

Emmett just prayed that the police weren't already at the nursing home.

He got to Russell in record time. The sleepy town was just starting to come to life as the farmers and long-haul truckers began to populate the lonely road in and out of the town. Emmett took the first turnoff into town and let the truck's speed bleed down to a more reasonable level. Luckily, Peaceful Hills was on the outskirts of town and Emmett was pulling into the parking lot a moment later.

King perked up when Emmett shut down the engine but he dashed the poor dog's hopes when he snapped his fingers twice and gestured back down towards the seat. King responded by quickly plopping his weight onto the seat and looking at him attentively.

Emmett left the truck and jogged towards the entrance into the home. Meredith was waiting anxiously on the other side of the door. When she caught sight of Emmett's frame, she promptly unlocked the front door and opened it for him.

"He's really out of sorts today, Emmett." Meredith looked at him with a stern face as she said the words. "Things have totally gotten out of hand. We've left him in his room, and he seems content with that, but there's something else." Meredith led the way towards his father's room as Emmett fished his tiny notepad and pen out of the breast pocket of his jacket. He was about to ask the head nurse what had happened this time to set his father off, but she spoke before he could get the words down. "He's got a pair of scissors with him, Emmett."

Emmett stopped in his tracks and madly scratched out what he had been writing and quickly started writing before Meredith could say anything else. Thankfully, the older woman patiently waited for him to finish. Emmett ripped the page out and showed her.

What!? Where did he get scissors?!!!

Meredith huffed a bit and her expression dropped to a look of guilt, like she was admitting to a mistake.

"He started causing a ruckus when we were prepping him for the morning. One of the orderlies was taking him into the bathroom to get him cleaned up, and your father just freaked out. He took the scissors off him and started threatening Dean with them." Emmett assumed Dean was the name of the orderly. He quickly started working on the pad again. Writing smaller to conserve space.

Is anybody hurt?

"No. Thank God." The stout, greying nurse looked at him with a mixture of concern and frustration that only a nurse of her years could pull off. "This is the third time this year, Emmett, and it's *only* March. I have to write this up Emmett," she said with some remorse. "He's dangerous. Not just to himself, but to others as well." Emmett was furiously working on his pad while she was speaking.

You don't have to write this up, Emmett wrote and he underlined the word *have* in hopes that Meredith would infer his meaning. Below that he wrote, *I'll take care of it.*

"Emmett, he has a weapon," Meredith said as if she was trying to reason with him. "We *should* be calling the cops. He *assaulted* someone." To that, Emmett furiously shook his head while scribbling his words down as quickly as he could.

No cops. I'll take care of it.

Emmett didn't even want to think about how the police would handle the situation, or rather, he didn't want to think of the situation his father would force upon the police as they tried to restrain him.

He couldn't blame the police. His father *was* dangerous. For a sixty-five-year-old, Carter Brooks stood slightly taller than six-feet tall and probably still weighed close to two hundred pounds. He was still an imposing figure.

Back when he was in his right mind, people regarded his father as a legend. In some small way, Emmett had to relent, that maybe he was. People still talked about the bar brawls his father had been in *back in the day* or the times he wiped the floor with some young roughneck who rubbed Carter Brooks the wrong way.

Nobody talked about the drinking though.

Nobody knew about the way his father's hands would shake in the mornings before he had his first cup of his *special* coffee. Emmett sometimes wondered how his father's many part-time fans would think of their hero if they knew about the regret his father carried around with him? How could they know? They only knew what they wanted to know about Carter Brooks. Emmett lived with the man his whole life; he knew the man's demons as well as he knew his face. He saw how the rot grew inside his father like a tumor. First, it was the assault charge that sidelined his fighting career, and then Tommy's conviction just sent him deeper into the bottle. Lastly, when the Brooks family was at its lowest point, the Lord took their last shining light.

But not all at once.

First, it was the diagnosis. His father didn't take that well at all. Neither did Emmett, if he was being honest. The following rounds of chemotherapy were hard to endure. It was hard watching her suffer like that and knowing that there was nothing he or his father could do. That didn't stop the Brooks boys from fussing over her during that time like she was a wounded angel. They took shifts and made sure that she had someone around to care for her. Even if that was the last thing she wanted them to do. Then she got sick, *really sick*, and the final damning prognosis came. By then, Grace Brooks was a shell of her former, beautiful self. When Emmett held her hand, he only felt the bones underneath her seemingly paper-thin skin. All the fight had been taken out of his mother. She didn't even fear the end. She was just glad the pain would be over.

As bad as her passing was for Emmett, his mother's death simply broke his father.

At first it had been little things. Small things that could be easily overlooked. After all, everybody loses their keys, or their glasses, and everyone forgets things sometimes. Then his father started to forget other things. He would often mistakenly call him Tommy, and he would frequently have to call the house to ask for directions to places he had been to numerous times before. Emmett started to get really concerned when his father started to forget how to sign, because as the story goes, it had been his father who taught Emmett and Tommy how to sign.

By the time Emmett could get his father into a doctor's office, the problem was pretty clear. Their physician told Emmett that chances were pretty good he had been declining for years, and it just went unnoticed. He said it was the stress of his mother's death that must have triggered the sudden decline. He was also quick to note his father's alcohol consumption over the years probably only exacerbated the problem. Medication was prescribed, schedules were made, and Emmett dug his heels in for the long haul. His father was the only family Emmett had left. He would make sure his father didn't face this alone.

It took Emmett two hard years, and three hospital visits for Emmett to finally accept he couldn't look after his father anymore. He couldn't provide him with the level of care he needed. He still had the farm to look after, and over the years the once proud operation was languishing noticeably. A terrible decision had to be made, and there was no one else around to make it.

It had to be Emmett.

He still remembered how his father wept and begged Emmett not to leave him in that home. Luckily, it didn't take his father long to forget he ever had a home, or was married, or had children. His father was still in there. Every now-and-then his true self would poke through the fog of his mind like a ray of sunlight piercing a dark cloud. Those times were getting farther, and farther in between. The rest of the time he was alone, confused, and afraid.

"They won't take me," his father's weak voice came as Emmett slowly approached the door from the side.

On the other side of the door, Emmett saw a young orderly nervously standing guard, just out of sight of the room's crazed occupant. Their eyes met and Emmett saw genuine fear in his eyes.

"I won't let them take me," his father said and Emmett focused on the door again. Emmett removed his coat and placed it on the floor by the wall. Then removed his ball cap and straightened his hair. His father always hated it when his boys looked disheveled.

Emmett stepped into the doorway.

"Oh! Who's this then?"

When he turned the corner, he spied the deep state of concentration his father seemed to be in. That all changed the moment Emmett's large frame came into view. Carter Brooks, lost and confused, fell back into old habits.

"You think I'm scared of you, *big boy*?" Emmett tried to look small as he held up his hands in front of him and slowly patted the air in front of him. "I've put bigger guys than you down in my time."

Dad? It's me, Emmett signed slowly. *You need to calm down.* Emmett's hopes were dashed the moment his father's expression twisted up in disdain.

"What the hell's wrong with you?" his father spat angrily and struggled out of the chair in the corner he had been sitting in. "You think this is some sort of dance contest?" His father moved out from behind the bed. That's when Emmett noticed the large pair of scissors that were clenched in his right hand.

Jesus Christ! Emmett cursed as he saw the weapon for the first time.

Those were not the scissors Emmett had envisioned when he first heard about the problem. Emmett had no idea why an orderly would need scissors like *that*. His father gripped them the same way he would grip a large knife. Luckily, there was no cutting edge to speak from but that was a small grace considering the menacing point that extended out from his father's clenched fist by at least six inches.

"This is *real*," his father growled angrily, but thankfully he held his ground by the bed's corner for the time being.

Emmett patted the air again, and tried to look as meek as possible. It was a stretch that a person his size would ever look meek, but it was worth a try. Emmett's eyes fell to an object on the floor and he quickly recognized the little orange pill by the foot of the bed. It stuck out on the ivory tile of the floor. After a quick search, Emmett soon found another pill. This one was white and smaller than its orange brother. He found it a few feet from the head of the bulky hospital bed.

Well, that's great, Emmett thought bitterly to himself as he assumed that was his father's medication from last night. The white one was his father's Alzheimer's medication, they helped with his mood swings, and the orange one was his father's anti-anxiety medication.

Emmett took a deep breath, and took a single step into the room.

"That's far enough, you motherfucker!" his father bellowed. "I'm warning you! You're *not* taking me! I don't care if I have to stick every last one of you!"

Aw, don't say that. Emmett just sighed.

Then he looked to his right, into his father's tiny bathroom. It was surprisingly spacious, probably to allow an orderly to help his father use the toilet and shower. Emmett immediately saw his reflection in the bathroom's tiny mirror.

Fuck sakes, Emmett hissed and shot an angry look back at Meredith. *It's goddamn amateur-hour around here.*

Emmett had warned the staff here, on many occasions, about his father and mirrors. It was simple. Emmett didn't know why it was so hard for people to understand the problem. His father doesn't recognize his own reflection. Well, he did, but he didn't see himself in that mirror. Carter Brooks saw his hated enemy in the mirror. Emmett couldn't explain it, he didn't know the hows or whys of it, but he had seen it enough with his own eyes to believe it. Before he had to relent and put his father into a nursing home, every mirror in his family's home was covered up with a blanket and secured in place with duct tape. Just in case his father felt adventurous and decided to see what was behind the curtains.

Emmett took another step forward, slowly and calmly, with his hands out in front of him. He wanted his father to see that he wasn't armed. He wasn't a threat to him. Emmett's heart broke slightly when his father's expression dropped to abject fear.

"Stay away!" he cried. "*Please*! Just leave me alone!"

Emmett was out of options. His father didn't recognize sign language, and he couldn't read anymore. Emmett had no way to reach him, save one. He had to act, because the alternative was for the police to get involved. He couldn't take that chance.

Emmett continued to step closer to his father.

"Why won't you just leave me *alone*," his father said with tears forming in his eyes.

Emmett readied himself for the next part, because when it happened, it was going to happen fast. He continued to move towards his father with his hands up and a sympathetic look on his face, like he was approaching a wounded child instead of an armed man. Emmett kept an eye on the tip of the scissors clenched in his father's hand and tried to imagine the line of attack. Emmett was taller than his father; he was a late bloomer. By the time his body was done growing, he was probably bigger than Tommy. With his hands up, Emmett was intentionally giving his father an opening, as if he was saying, *stab me here*. It was a gamble, but Emmett prayed a little bit of his father was still there.

Emmett suddenly darted in.

In an instant, he crossed the space between his father and himself. Emmett witnessed the flash of unbridled fear in his father's eyes. He didn't blame him, anything as large as him rushing towards you would be frightening. He was forcing his father's hand, he knew that. He knew if he miscalculated this move it might land him in the hospital. He was out of options, and it just seemed like what he had to do in that moment.

The tip of the scissors lunged forward, and Emmett dropped his left hand with his fingers splayed and caught his father's wrist. He held the wrist in a vice-like grip and watched as his father raised his left hand in an angry fist and Emmett did the only thing he could think of.

He rushed forward and wrapped his free hand around his father's bony shoulders. His father's fist weakly struck the back of Emmett's head. It stung a bit but that was the extent of it. Emmett just prayed that this was the end of it. His father struggled weakly in Emmett's embrace but there was no place for the withered man to go.

Then, as if a switch went off inside his father's mind, it changed.

"Tommy?" his father asked weakly as the scissors clattered to the floor. "Tommy!" His father returned the embrace in earnest. "Oh, Tommy, my boy." His father wept into Emmett's plaid work shirt. He didn't blame his father. After all, Emmett had to admit he did look a lot like his older brother. Their father always liked Tommy more anyway. Maybe it was better that he thought Emmett was his brother. Emmett held the shuttering frame of his father until he spoke next. "I'm scared, Tommy. I don't know where I am, and they won't let me leave," Carter Brooks, legend of St. Lazare, Manitoba, and the man who taught Emmett what it was to be a man, whined weakly into his shirt. "I want to go home, Tommy," his father wept, and a familiar piece of Emmett broke apart again on the inside.

Emmett used his foot and carefully slid the scissors across the floor and out the door of the room. He looked back in time to see them skidding to a halt in the hallway where Meredith quickly swooped in and snatched them off the ground. He then gently pivoted his father so he was looking away from the door and Emmett used his finger to spell out the word *pudding* for Meredith. He had to do it three times before the head nurse finally got the message and disappeared down the hall.

It took some doing, but Emmett finally wordlessly coerced his father to sit on the edge of the bed. His father's mood significantly improved when the pudding arrived. Emmett was thankful it was chocolate flavored; it would make things easier. Chocolate was his father's favorite flavor. When he wasn't looking, Emmett quickly scooped the tiny pills off the floor and used his thumb and forefinger to crush them into the pudding. He mixed the drugs into the pudding earnestly before he presented the tasty treat to his father.

"Oh!" His father looked at him with genuine surprise. "Thank you." He took the pudding from Emmett and looked at him with a big smile. "Well, that is just fine. Great, in fact." Emmett gave his father the plastic spoon Meredith had brought, but when his father held up his badly shaking hand to try and grasp it, Emmett decided it would just be easier if he fed the pudding to his father himself. He had already come this far; a little more wouldn't matter. "Thank you," his father said after the first spoonful went down, and every spoonful after that. Like clockwork.

Emmett slowly fed his father the pudding laden with his medication, and when it was done Emmett turned on the radio to an oldies station he knew his father liked and sat with him while the drugs took effect. When his father was calm, Emmett silently moved into the bathroom and tacked the small towel over the mirror with the thumbtacks that were left on the sink's rim. The sight of those tacks lying loosely on the sink's rim infuriated Emmett more. When he was done, his father was still and quietly listening to music so Emmett moved into the hall. Meredith was patiently waiting for him.

"It's amazing how you reach him, Emmett," Meredith said with an affable grin. Emmett just gave her an angry look and held up a stiff finger to her. He then reached down to retrieve his notepad from his coat pocket and began to furiously write.

You want to tell me why his pills were on the floor?

Meredith's grin fell away the instant she finished reading the note.

"I checked the logs from last night, Emmett. The nurse on-duty signed off on it, he took them." Emmett replied simply by underlining the words, *on the floor*, on his note and showed her again. "Yes, well...," she trailed off, defeated by the obvious facts to the contrary.

Emmett returned to his notepad.

You HAVE to crush up his pills into his food. He won't take them otherwise. You KNOW this.

"Yes. You're right," she quickly admitted. "There are instructions in his file to do just that. I don't know what to say, Emmett. It must have gotten overlooked. We have a few new people on staff," she said, like it explained everything. Emmett only huffed and went back to his pad.

And the mirror?!

"Dean admitted to that. He uncovered it because he was going to shave your father, and it's his habit to do that in front of a mirror. He doesn't usually work mornings. He was covering for one of the other girls." Emmett was already writing down on his notepad before she could finish what she was saying.

Quite the perfect storm of fuck-ups then, isn't it?!

He immediately regretted showing her the note.

"I don't think that kind of language is necessary, Emmett." She looked hurt, like she had expected better from him. "Do you?" She gave him a challenging look.

In one way or another, he had known Meredith for over twenty years. She was a friend to their family. Emmett took a deep breath and reminded himself of all the times she had been there for his family in the past.

You're right. I'm sorry. I'm just having a bad day.

Meredith gave him a sympathetic look after she finished reading the note, and reached out and gave his arm a gentle squeeze.

"I know, sweetie. We're all just trying to do our best here." Emmett looked at her suspiciously. "But Emmett, we have to be honest, we're not equipped to handle somebody as far gone as Carter is. I know it's hard to hear, but I think it's time you start thinking about putting him someplace that can care for him better." Emmett shook his head and went back to his notepad.

No. The closest one is in Brandon, and I can't afford that place long-term. And Winnipeg is too far away. Not to mention it was a mental institution. No, Winnipeg wasn't an option. At least,

Emmett prayed it wouldn't be an option. But after today, he wasn't so sure. *Are you still going to write this up?* Emmett showed Meredith the note with a guilty look, because he knew she probably *should* fill out an incident report over this.

"No," Meredith said with an air of finality. "If I did, I would have to write up Dean and whoever screwed up his medication last night as well. Maybe we can call this a learning experience about the importance of following the protocols in the files. This time," she warned gently. "But Emmett, a good portion of the people who work here are volunteers, they're not trained for the level of care your father requires." Emmett held up his finger to pause Meredith as he went to his notepad. He felt he had squeaked a win out of this encounter and he didn't want to spoil it.

Ok. Great. I'll go back in and get him cleaned up and ready for breakfast.

"That would be wonderful, thank you Emmett."

An hour later, Emmett walked out into the morning light and immediately noticed the R.C.M.P cruiser that was parked next to his truck. Emmett sighed and tried to keep an open mind. A moment later, the driver's door opened and Tommy's childhood friend Calvin Biggs stepped out in his full patrol gear. Bulletproof vest and all.

After Calvin finished university, he immediately applied for the Mounted Police, and being a university graduate, he was quickly accepted. He went on to work in British Columbia, which was lucky considering the higher-ups could have put him anywhere in Canada. Calvin did his time there, and when an opening for the Top Cop position in the small five-man station in Russell became available, which was close to his hometown, Calvin didn't hesitate.

"Imagine my surprise," Calvin started to say with gusto as soon as he exited his cruiser. "There I am, in my cruiser, enjoying a lovely cup of coffee and a donut." Emmett smirked at that. "Hey, it's a stereotype for a reason. Anyway, I'm just about to enjoy my end-of-shift treat when this ugly, shit-brown Chev blows past me doing one-hundred-and fifty-kilometers an hour. I ask you, Emmett, if you were me, what would you have done in that situation?" Calvin asked with a sly grin.

I would have finished my coffee, too. Emmett grinned when he finished signing. Luckily Calvin was smiling too.

"That's why I like you so much," Calvin said with some mirth in his voice and he stepped in front of his cruiser. "We think alike," Calvin said a moment before the two men embraced as only friends who had suffered through tragedy together could. After they released Calvin's expression changed to one of concern. "How's the old man?"

Don't ask and I won't have to tell you, Emmett signed like he had chains on his hands. He didn't want to tell his friend, because his father did technically assault someone this morning. He would avoid putting Calvin in a potentially awkward position like that if he could.

"That bad, huh?" he asked grimly. Calvin understood sign language perfectly. Tommy taught him a few phrases when they were kids, and after his death Calvin made a point of learning it. Though, he rarely signed himself.

Well, he's certainly not getting better, Emmett signed after a deep breath. *This disease only goes one way.*

"Well shit, Emmett," Calvin said softly. "I'm sorry to hear that. He was a good man. A lot of people liked him." Calvin let his words hang in the air between them for a moment before he perked up again. "On a brighter note, I was about to head over to the diner for some breakfast. You want to join me? My treat," Calvin said, sweetening the deal.

I appreciate that, but no. I have to go to Yorkton to pick up a belt for the Kubota. It died in the field a couple days ago. I have to get that thing fixed. I also have fences that need repairing. Emmett just shrugged.

"Farmer's life, eh?" Calvin was a third-generation farmer, and still helped his brother manage their family's farm in Churchbridge. He understood. "Well, don't feel bad, I have a crap load of paperwork to catch up on anyway. I'll talk to you later." Calvin smiled and wave his goodbyes before he turned and walked back to his cruiser. "And Emmett?" Calvin called back to him when Emmett reached the driver's door of his truck. "*Slow down,*" Calvin said in his stern cop-voice. "If my officers catch you going that fast, it's an automatic suspension, and there won't be anything I can do about that. So, slow down, and save us all the heartache." Emmett sighed and nodded his head.

You're right, I will. Thanks again.

.....

It didn't take Emmett long to get the belt onto the small Kubota tractor, and from there he hooked it up to the fencing trailer. It was just a small flat deck trailer that had about a dozen four-inch wooden posts, a couple spools of the stainless-steel double-twist barbed wire he liked to use, and a box of fasteners. The necessary tools were in the toolbox that was welded to the passenger fender. It would have been easier to just hook the trailer up to his truck, but there were a lot of patches on the dirt track into the east field that were wet, and he didn't want to get his truck stuck in the field again. Considering the day he was having, he wasn't about to take the chance.

He didn't have to do this today, it would easily be another month before his meager herd would be ready for the pasture, but it was easy work. Honestly, Emmett couldn't think of anything he'd rather do right now than sit in the quiet afternoon sun, drink a couple cold beers and pound some fence posts into the ground.

The Brooks farm was a giant square-shaped piece of land that was just over a kilometer and a half on all sides with the farm itself being nestled in the center. The main fence lines neatly sectioned the land into quarters. The eastern fence line was always a problem. In the winter, the fierce southern wind dumped snow at the base of the posts. Over the winter, the weight of the snow built up. Each year at least four posts had to be replaced on the back half of the seven-hundred-and-fifty-meter fence line. The front half is protected by a wind shield of tall bushes his father had the forethought to plant over a decade ago. At the time, his mother wanted him to create the shield using saskatoon bushes. That way, every summer they could harvest the sweet berries for pies. They were far too expensive though. Instead, his father planted the cheapest shrubbery he could find. Emmett didn't even remember what they were called, but they were hardy and stood up well against the high winds of the winter.

Emmett had been planning to finished the back half of the wind shield for years, but he never got around to it. Something more important always seemed to pop up.

Emmett had the tractor and the trailer parked on the dirt track that ran parallel to the fence line all the way to 164 W. In school, Emmett learned that all the gravel roads that travel north and south were numbered according to their distance from the *principal meridian*. Emmett didn't know where that was, but he knew that that gravel road to the east was one-hundred-and-sixty-four kilometers to the west of it.

Emmett twisted the post partway into the ground, then placed the large driver over top. Normally post drivers weighed about twenty pounds, but he had welded six five-pound weights onto this one. His father taught him how to weld, so that meant his welds were solid, but they weren't very attractive to look at. Farm tools had to work; they didn't have to look pretty. Emmett grabbed the handles at the side of the driver, and began to hammer the post into the ground.

It was only his second post, with three more to go. Winter had not been kind to his fence. Emmett was sweating, on his fourth beer, and starting to feel a buzz. The poor start to the day wasn't forgotten; he drove each post into the ground with all his frustration. Tommy's sudden death, his mother's illness, and of course, his father. He used all of it to pound those posts into the hard packed earth, hissing angrily with each stroke.

Emmett used to do this job with Tommy. Tommy made him hold the post while he swung the sledgehammer from the truck bed to drive it into the earth. Back then Emmett was smaller, and each strike made him fear his brother might miss and crush his hands. It never happened though. Tommy never missed.

Wham!

On hot days, his mother would bring them a giant thermos filled with ice-cold lemonade, and a plate of homemade cinnamon buns for them to snack on. Emmett loved those cinnamon buns. He tried to make them, but he could never get the recipe right.

Wham!

The look on his father's face from this morning, when he used a pair of scissors to attack him with lethal force.

WHAM!

Ping!

The sharp sound didn't escape Emmett's ears. It sounded like a pebble had hit the side of the tractor with some force. Emmett turned away from the driver and the post he was currently beating into the ground and looked back to the open field. He didn't know what he expected to see, but it was just the open field beyond the tractor. King furiously sniffed the ground in search of a mouse. He didn't eat mice, but he sure liked playing with them. Emmett suspected the dog was chasing a mouse. He was about to return to the post when King's body jerked unnaturally to the side with a sharp yelp.

King?

Emmett quickly snapped his fingers. King only turned towards him and staggered forward a step before he whined again and settled into the ground.

Emmett sprinted towards his dog.

Once he passed the tractor and trailer something bit him in the side of the leg. The sharp pain made Emmett stumble slightly but it didn't slow him down much. He dropped to King's side and put his hand on his dog's wet fur by his shoulder. His breath caught in his throat when his palm was slick with blood.

He's been shot!

Emmett didn't need any other information. He scooped King up into his arms and madly ran the five-hundred meters back to the farm where his truck was. He didn't bother with the tractor, it wouldn't get him there fast enough. The knot in his leg flared wildly with each step, and King whimpered in his arms the whole time.

No, Emmett screamed inside in his head, *not King.* Emmett forced all other thoughts out of his mind and just ran.

For the second time today, Emmett's truck fishtailed dangerously down the lane as the truck roared towards the road that would take him to the highway to Russell. *Hang on,* Emmett wanted to tell his dog. *You're a good boy, just hang on a little longer.* But he couldn't. So, Emmett wiped the tears from his eyes and angrily slapped the top of the truck's dash as the truck sped down the narrow highway.

Emmett broke his promise to Calvin.

Luckily no police were watching the highway between St-Lazare and Russell. Not that Emmett would have stopped.

Emmett burst through the doors of the Russell Veterinarian Clinic like someone had pushed him. Immediately he noticed the reception area was vacant. Desperate, Emmett stepped towards the large reception counter and started to loudly bang his foot against it.

Seconds later a voice came from the back area.

"Hey! Hey! What do you think you're doing-," Carol spoke fiercely from the back until she rounded the corner into the room. "Emmett?!" She then noticed the furry, bloodied shape in his arms and Emmett's tear-stained face. Things happened quickly after that. "David!" Carol shouted into the back before she rushed towards Emmett. "Bring him into the back!" she called to Emmett and rushed him through the doorway to the back care area. "What happened?!"

Emmett struggled with King in his arms but he managed to make his hand into the shape of a pistol and he showed it to Carol.

"What happened?" The vet appeared through another doorway and rushed towards the scene.

"Gunshot," Carol answered as she led Emmett into a small sterile-looking, operating room.

"Here! Put him on the table," the vet said and loudly called others into the room as he rushed to snap his medical gloves on. "I'm sorry, but you're going to have to wait outside."

Carol gently led Emmett out of the room. Before he left, Emmett looked back to King and witnessed his dog weakly lull his head to the side, as if he was searching for him. Then he quietly whimpered, and then Emmett was ushered out of the room and back into the waiting area.

Emmett waited anxiously for over an hour while King's blood dried on his clothes and hands. When he looked up and saw Carol's face, he knew.

"Emmett?" Carol began in a soft, remorseful voice. "We did everything we could." There was more that she was going to say but Emmett didn't want to hear it.

He just left before Carol could see the first tears seep down his cheeks.

He didn't worry about the bill. Whatever fees were involved would just be added to his account. He just wanted to leave. Emmett got into his truck and pushed every bit of air out of his lungs in an angry hiss that lasted several seconds and struck his steering wheel a number of times.

There was only one other property that Emmett could think of where the shot that killed King could have come from. He wasn't surprised by the revelation. Those fucking people have caused him so much pain over the years.

Adlers.

Emmett started his truck and glanced at the dash clock. It was just after seven. He knew where they would be. This time of year, most farmers were prepping their equipment and fields for the planting season. They would be in St-Lazare, having a few beers at the end of a long day and shooting some pool with friends. The Adlers were blessedly predictable.

Emmett backed his truck out of his parking stall and the engine roared as he angrily accelerated out of the parking lot.

He didn't speed this time. There was no reason to. Part of Emmett, a small part, prayed the Adlers wouldn't be at Maggie's bar. A much larger part of Emmett thought about when he first saw King. His mother had been carrying him around in a large cardboard box.

"This place could use a little life," his mother had said with a guilty smile. She knew he didn't want a dog to replace Tommy. Just like she knew that King would soon fill the void inside him that was left from Tommy's death.

My last good thing, Emmett kept telling himself as he sped toward St-Lazare. *They took the last good thing in my life.* Emmett gripped the steering wheel like he was trying to strangle it with hands that were still caked with his dog's blood.

His truck came to a skidding halt in the gravel parking lot of the Fort Ellice Motel. Everyone Emmett knew just called it Maggie's bar though, because that's what it was. He didn't think about any of that though as he stormed towards the front door and threw it open like he was trying to rip the heavy door right off its hinges.

Emmett turned at the reception area of the motel, that also doubled as an off-sales counter, and made a sharp right into the bar area. He saw the regulars at the VLTs by the door; they didn't even look up from the screens when he stormed into the bar.

"Emmett?" he heard Maggie's concerned voice sound off from behind the bar. "Are you alright?" He didn't even turn to look at her, he just walked up to where the Adlers sat.

The whole damned clan was in the bar tonight.

John Adler Sr, the patriarch of these shitbirds, sat in the corner with another old timer Emmett recognized but his name slipped his mind at the moment. Emmett spied Senior's cane leaning against his chair. Sitting in front of the pool table was John's first born, William Adler, though everyone knew him as Bill. Growing up, they called him Big Bill, because he easily towered over the other kids. He was two years older than Clive, who died by Tommy's hand in this very same bar over a decade ago. Big Bill was sitting at the table with his long-time friend, Chris Dupuis. Playing pool were the other two Adlers. Owen, who was Emmett's age, was leaning in to take as shot as Emmett approached. Owen was the only Adler who was married so far. He married his high school sweetheart, Lisa DeCorby right out of high school. He had two boys, Lucas and Josh. It was Owen who gave Emmett the nickname *R-Two* in junior high. Robert was the youngest of the Adler boys. He stood sheepishly in the corner waiting for his turn to shoot. He was the only one who noticed Emmett when he first walked in the door.

He walked right up to Bill's table and didn't waste a second making his presence known. Emmett grabbed the edge of their table with one hand and violently flung it to the side. Their drinks went flying through the air. The table landed with a crash on the neighboring table and toppled over the other side of it before it clattered loudly to the ground.

He had their attention now

"What the fuck!?" Chris yelped at the sudden chaos.

There were other cries from the pool table but Emmett didn't pay any attention to them. He leveled his stony glare solely on Bill. Since Senior's retirement, he was the man in charge of the Adler operations. He was responsible for what happened on their property. So, in Emmett's eyes, he was responsible. Period.

"Well, hello Emmett," Bill said with a certain amount of amusement in his tone. "Something I can help you with?" he asked in a calm demeanor that Emmett didn't appreciate one bit.

Emmett simply huffed heatedly and then moved over to the chalkboard next to the dartboard that was on the wall.

"What? You're not going to do some charades for us there, R-Two?" Owen said angrily as Emmett took the piece of chalk and began to write for them all to see.

You killed my dog.

There was a chorus of scoffs that sounded off around him but Emmett kept his eyes on Bill, who remained in his seat and crossed his large arms in front of him.

"I don't know what to tell you, Emmett. We were prepping equipment all morning and spent the afternoon in Brandon doing some shopping. Me and the boys here had a nice meal at Montana's, got back and finished up our work before we came here." At that point, Bill rose from his seat. Chris was right behind him. "So, you'll excuse me if I don't know what the *fuck* you're talking about." Unphased, Emmett angrily wiped his previous words away and started again.

Somebody at your place shot my dog! He's dead because of you.

"He already told you we weren't there!" Owen said loudly and took a step towards him with his pool cue held in both hands. Like a weapon.

"Owen!" Bill called to his younger brother with some annoyance. "Cool it." Bill turned back to Emmett and held out his hands. "I'm sorry to hear about your dog, Emmett. I don't know who did it, but it wasn't us."

Emmett used his fist to hammer the chalkboard, and promptly broke it into five pieces.

"Hey!" Maggie cried from behind the bar. "Take it outside!"

"Emmett," Bill, Chris, and Owen moved into a loose circle around him. "Why don't you fuck off before we all do something we're going to regret in the morning? We all have work to do tomorrow."

He's right, A voice inside him said, *you don't know for a fact what happened.* Emmett gave each of them a challenging look before he let out a long sigh. *Remember what dad always said, 'It's always better to walk away from trouble, when you can.'* Emmett felt a bitter sting when he remembered the same person who told him that, tried to stab him this morning.

Emmet used his hands to cut the air in a gesture that meant, *fine.* He turned and moved towards the exit. He promptly shoulder-checked Chris out of his path when he refused to move and started to walk away.

"You're just as bad as Tommy was for fu-," Owen started to say while chasing after him.

Emmett didn't allow him to finish.

He pivoted around in a flash. He reached up and wrapped his one hand around the front of Owen's mouth and strong-armed him all the way back to the wall. He pinned him there and used his other hand to vigorously point at the man. As if he was saying, *not another word.*

Owen Adler just looked at him with utter fear and confusion in his eyes.

"Let'em go!" a voice cried weakly from the side. Emmett turned just in time to see Robbie Adler rushing forward with his pool cue raised over his shoulder to strike.

Emmett raised up the hand that was pointed at Owen to block the attack like it was the simplest thing in the world. The pool cue struck his forearm close to the elbow and promptly snapped in two, sending the lower half of the cue flying across the bar room. Emmett released his hold on Owen and turned his attention towards the younger, and considerably smaller, Adler.

"Now Emmet," Bill cautioned quietly as the air in the room seemed to grow thicker. Emmett just smiled.

This is what he wanted after all.

Emmett turned and struck Owen across the face with a quick backhand.

Everything happened rather quickly after that.

When Calvin showed up in his cruiser, the other constables had Emmett cuffed and sitting cross-legged on the gravel in front of the steps that led up to the entrance. He gave Emmett a single heated glance before he ascended the steps and disappeared into the bar. He was inside for what seemed like a long time before he walked back out with a sort of defeated look on his face.

"I got him," Calvin said to the female officer watching over him.

"You got it, boss." Emmett heard her climb the steps behind him and enter the bar. Emmett didn't know what the other two constables were doing in there, but he was glad to have the time alone with his friend. Even if Emmett spent the first few seconds shamefully staring at the gravel in front of himself.

"Bad day?" Calvin asked with amused disappointment when Emmett finally did look up.

Emmett just shrugged.

"So, Maggie hit you with the beanbag round, did she?" Calvin was chuckling slightly when he asked.

It was the thing that actually brought the fight to an immediate conclusion. A shotgun blast in a confined space had a way of doing that. Thankfully, Maggie had been looking for the perfect shot the whole time he was fighting the Adlers, and Chris Dupuis. She waited until she had a clear shot, and she didn't hesitate when she found it. The non-lethal beanbag round struck Emmett in his chest, on the left side. The impact knocked Emmett clean off his feet and left him gasping for breath on the floor. That's where he stayed until the police arrived. Maggie profusely apologized as she held him at gunpoint on the floor. Maggie was a friend of his mother's, after all.

Emmett nodded.

"Serves you right," Calvin chuckled before he bent down and gently slapped his chest on the left side. He didn't hit the impact point exactly, but he didn't have to. Pain flared up his spine, and Emmett winced and hissed loudly. "Dumbass." Calvin lowered himself in front of Emmett and looked at him with a sympathetic expression that made Emmett look towards the ground again. "What are you doing, Emmett?" he asked cooly. "Like what the *actual* hell are you *doing*? You're thirty-years-old. You know better than this. You know what this is, Emmett? This is a felony. Five of them actually." He held up his hand with his fingers splayed. "Some poor asshole got hit in the back of the head with the pool cue you broke." Emmett sighed because he didn't technically break that pool cue. Robbie did. But he was in no position to argue. "Some of those guys are going to need stitches, Emmett. After we're done here the whole Adler clan is going to the hospital."

Calvin waited until Emmett was looking at him again before he continued.

"You're goddamn lucky nobody is pressing charges. You can bet your ass you're banned, though? Maggie is super-pissed with you. She doesn't want to see you again until you have the check for the damages in your hand. Even then, she'll probably have a few stern words for you. Judging by the state of that place, I'm thinking that's going to be a pretty hefty bill. Again, she's not pressing charges. We made a trade. She won't press charges, and I'll forget she just shot someone with a firearm in my jurisdiction."

Emmett looked to his friend and slightly twisted his body to bring his cuffed hands forward, hoping Calvin would pick up on the gesture. He was usually pretty sharp.

"Oh, *hell* no. You're staying in the cuffs until we get to the station. You're spending the night in the *tank*." Emmett sighed.

It wouldn't be the first time he slept in Russell's infamous drunk tank. A small section of the prison was reserved for people to sober up in. It usually stunk of piss and vomit. "Which brings me to my next point," Calvin said as he pulled the small flashlight from his belt. "Something John Senior brought to my attention actually." He looked at Emmett with an amused smile. "Are you injured, Emmett?"

Emmett just shrugged.

At this point in the evening, pain flared from several spots on his body. To Emmett, it seemed like a dumb question. Calvin turned the flashlight and pointed its beam towards Emmett's leg, the same one he had pulled the muscle in when he sprinted towards King's dying form. There was blood on his pant leg, but Emmett didn't think much of that. He had King's blood all over the front of him, it wasn't a stretch to think that some dropped onto his pant leg as well. Calvin moved in closer to inspect the area. Emmett watched with interest as Calvin probed his finger into a small hole he found.

Emmett suddenly winced in pain and hissed.

"Jesus Christ, Emmett!" Calvin exclaimed. "Have you been shot?!"

CHAPTER 2

Nicole Jones

Jones, she thought sitting on the old deck with the peeling paint on the boards, and looking out over the overgrown yard, *this just might be the dumbest idea you've had yet.*

She couldn't deny that it was impulsive. Hell, she used a week's worth of vacation time and spent her own money to get her ass out here, to the exact middle of nowhere. On paper, she knew this looked like a rash decision made by a flighty government worker who was out to prove a point. The type who was still naïve enough to still believe in happy endings. She couldn't help that.

Just like she couldn't help this feeling in her gut.

When she left the Toronto Metropolitan Police Department after twenty years, the few colleagues within the department she still considered friends told her it was a mistake.

"Ride it out," they said. "Once you have that pension in your pocket, then you can do whatever you want."

They didn't understand. She didn't blame them for that.

Everybody joins the force with aspirations of making a difference, of helping people. She wasn't alone in that regard. She was different because she never stopped wanting to help people, and the hard truth about being a police officer was that they didn't help people. Not really. That wasn't their job. Their job was to investigate the crime that happened, collect the appropriate evidence of that crime, hopefully find the person responsible, and bring them to justice. That's it. Nicole was a good cop, but after twenty years, that wasn't enough.

She joined the Ontario Ministry of Children because her years on the force had shown her that children were the most vulnerable, the ones most likely to slip through the cracks of the system. Nicole told herself she wanted to get to those kids before the police did. Too often kids just move from one system to the other. It was ultimately her job to make sure the kids in the family services system stayed out of the criminal justice system. The Ministry's official mission statement was, *To improve outcomes of children, youths, families, and individuals who need support, and advancing interests of women across Ontario.* Which was great, really, but Nicole had a much simpler mission statement. *Keep them safe, keep them off the streets, and get them out of the system if you can.*

That's why she was here, sitting in an uncomfortable lawn chair that creaked and groaned with every move she made, threatening to collapse under her weight. When it was obvious nobody was home, she moved the chair to a spot on the deck where she could watch any approaching vehicles. She had a good overall view of the entire yard.

She wasn't thrilled with what she saw.

After a twelve-hour drive across two provinces, Nicole had a lot of time to envision what kind of household was waiting for her in St-Lazare, Manitoba.

The hopeful side of her was thinking of a nice manicured space, with clean buildings and bright, new-looking farm equipment. Nicole wasn't a farmer, and had never set foot on a farm. She didn't know what to expect in that regard, but she knew what she wanted to see. The pessimistic side of her, the one all those years on the police force brought out in her, expected something similar to what she was looking at.

There was a large metal vehicle shed, that was big enough to house a full-size school bus within it, that stood out prominently on the corner of the yard by the lane. She could see several spots where rust stains ran down the side of it, like tears. Nicole, during her initial search of the yard, found it to be locked up tight. Through the crack in the door though, Nicole could see a large tractor parked inside.

Across from that, was a dusty-looking building with cracked white siding and old, patchy shingles covering the roof. There was a moldy window in the front of it that was really just for show, because it was impossible to see anything on the other side. The door was unlocked, and Nicole nudged it open for a quick look before she had to remind herself that she wasn't a cop anymore. She didn't have the right to search the premises. She stayed at the entrance of the opened door and was assaulted by a smell that she only hoped was related to farm work somehow.

It was like manure and rotting vegetation had a baby.

Nicole wrinkled her nose and peered inside. There was a small room with a large sliding door across from her that led into another part of the building. The room had two large freezers on the adjacent sides of the room that instantly made the hairs on the back of her neck stand on end. On the walls, Nicole spied several weird instruments, that again, she hoped had something to do with whatever kind of farming operation this was.

"Jesus Christ," she said quietly and backed away from the entrance and closed the door.

That was the first time Nicole Jones questioned her decision to seek this *Emmett Brooks* out. After that, Nicole resigned herself to quietly waiting on the neglected deck on the side of the house.

That didn't stop her from seeing other things she would consider *red flags.*

The grass, if you could even call it that, had been neglected for so long it looked like the lawn was slowly trying to retake the property.

At this time of year, the grass was still brown and pressed flat from the weight of the winter snow. She couldn't help but wonder what manner of creatures might be scurrying freely within the jungle of grass around this place. Nicole took a deep breath and tried not to think about it.

Just like she tried not to think about the trio of cars that were abandoned on the east side of the property, close to the metal vehicle shed. They too, were slowly being consumed by the grass and weeds of this place.

On that side of the property, there was also an ominous set of vehicle tracks that led into the narrow path that had been cut into the dense clutch of trees and led to only-God-knows-where.

Off in the distance somewhere, cows were mooing.

Nicole checked the time using her phone, and huffed a bit. It was ten o'clock. She had been waiting here in the chilly morning air, quietly watching the morning frost melt away, for two hours.

"Jesus, Nicole," she cursed herself aloud. "What the actual fuck are you doing out here?" She adjusted herself in the lawn chair again.

Quickly, a nagging voice inside her responded. *We can get one out!* It said excitedly, almost like a child would.

Sometimes, Nicole hated that voice.

Isabelle Lamoine wasn't a special case. If anything, her case was all too familiar. It started with her mother, Rebecca, applying, and being approved for social assistance. Just like that, Isabelle was *in the system.* Less than a year later a child protective order was issued after a noise complaint led to Toronto Metro to a small apartment where the mother had overdosed and was unresponsive on the floor with a toddler nearby. Isabelle was sent to stay with relatives until the mother cleaned up, which she did. According to the file. A few months later there was a restraining order issued, against who Nicole didn't know, but then there was a grace period of a couple years where it seemed like Miss Lamoine and her child were actually out of the system.

Nicole knew all this because when Rebecca died of cancer, Isabelle's file landed squarely on her desk.

In the beginning, it seemed simple. Rebecca had an aunt in the Toronto Metropolitan Area that was more than willing to care for the small girl. Cassidy Cadieux was an older lady, sure, Nicole wouldn't have considered her *elderly* though. A bad fall from a ladder and a broken hip had changed all that, almost overnight. Isabelle had only been in her care for two months when it happened.

For the second time, Nicole had to show up at the child's door to take her away from her home. It was hard, sure, but nobody said this job would be easier than being a cop. In fact, the exact opposite was mentioned to her on more than one occasion.

She got Isabelle set up with a nice foster family in the city that had four other kids in their care. It was a full house, but Nicole knew the people personally. They were good people. They would do the best they could.

Then Isabelle's Golden Ticket came in.

Nicole still didn't know who it was that sent the Guardianship papers to her office. The best she could do was to find out some bank officer found it when cleaning out a safe deposit box at the request of Rebecca's estate, and someone must have thought to mail it into the Ministry. From there, she didn't know what happened, but one day it ended up on her desk. Like it was a gift from God.

We can get her *out,* the voice continued to nag.

She'd seen cases like Isabelle's before. She knew what could happen, even under the best conditions in foster care. She still had a list of names of kids who had runaway from their foster homes and basically disappeared onto the streets of Toronto. Nicole had lived in Toronto her whole life, she loved the city, but she knew the disturbing ease in which the streets could grind a kid up and spit out a criminal, or a corpse.

She checked the time again, only five minutes had passed since she had last checked. Nicole let out a long breath and decided she would wait another half hour. From there, she didn't know. She supposed the only option would be to try again later on in the day, and then tomorrow morning, and so on. She could do that for a couple of days and then maybe she would check in with the local

R.C.M.P detachment and see if they could give any insights into the whereabouts of Emmett Brooks.

Twenty-two minutes later a truck pulled into the yard.

Nicole perked up the moment her ears picked up on the sounds of a vehicle coming down the gravel lane towards the property. The time she served with the police didn't allow her to travel unarmed. She didn't have a firearm, of course, but she had a hand-held taser that would put any human being on their ass, and she still carried her retractable steel baton from her police days on her person at all times. More than a few sets of teeth had been knocked out with that baton. The taser went into her left jacket pocket, and the baton was stuffed into the back pocket of her jeans. She wasn't taking any chances.

Soon enough, a dark brown truck pulled into the yard, leaving a dust trail behind it. The beat-up truck promptly slowed to a crawl when the driver noticed Nicole's rental vehicle parked to the side of the driveway. She lifted herself out of the chair and reached down to pick up the large leather satchel she carried with her before she gave the driver a curt wave.

It's about damned time, she thought to herself and prayed this was her guy.

The large figure behind the wheel parked the brown truck with the rusted fenders beside her SUV and regarded her through the window of the truck.

Then he got out.

Christ! Nicole thought to herself and instinctively her hand felt for the taser in her pocket. *This guy's a freaking giant.*

The truck visibly lifted up when the man's weight exited it. He wasn't fat, just large. The serious looking man stood easily over six-feet and had wide shoulders that were slouched forward. He turned and fixed his gaze squarely on her, Nicole could see by the bruises, cuts, and swelling on the man's face that he had recently been in a fight.

Worse yet, the front of his clothing was caked with dried blood.

Nicole kept her hands at her sides and forced herself to keep a neutral expression as she approached the bruised giant with the blood on his clothing.

"Mr. Brooks? Mr. *Emmett* Brooks?" she asked politely as she walked down the steps from the porch and stood in front of the door the man was approaching.

The man stopped in front of her and sighed deeply before he lazily lifted his massive arm, that looked bigger than Nicole's thigh, and pointed towards a placard that stood out prominently on the door.

No solicitors.

"You think I'm here for a donation?" she asked incredulously as she thought of the drive out here.

The big man literally looked down at Nicole's five-foot-six-inch frame and shrugged his massive shoulders once. He then took a moment to pat down the breast pockets of his jean jacket, as if he was looking for something, and his shoulders slumped even more when he didn't find it.

Then he used his hands to deftly sign, like he'd been doing it his whole life.

"Oh, shit," she exclaimed. "You're deaf."

Nicole then watched the big man frown slightly before he rolled his eyes at her, like he not only understood what she had said, but he was also disappointed by it. The expression on his face seemed to cause him some discomfort.

And, he can read lips apparently, she thought to herself with some shame, *smooth move Jones.*

She gave him an apologetic smile.

"I need to talk to you about something," she said, speaking slowly, and making an effort to enunciate each word. "Something important."

The large man just looked at her before he ran his large hand down the front of his face, like he was trying to wipe away the ugly look he was giving her. Then he checked his palm.

Probably to check to see if he's still bleeding, she thought cynically.

When he was done, he looked at her and slowly brought up his hands and tapped his right hand to his left wrist. Like he was tapping his wrist-watch, if he had been wearing one. He then shook his hands out in front of himself, and calmly shook his head, like he was disagreeing with something. He finished the display by tapping his wrist again and making a slow circle with his hand.

Is this guy blowing me off? Nicole thought to herself and couldn't help the expression that washed across her face when she finally understood the man's gestures. *Now's not a good time, come back later.*

Then his bulk suddenly shifted towards her.

"Whoa!" Nicole barked softly in her *cop-voice* and took a step back as her hand shot into her pocket.

The man immediately halted his motion and took a step back in surprise. For added measure, he threw up his hands in surrender as his eyes dropped down to her hand that was clearly holding onto something in her pocket.

"Easy there, big guy."

She leveled a hard look at him, and kept her hand in her pocket. It was probably best for her if he didn't know what she was clenching in her hand. A simple taser might not be sufficient deterrent for someone as big as this guy was.

The man looked at her, frowning again, and motioned to something behind her. Nicole then remembered that the door to this man's house was behind her. It was then Nicole's turn to slump her shoulders as she visibly relaxed her stance. The man in front of her then slowly raised his hands up in frustration, or maybe it was confusion, she didn't know for sure. One thing was clear, though. She had mistaken his intentions.

"Sorry," she said and promptly released her death grip on the taser, pulled her hand out of her pocket and showed it to him before she quickly stepped to the side. She watched his bulk move towards the door, but not before using his hand to dismiss her. Like he was shooing a child away. That was the last straw.

Nicole reached out and grabbed his arm.

The big man stopped in his tracks, even though if he wanted to, he could probably pull Nicole right off her feet if he chose to keep moving. She felt the muscles of his massive forearm tense up and come to life under her grasp. His whole frame shifted slowly as he looked back at her with a heated gaze that hinted towards a person that didn't like to be touched.

Nicole gave him a glare of her own before she spoke.

"Isabelle Lamoine," she said slowly and watched his expression change before she even finished saying the name. "You know the name?" It was clear he did. He turned back to her. Nicole had the big man's attention now. "If you're Emmett Brooks, then I need to talk to you, because Isabelle needs your help." She released her grip on his arm and leveled him with a hard look. "*Are* you Emmett Brooks?"

The big man nodded once and turned back to the door of the house, he opened it, and looked back to her as he held it open. With his free hand, he slowly gestured for her to enter.

Nicole's finely honed survival instincts flared up at the thought of entering this giant's house, alone. Nicole Jones was an athletic forty-five-year-old, she was a daughter of a military man, and she served her time on the unforgiving streets of Toronto. She knew how to take care of herself. She wasn't afraid, per se. She was just hyper-aware of the risk she might be taking.

Nicole thought of Isabelle, and walked into the man's home.

The small entranceway had a set of stairs that descended into a dark basement, and another few steps that led up into a small kitchen. Nicole immediately ascended the stairs into the kitchen and turned back to face the man once she was in the center of the room, so as to give her the most amount of room to move. As her host removed his jacket and cap at the entrance, Nicole scanned her surroundings.

Again, like the exterior, she wasn't thrilled with what she saw.

The countertop that lined the east wall, was cluttered with dirty dishes, empty food containers, and partially crushed beer cans. In the corner by the door was a pile of unopened mail and promotional flyers, and underneath that was a loose garbage bag that was half full with what she imagined was household waste.

Through the rounded archway that led into the dining and living rooms she saw a large china cabinet that was filled with *the good dishes.* Nicole smiled. Her mother had a similar cabinet that housed the dishes that were reserved for special meals. Sitting prominently on a shelf inside the cabinet were two metal containers that looked out of place.

Beyond that, in the living room she saw clothes strewn about the room, empty drink containers on the coffee table, and more dirty dishes.

Seemingly everywhere she looked she saw red flags.

This isn't going to work, a part of her said loudly inside her head, *look at this shithole.*

Nicole took a deep breath and forced herself to remember her mother's motto. *Don't look at the problems, dear. Look at the potential.* Her mother was the kind of person who would take one look at this Emmett Brooks person, and she would see right past the bruises, the scrapes, the blood stains, and she would instead comment on the sadness in the man's eyes. She would look at this mess and insist Emmett just needed a good reason to have a clean house. Her mother was an unrelenting optimist, it was one of the things that caused them friction in the past, but right now, she prayed her mother's worldview was right. This man held Isabelle's future in his hands, after all. Nicole just prayed that he didn't fuck it up.

Emmett Brooks finished hanging up his jacket and depositing his cap on the shelf by the door and stepped up into the kitchen. Nicole noted the man had to slightly shift his shoulders to fit through the entranceway. He gave himself a quick once-over before he looked to Nicole with a sheepish expression. He then quickly removed a soiled article of clothing from the nearest chair at the modest-looking table, and pulled it out for her to sit in. Emmett slowly motioned for her to wait a moment after she took her seat and disappeared through the archway into the dining room.

It was the first time she noticed the large man was limping.

Nicole could hear sounds of running water, and frantic movement coming from another part of the house. When he returned, Emmett was wearing a clean pair of jeans and a fresh shirt, he even washed the dried blood from his face and combed his dark hair.

He still looks like shit, Nicole thought to herself.

The man moved towards the refrigerator, which she noticed had a chalkboard affixed to the freezer door of the fridge. He reached up and retrieved a piece of chalk from a small container on the top and began to write.

I'm not deaf. I'm a mute.

Then he went on to simplify it even more, just in case Nicole didn't know what a mute was.

So, I hear just fine. I just can't speak.

"Okay," Nicole said, unsure what else she could say on the matter and watched as he reached up with his free hand and grabbed a blackboard eraser, like the kind teachers used decades ago. "That's good to know." Emmett wiped the previous message away and began to write again.

What's this about Isabelle? You mean Becky's daughter?

"Yes. I mean *Rebecca Lamoine's* daughter, Isabelle. Are you aware of her situation?" Nicole eyed him closely as Emmett Brooks looked at if he was lost in his own thoughts for a moment. She watched as he slowly turned his gaze into the dining room, where he seemed to be staring at something.

Then he went to the chalkboard.

I know she's my brother's kid.

What about Becky?

"I'm afraid she died, over a year ago. Cancer. I don't know much more than that. Isabelle's file landed on my desk shortly after that."

Nicole proceeded to tell him Isabelle's whole sad tale as she knew it. While she did, he made himself a cup of coffee from one of those fancy coffee makers that used *pods* instead of the paper filters her generation had used. He offered her a cup, she agreed. It was actually pretty good. She was impressed Brooks had managed to find a clean cup.

"So that's the long and short of it." She concluded and looked at the giant, letting him soak it in. The coffee mug looked small in his massive hands

What am I supposed to do about any of that? He wrote on his little blackboard.

Not exactly chomping at the bit, is he? Nicole thought cynically to herself as she reached down and unzipped the top of her satchel. She pulled out the document from the sleeve she meticulously filed away for safe keeping. She placed the guardianship paperwork onto the table, in clear view of the big man, and then tapped it with her fingers.

"This look familiar?" She could clearly see by the change in his expression, that he did.

That was a long time ago. A lot of things have changed for me.

"Oh, trust me," she started with a dry, cynical chuckle. "Things have *really* changed for her too." She tapped the guardianship papers again. "My point is she needs you." Nicole gave Brooks a hopeful look she wasn't proud of and watched him return to the board.

I can't. I'm not a parent.

She just frowned at him. Nicole Jones had *officially* had enough.

"You mind if I call you Emmett?" she asked politely. The large man simply nodded and motioned for her to continue. "Do you think I'm *fucking* stupid, Emmett?"

That got his attention. The question seemed to hit the man like it was a physical blow. He looked at her dumbly and raised his hands in surrender, as if he didn't know what the proper response to that question might be. She paid no attention to it.

"Do you think I don't see the dirty dishes and garbage all over your counter back there? You think all the clothes scattered haphazardly around this place just missed my attention? What about the garbage bag over there?" She quickly pointed to the trash bag slumped on the floor at the end of the counter. "Jesus Christ! The signs of how much you are *not* a parent are all around me." Nicole spread her arms and waved them about the room. "You think it slipped my notice that if you *were* a parent, maybe you would have followed up on this sooner." Nicole slammed her hand down on the guardianship papers with fury in her eyes. "Maybe you would have been there when Isabelle needed you, but you weren't, and now here we are."

Emmett moved towards the chalkboard, but Nicole halted him with a stiff finger.

"No! I didn't come all this way to hear your *reasons* or *excuses*." She said the words with disdain. "What's done is done. What I want to know Emmett, what I drove almost half a day to find out is, can you *be* a parent?" Nicole's fury held the large man in place, and she did not let up. "Because that's what she needs. Isabelle needs a good stable home. Someone who loves her and can provide for her, and if I'm being a hundred percent honest right now, that's not you. Not from what I've seen so far." Nicole let out a long breath and let her words sink in. "Nobody knows about this," she said quietly and softly tapped the papers on the table. Emmett looked at her quizzically. "I didn't file it, because if I did, then it would be in the system. You would be contacted by my people from my office, we would set up an initial interview to assess your viability to be Isabelle's *legal* guardian. It would all be very *official*." She smirked at him. "It's a process, a *long* process. There are ways to speed it up, though. That's why I'm here, Emmett." She took another breath and laid it all out for him. "Listen, right now, you have two choices ahead of you." Nicole held up a single digit. "One, you can take these papers," she said softly and slowly placed her finger on the guardianship papers. "And rip them up and throw them in that trash bag over there, and you'll never hear from me, or Isabelle ever again." Nicole paused and was pleased to see Emmett tilted his head for her to continue. "Or, we can sit down and come up with a plan. Keep in mind, though," Nicole cautioned gently. "You have to be completely committed to this, Emmett. A lot of things have to change around here for this to work, and I haven't even *seen* everything." Nicole began to check off the items on her fingers. "I'll need to see your financials for the last five years, which includes your tax returns, we'll need to do a credit check, as well as a full criminal records check. And Emmett," she dropped her brow towards him. "*That* needs to be spotless. So, I hope whatever caused those marks on your face isn't going to be a problem."

He looked at her like she caught him with his hand in the cookie jar, and slowly shook his head.

"Keep in mind, your biggest problem isn't convincing my colleagues you can do this. Your biggest problem is convincing *me*. Isabelle is in an *okay* place right now," Nicole said with some reluctance, but she felt she should put all her cards on the table. "She has a roof over her head, three square meals a day, and people who care for her. I'm not going to take that away from her if I don't think it's the best thing for her. So, you need to take a big step up for your brother's daughter if you want this to work," she challenged him and left it at that.

Emmett looked again into the dining room, and something held his gaze for a full breath before he finally moved towards the chalkboard. Maybe it was Nicole's imagination, but when he did, Emmett seemed taller.

What do I have to do?

It wasn't his words that sparked the hope inside of herself, they definitely helped, but it was the look of calm determination on Emmett's face that really sold Nicole Jones on the prospect that this just might work.

"Well," she said with an encouraging smile. "Why don't you give me a proper tour of the whole place, and I mean *everything*? Then, we can sit down and make a list."

CHAPTER 3

Brooke

Brooke Talbot backed out of her parent's driveway and onto Seventh Avenue of Binscarth, Manitoba. It was the last avenue in the town, and her parents' backyard was a stone's throw away from the highway.

Her father had converted the basement into a suite, exclusively for her to use. It even had a separate entrance into her space from the garage, for those days she didn't feel like talking about her day. She usually fell asleep listening to the sounds of the large tractor-trailer units plummeting down Highway 83. In the mornings, she was usually greeted with the sound of the train's horn blaring as it cruised passed the town's south end.

She paused before *her* stop sign. She didn't own it or anything, and in no way, shape, or form was she responsible for it, but it was still hers. In a way. She and this sign had been through a lot together. They were like friends.

When Brooke returned to her childhood home, the place she swore she'd never return to, she stood in front of that sign and cried for a long time.

Some days she screamed at it like she was a crazy-person. Other days she looked upon that simple stop sign like it was the only stable thing in her life. The only thing that wouldn't change.

So yeah, after almost a year of this, she kind of claimed it for herself.

Today, she gave her sign the smallest of nods before Brooke turned left. She approached the highway before she quickly turned onto it and accelerated towards Russell.

Today was the hardware store.

Brooke had a plethora of odd jobs she did around the area. She didn't need the money, not really. She was saving up for a place of her own, but right now she wasn't in any sort of hurry to leave her parent's house. As demeaning as it was to be a thirty-five-year-old and still living with her parents, she had to admit she enjoyed their company. It was nice to have someone to talk to if she wanted, and her father was always up for a game of cribbage.

She had a plan.

She planned to save up enough money to buy a house in town when one came up for sale, or maybe in Russell. She hadn't decided yet. The one nice thing about rural Manitoba is that house prices were incredibly cheap. She had no doubts she could find a nice two-bedroom house in the area for under a hundred thousand dollars. Compared to the housing market in Winnipeg, that was an insane bargain. It made it feasible for a person to own their own home. The prospect of owning her own home was very appealing to her, even if she didn't have anyone to share the space with. That was okay. She didn't need anyone else. She would never again put her dreams in the hands of another person. Those people will only let you down.

Her ex-husband taught her that.

She no longer blamed Graeme for what he did, or at least she didn't think she did. If she was being honest, she wouldn't trust herself if her ex-husband were to appear in front of her for whatever reason. She didn't have to worry about that happening, though. Her ex-husband has officially moved on to his new life. With his new wife, and his new baby boy. Graeme always wanted a boy. So, in a way, she was happy for him. Graeme Read was a good man and a good provider. He never hurt her, except for that one cold, devastating act. In every other way, he was the perfect husband.

When they were having troubles conceiving, he was the most empathetic person you could ever imagine. He went with her to every doctor's appointment, he held her hand at the fertility clinic, and he even cried the first time he gave her the hormone injection. It was the happiest moment of her life when she could finally tell him she was pregnant, only to have that feeling trumped by the utter horror she felt in the pit of her stomach when the cramping started in her second trimester. And then the bleeding started. Graeme met her in the Emergency Room just in time to hear the doctor shatter her world with a single word. *Miscarriage.*

"Don't worry, babe," Graeme whispered in her ear as he held her. "We can try again."

It was the light at the end of her dark tunnel. She could try again. *No problem. Just dust yourself off and get back on the horse. Easy-peasy.*

She went in for a simple procedure to remove the unviable fetus from her womb, but when she came out, a piece of her was missing. A very important piece. *Pre-cancerous cysts.* Brooke never even heard the term before, but apparently her uterus was full of them. *Luckily, we caught it in time,* they said to her, as if they were waiting for her to thank them for removing her womb.

The recovery from the hysterectomy was incredibly painful, but it was dwarfed by the soul-crushing feeling she felt when Graeme told her he wanted a divorce just a few months later. He had always wanted children. It was the one thing he always talked about when they were dating in high school. Brooke just never imagined that it was more important to him than she was, especially after ten years.

After all this time, she was mature enough to admit that whatever they had at the end of their relationship, it wasn't love. It was too *transactional* for that. Graeme had gone into business, after all. He always had a good mind for it. She didn't realize it at the time, maybe she was too caught up in her own aspirations, but at some point, their relationship started to devolve to unspoken obligations. Maybe that's what it had always been. Maybe they had just been using each other. She used him to get her out of Binscarth, and provide her with the kind of life she could brag about to the people who never left on the rare occasions she returned to this place, and she was to provide him with a child. She imagined in Graeme's cold, business-like brain, he believed she simply was in breach of contract, and any previous agreement they had was null and void.

It didn't matter now. It was over.

She still stalked him on Facebook now and then, though she tried not to anymore. She still had some of the same friends on the platform that Graeme did. She was following him through their accounts. Last year, one of their mutual friends liked a picture of Graeme and his new wife while they were on vacation in Mexico. It was before their son was born. Diane, that was the new wife's name, was too far along in her pregnancy for her to be traveling like she was. That's what Brooke thought anyway when she saw the picture.

It's over, she told herself and refocused on the road in front of her. Sometimes there were deer on the side of the road this early in the morning, threatening to bolt across the road at any moment. She needed to focus on the road, not the life that had slipped away years ago. *Today is the hardware store.*

It was ten minutes past noon, and the majority of the staff had either left for lunch at the local diner that was a few blocks away, or else they were quietly sitting in the break room eating with Dale. Who always ate the lunch his wife had prepared for him the night before. Brooke didn't know for certain, but she was pretty sure Dale was the oldest employee at the store. He had been working the service counter at Bale's Home Hardware since she was a child and came here with her father. He had been working at this store longer than anyone else, even the owners hadn't worked there as long as Dale.

Brooke lazily swept the area around the service counter, and generally tried to keep herself busy. She had only been at the store for six months, and she was still part-time. If she was lucky, she might get sixteen hours a week at the store. Today, she was covering for Rachel, who had a sick kid at home. Brooke didn't mind. She needed the hours, and the distraction. Plus, she was trying to convince Bruce to put her on full-time. Which would be amazing. Permanent full-time employment was a hard thing for a completely unskilled middle-aged woman to secure in a rural town.

Well, that's not totally true, Brooke thought cynically as she swept. *I do have my Bachelor of Arts in Interior Design. That's sure come in handy so far.*

Just then, through the large front windows of the store, Brooke noticed a brown truck pull into the parking lot. *Chestnut,* Brooke thought idly trying to put a name to the exact color. It was something she always enjoyed doing. *No, deeper than that. Chocolate maybe, leaning heavily towards a more Sepia tone.* Brooke smiled and decided whatever the actual color was, it wasn't a good color for a truck. It hid the rust around the fenders well, though.

Then the largest man she had ever seen stepped out of the cab.

"What the-?" she said dumbly as she watched his massive frame approach the front doors of the store.

He looked like an NFL linebacker that was dressed up to look like the Marlboro Man, like this giant had just left a photo shoot or something. It was pretty common to see a large man dressed in denim around town, but those men usually wore their weight around their middles. This guy wore his weight...well, everywhere else. When he entered through the front door, he almost had to turn sideways in order to fit through the door. He had shaggy, unkept brown hair that hung down his forehead. Brooke caught a glimpse of the man's light, focused eyes and chiseled features as he turned to retrieve a shopping cart from the line of parked carts to the side of the door.

Then the giant started down one of the aisles.

Brooke quickly flagged down the other part-time worker on shift, Tim, and waved him over.

"Hey," he said when he approached. Tim was fresh out of high school, and it slightly irked Brooke that he was her direct competition for the full-time position. "What's up?" he asked with a slack face and ran his hand through his blonde hair.

"Who's that guy?" Brooke asked and pointed towards the aisle the giant disappeared down.

"What guy?"

"The guy who just came in." Tim clearly wasn't aware of whom she was speaking. So, Brooke gestured for him to wait and soon enough, the giant of a man reappeared for a brief moment before disappearing down another aisle.

"Him?" The man was currently the only other person in the store, but Brooke nodded patiently anyway. "That's Emmett Brooks," he said with some amusement, like it was something she should have known already, and it pleased him to be able to enlighten her.

That's Emmett Brooks?! She didn't blame herself for not recognizing the boy from her past, because the last time she saw him he definitely didn't look like *that*.

"You know? R-Two," Tim said off-handedly and Brooke just cringed at the nickname.

"Gawd," Brooke exclaimed breathlessly. "Tell me they don't still call him that." Tim just looked at her with a surprised expression.

"No," he responded quietly. "Not to his face anyway. Look at him!" Tim chuckled. "Do you know him, or something?"

"I went to school with his brother." Tim's somber nod told her he was well aware of the grim story behind Tommy Brooks and Clive Adler. Everybody did. It'd been over ten years since those events, but small towns have long memories, and something like that isn't soon forgotten.

"Shit! People still talk about the shit that went down with his brother. That shit is fucking legendary around here." Brooke frowned slightly at Tim's youthful enthusiasm.

He doesn't know the truth of it, she told herself. *He only knows about what people still talk about.*

People Tim's age only knew about the gritty details of the fight that ended Clive Adler's life, and ruined Tommy's. Brooke had first-hand knowledge of the event that was burned into St-Lazare's history. Hell, she *knew* Rebecca Lamoine. Brooke had gone to bush parties with her and Tommy in high school.

"You hear about what went down at Maggie's a couple nights ago?" Tim asked suddenly, delighted to have more news he could divulge.

"No. What happened?"

"Big man over there," Tim started and pointed to the aisle Emmett had gone down. "Went into Maggie's and beat the shit out of the whole Adler clan." Tim chuckled heartily. "Man! I wished I could have seen that."

"Seriously?!" Brooke asked shocked by what she had heard. From her memory, Emmett was a sweet, quiet kid who always stayed in the background. "Why?"

"They shot his dog, or some shit like that. That's what I heard. Whatever it was, R-Two tore a strip off the Adler's. Sent most of them to the hospital too, that's what Jenny said. Emmett was so riled up, Maggie shot him with that shotgun she has behind the bar"

"What?!" Brooke couldn't help raising her voice a bit.

It was always rumored that Maggie kept a loaded shotgun behind the bar. It was supposed to be non-lethal somehow. Brooke didn't understand how something like a shotgun could be non-lethal but that was what people said. It was a rumor because she had never heard of it actually being used on anyone. Much less someone she knew.

"Yeah," Tim said with some amusement. "The Mounties showed up and everything. It was a real mess." Brooke suspected, by the way he was talking, that Tim also regretted not being there to see the action.

Then Emmett emerged from the aisle and made a bee-line for the service counter. Tim made a strange noise and suddenly scurried away. Brooke promptly put her broom aside and moved in behind the counter.

"Hi, Emmett," she said, trying to sound friendly. "How've you been?" she asked and watched with some disappointment as his expression changed.

Clearly, he didn't remember her.

Why would he? A familiar voice said inside her head. *You've gained thirty pounds, all of it in the wrong places, and you're a decade uglier.*

She kept the friendly smile on her face as he set the papers in his hand aside and reached into his breast pocket. Emmett pulled out a small notepad and a cheap-looking pen before he started to write.

Do I know you? It was written in the most beautiful cursive Brooke had ever seen.

"Brooke," she said swallowing her pride. "Brooke Talbot. I went to school with your brother." He still looked at her with some confusion in those sky-blue eyes. "We went to a few bush parties together."

Jesus, now you just sound sad, she thought bitterly but then Emmett's expression changed and he gave her a big knowing smile. He nodded like the lost memories of her came flooding back to him. Then he went back to his notepad.

While he wrote, Brooke looked over the marks on his face. He had definitely been in a fight recently. There were several spots where she could see the slight discoloration where some bruises had yet to heal completely. On his left cheek was a nasty abrasion that looked like it still might be a bit sore, as well as a small cut on his lower lip.

Yes! I remember you now. Wow. It's been a long time. How have you been?

Brooke looked at the pad for a long time, trying to summon the courage to answer the question. *I'm trying desperately to rebuild my shattered life after the man I loved and trusted for eleven years took my heart and broke it into a thousand pieces. That, and I'm struggling to see where I even fit in this life anymore, and, for added flavour, I'm also questioning my worth as a woman.*

"Great," she answered with a convincing smile. "Really good," she added, immediately downgrading what she had said, because *great* just felt wrong. "You?"

Emmett replied with a broad smile and a thumbs-up gesture. Brooke thought his eyes told a different story though.

"What can I help you with today?" she asked, hoping to steer the conversation towards safer topics. Thankfully, Emmett was more than willing to oblige.

He picked up the papers he was carrying and took one and unfolded it before he placed it on the counter and slid it towards her. On it, written in the same delicate handwriting as the notepad, was a long list of building supplies. At a glance, Brooke would have thought Emmett was building a house with the materials she was reading.

Oh shit!

Brooke swallowed hard as she looked at the intimidating list. Dale and Meredith could work through a list like that in a heartbeat, but Brooke had only worked the service counter over lunch, and nobody ever came in over the lunch hour. Thankfully, upon closer inspection she saw Emmett had listed everything in meticulous detail. The only way it could have been easier for her is if he also included the stock numbers.

Okay, you can do this.

"This might take me a minute," Brooke quietly confessed as she went to the computer and started filling out the stock order. *Jesus! This is going to be expensive,* Brooke thought excitedly as the amount at the bottom grew with each item she added.

She was going to get on the Sales Board.

Bruce had a board in the break room that listed the number of sales each employee made. It was meant to be a friendly competition. At the end of each month, the employee with the most sales gets a small bonus on their check, and a gift card to Tim Horton's. Normally, being a part-timer, Brooke and Tim were always near the bottom. With this one order though, she could rocket to the top, with a comfortable lead.

Emmett returned to his notepad, and caught her attention with a click of his tongue when he was ready to show her.

I'm also going to need some paint.

"Sure. Just give me the swatch of the color you want, and I can mix that up for you," Brooke said, thinking of the look on Dale's face when he sees this order. Again, she had never actually mixed paint before, but Dale had shown her how to use the machine and it seemed easy enough to operate.

She looked up at Emmett and he seemed confused about something. Brooke just went back to entering the items into the sales order. Out of the corner of her eye, Brooke seen Emmett return to his notepad and she looked up just in time to read the note.

What color do girls like?

Why Mr. Brooks, Brooke thought with childish amusement. *Is someone having a lady-friend over to the house?* Eve gave Emmett the slightest of grins before she considered the question. Then she chuckled.

"I guess it depends on the girl."

Pink? He wrote a second later.

"Pink?!" Brooke just looked at him with a quizzical look. "You think *all* girls like the color pink?" she asked him with a serious look on her face, before she leaned in to him, like she was telling him a secret. "You know, some of us like the *manly* colors, like *blue*." She gave him a warm smile as she backed away from him. She could see by the expression on his face, he knew she was teasing him a bit. She just hoped he was okay with it. "Besides which," she said bringing it back to a semi-professional tone. "There's like a dozen different shades of pink down there," she warned him, and absently pointed in the direction of the paint aisle. "Just go down and have a look at the swatches and find one you like. I'll be a while putting this in, anyway." Emmett just nodded and gave her a curt wave as a way of a thanks before he retrieved his cart and moved into the paint aisle.

Brooke finished with the massive sale order, and busied herself at the counter for a minute or two before she decided to check in on Emmett. She knew the store had surveillance cameras, just like she knew they weren't there to catch shoplifters. *Who's going to steal a hammer in this town?* No, the cameras where there so Bruce could keep an eye on his employees. Everybody knew it, and they were all fine with it. Right now, though, she was counting on the fact Bruce would be watching later on, and she wanted him to remember this when it came time to fill the next full-time spot.

When Brooke turned down the aisle, she saw Emmett towering over the display with the seemingly endless rainbow of colors that were available. She couldn't help but smile when she saw the way he was looking over the myriad of options with some distress. Emmett was looking at the few swatches in his hand like they had an algebra equation on them he had to solve.

"How are we making out?" she asked politely as she approached. Emmett looked at her like he was a lost child and shrugged his massive shoulders. *Holy shit,* Brooke thought to herself with some sarcasm. *I actually might have a use for my college degree.* "Did you want some help?"

Emmett thought for a moment before finally nodding reluctantly.

"Does the room you're painting get a lot of light?" Brooke began. "Because if it does, you probably want a deeper shade to soak up that light. We don't want a glare or anything like that. If it doesn't get a lot of light then we can probably drift into the lighter shades. So, does it get a lot of light?"

Emmett shrugged.

Typical, Brooke thought and let out a quiet sigh.

"Which direction does the window face? I'm assuming this room has a window," Brooke added and watched as Emmett thought for a moment before he used his whole arm to chop in the direction of the back of the store. "Okay," Brooke said with some disappointment. "Which direction is that?" she asked absently, trying to answer her own question.

North, Emmett wrote onto his notepad.

"Okay, so it probably doesn't get a ton of light during the day. Now, what kind of theme are you going for?" She didn't blame Emmett for the look he was giving her. She just approached the issue from another direction. "What do you want this person to feel when they walk into the room?"

Jesus, look at who you're asking, Brooke thought immediately after she spoke the words. However, Emmett knew the answer immediately, and quickly returned to his notepad.

I want her to feel at home.

Brooke looked up and saw how tortured Emmett was trying to find the perfect color for his special lady-friend.

That's sweet, Brooke thought to herself and felt a sting of envy in her gut she wasn't proud of. *Whoever she is, she's a lucky girl.*

"I like this one," Brooke said quietly and reached out and pulled one of the swatches off the display. "It's called Artic Blue, but I think it should have been called *Morning Sky,*" Brooke said and thought of all the mornings she spent in front of her stop sign, looking out at the expansive eastern sky to see the horizon beginning to come to life. "It's a lighter shade, so it will utilize the natural light of the room without being too overpowering to look at."

Brooke took a deep breath. In another life, a different version of herself once contemplated painting a nursery a similar color.

"It's the color that makes me think of home. I don't know," she said suddenly, diverting herself away from that ugliness. "I like it."

I'll take two gallons. Emmett showed her the notepad with a smile on his face, like he approved of her selection. He then pulled back his notepad and began to write something else. *What about something for the kitchen? Bathroom? Living room?*

Brooke just smiled.

They went with a mint green for the bathrooms. For the kitchen, they went with a deeper shade. Forest Green. Emmett explained the kitchen got the most light in the house, and she wanted something darker to soak up all that light. She went with a green color because she personally believed the rooms with water features deserved earthier tones. In the living room, they went with Classic Pearl. When they were done, Emmett bought fifteen gallons of paint.

Back at the service counter, Brooke was finishing up with the sales order, the whole time thinking of that gift card she could wave in front of Tim's face. The order came to just over twenty-five-hundred-dollars. Not too bad for a part-timer over the lunch hour. She was checking the sales order for the third time before she finalized it when Emmett slid a cue card towards her.

On account, please, the worn card said.

"Sure. No problem," she said and brought up Emmett Brooks' account information. Then she saw the flashing red warning banner on the account header.

You got to be kidding me, Brooke thought and internally saw her gift card go up in smoke.

"Umm," she started timidly. "Looks like your account has been suspended, Emmett." She looked up at him and gave him an empathetic look. "I could put it on a credit card if you'd like?" Brooke offered lightly, secretly suspecting what the answer would be.

Emmett's expression dropped and he sucked on his teeth loudly before he perked up and his finger shot up between them. *One moment,* the gesture said. Emmett took out his phone and began to furiously write a text message. Brooke busied herself behind the counter with things that didn't really need to be done and prepared herself for disappointment.

Oh well, Brooke thought to herself. *It was still nice to see Emmett again.*

Behind her, she could hear the bell on Emmett's phone go off maybe four more times.

Then the police showed up.

What the fuck? Brooke snapped to attention when she first saw the cruiser pull into the parking lot. Immediately she felt dread in the pit of her stomach. *What if this is about what happened at Maggie's?*

Then, with a certain amount of horror, she saw Calvin Biggs exit the cruiser and move towards the door. Brooke swallowed and shot Emmett a worried look.

Jesus! How fucked up would it be for Tommy's best friend to arrest his brother? Right in front of me!

Emmett saw her turn towards the door just as Calvin walked through it and locked his gaze on the two of them.

Emmett stepped closer and quickly began signing something.

"No, no," Calvin said with a modest smile. "It's fine. I was just getting ready to leave the office and head home. I'm on night shift again tonight. So, you caught me at the perfect time. This was on my way home."

Brooke frowned at the unexpectedly light exchange between the two. *Are they friends?* She wondered and then thought back to how close Calvin had been to Tommy and the whole Brooks family. *Of course, they're friends.* Suddenly she felt silly for thinking otherwise.

"Hey, Brooke!" Calvin said with a bright smile. "Good to see you. How are the folks?"

"Hey, Calvin," she greeted her old friend warmly. "It's nice to see you too. I heard you 're the Top Cop around here now." Calvin's smile deepened and he just waved off the comment.

"Same job, different place. That's all. Just another cog in the great machine of law enforcement," Calvin said with his usual cheer. *What's wrong with you?* Brooke thought bitterly as she smiled at him.

Calvin, as the story goes, graduated from the R.C.M.P Academy in Regina with honors, and was almost immediately snatched up by a detachment in Surrey, British Columbia. Straight out of the academy he was thrown into the thick of it. As her mother told it, Calvin worked as a patrol officer where he was shot at twice, and the second one found its mark. Luckily Calvin had been wearing a bulletproof vest at the time, but still. After he served his time on the streets, Calvin moved into homicide. Her mother visibly shuddered when she tried to imagine the kinds of *ugliness* Calvin must have seen during his time in the homicide division. Calvin Biggs was making a name for himself out there in the promised land of Canada. Then, the second an opportunity presented itself, Calvin moved back home. As her mother told it, taking a sizable pay cut along the way.

That's not what annoyed her though.

What annoyed Brooke the most about the man was how he always seemed to be right where he wanted to be.

"Is Lester going to make it out to the *Beef and Barley* this year?" Calvin asked resting his elbow on the counter. The Beef and Barley Days were Russell's annual...Carnival? Brook didn't know what the best word was to describe the three-day-long celebration that happened around town in October.

"I don't know," Brooke said absently. She had no idea what her father's plans for the event were. "Maybe."

"Tell him he should at least come out to the tractor pull." Calvin had an excited air about him as he spoke of the tractor pull, like it was the greatest thing ever. "I hear the Hendersons are bringing out their big John Deere this year. Should really heat up the competition."

"I'll let him know," Brooke said and discreetly slid Emmett's sales order toward him.

"Let's see what we got here," Calvin said and then looked at the order in front of him. Brooke was amused by the little noise that erupted from Calvin's throat. "Just give me a minute with my large friend here." Calvin smiled and grabbed Emmett by his large arm and led him to the side.

Emmett signed effortlessly with a concerned look on his face.

"Well, it's a lot of money," Calvin said in hushed tones.

Again, Brooke busied herself behind the counter, but made sure to stay close enough to eavesdrop a bit.

"No, that's not the problem. Yes, I know you'll pay me back. I still have to tell Joni why I dropped so much on our credit card. Like, what the hell are you building out there?"

Brooke briefly looked over and saw Emmett furiously signing in front of Calvin. Whatever Emmett was communicating to Calvin, was a genuine surprise.

"What?!" he exclaimed loudly, interrupting Emmett's signing. "Why is this the first I'm hearing about this?" Now, he sounded hurt by whatever Emmett was telling him. "And when were these papers signed? You're kidding me. And nobody tried to reach out? Even after Tommy died? So, how did she die?"

What?! Brooke's ears perked up as the conversation turned a corner.

"Well, shit," Calvin said with some remorse and turned away from his friend for a moment, like he was trying to collect himself. "So, this woman who told you all this, she drove all the way from Toronto, and just showed up on your doorstep? Did you ask for some form of identification? You never know, this could be some sort of scam or something."

There was a long pause in which Brooke assumed Emmett was signing. She couldn't see because she began wiping down the counter's shelves close to where Emmett and Calvin were talking.

"So, it's not official yet. Well, you can't blame her for that. Have you seen your place lately? Jesus. All this is you working through her list? Why didn't you say so, Emmett? Are you up for that? That's life-changing, buddy."

Then the service counter's phone rang. *Dammit,* Brooke thought as she was forced to abandon the juicy conversation she was eavesdropping on, to answer the call. When she finished up with the caller, Calvin was waiting in front of the counter for her.

"I guess we're all ready to go here," he said before he pulled out his wallet and fished out his credit card. "That'll be on Mastercard."

Brooke finished up the transaction, stapled the receipt to Calvin's copy of the sale order and handed it to him.

"You guys are all set," she said with a big smile she couldn't help. "Have a great day."

"You bet," Calvin said and then turned to Emmett when he clicked his tongue. Emmett signed and looked at Brooke. "Emmett says you look nice." Brooke slightly chuckled as Emmett playfully slapped his friend on the arm. "Oh," Calvin said light-heartedly. "My mistake. He said it was nice *to see you.*" The two walked away after a friendly wave. Emmett struggled as he pushed the cart and signed at the same time. "What?! It was an honest mistake."

Shortly after that, Dale returned from the break room with a big smile of his face, and some mustard on the corner of his mouth.

"So, Sport?" That's what he liked to call her, *Sport.* It was the same nickname he called her when she was a child. "How'd it go?" he asked lightly and with a warm smile.

Brooke couldn't hide the shit-eating grin on her face when she turned to him and told him he was no longer at the top of the sales board.

CHAPTER 4

Belle

Belle had to hurry. Latesha would be out of the shower soon. She had observed the girl's schedule and noticed that she usually took a long shower after she got home from her shift at the coffee shop.

Latesha Harris was a tall, slender sixteen-year-old African-American girl who had lived at the Burke household for two years and was two years from *aging out of the system*. That was the magical age when kids could leave foster care and try to be whoever they wanted, if they had the means. Most foster kids spoke about that age with wonder. Latesha was no different. Latesha was no different. She was saving up for university; she had big plans to get a scholarship and become a veterinarian. She talked about moving out to the coast all the time.

Belle was sitting cross-legged beside the bed that came with the small room they gave her. Belle couldn't complain, at least she had her own room. The two boys, Kevin, and Darryl, they had to share the bedroom further down the hall. Belle had the door to her room closed. She had Latesha's earbuds in and was watching the latest episode of Crimson Tides. It was a teenage romance-drama set in Malibu where the main characters were all vampires. It was *uber-trendy,* that's what Kendra said. Belle didn't even know what that meant, but she knew it was important in her little group of would-be friends.

She couldn't even say with one-hundred-percent certainty those girls were her friends. They tolerated her presence at their table during lunch time, and sometimes they even laughed at the few times Belle would speak to interject with a witty remark. They didn't ask questions, though. That was one thing Belle liked about them. She did know one thing, she wanted to be liked by these girls.

Lately, this stupid show was the only thing they talked about. Latesha's phone was the only device in the house that was even capable of streaming it. Latesha used her own money to pay for the phone, as well as the streaming service. Belle figured she had fifteen minutes. Surely, that would be enough to quickly skim through the episode and get enough information to be able to enter into the conversation about it the next day at lunch.

Those girls aren't your friends, a wicked little voice pestered her from inside her head.

It was true, but she couldn't help that. Just like she couldn't help the part of her that wished they were. There was nothing special about Amber Stone, Petra Riley, or Kendra Kwon. They were just the girls who were the first to talk to her, and they didn't mind if Belle sat with them at lunch. That, so far, was the length and width of her relationship with them.

She had started halfway through the school year. After her aunt had fallen and broke her hip, Belle had to move to an entirely different part of Toronto, which meant a different school division. It sucked. Not because she had a lot of friends at her old school, she didn't. She didn't have any friends there either, but she had people she was *friendly* with. It was a start though. Now, she had to try again with a whole new bunch of strange, happy kids she couldn't relate to.

Who would ever want to be friends with you? The voice persisted. *You're an orphan.*

Belle tried not to think about that word too much. Just like she tried not to think of her mother, even in the times she really needed to. Belle knew if she let her thoughts drift to the only person who ever really loved her, she would be tormented with the memories of the last eight months of her life. The hard months.

None of that matters now, you dumb kid, she told herself.

She tried to focus on the stupid teen drama and looked for things she could mention at lunch tomorrow. Well, she wouldn't be the first one to bring the subject up, but maybe if the girls started talking about it, she could add to the conversation. Belle knew she should be studying, but this somehow seemed more important. She had horrible grades, and it wasn't like that was going to change in the next few months. And, summer was coming. If she could manage it, it would be nice to have some friends to spend it with.

Then the sounds of heavy footfalls echoed in the hall outside her door. Belle looked up just in time to see the tiny bedroom's door fly open and Latesha was standing there in her sweats and a t-shirt.

She did not look happy.

"You little bitch!" she loudly cried out when she saw her smartphone in Belle's hands.

"You said I could use it," Belle shot back quickly. She knew that wasn't the truth, but she had to say something.

"That was one time," Latesha said and stormed into the room. "That doesn't mean you get to use my shit whenever you like. Give it," she said with an angry expression as she stopped in front of Belle and held out her hand. Belle looked up at her with a desperate look on her face.

"I need it, *please*. Just five more minutes. I swear, I'll-." Belle was cut off when Latesha bent down and slapped her hard across the face. She ricocheted away from the blow and her head struck the wall, Belle saw stars swimming in front of her eyes.

"Fucking bitch! I told you! This is *my* shit. You don't take my shit without my say-so." Belle's head still swam as Latesha leaned close. "You hear me?" She then took her index finger and aggressively pushed Belle's head away from her. "Get it through your thick skull." Latesha sneered at her before she rose and started to leave.

That's when Belle saw red.

When Latesha reached the door, Belle sprang up from her spot in the corner by her bed and ran full speed at the full-bodied, teenage athlete. Screaming at the top of her lungs, Belle's body struck Latesha's body just as she was turning back. Belle's momentum propelled them out into the hall and Belle kept pushing until Latesha slammed into the wall of the hallway. She reached up and grabbed a handful of Latesha's white t-shirt and savagely yanked her backwards and down to the hall's floor. Now, it was Belle who was taller. Belle descended on Latesha, quickly straddled her waist, and rained blows on her shocked face.

Belle never learned how to fight, and if she was being honest, she didn't know what she was doing. She just hit whatever was open. Belle used her fists and beat down on the teen's chest a few times, and in her mad flailing Belle suspected she even struck one of Latesha's boobs. When she could, Belle slapped the ebony skin of Latesha's face, and when she could she smacked the sides of her head. The two of them were madly screaming and flailing at each other. Latesha was trying to buck Belle's weight off her hips, while at the same time, thrashing at her wildly from the ground. She took a sharp punch to the mouth, quickly tasted blood, but Belle didn't stop. She just grabbed Latesha's arm and spread them wide before she screamed full-force into her face.

Then she bit her.

Belle chomped down on Latesha's left forearm, the same one that struck her, and bit down hard. Latesha screamed in earnest, but the African-American teen wasn't a push-over, by any means. She grabbed a fistful of Belle's dark hair and simply threw her to the side with enough force her back slammed painfully against the wall.

Then Latesha kicked her in the midsection, and the fight was over. For Belle, anyway.

"You fucking nasty bitch!" Latesha growled as she wrestled herself back onto her feet and looked down at her crumpled form.

"Girls!" Brian Burke's voice rang out in the hallway as he rounded the corner from the stairs. "Stop it! Right now!"

"Oh, great timing, Brian." Latesha scowled at the man.

"What the hell is going on?!" Brian asked and looked down at them with heated disapproval.

He wore blue jeans, and a white button-down shirt with a blue sweater vest over it. Brian Burke was a nice enough man, as far as Belle could tell, but he wasn't the kind of person who put up with *foolishness.*

"I'm waiting," he said after neither of them spoke.

"She keeps taking my shit, Brian." Latesha broke in first and reached down to snatch her smartphone off the floor. She checked it over once before she turned to Belle, who was still on the floor. "You're lucky you didn't break it."

"Hey," Brian cautioned. "Let's just simmer down a bit here."

"No, Brian. I won't *simmer down*," Latesha mockingly repeated the man's words back to him before she continued. "This is my shit. I bought it, with my own money. My *own* money! You don't get to tell me how to feel when someone straight-up steals my shit."

"You said I could use it," Belle said. It was a moot point, because Latesha was right. Still, it was the only point she had in her favor.

"That was one time, you little *cunt.*"

"Hey! Enough!" Brian held up his finger to Latesha, who looked to him angrily before she huffed and visibly relaxed her shoulders. Then Brian focused his attention back on Belle. "Are you bleeding? Show me your teeth," he asked in a way that didn't allow for debate. Belle reluctantly obliged. "Did you hit her?" he sternly asked Latesha.

"She bit me!" Latesha held up her wounded arm. It had a full bite mark on it, and on a few of the marks Belle's teeth left behind were trails of crimson that seeped down her arm.

"Jesus!" Brian leaned closer to the wound. "That looks bad. Isabelle!" Brian looked at her with a shocked expression.

"Yeah," Latesha said pulling her arm back. "And I have a game in two days. What if this shit gets infected?" Latesha looked at him like she was waiting for his answer.

"I know," Brian said and motioned Latesha down the stairs. "Go have Moira clean that up and get a bandage on it."

"What about her!" she cried out and angrily pointed in her direction. Belle flinched away from the sudden gesture,

"Hey!" Brian shot back. "Don't push it. You're on thin ice as it is."

"What did I do?!" Latesha looked hurt.

"It's what you didn't do," Brian said quickly. "She's like half your size, Latesha. I expect *you both* to find other ways to resolve your problems than beating the shit out of each other." He paused to give them both a hard look.

"I *was* walking away, until she jumped me from behind." Latesha gestured angrily at Belle. "Then she pulled me to the ground and jumped on top of me. What was I supposed to do?" Again, she looked at Brian like she expected him to answer the question, but this time, she didn't wait for his reply. "Don't be preaching your *turn-the-other-cheek* bullshit to me."

"Latesha," Brian said wearily and pinched the bridge of his nose. "That's enough, okay?" He gave her a tired expression and motioned down the stairwell again. "Go get your arm looked at. Go."

Latesha huffed, brushed past Brian and loudly walked down the stairs.

"Isabelle, go to your room," Brian looked at her with mild disappointment. "You're on an official *time-out* for the rest of the night. Maybe the week, I don't know. I'll have to talk to Moira and see how bad that bite is." Brian pinched his nose again. He did that when he was stressed. "We'll talk later. Go." Brian waved her back into her room. "But Isabelle," Brian called after her when she crossed the threshold to her room. "We expect you to try harder to fit in around here. We all have to show each other respect, if we're going to make this work." Brian then spread his arms out in front of himself, like he was offering something to her, before he turned and walked away.

Belle moved back into her room and quietly closed the door.

She scurried back into her quiet little corner, pulled her knees up to her chest, and hugged them tightly.

"You're so stupid," she hissed quietly into her knees as she felt the sting in her eyes.

You think those girls are going to like you because you watched a television show they like. Oh, you silly, silly, little girl. Sooner or later, they're going to find out you're an orphan. That nobody loves you. Then the questions will come. You think those girls, or anybody for that matter, wants to be friends with someone who slept in a car for a month?

"Shut up," she whispered angrily into her jeans as the first bit of wetness streamed down her cheek.

No, of course they don't. Anybody who tells you different is just saying that because they feel sorry for you. The little misfit child that nobody wants. One person in this world loved you, and now she's gone. You're all alone. Where do you think you're going to go if the Burkes suddenly decide you're not worth the tax break Latesha said they get for having you in their home? What? You think the next foster home is going to be as nice as this one?

Belle didn't want to think about that, either. Kevin, one of the other boys at the Burke's, he had told her stories of some of the places he had been to. If anything, he just reinforced what Latesha had already been telling them. *Keep your head down, stay out of trouble, because this was about as good as it gets.* Belle felt that familiar dread descending upon her. Not for the first time Belle worried about where she would go if, for whatever reason, she had to leave the Burke's. Where would she go this time? Would she have to change schools again? What if there wasn't anywhere left for her to go?

"It wasn't supposed to be like this?" Belle wept quietly and let her jeans soak up the wetness from her eyes. "It wasn't." Belle couldn't continue because the first real sob stole her voice away. *Why did she have to get sick? People get cancer all the time, why did she have to die? It wasn't fair.*

Not for the first time, Belle felt very small. Like a tiny, insignificant...*thing* that was left somewhere and forgotten about. Like a child's toy that was lost out in the real world, and being of no use to anyone, it just sits there, slowly rotting away. That's all she was. Just a broken little thing out in the world, that nobody had a use for.

CHAPTER 5

Emmett

When Emmett heard the sounds of Calvin's cruiser coming down the lane, he sat up a bit straighter in his chair on the patio. All the patio chairs, as well as the small four-person table, were made with a sturdy, light-weight steel. Emmett took the steel brush to all of it, scrubbed the rust from it before he painted the whole works a deep blue color. Brooke helped him pick out the color.

She was good with that stuff.

Emmett took a generous swig from his beer bottle as Calvin's cruiser came to a slow stop in front of the house. He set his bottle down on the newly painted deck, and groaned a bit when he rose off the new cushion of the deck chair.

"I'm sorry," Calvin said loudly and with obvious mirth the moment he stepped out of the cruiser. "I seemed to have taken a wrong turn somewhere. I'm looking for the Brooks' farm." Calvin closed the door to his cruiser and smiled at Emmett. "Maybe you could help me out."

Emmett laughed soundlessly. It sounded a bit like a dog panting. He didn't blame his friend for acting surprised. It had been a busy month.

It started with the lane and yard.

"This place looks like it's straight out of a horror film," Nicole Jones had said. *Nic, she prefers to be called Nic,* He reminded himself. "That might have been fine for you, but it's not fucking good enough for your niece." She didn't pull any punches when they sat at the small table in the kitchen coming up with the list of things that needed to be done.

It was two pages long.

Before she left, Nic showed him a picture of Isabelle Lamoine. In the picture, Emmett saw a small girl with dark hair that hid her face. She was standing in front of a bare, white wall in jeans and a light blue shirt that had a logo on it that Emmett didn't recognize. It was obvious the clothes didn't fit her well. The thing that struck Emmett, though, was the expression on her face. Emmett recognized that look. He wore it himself more than a few times in his past. The look you made when you just wanted to disappear. Like the last thing you wanted in this world was to be noticed. Emmett didn't like seeing that look on this little girl, his niece.

After that, Emmett looked at his home with fresh eyes, and he didn't like what he saw. Not one bit.

He started by cutting the grass, and quickly found that it wouldn't be as simple as he thought it would. The riding mower growled angrily as it worked its way through the tall grass. Emmett had to take his time. Worse yet, the sheer volume of grass made it impossible to mulch properly and left large clumps behind that had to be raked up. On the plus side, it made for a nice treat for the cows, but it took an entire day to just mow the grass on the property. Emmett felt a sting deep inside every time he found one of King's toys out in the grass. On more than one occasion, Emmett promised his riding mower if it just kept going, he would never let the grass get that long again.

Then, Emmett mixed a potent herbicide into the small, pull-behind sprayer and hooked it up to the Kubota. Emmett sprayed the approach all the way to the gravel road, and then did the gravel in the yard. It took a couple days for the grass and weeds to die, but when they did, he ordered a truckload of gravel and used the small tractor to spread the fresh gravel around the yard and down the lane. Then Emmett paid Darren Peters to come by and spray the whole works with a fresh coat of tar to keep the weeds away, and keep the dust down to a minimum.

When he wasn't working on the yard, Emmett was prepping the Quonset, as well as the fuel tanks, for painting. He used the electric angle-grinder with the wire-wheel on the majority of the rust, but on the places he couldn't he was forced to used the hand brush. The actual painting went pretty quickly. Emmett used an air-powered paint sprayer to first spray the shed and the two fuel tanks with the primer before he could spray the final coat of white paint over top. Emmett was thankful on more than one occasion that no one from Manitoba Health and Safety were around to see the poorly constructed scaffolding he was using to paint the shed. The fuel tanks were easier. He used the bucket on the Kubota to reach the top of the tanks that were nestled on their scaffolding.

After that, Emmett focused on the animal shed. He removed everything from the front rooms of the shed and sprayed the front rooms with bleach before he took the pressure washer to the floor, he washed the concrete floor while slowly working his way into the animal pens, and out the back. Emmett dry-heaved more than once as the smell of wet manure filled his nostrils and burned its way down his throat.

When it was clean, Emmett painted the front room with the pearl-white Brooke helped him pick out for the living room. The two rooms in the shed were small, he didn't think it would take much paint. He was wrong. It took a whole gallon of paint before he was happy with the job. He then added some plain-looking moldings along the bottom of the drywall, and around the two man-doors. Then he moved the freezers back in, after he thoroughly cleaned them. As per the list taped to the refrigerator, Emmett added a padlock to the medical freezer he used for the livestock's antibiotics. In the small, adjacent room, the one he used to store the numerous empty beer cases he had collected over the years, he turned into a medical room of sorts. He repurposed one of his father's many rusted toolboxes and emptied it out to house the various dehorning implements he had, the castrating tools, and the farrier rasps for trimming hooves. When he was done, the room looked downright orderly. For good measure, he added a lock to that door as well.

"Seriously," Calvin said as he spread his arms wide and looked over the new yard. "I can't believe this is the same place." The two men crossed the space between them and embraced each other warmly. "How you doing, buddy?"

Good, Emmett signed when they parted. *So, as you can s-.* Emmett started to sign but Calvin absently pushed passed him.

"Did you redo the *entire* deck?!" Calvin quickly strode up to the new deck and fawned over it. "Hey! This is good work," he said inspecting the joints closely and giving the railing a hearty shake.

Emmett whistled loudly.

Well, don't wreck it.

"I'm not wrecking it," Calvin said defensively. "Just testing it out a little. This is solid. I should get you to do my deck."

You should see the inside of the house, Emmett signed when Calvin finally looked back at him.

"Inside?" Calvin said with keen interest.

Emmett eloquently motioned towards the house door, like he was presenting a princess with her chariot.

"How fancy," Calvin chuckled and moved towards the house. Emmett held the door for him and waited. "Oh my god," Calvin said quietly when he saw the freshly painted kitchen.

It was spotless.

Emmett scrubbed every inch of it before he painted. He found a place for everything, and everything was in its place.

"Jesus!" Calvin exclaimed when he approached the bathroom. "Will you look at that," he said as he pulled the lever up on the new faucet Emmett installed, and flipped the light switch a few times to test out the new LED light he put in. "I really like the color you went with," Calvin said poking his head out the door. "What is that?"

Mint green.

Calvin disappeared into the bathroom only to poke his head out a second later.

"Did Brooke help you pick out the shower curtain too?" He cocked his eyebrow towards Emmett.

Maybe.

Calvin chuckled heartily as he moved into the bedroom across the hallway.

"You know, I've noticed your truck in front of Bales' hardware a few times over the last month," he said as he looked around the room.

Emmett worked it so, if he needed something, he went during the lunch hour on the days he knew Brooke would be working. Everybody knew about the incentive program at Bales'. Just like they knew Dale and Meredith were usually in a fierce competition for the bonus at the end of the month. That all changed after Emmett and Brooke's first meeting. Since then, Emmett was tickled with the prospect of stealing the bonus away from both of them and giving it to a lowly part-time worker. It was just a bonus that worker happened to be Brooke Talbot. At least, that's what Emmett wanted people to believe.

The heated pulse in his cheeks told a different story, though.

"Aww!" Calvin cooed warmly. "Where'd you get this?"

Emmett suspected what Calvin was referring to, and he took a deep breath as he moved towards the room. As soon as he entered the artic-blue room he had put together for his niece, he spied Calvin in front of Tommy's old dresser. Calvin held the small-framed picture of Tommy and Becky from the graduation dance in his hands. Emmett had placed it on top of the dresser; he thought his niece would like it.

"Jesus! They looked so young," he said and looked to Emmett.

No, we're just getting older.

"Don't remind me," he said with a grin and placed the picture back onto the dresser's top. "So, is this going to be Isabelle's room?" Calvin asked. Emmett suspected he already knew the answer. If he didn't, he wasn't much of a cop.

Yeah, I moved into the main bedroom.

Emmett called it the main bedroom, because it seemed silly to still call it *his parent's room*. Especially since it has been vacant for almost five years now. When his father went into the home, Emmett went in there to pack the necessities his father would need. After that, he closed the door on that room and never opened it again until the news of Isabelle came. Then something changed. Emmett knew what it was too. He could no longer afford to keep that door closed anymore. He had to enter his parent's room, to dive back into the quiet little life Grace and Carter had made for themselves, and box it up.

He didn't expect it to be easy, but he was surprised with just how hard it was to empty out the room. He took the pictures down from the walls, then he removed the frames from the large wooden dresser at the foot of the king-sized bed, and he packed them into a large box along with the other little knickknacks that had collected around their space. He packed it all into the box he marked *precious memories*. That had been the hardest part. After that was done, it seemed less like his parent's room and more like a room he simply had to clear out.

He did it for Isabelle.

That made it easier too. Seeing this as another thing that stood between him and his niece made the job easier. He *had* to do this. He *had* to pack up what he could of his parent's life, and throw away the rest.

Well, he didn't exactly throw them away.

Emmett used the Kubota to remove the weed-infested topsoil in his mother's garden, which he piled to the side. He then took a shovel and basically dug a grave. He didn't start out with the dimensions of a grave in mind, he knew he wanted something long, wide, and deep. A grave is what he dug, though. It wasn't easy, but it wasn't supposed to be. The fact it was hard was the point. He *wanted* it to be hard. He wanted to feel the sweat roll down his skin and that familiar deep ache of exertion in his muscles. He wanted to suffer.

When it was done, Emmett took that garbage topsoil he took off the garden and lined the bottom of his grave with it before he threw the unimportant remnants of his parent's lives into that grave. Clothes, shoes, coats, toothbrushes, combs, brushes, eye glasses, every little insignificant piece of their life went in. Then Emmett poured about two liters of gasoline around the inside of the grave, and moved back to a safe distance before he threw a road flare into the grave and watched the resulting fireball spread out to nothingness above it. Then the flames came in earnest. It was still the dry season before the rains of June came, there was a lot of dry grass still out there. Emmett stood guard and watched the fire until it burned itself down to flaring embers.

He grabbed some beers and made a night of it. He cried a few times too.

He didn't tell Calvin any of that though.

"Emmett!" Calvin cried out when he passed into the dining room. Emmett smiled with a certain amount of pride. "You refinished the floor?!"

When Emmett rounded the corner into the dining room, Calvin was crouched down by the dining room table, running his hand along the smooth surface of the wood. Emmett snapped his fingers to get his attention.

You like that? I sanded the whole thing down to the good wood and then stained it and varnished it.

Emmett knew Calvin would appreciate the floor the most because he was a bit of an amateur woodworker. He kept a small shop in the back of his property where Calvin liked to do little projects. His last coffee table was pretty nice.

"You know, I didn't want to say anything," Calvin said, sounding a bit sad. "Because I know things haven't been easy for you these last couple of years, but the state of this floor was driving me fucking crazy." Emmett couldn't help himself when he saw the distressed look on his face when he said the words. Emmett chuckled with amusement. "Like, this is a *good* floor. You don't see workmanship like this anymore."

I was actually thinking of ripping it all up and putting in linoleum, Emmett joked, *but this turned out to be easier.*

"Don't even joke about that," he quickly shot back, he even managed to sound hurt by the suggestion. "Are you thinking of getting new furniture?" Calvin asked and thumbed back to the living room.

The whole room had several coats of Brooke's pearl white paint. Emmett had rented a steam cleaning machine and repeatedly cleaned all the carpets in the house. The living room looked immaculate, except for the furniture. The couch along the north wall had been in that exact spot for all of Emmett's life. Its faded floral print hinted towards its age, and anyone who sat on that couch sank deeply into the worn cushions. It was a perfect couch for napping, but Emmett couldn't deny it looked out of place in the room now. Worse than that, it looked ugly.

Next to it, was his father's chair, the big, reclining *La-Z-Boy* chair. It wasn't an actual La-Z-Boy, that's just what his father called it. Every memory he had of his father in this room, was of him sitting in *that* chair. It had a tear in the leather on the armrest, and the chair creaked horribly when someone sat in it. Across the room, in a quiet corner, like it was trying to hide itself away, was the chair his mother usually sat in.

I was thinking about it, Emmett said with a sad expression on his face. *Honestly, I'm getting a little concerned with how much this is all costing.* Emmett spied Calvin's expression shift and quickly started signing again. *I'm not asking you for anything else. I'm just saying. You letting me use your account at Bale's was a huge help.*

"Yeah," Calvin broke in and rubbed the back of his neck. He usually did this when he had to deliver unfortunate news. Emmett could guess what it was. "I'm going to have to pull the plug on that for a little while. Joni has been keeping an eye on our account online, and she's getting...," Calvin struggled with the next word. "*Concerned.*" Emmett nodded and let his friend continue. "You know she loves you like a brother, but with summer coming up, we have to start thinking about our vacation with the boys." Calvin gave him a remorseful look. "We're not rich people, Emmett."

Stop, Emmett signed, and interrupted his friend. Emmett reached out, placed his hand on his friend's shoulder, and gave it a gentle squeeze. *You've done more than enough. I don't know how to thank you.*

"You could pay me back," Calvin offered quickly, and with a grin. Emmett panted out a quick chuckle and pointed towards *his* room.

I got your back.

Calvin stepped down the few steps into the living room and proceeded through the bedroom door. Again, he cooed at the state of the room, then Emmett saw his eyes lock onto the bed.

"Huh? Emmett?" he asked cautiously. "Were you going to pay me back in guns?"

Emmett walked into the room and stood beside Calvin. There on the large bed, was every firearm on the property. Turns out, it was quite a collection.

Well, I have to get rid of them all anyway. You might as well sell them and keep the money for yourself. There's got to be more than enough to cover what I owe you.

"Are you kidding me?!" Calvin looked at him with shocked disappointment before he returned his gaze to the bed.

There, spread out lovingly, were five large rifles of various calibers, two which were meant for hunting. The other three were more for fun. In addition, there were also two shotguns, four revolvers, eight pistols, and two small .22 pump-action rifles that looked out of place amongst the other larger rifles.

"What the hell do you think Joni is going to say when I walk into the house with this goddamn *arsenal*?"

Emmett shrugged.

"Is that an AK-47?" Calvin pointed to the imposing looking weapon on the bed.

Maybe.

"Jesus Christ, Emmett!" Calvin complained loudly. "You're not even supposed to have that!" Then Calvin's eyes landed on the small snub-nosed .38 amongst the other revolvers. "Or that!" He then looked at Emmett with an exasperated look before he took a deep breath. "Where did you even get all these?"

They were in my dad's gun safe. I had to pay a guy to come from Brandon to get the thing open. You should have seen the look on his face when he opened it. Emmett did his best to mimic the look of utter surprise that was on the young tech's face. Calvin didn't look impressed.

"I bet," he said sourly.

Look, I thought this would be a quick way for you to get your money back, and then some. If it's a problem I can find another way to get rid of them. I have an appointment with the bank at the end of the month. I'm going to transfer some money from my mom's life insurance account. I'm paying off all my bills, and padding my account a little for the Ministry of Children people. I can pay you back in full then. Emmett gave his friend a knowing look. *But that's going to take some time. This way, you get your money sooner, and make get a nice bonus for yourself. I didn't think it would be a problem, because your family is a bunch of gun nuts.*

"Gun *enthusiasts*," Calvin playfully corrected. "I suppose I could store them at my brother's place. You sure, there's a lot of coin on that bed." Emmett nodded eagerly. "Okay, well, these two." Calvin singled out the AK-47 and the snub-nosed revolver and placed them aside. "Are going to be anonymously turned over to the detachment for destruction."

When Emmett gave him a hurtful look, Calvin simply swiped his hands down the front of his uniform.

"Still a cop," he said incredulously, like Emmett should have known better.

He wasn't thrilled with the news, but he wasn't surprised about it either. He shrugged, reluctantly conceding the point.

"The rest?" Calvin looked over the collection again and scratched his chin as he did some calculations in his head. "Yeah. Okay. I can take them. Honestly, it shouldn't be too hard to offload to someone around here. Some of those pistols are pretty nice. Where's the Mossberg?" Calvin asked, amused.

I'm keeping that one. It's locked up in the closet.

Nice try, Emmett thought to himself as he remembered the sleek-looking shotgun Tommy bought him as a graduation gift. Calvin had offered to buy it on more than one occasion. Nic Jones warned him about having firearms in the house, and it was a shame the tech from the locksmithing place had to render the safe completely useless before he could get it open. Emmett had to buy a nylon case, and a trigger lock for the weapon. He had it stored on the high shelf in the closet, near the back where it would be out of sight. He didn't plan on telling the Ministry people about it, and he just hoped their home inspection would miss it. He would hate to get rid of it. It was a nice memento of when he and Tommy took a trip to Minot, North Dakota.

"Fine," Calvin said somewhat deflated. "You got a deal." Calvin stuck his hand out and Emmett shook it. "You got some zip-ties?" Emmett gave him a quizzical look. "So, we can make them safe for transport." Calvin shook his head in disbelief. "This isn't the old west, Emmett. You put a zip-tie through the breech so law enforcement can see the weapon isn't a threat. Don't think it slipped my notice none of these guns have trigger locks, either. Go get those zip-ties." Emmett held up his hands and turned to retrieve the ties.

At the back of Calvin's cruiser, the two of them began to haul the weapons into the trunk. Calvin stayed by the trunk to make room and organize the weapons and Emmett hauled them in from the house. Each trip he took he walked past the old, ratty-looking furniture in the living room.

It's not good enough, Emmett thought to himself as he headed through the house.

How much do you think new furniture would cost? Emmett stopped to ask after the first trip. Calvin noisily sighed as he thought about it.

"About a thousand bucks, maybe," he said after some thought. "When we were at The Brick in Yorkton, I saw a set there that was pretty nice for eight hundred."

Emmett went back into the house, and once again looked into the living room and tried to imagine what new furniture would look like. *It's impossible,* he reminded himself as he scooped up the next load of firearms to haul back. By the time the bank freed up the money, he wouldn't have enough time to drive all the way to Yorkton to buy a new furniture set. Plus, he would have to get it delivered, which would take probably at a least a day or two, and it wouldn't be free. Yorkton was over an hour away, after all.

Isabelle.

You know anyone who's looking to get some work done? Emmett signed after Calvin took the last firearm he was carrying.

"What kind of work?"

The kind I can do, and the kind that pays.

"You're thinking about that living room, aren't you?" Emmett nodded. "I thought you had some money coming to you?"

I won't get that in time. I'll be lucky to get everything transferred over in time for the home inspection. I need something right now. Emmett had set himself a two-thousand-dollar budget for the furniture. He didn't want a *nice* set, he wanted a *great* set. There couldn't be any half-measures when it came to Isabelle. Maybe, if there was money left over he could buy a desk for Isabelle's room.

"Well," Calvin started to say after he thought about the question for a time. "Nothing that would produce that sort of *right-now* cash you're looking for." Calvin looked up at him sheepishly. "There *is* one thing you could do," Calvin said with enough reluctance to catch Emmett's attention.

I'm not stripping, Emmett signed with a smile, but Calvin wasn't having any part of the joke. *What? What is it?*

"Well, no, it's not stripping. Though, you would make a wonderful male stripper," Calvin joked. "What I'm thinking of is a little more up your alley, but it's still a little trashy," he said and looked at Emmett, wanting to know if Emmett was still interested. Emmett motioned for him to continue.

How bad could it be, he thought.

"Have you ever heard of *Hillbilly Fights*?"

***

The drive to Churchbridge, Saskatchewan was quiet. The sleepy town sat just over the Manitoba-Saskatchewan border on Highway 16, about half an hour east of Russell. Calvin insisted on driving him out there, even though Emmett knew the way to the Dupuis' farm. His family had pastured a good number of the Dupuis' herd back when his father still ran things. The Dupuis family were prominent around the St-Lazare area. They were one of the few families that had been in the area since the turn of the century. As a result, they were spread throughout the whole region. In St-Lazare, it was Roger and Caroline Dupuis. They had two sons who ran the local repair shop, Bryan and Jaiden. In Churchbridge, it was Rene Dupuis, his wife Michelle, and their three kids. Martha, Greg, and Chester. Emmett knew Greg from his teenage years. He played against Greg in Midget hockey a number of times. That's how he knew Martha, as well. She would sometimes drive Greg to the games that were played in Russell.

Emmett didn't know Chester.

Chester was almost ten years younger than Greg. Emmett wasn't even aware the family even had a third child until Calvin explained the whole *Hillbilly Fights* idea to him. According to Calvin, once young Chester graduated from high school, he went to his father with a business plan. Like, an actual business plan that was arranged into a pretty convincing power-point presentation, as the story goes.

Apparently, it was so convincing, his father rented a sizable portion of his eastern field to Chester, who prefers to be called *Chaz*, to produce his internet fight videos.

"I'm having second thoughts about this," Calvin said as he turned his pickup down the gravel road that led to the north, right before the town's welcome sign. Emmett snapped his fingers and waved down the road they were currently travelling on.

Keep going.

Emmett wasn't having second thoughts. According to Calvin, fighters were paid a thousand dollars. Win, lose, or draw. Emmett would only have to fight twice to pay for the new furniture set. Assuming he could fight twice in one day. He didn't know the specific rules to this *Hillbilly* operation, but he had less than a month before the home inspection and couldn't risk visible marks when the Ministry arrived.

He would have to be careful.

"I'm just saying it's a bad look," Calvin continued. "A real bad look. I don't know what the Ministry folks would think of you doing something like this. I know I said Chester doesn't use the fighter's real names, but it's still your face out there. It's still *you* fighting. What if the wrong people see that video and recognize you?"

Emmett snapped his fingers again, and chopped his hand in the direction they were going.

Keep going.

Thankfully, Calvin remained silent for the rest of the journey. Driving made keeping a conversation going difficult, because you had to see the signs to understand them. Emmett's vocabulary then devolved to yes-or-no answers and simple hand gestures. So, he couldn't tell his friend he had already considered the possibility that someone from the Ministry of Children might see the video, and he thought it was rather slim. However, they would definitely see that old furniture in his house. Emmett dreaded the thought of one of them actually sitting on the couch and sinking into the cushions like the sofa was trying to eat them alive. No, it wasn't good enough. She deserved better.

Isabelle.

Ten minutes later, they saw the crudely painted sign on the side of the road.

CDA Productions

NEXT RIGHT

Emmett pointed to the sign and made a questioning gesture.

"Yep, that's our place. It stands for Chester-Dupuis-is-awesome," Calvin said like his confidence in this endeavor was waning the closer they got to the turnoff.

It was a nice approach. Emmett was expecting some packed-dirt track that led into a clearing somewhere. The gravel approach was big enough to support two vehicles and looked nicer than Emmett's own lane. They followed it into a large clump of trees. The nicely manicured road led to a gravel parking lot where dozens of other vehicles were already neatly parked in tight rows. Ahead of them, a small teenager wearing a reflective vest was directing them towards their assigned spot.

"What the fuck?! He has a parking attendant?!" Calvin said with stunned amazement as he followed the skinny attendant's directions and parked next to a similar-looking truck, but it had a nice set of chrome running-boards, and it was blue. The two of them got out of the truck, walked around to the front of the vehicle and looked at the operation in front of them.

The whole area was cut out of a grove of trees. All around them tall, deciduous trees sheltered them in all directions. The large parking lot was fenced off with a solid-looking wooden fence that made Emmett a little envious. From there, a small fenced-off path led to a manned-booth with a banner that read, *admissions.* Beyond that, they could see crowds of people lingering around the open area. There was a large metal vehicle shed, similar to the one Emmett had in his own yard, and off to the side of that he could make out another fenced section of the yard.

Emmett whistled.

I thought you said this was run by some kid.

"I thought it was," Calvin said while shrugging his shoulders. Clearly, he was as surprised with what he was seeing as Emmett was.

You have never been here? Emmett said giving Calvin a look.

"No, this is my first time. I only heard about it. I never imagined...*this*." Calvin gestured to the neatly manicured grounds ahead of them. "Come on," he said, gently slapping Emmett on the chest. "Let's go find Chester." He gave Emmett a fatherly look. "You're sure you still want to go through with this?" Emmett just smiled at him.

You could always lend me the money for the furniture set, Emmett signed as a joke. Calvin looked at him with an unimpressed expression.

"Okay," Calvin replied quickly. "Let's go get you signed up."

They followed the fenced path to the admissions booth, a bored-looking young woman with short blonde hair in jeans and a tight-fitting halter top looked up at them from her phone.

"Twenty-five dollars," she said like it was the hundredth time she had those exact words. Emmett quickly surveyed the people on the inside and did some quick math before he let out a low whistle.

"We're here to talk to Chester," Calvin said quickly.

The woman with the short blonde hair then reached under her counter and produced a small walkie-talkie. It made a single beep when she pressed the button on the side.

"Chaz, there's some guys here to see you." She looked at them with the same bored expression as she held the radio loosely in her hand.

A few seconds later it came to life.

"Okay, cool. Let them in. I'm on my way." A high pitched, excited voice said over the radio.

The girl behind the booth waved them threw with a certain lackluster that Emmett had already come to expect from her. Like she was annoyed with the whole interaction.

Emmett and Calvin walked into the main area of the grounds and meandered around the admissions area, waiting for Chester Dupuis to arrive.

"They even have a goddamn food truck," Calvin said and pointed towards the panel van with the smoke stack on top, and an awning on the side that provided a nice bit of shade for the serving counter. The line was six people deep. Emmett spied two teenagers shuffling around quickly on the inside.

"Yo, yo, yo!" a voice called loudly behind them.

When they turned, he and Emmett saw a short, skinny *man* in pants and a white t-shirt that was at least two sizes too big for his frame. He had a blue bandana tied tightly around his small head, and a large gold chain that slapped against his chest with each animated step the little man took.

"My man *Calvin Biggs*!" he said Calvin's name like he was introducing the man to wrestling fans and used both his hands to point towards Calvin, who stood, clearly unimpressed, with his hands perched on his hips. *"They call me Mister Biggs!"* Chester chuckled, clearly pleased with himself. "And if it isn't the *man, the myth, the legend, R-TWO!"*

Emmett quickly stepped towards the small man with the ridiculous grin on his stupid face and gave him a challenging look that warned him against using that name again. Chester looked wide-eyed as he quickly halted all forward motion and even jumped back a bit.

"Yeah, don't call him that," Calvin said smugly. Chester just smiled.

"No, yeah, I feel you. My man has this whole air of danger around him. I feel it, I feel it!" Chester fanned his grinning face. "It's like a heat. It's radiating off my dude here. Jesus! Look at the size of you, my guy." Chester looked at Emmett with an expression of awe. He reached out and grabbed Emmett's bicep and gave it a squeeze. Emmett promptly slapped the man's hand away, much to Chester's amusement. "Feisty! I like it."

"Jesus, Chester," Calvin began.

"Chaz," Chester corrected.

"What the hell is all this?" Calvin said and motioned around himself. "Is this even legal?"

Chester just laughed.

"Legal?!" Chester chuckled and shielded his shocked expression with his hand. "Is this shit *legal*? This is a *full-fledged-entrepreneurial-enterprise*, my guy! Yo, check it, I got me a business license." Chester checked the point off on his finger.

"You have a business license from the Town of Churchbridge?"

"*And*, I have a *special promotions* permit from the town that allows me to hold events *in-perpetuity*," Chester said excitedly. "As long as I do it on the weekends, and on my own land. I also can't have more than five hundred people on-site during events. *Fire regulations*," he said it like it annoyed him.

By the look on his face, Calvin wasn't expecting the news.

"The town knows you're doing this?"

"Fuck yeah, son!" Calvin said excitedly and pointed to an older man in the distance in jeans and a faded black polo shirt. "That's Councilman Bailey, right there." Chester then waved vigorously at the man and called out to him.

Yo! My Dude! Councilman Bailey! Good to see you, my guy! Enjoy yourself out there!"

The man turned and sheepishly waved towards Chester. Emmett could see the man had a half-eaten hotdog in one hand and a beverage in the other. After that, he tried to discreetly move off and blend into the meandering crowd. Chester laughed weirdly and playfully slapped Calvin on the chest.

"Check this shit out, I even have a few dudes from the Langenburg detachment doing security."

"What?!" Calvin clearly couldn't believe what he was hearing.

"Fuck yeah, those dudes are keeping my shit tight out there. You wouldn't believe the shit people try to pull on me." Chester searched the grounds until he spotted a serious-looking man in a black hoodie with Security written in bold, yellow letters on the back.

"That's my guy. Jimmy." He quickly pointed the man out to Calvin.

Emmett watched with amusement as the serious-looking man turned and recognized Calvin. He locked eyes with him and Calvin threw his arms wide in the classic *what-the-hell* gesture. Jimmy suddenly didn't look so serious as he quickly turned and walked in the other direction.

"So," Chester said as he turned back to focus his attention on the two of them, and clapped his hands together loudly. "What's the *dealio* here, gentlemen? Are we here to *participate* or *spectate*? Today's fight will be in the outdoor ring. First time this season!" he added excitedly. "The sun's out, it's time to bring the guns out, am I right?"

I hate this guy, Emmett signed to Calvin.

"What'd big-man say?" Chester looked to Calvin.

"He said he's here to fight."

"Fuck yeah, he is! I got the perfect guy all lined up, and chomping at the bit to go. I thought I'd have to bench him, because I didn't have anyone lined up that's this guy's size, but you'll do nicely." Chester stepped forward and slapped Emmett on the arm.

"It's a thousand bucks a fight, right?"

"Five hundred," Chester quickly corrected. "Five hundred per fight. A thousand if he wins. If he gets fight-of-the-night, I'll pay out a cool fifteen to his ass." Emmett didn't even have to sign anything. Calvin was quick to speak.

"What the hell is fight-of-the-night?"

"Yo, check it Last month this guy smashed this dude's nose, fucking blood everywhere. Presto, Bitch! Fight of the night! People love that shit. My views go through the roof when crazy shit like that happens. So, I try to incentivize performance with a little bonus." Chester smiled widely when he finished, as if he was proud of his business acumen. Inwardly, Emmett smiled at this new development.

He signed again.

"How many times can he fight?"

"Big-man's looking to make some money, is he? Alright, alright, alright! I can respect that. We're all chasing those dolla bills y'all. As long as he clears medical, and I can find someone who wants a piece of him, he can fight all night. But I only pay the win-lose-or draw money once though. SO, if you lose your second match, you're not getting anything. You lost that shit for free, ya feel me?" Emmett nodded. "Okay, let's get you set up with a waiver, and get this shit going."

The ring was at least twice as large as a standard fighting octagon, Chester explained the added area was to allow his cameraman to freely roam within the fighting arena. He warned each participant that there would be dire consequences if his employees or his equipment were to be damaged during the fight.

Emmett looked around at the other fighters, which was a generous term for them. Brawlers most of them, a few of them had nervous looks on their faces, like fledgling gladiators at the gates of the coliseum. *Hardly a coliseum*, Emmett thought as he looked back to the large animal pen that was lined with hay bales. The ground was covered with a deep sand, that was fine enough to be from a beach on the coast somewhere.

The rules were simple. It was a standard MMA match, and the participants were expected to fight three five-minute rounds until they couldn't fight anymore, or until the *referee* blew the whistle. Chester was also adamant about that point. Once that whistle blows, you stop fighting and move to your corner, or else. He had a serious expression on his face, a threat that Chester wanted to strongly imply. If, by some chance, the fight ended in a draw, both fighters would only be paid the five hundred for the match.

Emmett wasn't worried about any of that. He wasn't here to prove anything, just make some quick cash and slip out unscathed. Hopefully.

Emmett's fight was the third one in Chester's line-up. He came to the area that was set up for the fighters to wait until their fight was called. It was just a bunch of benches that were set up in the back of the vehicle shed. When he called his name, Emmett stood, and then Chester called a name he didn't recognize. Across from him, a large, young man with wide shoulders stood up and looked defiantly at Emmett. They both silently filed out of the vehicle shed and followed Chester to the arena. Emmett quickly spotted Calvin sitting in the raised bleachers that were set around the animal pen. He also spied the bag of popcorn in his hands. Emmett moved to his end of the ring where he removed his shirt, shoes, and socks. He waited for Chester to call him.

Emmett used the only pseudonym he could think of.

"And in this corner, we have *King*!" Chester boisterously said and Emmett took that as his cue to climb the side of the pen and hop into the ring.

The two fighters moved to the center of the ring, while some teenager in a striped polo shirt recited their instructions.

They both had mouthguards in, even though it was considered optional. Emmett had the same mouthguard he had when his father took him to the dentist to get a custom-fit guard that was molded to his teeth. Luckily, his teeth hadn't changed much in the decade or so since he last wore it. The blonde-haired bruiser staring at him had one that you could buy at Wal-mart for less than twenty dollars. Emmett returned the young man's gaze with one that lacked any emotion at all. His opponent looked like he came straight from a university football team. He stood as tall as Emmett did, but he was considerably leaner. Emmett guessed the man had less than five-percent bodyfat on him. Except for the angry scowl on his face, his opponent looked like he could pass for a fitness model.

They touched fists and moved to their corners. Emmett rolled his head to loosen his neck muscles and waited for the bell.

An airhorn blew to signal the start of the round. Emmett took a deep breath.

For Isabelle.

His opponent lived up to his youthful looks.

He charged angrily across the sand towards Emmett and started throwing a fury of blows at him, all off a weak-looking jab. Emmett considered his face as he blocked the shots he could, and covered up the ones he couldn't. A few punches dug painfully into Emmett's bicep as he raised his hands up to cover the man's devastating hooks.

Then a round kick battered Emmett's side before he backed off a step and begun anew. Again, starting off a weak jab. The punches came from all directions, Emmett was careful of his face, which meant he had to sacrifice his body on a few occasions. As before, the man sent a savage round kick to Emmett's side before he backed up the step.

Outwardly, it probably looked like the blonde-haired man was punishing him the entire round. Like this fight between giants was wholly one-sided. Emmett even imagined when the round ended with a second air horn blast, a few spectators had already written him off. Emmett went back to his corner, drank from the water bottle Chester provided, and looked up at the stands.

What are you doing? Calvin signed clumsily with the popcorn bag in his hand. Emmett just waved him off and took another drink from the bottle before the next round started.

As before, when the airhorn sounded, the blonde bull charged across the ring. Emmett met the weak jab, breathed normally as he blocked the incoming punches, and he waited for the round kick to come.

When it did, Emmett clenched his forearm, twisted at his waist and brutally chopped his opponent's shin bone, right below the knee. The man's leg struck Emmett's forearm, close to the elbow, and he watched with great satisfaction as he winced and staggered back. *Yeah, I bet that didn't feel good,* Emmett said to himself as he stepped closer to the man, keeping the pressure on. Almost begging him to react.

When he did, it was the only mistake Emmett allowed.

Emmett moved in close as the tall blonde man staggered back, and almost on cue, the weak jab shot out. Emmett didn't even slow down his approach. He lined up the punch and ducked his head down at the last second.

Crack.

Emmett felt the blow land solidly right above his hairline. Emmett didn't know what exactly broke in the man's hand as it struck the thickest part of the skull, but something definitely broke. Emmett could tell by the sharp way the man withdrew his hand. The blow didn't bother Emmett at all, but his opponent didn't see that. He was on autopilot. When his opponent's right hand came, Emmett easily blocked it and sent a nasty hook to the left side of the man's face.

When the blow landed, it made a loud slapping noise that reverberated around the ring. Emmett heard the spectators suck in a collective breath in horror. Emmett's opponent was badly stunned, but too inexperienced to know how to deal with it. He just kept on the attack. He recovered from the blow and Emmett could see the attack in the man's eyes a half second before he moved in for the body shot.

Emmett almost felt sorry for him.

He just ducked down, moved forward inside the punch, and delivered an uppercut to the man's downturned face. *Sorry kid*, Emmett grunted as the blow lifted his opponent up onto the tips of his toes, and followed it up with a stepping elbow to the man's sternum.

The stepping elbow was an unconventional attack to say the least. It was a favorite of Emmett's. Though, he'd never hit a person with it, until now. He hit the hundred-pound punching bag at the back of his vehicle shed with the same blow a thousand times. Each time the bag always swung dangerously back from the blow.

Last time he weighed himself, Emmett was two-hundred-and-forty-two pounds, that's a considerable amount of weight to be accelerating towards you. Plus, the area of the elbow he used was probably the size of a large pine comb, which wasn't very large at all. He didn't know the physics behind it, but Emmett suspected that blow landed with a force comparable to Maggie's beanbag shotgun round.

His opponent didn't seem to like it too much.

The spectators gasped when the blonde man's feet left the ground. They held their collective breath the whole time his opponent was in the air, and winced when he finally came to rest in the fine sand a short distance back from where he started. Emmett saw his opponent's panicked face as he hugged himself and struggled to breathe as he writhed in pain.

Then the whistle blew. The fight was over.

The crowd cheered.

Emmett fought two more times before Chester cut him off, saying there was nobody left who was willing to fight him. It was a shame because Emmett could have kept going. No one had landed a solid blow on his face. He left Chester's little operation virtually untouched with a cheque for four thousand dollars in his pocket.

***

Emmett waved at the black SUV that pulled into the yard. He wore his best shirt and a pair of freshly washed blue jeans. He didn't want to look like he made an effort, he needed these people to think this was how he had always lived his life. He needed to look clean, but natural. Nic Jones had called from the airport in Winnipeg when her party was renting the SUV they used to drive out to his place.

It was a four-hour drive.

Emmett spent the first two anxiously running through the house making sure everything was in order. The last two hours he spent sitting on the porch, rubbing his hands together, nervously waiting for the people who would decide his and Isabelle's future to show up.

As they filed out of the vehicle, Emmett took a deep breath and put on his best smile. The driver was an older gentleman with short salt-and-pepper hair and a pleasant looking face. He wore a dark suit with a white shirt, no tie, and the top two buttons of his shirt were unbuttoned. There was a smaller, neatly dress man who exited from the passenger side. Emmett quickly recognized Nicole Jones as she exited the back in a sharp-looking pant suit, and on the other side, an older lady exited the vehicle. The group took a moment to scan their surroundings as a group before the driver moved towards Emmett with a broad smile on his face. Behind him, the smaller man kept close by his side.

"Mister Brooks, I presume?" he said and extended his hand towards Emmett. "I'm Edward Maye, Director of the Ministry of Children for the Ontario Government." Emmett quickly shook the man's hand. "I'd like to first introduce you to Norton Mills. He'll be our translator for today."

"Mister Brooks." The smaller man stepped forward with his hand. "I understand your speech impaired," he said and Emmett nodded. "Would you like me to translate what my colleagues say as well as your words?"

No. That's okay. I can hear just fine. Might as well save yourself some work.

"As you wish," Norton said with a small grin. "From this point on I'll translate for you. If, at any point, there's something you don't wish to be translated, like if you want to address me personally, simply raise your hand." Emmett nodded his understanding and signed. "Thanks," he said, officially beginning his translation. "I appreciate that."

Edward introduced his subordinate from the Ministry of Children, Nicole Jones, Emmett smiled affably, stepped forward and shook her hand like it was the first time he was meeting the woman. The older lady was the Liaison Officer from Manitoba's Child Services agency, Joan Linns.

Just like that, the home inspection had started.

Emmett was quick to learn that Edward Maye wasn't the kind of man that wasted a bunch of time on small talk. With Edward in the lead, Emmett took the group on a tour of every building on the premises, and once that was done, they moved into the house. Where Emmett led them into every room and stepped back as the small group poked around the space. They opened cabinets, drawers, and closets. They even checked under the beds.

As the group went through his bedroom, Emmett stood in front of his brand-new coffee table that was part of the cream-colored leather furniture set he purchased. He caught Nic Jones passing by his bedroom door. She cautiously glanced in his direction, smiled and used her free hand to give him a subtle thumbs-up.

After that, Emmett relaxed.

CHAPTER 6

Zeke

"Get going, shit-bird," the guard behind him said angrily and gave his shoulder a gentle shove for him to pick up his pace. Zeke grimaced as the slight touch sent shockwaves of pain up his spine and caused him to stumble on his next step. "I ain't got all day."

"Putain de connard!" fucking asshole, Zeke grumbled as he caught himself and continued to hobble down the wide, sterile-looking hallway with the colored lines on the floor.

Millhaven maximum-security prison, in Bath, Ontario, was supposedly the most modern prison in all of Canada. Not the newest, not the best, or the most secure. The most *modern.* Zeke didn't even know what that word meant in relation to a prison. As far as he could tell, it meant they added new doors, more cameras, and then put on a fresh coat of paint to cover up the rotten bits. He still saw it though, in the corners, all the little nooks and crannies they overlooked during the renovation. They weren't hard to find, if you knew where to look. Zeke prided himself in always knowing where to look to find the rot in the world. This place was no different. They hid it well, but he still saw the tiny bits of decay in the fifty-year-old prison.

It comforted him.

It was still a prison, though. Things still happened. Unfortunate things.

He was six months away from the end of his sentence. Five years, no parole. It was like skating on ice to him.

Well, until recently.

The Organization was paying for his ride, it was one of the perks of being a member. Zeke still didn't know what the actual organization was called, it didn't have a name. At least, not one he was aware of. He asked, of course. He was French, after all. French people were curious about the world. The answer he later got was to stop asking questions. Even after he was initiated into the group, and cut his pinkie finger off at the second knuckle as the admission fee, they still didn't give him any details. What they did give him was an assignment, perfectly tailored to his talents.

Cook.

They called it cooking meth because it was surprisingly similar to actual baking. You have ingredients, and a set of instructions for the correct preparation of the illicit drug, much like a recipe. Zeke first learned the process from a crew he used to run with in Montreal. It wasn't hard, but if one was to be successful at it, one had to pay attention to the details. That's what he was good at.

That, and people.

He was a people person. That's what got him out of the *lab.* Zeke was a humble person, he had to be. He knew there were people out there who could make a better-quality product than he could.

Like a chemist.

That's how he met Remy Lacroix, a promising chemistry major who had a budding marijuana habit. It didn't take Zeke long to convert the energetic, young student into a criminal. He just needed a taste of the good life before he forgot all about his aspirations of graduating.

He was the first piece.

The rest of his crew came together like moths to a flame.

"Don't give me that French-bullshit, just move your ass." The guard nudged him again in the spot on his shoulder that was brutally, and repeatedly, stomped on a few days ago.

"Ey man," Zeke cried back. "Can't you see I'm urting ere?" His thick French-Canadian accent made the words sound more musical than he intended.

He was only released from the medical wing yesterday, his injuries were far from healed, but he was out of danger. So, he was sent to his cell to struggle through the rest of the healing process. His list of injuries was numerous.

From top to bottom, the more impressive injuries included a fractured orbital bone on his left side, Zeke was pretty sure he knew the exact punch that broke it. A dislocated collarbone from the barrage of kicks he received once he fell to the ground, that's where he got the two broken ribs as well. The three broken fingers were from a slippered-foot that stomped down on his left hand. That happened right before he was about to wink out. It brought him back from the merciful abyss of unconsciousness and into the here-and-now real fast. The severely lacerated rectum however, that was an ugly bit of business. One he didn't appreciate, not one bit.

It seemed personal.

As far as Zeke knew, he was getting along fabulously with the other inmates he shared this space with. This wasn't his first stint in prison. He knew how to keep his head down and blend into the surroundings. In prison, the people who stood out were the fresh fish, the poor fools who hadn't been initiated yet. The ones who had yet to learn. That's what Zeke couldn't figure out. He hadn't made any moves on anyone in here, nor had he made any ripples amongst the other inmates. So why the assault?

He intended to find out.

"Yeah, that's right," the guard said with some amusement from behind him. "I heard you got into a *lover's spat*." That's what the guards called rape in this place, like it was a joke. To them, it probably was. To those uptight fuckers, it was probably the funniest thing in the world.

"Et si je mettais ma bite dans ta cul, nous verrons ce que ça fait," Zeke said with a sort of musical venom. *How about I stick my cock up your ass, and we'll see how it feels?*

"Yeah, whatever Frenchie." Zeke just smiled at the man's ignorance.

"Aren't you guys supposed to be bilingual?" Zeke asked lightly.

"I know enough," the large guard said quickly, like his feelings had been hurt. "Keep moving."

"It's da official, goddamn language of Canada," Zeke said looking back and giving the dumb-looking guard an incredulous look.

"It's *one* of the official languages," the guard shot back.

"Yeah, da first one. Dis is a federal prison, man!" Zeke threw his head up in mock frustration. "You're supposed to be able to interact wit da inmates using *eiter* of da official languages. Jesus, Man! Were's da representation?"

"This is Ontario, dipshit. Nobody speaks French in Ontario." Zeke just groaned.

"Tu es un idiot tellement inculte," Zeke clearly said, almost challenging the man. *You are such an uncultured idiot.*

"Give it a rest," the guard complained. "Save it for your lawyer, you can speak that bullshit with him all you like."

Zeke remained silent after that. The burly, uneducated guard directing him down the hallway had a good point. He should be focusing his energy on his meeting with The Barrister.

The Organization could get to you anywhere, and of course, if they needed to get a message to someone who was incarcerated, you sent a barrister. It was just another fancy word for a lawyer. The Canadian court system was a throw back from the UK system, so they even wore goofy black robes in court too. The best thing about barristers though, was that they required client meetings to be conducted in a private conference room, away from the riff-raff and the prying eyes of the government.

If he was here, Zeke thought to himself as he hobbled closer to the conference room. *That means they must already know about the attack.* Part of Zeke was even hopeful they had plans of retribution in mind. One of the many perks of being a member of The Organization was knowing that whatever was done to Zeke, was also done to them. So, whoever it was that rammed their prick into his asshole, also rammed it into The Organization's. His handlers even sent their man to reassure Zeke personally that everything was under control, his attackers would be caught, punished, and a message would be sent.

Half way down the corridor to the official visitor's room, the guard stopped him in front of a solid steel door. He made him stand so close to the door that Zeke's nose was practically touching it while the guard reached around and open the door. There behind the plain square table was a serious-looking man in a beautifully tailored dark suit. The Barrister. John Cole, The Organization's bagman sat looking quite comfortable in the dull room. His dark hair was slicked back; it framed his flawless face perfectly.

If you're going to be the face of The Organization, Zeke mused to himself as the oafish guard removed his cuffs and shackles, *I guess you better be good looking.* Cole was more than just *good looking.* He looked like the devil himself was sitting behind that conference table, quietly waiting to claim his next soul.

"Ezekiel," The Barrister said coldly as a way of a greeting once Zeke stood across from him. John Cole insisted on using people's full names, it was a quirk of his that Zeke found annoying. He didn't like hearing his full name, he didn't like the sound of it.

"Mister Cole, so good to see you again. To wat do I owe da pleasure of your company?" Zeke gave the man a side-eyed glance as he watched the guard exit the room and close the door behind him.

"Please, have a seat, we have much to discuss." The Barrister gracefully motioned to the empty seat across from him.

"I'll stand, tanks."

"I'm afraid I must insist," Cole said with an apologetic grin, and again motioned towards the empty metal chair that had little cushioning for his tender rear. "Have a seat," the face of The Organization said again. Zeke raised an eyebrow at the request but he could do little else. When The Barrister spoke, it was The Organization speaking.

Zeke slowly eased himself down into the uncomfortable chair, winced several times when barbs of lightning erupted from inside him and coursed up his spine, but he managed to finally settle into a semi-comfortable position. When done, he looked towards Cole and spread his arms wide with a quizzical look. *Happy?*

"You have, I have no doubt, received the message from our employers," Cole said as a matter of fact.

Message?! Zeke hadn't received any communications from any of his contacts. Besides that, if he was to get direct instruction from The Organization, it would come through John Cole.

"I am here to log your response to said message."

"Wat da fuck are you talking about? Message? Wat message? I've been too busy getting beaten witin an inch of my life." Zeke quickly motioned about his bruised and battered face.

He didn't know what the hell The Barrister was playing at, and he frankly didn't have the patience to play along. Christ's sakes, The Organization was supposed to protect him while on the inside. Zeke wanted to know what they were going to do about his attackers.

John Cole chuckled coldly once.

"Ezekial," he said with some amusement. Like he was patiently teaching an ignorant child. "I assure you, you *have* received the *message.*" Then Cole gave him a knowing look that caused Zeke to pause.

Wait a minute!

"The only real question that remains is, did you understand it?"

Membership into the elusive criminal empire definitely had its privileges, but it also came with a hefty number of obligations. Zeke would be taken care of while in prison, but the price was the meth supply from his crew didn't stop or even slow down. Zeke was a facilitator. He didn't need to be physically present to run his operation. At least, that's what he told his handlers.

Motherfuckers!

Zeke huffed angrily in front of Cole, but he didn't say anything. Not yet. The news was still too raw. He didn't trust himself to act professionally. His current position put him at a disadvantage. The only reason The Organization hadn't *terminated* him for his incarceration was because it was technically the higher-up's fault that he got pinched in the first place, and Zeke kept his mouth shut and pled no contest to the charges. Just like John Cole instructed him to do. That, and the drug supply wasn't interrupted in the slightest. Problem with that was, that also meant Zeke wasn't an instrumental member of the process. He was riding the razor's edge with his employers as it was, he couldn't afford a misstep now.

Zeke breathed in deeply and ran his hand through his long, jet-black hair.

"Ow can I be of service?" he asked with a sweet smile on his face, that John Cole no doubt saw right through. It was all part of the game. His handlers didn't expect him to like it, but he still had to play along.

"Your family's bakery is producing less bread," The Barrister said quickly.

"Oh?"

"Twenty percent, actually." Zeke was somewhat surprised the man didn't produce a spreadsheet from the briefcase on the table. "Not to mention the deliveries have been, how can I put this gently, *erratic*. The distributors have been complaining. With no bread, their restaurant's bottom-line suffers. Profits go down."

"I understand," Zeke said lightly, hoping to inspire confidence. It didn't work.

"Do you? You and your family's bakery were brought into this organization for one reason, and one reason only, you make good bread. But don't delude yourself into thinking you're the only ones who make bread. You're not, you never were. Production goals were set, *and* agreed upon. As a token of goodwill, our employers have given you considerable leeway already."

"Dis is da first I'm hearing about it," Zeke cut in but was silenced by a single finger from John Cole.

"Then you're not paying attention to your operation," he replied sharply. "An effective manager does not need to be informed on how well, *or* how poorly, his business is doing. It is his responsibility to know that information. If your business partners have to inform you of your failings, that means you have already severely dropped the ball." Zeke bit his tongue while The Barrister preached at him. "Now we realize your current situation may make your job challenging, but management has fulfilled its side of the contract. Have you not enjoyed a relatively calm and peaceful incarceration?" Zeke nodded slowly. "Until recently, of course. Management thought it was important to demonstrate what the rest of your incarceration would be like if you continue to fail to fulfill your obligations." He breathed in deeply and scratched his hawkish nose.

There it was, the threat. Actually, in reality, it was more akin to a promise. There was no place in Canada he could go to escape them, and people like himself weren't exactly international travellers.

"Sounds like a real pain in da ass," Zeke said without a hint of humor. None-the-less, The Barrister chuckled a bit. "I'll take care of it."

"See that you do. Now, I have also been authorized to inform you that our employers have big plans for you when you do leave this *unfortunate* place."

Here it comes, Zeke thought and allowed himself a slight grin. The Organization liked to show the stick first, then the carrot.

"They are thinking of expanding your operation. Moving it to a secure location, away from prying eyes. More staff to help you with the day-to-day operations. You've proven yourself, in a way, and our employers are ready to give you an opportunity to see how you handle *the big leagues,* as they say." The way the man said it, Zeke suspected he wasn't much of a sports fan.

"Sounds to me like dere's going to be a lot more bread out dere," Zeke said dryly.

"*And*," John Cole added excitedly. "More money for you and your associates. You're moving up, Ezekial. This is what you wanted, what you sacrificed for," John Cole said and briefly motioned towards his partial pinkie finger on his left hand. "If it makes you feel better, because you still look a little...*sore,* each of us had to suffer certain *indignities* in order to advance through the ranks."

"Huh-uh," Zeke said unconvincingly. He wondered, if he had reacted differently to the stick, would they have even offered him the carrot? Was his sodomy arranged to be some sort of sick test? It made sense to him. Zeke couldn't actually argue with their methods. Honestly, it was cleaner and less disruptive, than killing one of his crew, or himself, for that matter.

"Now," The Barrister pressed his hands together. "When you return to your *enclosure,* you will find a burner phone under your pillow with enough minutes on it to call your associates and get this nasty supply issue taken care of." Zeke was keen to notice that the man didn't specify exactly how long that was. "Thirty minutes later, a man will arrive at your door to retrieve the phone. After that, assuming there are no further supply issues, your privileges will resume. Now," The Barrister clapped his hands together once and wiped them together a few times, like he was cleaning them. "This concludes our business. You may return to your enclosure now, unless, of course, there is some other business you would like to discuss."

Zeke gave the man a cold smirk. He actually did have other business he felt was important.

"Wat about da guy who fucked me up da ass? He just gets a pass?" Zeke held up his left hand and wiggled his pinkie knub. "I'm a goddamn member. Doesn't dat mean someting? Our employers have no problems with its members being disrespected like dat? Eh?"

"Mr. Simard," John Cole cautioned with a bored expression. "You are half a year away from your freedom, *and* a promotion.

Surely, even you, can see the stupidity of jeopardizing that with petty aspirations of vengeance."

"Easy for you to say, you don't ave a lacerated asshole." The Barrister seemed unimpressed with his approach, so Zeke changed his tactics. "Ow do you tink it's going to look if one of your own guys gets attacked like dat witout any sort of repercussion?"

"You realize, of course, we were responsible for your attack, right? Like, you do understand that part of it, correct?"

"Yes, I believe you made dat part of it abundantly clear, and dat's fine. I get da necessity of it. A bit over da top for my liking, but who am I to argue wit your methods. You got a business to run, and a reputation to upold," Zeke looked at him with a cold indifference. "So do I." Zeke scratched the bridge of his nose with his bandaged fingers. "Da street is a nasty place. Tings like dis get out, people start to tink they can get away wit shit. Dis our esteemed employers must know. We can solve a lot of problems in da future by tying up a few loose ends now."

"You're not going to let this go, are you Ezekiel?"

"Would you?" The Barrister just shook his head in disappointment.

"I would see the benefit of letting it go. That's what I would do, but I can see by the animalistic look in your eyes that this is a thorn in your side. Fine, I will text you a name on the burner phone. This person will be the one responsible for your...*pain*, but more importantly, this person will mark the end of this issue. Do with the name as you will but," John Cole paused to emphasize his next words. "Don't get caught. Whatever fate befalls this man can not lead back to you in the slightest. Do you understand me, Ezekiel?" Zeke smiled and nodded fractionally. "Not even a whisper of a suspicion."

"Like a ghost in da night," Zeke said with a sly smile. "Trust me. I can be very discreet."

"See that you are. Is there anything else?" The Barrister asked with a certain amount of annoyance. Zeke smiled affably.

"Nope. I'm good."

"Okay, then *shoo*!" The Barrister made a tiny sweeping motion with both his hands, like Zeke was a spot of dirt he was trying to clean of the table. "Back to your cage." Zeke sucked air in through his teeth as he leveraged himself off the hard chair. "Next time we meet will be a few days before your release. We have to go over the conditions of your release and subsequent probation."

"I look forward to it," Zeke said and hobbled towards the door while The Barrister remained seated. It was one of the man's kinks. Other lawyers would rise off their chairs, and maybe even shake their client's hands. Not John Cole. He just gave you an icy look as you exited the room, like it had been his room all this time, and he simply allowed Milhaven to use it.

"And Ezekiel?" John Cole called to him a moment before he was about to knock on the door to alert the guard. "You do not want to see me before then, so make sure you don't."

Zeke gave the man a brief wave before tapping on the door with his uninjured hand.

Back in his cell, Zeke waited until the guard closed the door and disappeared down the corridor. Even then, he counted out a full minute before moving toward his pillow. Zeke quickly opened the small flip phone and awkwardly punched in Remy's digits as he held the phone weakly in his bandaged fingers.

"Hello?" Remy's voice came over the line after only one ring.

"It's me," Zeke said in his native tongue. The guard had been wrong when he said no one spoke French in Ontario, but few enough did that he and Remy could use it to avoid prying ears.

"Zeke? My god! Whose number is this? How are you calling me? Oh shit! Did you get out early?" Remy fired off the questions with his signature nervous energy. He probably would have kept going with his incessant questions if Zeke hadn't cut him off.

"Shut up, you idiot!" he said sharply. *"I don't have time for bullshit right now. I know Remy, I know about what you've been doing with the shipments."*

"What?" Remy acted like he was surprised by the accusation, and doing a poor job of it as well. *"What do you-."*

"I know about all of it. You've been shorting the shipments." He didn't say it like an accusation, Zeke said it like it was a cold, hard fact. *"My numbers are telling me by at least twenty percent. You mind telling me just what the fuck you think you're doing?"*

"How did-," he started to ask, but again Zeke cut him off.

"It's MY goddamn operation, Remy. It's my job to know these things. Did you really think I wouldn't find out?"

"I'm sorry, Zeke. It's not my fault. It's just, well," Remy's voice sheepishly drained away to nothingness.

"Well?" Zeke barked. He kept his voice down because he didn't want to attract any attention to himself. He was more than sure this little conversation was cleared with the guards, but he didn't want to take any chances. Cell phones were strictly prohibited. *"Speak up. I don't have all day."*

"Some of the other guys were wanting to make a little extra cash on the side." Zeke ground his teeth together.

"You greedy assholes! There's plenty of money for the four of you."

"Seven."

"What?"

"There's seven of us in the crew now, Zeke."

Zeke growled his frustration into the receiver of the tiny phone. *What the hell is going on over there?* He pinched the bridge of his nose with his good hand.

"Explain," Zeke simply said, *"quickly."*

On the other end of the line, he heard Remy take a deep sorrowful breath.

"A couple months back, Richard got beat up at a bar, like really bad. He spent the night in the hospital, boss." Remy said, like it explained everything. *"Anyways, after that, me and Richard decided it would be a good idea to have some more muscle around."*

"Muscle?" There was no doubt in Zeke's mind that Richard was hitting on someone else's girlfriend, and that's what got his ass kicked.

"Yeah, you know, to make sure people don't fuck with us when we're out in the clubs." Zeke breathed loudly over the phone, but he didn't interrupt. *"So, Levi has this girlfriend."*

"Levi? Like the fucking jeans?!" Zeke asked with obvious disdain. It sounded like it was the name of the first musclehead they came across.

"Yeah. So, anyways, he has this girlfriend, Charlotte. She's a lot of fun. She knows all the good places to party in the G.T.A, and she has a brother. Travis. He's a pretty big guy too. When we go out with those guys, nobody fucks with us. They were pretty cool in the beginning, but now..." Remy trailed off.

He didn't have to say anything else.

"Are you letting them take over my operation?"

"No," Remy said defensively, like he knew better than to let something like that happen. *"But they are starting to push their weight around a lot more than they used to. Then the whole money issue came up, and I didn't know what to do, so I let them skim a bit off the top. To make up the difference."*

"Jesus Christ, Remy! Twenty percent is a lot more than just skimming off the top. That's taking a goddamn shovelful off the top. I can't believe you could let this get this far. Shit, if you needed some protection, I could have arranged something."

"Yeah, but you're locked away, Zeke. You're always telling me I should take the initiative, and I thought I would try to solve this on my own."

"Well, good job, dipshit. Now, The Organization is involved. You've gone and fucked things up so badly they've taken notice, and they're not happy."

"What!?" Remy gasped.

Good, Zeke thought wickedly.

"Oh shit, oh shit, oh shit," Remy said in rapid-fire succession. Zeke could practically see him pacing around the room he was in, scratching the back of his head, like he did when he was worried about something. *"Fuck, man! What are we going to do?"* Hearing

those words, mixed in with the sweet desperation in his tone, was like music to his ears.

"Relax," he said quietly, now actively trying to bring the anxiety down. *"I have a meeting with them in a couple days. I'll smooth it over. Don't worry, but Remy, all this bullshit has to end. Immediately. No more skimming, no more fucking up the deliveries, and no more new faces."*

"What about Levi and Travis?"

"Are they using our product?" he asked with deep suspicion he already knew the answer.

"A little." Zeke clenched his fist at Remy's weak answer.

Rule one of cooking meth, don't use your own supply. Meth is a highly addictive narcotic. The second you start using your own product, you're taking money out of your own pocket. Plus, meth-heads are not known for their sense of moderation.

"Remy," he said with contained frustration. *"Are you, or any of the guys using our product?"*

"No, Zeke. I can't speak for the others, but you know I'm off that shit for good." Zeke touched his fist to his lips and said a silent prayer before he asked the next question.

"Do they know where the lab is?" He tried to asked the question lightly, he needed Remy to be truthful, and that little coward had a way of lying when he thought it would save his own hide.

Silence.

Zeke counted off a full thirty seconds before Remy spoke again.

"Yeah," Remi breathed out the answer finally.

Zeke wanted to crush the tiny phone in his hand, but his broken fingers could barely manage to hold it, much less break it. Instead, he moved the phone away as he hissed out a few choice curses and punched the air in front of him. Internally, he imagined he was smashing Remy's stupid face.

"Let me guess," Zeke said with scorn when he returned to the call. *"One of those fucking knuckleheads suddenly developed a keen interest in chemistry, and just wants to help you out with the cooks, right? Probably telling you some bullshit like it was a good idea to*

have someone else who knows the business side of things. Am I getting warm?"

"Charlotte did mention that she thought it was a good idea if someone else knew the process," Remy said with muted awe, like he was finally waking up to the danger he had brought to his crew.

"Remy, Jesus, use your head. These dirty little weasels are trying to take over the operation."

"What should I do? Like, I don't know, Zeke, those guys are some bad dudes. It's not like I can just tell them to stop coming around anymore."

"No," Zeke cut in, before he repeated himself, quieter this time. *"No, the main thing to do now is not to ruffle any feathers. I'll talk to the accountant, and I want you to get them on the payroll. Three thousand each."* A part of Zeke couldn't believe he was actually going to pay people not to take over his own operation. *"Tell them they are doing a great job. Also, you're going to have to cook three days a week to make up for the shortages, but only you and Richard are allowed in the lab. That's rule number-fucking-one, buddy. Under no circumstances can you break that rule. I'm serious here! Skim off the third cook. Give twenty-five percent to the meatheads, and the rest goes to our buyers to make up for the losses you've accrued. Maybe if we're lucky your new friends might party themselves to death."*

"Or get arrested," Remy said and perked up. Zeke just groaned again.

"No! We don't want that, because that bitch knows where the lab is. If they get pinched that will be the first thing she'll tell the police. No, just keep them happy and keep them out of the way." Zeke breathed deeply. *I'll deal with them when I'm on the outside,* he thought bitterly as his various injuries flared up angrily. *"Six months, Remy. You just have to keep your nose clean for six months."* His release suddenly felt like a lifetime away to him. *"Just keep our buyers happy. That's all that matters now. We can deal with the rest later."*

"What if something happens," Remy whined nervously. *"Jesus, Zeke, what are they going to do?"*

"They will start mailing pieces of your mother to you until you learn to walk-the-fucking-line!"

On the other end of the line, Zeke could hear Remy sniffling a little. Remy wasn't cut out for this kind of business. He was a great cook, but he lacked the balls to be upper-management material.

"They know where my mother lives?"

"They know where everyone's mother lives, fool! If they don't, they will find someone else you care about and put the squeeze on them to get what they want, what WE promised them! Listen, stop your moaning, it will be fine as long as you do what I say. Okay. I know exactly how to get us out of this. We're going to up the cooks to three times a week, you and Richard do the cook and the packaging, and Kevin and OJ do the drops. Same as always. No more fuck-ups. If my math is correct, with the increased production, we should make up for the shortages by the time I get out." Zeke knew that part wasn't required, but with The Organization, you went the extra mile to keep the higher-ups happy. That's how you got ahead with them. He knew his handlers had a long memory, and debts with them were never forgotten.

"Okay, yeah, you're right. I can do that. What about Travis, Levi, and Charlotte?"

"Don't worry about them, you probably won't see them until they burn through the cash and the meth. Hopefully that will keep them occupied until I can deal with them." Between the three of them, that's nine thousand dollars they could burn through, each and every month. Plus, enough drugs to kill a herd of horses. Zeke just prayed if he fed these losers enough cash and drugs, sooner or later the problem would deal with itself.

If he could only be so lucky.

Suddenly the little phone in his hand beeped three times in quick succession. Zeke pulled the tiny phone back to check the screen and was quickly informed he only had five minutes left. *Shit,* he thought as he quickly ran through the instructions he had given Remy. He needed to make sure nothing had been missed. The silence between them stretched out until Zeke was sure all the important bases had been covered. He could allow himself this one small thing.

"*Listen, I don't have much time left. Tell me what you know about* my little beautiful," Zeke said with a hushed tone.

He hadn't thought about her for such a long time, he couldn't. Thoughts of her made time stretch out into an eternity. She was his small, precious thing that he placed it into a dark corner in his mind. He had to put her out of his mind. If he didn't, it would drive him crazy knowing she was out there, in the cruel world, and he was stuck here, hundreds of kilometers away from her. A place where he couldn't keep her safe, shield her from the world's evils, or hold her in his arms again. No, he couldn't allow himself to dwell on how he had failed her by getting put in this place. He kept himself sane by thinking of the life he would make for them. Now that her mother was out of the way, it was up to him to make sure she had everything she needed.

She needed him, and he needed her. That's how love worked. That's how love was *supposed* to work. That's why what they had was so special, because it was pure.

"*Sure, Zeke,*" Remy responded obediently. "*Kevin has been keeping an eye on her, what do you want to know?*"

Zeke breathed in deeper, and shuddered. Suddenly, he felt a bit lighter.

"*Everything,*" he breathed.

CHAPTER 7

Belle

Belle sat on the edge of her bed and looked at her packed suitcase that her feet were resting on. She had gotten up earlier than usual today. Miss Jones had said she would be here at eight in the morning, and she was always very punctual. It was something people could rely on, and one of the things Belle liked about her. When Miss Jones said she was going to do something, she did it.

Mrs. Burke insisted Belle got up two hours early to get ready for her *big trip*. Belle enjoyed unlimited hot water in her shower, and a full breakfast that included bacon, eggs, *and* toast. Mrs. Burke cooked the food while Belle was in the shower, and when Belle sat down to her breakfast, Mrs. Burke sat across from her with a cup of coffee in front of her.

"Are you excited to meet your uncle?" she asked with an upbeat curiosity adults liked to use with her. As if she should have been excited to meet this stranger from another province.

"I dunno," Belle responded quietly after swallowing her mouthful of eggs. "I guess."

Truth was she wasn't excited about it, not one bit. She didn't want to leave Toronto. She spent her entire life here. It was all she had ever known. The life her mother made for them was here. Part of Belle had fantasized about reclaiming that life for herself when she was older, and out of the system. She even had daydreams of renting her and her mother's old apartment in Moss Park. Belle thought about eating at the same Thai restaurant her and her mother would eat at when she didn't feel like cooking. Across the street, Belle would stroll around the little park her mother took them to in the summer time when the interior of the apartment was sweltering.

Now, those dreams disappeared like wisps of smoke in a strong breeze.

"Manitoba is supposed to be nice," Mrs. Burke kept on with her upbeat offensive. "Lots of fresh air."

"I guess," Belle said noncommittedly, mostly because she felt she had to say something.

"Oh, sweetie," she said and reached across the table to place her hand on Belle's forearm. "I know it's hard starting over."

Not really, Belle thought, *this is my third time.* The hard truth of it was that it wasn't that hard starting over when you had nothing to lose. Belle ended her school year with subpar grades, and not one friend.

"This will be good for you, I promise. Your uncle sounds like he's a good man, and maybe a fresh start is just what you need. Don't get me wrong," she was quick to add. "We're going to miss you something terrible, but this is the best thing for you, to be with your family."

He's not my family, Belle quickly responded in her head, *he's just another stranger.*

"I know you may not be excited to leave, but I'm excited *for* you.

Belle said nothing further, and thankfully Mrs. Burke took the hint and let her eat what remained of her breakfast in peace. Afterwards, she was dismissed and she went upstairs to pack her small suitcase with her meager belongings.

Now, with everything she owned packed away neatly into her suitcase, and with no one else to say good-bye to, Belle just waited on her bed.

A half hour later, the doorbell rang and the front door was opened. Belle could hear a brief conversation take place before she could hear people begin to ascend the stairs. A second or two later, Miss Jones stood at her door with a sympathetic smile on her face.

"Hey kiddo," she said warmly. "You ready to go?"

"I guess."

Two minutes later Belle was ushered into the back seat of a plain-looking sedan while she held tightly onto her suitcase. It was important, after all. Everything that was still dear to her was in that suitcase. Belle didn't want to let it out of her sight.

There was a neat-looking young man that was in the driver's seat, and Miss Jones soon filed into the passenger seat.

Just like that, her time at the Burke's had come to an end. Belle didn't even look back as they drove away.

It took a full hour in morning traffic before their driver pulled up to the departure lane of the Pearson International Airport. Miss Jones said a few quick words to the driver before they said their goodbyes, Belle watched him depart and quickly disappear into the throng of cars passing by.

"Have you ever been on an airplane?" Miss Jones asked as they passed through the automatic doors of the airport.

"No."

"Oh, well, you're in for a treat." She said ominously and then said nothing further.

She moved straight to a ticket kiosk, punched in the appropriate information, and printed out their tickets and baggage tags. They both had small suitcases that could easily be considered carry-ons. After that, they went through security, where Belle had to sit quietly on a chair beside the security station while Miss Jones went over some paperwork with the guards. Apparently, taking her into another province required some form of special permission. Miss Jones had all the right forms, they were eventually cleared, but she was still rather bothered by the interaction none-the-less. From there they wandered the secured area while they waited for their flight to board.

"Here," Miss Jones said after she returned from the checkout at a small convenience store and handed her a small pack of chewing gum. "For your ears, when they pop."

"My ears are going to *pop*?" Belle asked suddenly. "Does it hurt?"

"Not really," Miss Jones said off-handedly. "It just feels kind of weird. Chewing gum helps with it." Belle gave the woman a quizzical look because she couldn't understand how something like chewing bubble-gum was going to help with spontaneously popping ears. Regardless, Belle stowed the gum in her pocket, along with the small packet of M&M's that she subtly slipped into her pocket as she was wandering aisles waiting for Miss Jones to complete her purchase.

Belle was disappointed to find out planes were kind of noisy. The loud whine of the engines reverberated around the cabin as the other passengers sat quietly in their small seats. A lot of them looked rather uncomfortable.

The take-off was fun.

Belle didn't know what to expect, which added to the sensation of them lifting into the sky. Her stomach dropped into her gut. It reminded her of the time her mother took her on a ferris wheel once during a carnival that was being held downtown for some reason. After that though, the fun quickly died away as the tedium of the flight took over. It was only an hour, but time seemed to stretch on as the engines filled the cabin with their white noise. Miss Jones read a magazine she bought at the same shop Belle procured her packet of M&M's. When she got to the end, she did the crossword. Every now and then she would lean over and ask Belle a question that had her stumped.

Mostly they stumped Belle as well.

"Lead character in Crimson Tides?" she asked, like she didn't even understand the meaning of the question. Belle sighed loudly as she thought of her failed attempts to make friends with the other girls at her old school.

"Malcolm," she answered coldly.

It doesn't matter now, she told herself. *Even if I did make friends with one of them, we wouldn't be friends for long.* They wouldn't be good friends, not the kind of friends that write letters to each other. No, she would have needed a lot of time to make a friend like that. *Maybe I never will.* The mean-spirited thought caused Belle to shrink in her seat a little bit.

Outside her window, the world slowly passed by beneath them. Miss Jones let her have the window seat, probably thinking it would be fun for Belle to gaze out at the wide world beneath them. Belle didn't like it so much.

It just reminded her of how small she really was.

She looked down at the vastness of a world that was just waiting to swallow her up. It reminded her that she was just some broken thing that was bouncing around, living off the tired mercies of others until she was old enough to be sent on her way. She was suddenly overwhelmed by a familiar sense of loneliness.

Belle turned away from the window and wept quietly in her seat, trying desperately not to draw attention to herself.

She soon felt Miss Jones's warm hand reach over and gently rub her back.

"It's okay, kiddo," she soothed. "You go ahead and cry, if you need to. Nobody will blame you for that. It'll get better," she said. "I promise."

"Nobody loves me," Belle said weakly between sobs. She didn't mean to, it just slipped out. She had inadvertently exposed the raw center of herself to the world.

"That's not true. I know one man who loves you," Miss Jones said with utter confidence. So much so, Belle looked up at her with her tear-stained eyes. Miss Jones had never lied to her before. "And I'm going to take you to him."

Their flight landed in Winnipeg, which was in Manitoba. Uncharted territory. It looked much like the airport they just left except smaller. Belle felt that if she stepped the wrong way and got lost in the crowd, she might just disappear entirely. She stuck close to Miss Jones as they made their way to the entrance, where there was another neatly dressed man. He had shorter dark hair, a warm-looking coat and was holding a sign with her name on it. Belle stayed close to her as she stepped towards the man.

"Norton," she said with a broad smile and extended her hand towards him. "Good to see you again."

It became apparent they knew each other as they exchanged pleasantries as people streamed past them.

Outside, Mr. Mills led them to a plain white SUV with *Government of Manitoba* stenciled on the side with a crest that Belle didn't recognize. She held on tightly to her luggage as she filed into the backseat. It was shortly after the vehicle pulled into traffic when Belle first learned this leg of their journey would take four hours. Belle groaned silently to herself as she stared out the window and watched the strange landscape pass her by as the adults spoke in the front.

They stopped for some fast food, so it wasn't all bad.

Soon enough, Winnipeg fell away and she looked out the window and marvelled with equal parts awe and horror at the vastness of the open countryside that spread out around them. They passed bright yellow fields that looked big enough to hold an entire city within their boundaries, stretched out as far as her eyes could see with mind-boggling uniformity. She watched as the wind moved through the plants in gentle waves that spread across their surface.

A half hour later, Belle let her suitcase slide between her legs to the floor, where she rested her shoes on it and tried to find a comfortable spot in the seat. She closed her eyes and thought of her mother, letting the memories of her play out inside her head like little movies while their SUV hummed its way down the road.

I'll be okay, she tried to reassure herself and thought about the suitcase at her feet. *As long as she's with me, I'll be okay.*

She didn't know why that would be true now, when it was never true before, but she hoped this time was different.

Belle perked up and opened her eyes to look out the window every time the vehicle slowed down. After about a dozen false alarms from the numerous small towns they passed through, she forced herself to just settle into her seat. The car slowed down again, but this time, she heard the crunch of gravel underneath the tires. She looked out her window and saw a small planted field swaying graceful in the breeze. Beyond that, she saw a clump of trees with some buildings hidden in the interior.

That's it, she said to herself. She didn't know how she knew that would be the place they would take her. She just knew. She wore a grim expression as they approached.

To her, it seemed like a lonely place.

Up ahead, there was a turnoff marked with a small, round reflector that stood atop a narrow pole planted in the ditch. Belle's heart kicked up a notch when they turned down the lane and slowly drove towards the sheltered property. Their SUV moved slowly past a large white building that had a small concrete foundation and a large metal top that was rounded at the peak. It was big enough to fit a full-size school bus inside. Belle looked on with curiosity at the rest of the yard as the driver spoke up.

"Should I honk the horn? You know, to let him know we're here."

Miss Jones chuckled slightly, for some reason.

"Trust me, he knows we're here."

As if on cue, the door to the small house ahead of them opened.

Oh my god, a voice inside Belle's head yelped as she saw a very large man exit the house. *He's a giant!*

Belle had seen large men before. The streets of Toronto had all types of people walking on them. The large men she saw there were usually large around the middle with the rest of the body proportioned to support it. They usually could be seen waddling down the street, or sometimes they drove little scooters. She'd also seen men who worked out a lot, like bodybuilders. The well-muscled individuals who strutted down the street in their muscle shirts and sweat pants.

This monster who appeared through the doorway was a completely different kind of man. He was tall, maybe taller than anyone Belle had ever met, but not only that he had broad shoulders and large proportions that warned of the dangerous strength that he carried with him. She had to admit, the man's short sandy-brown hair and broad smile made him look almost friendly, but his sheer size gave the man an air of danger that just seemed to radiate off him. Belle could only watch his bulk with wide-eyed amazement as the SUV came to a slow stop in front of him.

"Here we go, kiddo. You ready?" Miss Jones said and turned in her seat to look back at Belle. She must have seen the expression on Belle's face because her own expression softened slightly and she spoke in gentle tones. "Don't worry. He just looks scary, he's really a big teddy bear." She smiled warmly. "Let's go."

They filed out of the SUV and Miss Jones and the driver led the way towards the man. Belle stood back from Miss Jones a bit while the adults exchange their pleasantries. She had already explained to Belle that the large man, Mr. Brooks, was a mute. That meant he couldn't talk, but apparently, he could hear just fine. Belle didn't understand but she didn't question it. The driver was translating the large man's hand signals for Miss Jones. While they talked Belle scanned her surroundings. The trees around the property sheltered them from the vastness of the countryside and gave it the illusion of seclusion. Off in the distance, she heard cows mooing.

Soon enough, Miss Jones turned back and slowly waved Belle forward.

"Emmett, this is Isabelle." Belle took a single step closer and stood close to Miss Jones and looked up at the man.

He looked down at her from where he was a few paces from her and waved slowly.

"You're really tall," Belle said when she couldn't think of anything else to say while she craned her neck to look at his face.

He chuckled slightly.

Belle flinched away from the weird sounding rasp that emanated from the man's throat, and immediately felt embarrassed when the man caught the slight movement. The man's amusement quickly evaporated away and he just stood there looking down at her with a slightly embarrassed look on his face. The large man let out a deep breath, stepped forward and dropped down onto one knee. Belle instinctively retreated away a step as his bulk settled in front of her. She watched him closely as he reached into the breast pocket of his white button-up shirt and pulled out a small stack of cue cards. He pulled off the top card and handed it to her.

I'm so happy to meet you, the card read.

She was quick to notice he underlined the word *happy,* and he ended the statement with an exclamation point. It was nice.

Belle read the card and looked to Mr. Brooks, who slowly spread his arms wide in front of him and raised his eyebrow a bit in a quizzical expression. Mr. Brooks might not be able to talk, but Belle understood immediately what he was asking.

She looked at the invitation for a hug that threatened to crush her small body within his grasp, and then looked up at his face and shot her hand out in front of her.

Belle could immediately tell he was disappointed, but he recovered quickly and nodded at her before he extended his large, meaty hand and engulfed hers with his. It felt like a warm rock had gently formed around her palm. He shook her tiny hand slowly while looking at her with eyes that were the color of the midday sky.

Then he pulled out another card from his tiny stack.

I've spent a lot of time getting this place ready for you. I hope you like it. She looked at him and he handed her another card. This time, with a bit of a playful grin on his face. *Do you want to see your room?*

"I guess," Belle said and shrugged. Miss Jones looked over and Belle showed her the card Mr. Brooks had just given her.

"That's a great idea. Let's go inside and get settled. There's a bit of paperwork we need to take care of, and I don't know about you Norton, but I could use a cup of coffee before we hit the road again."

Mr. Brooks rose back up onto his feet and slowly reached down towards Belle's suitcase.

"No!" Belle said sharply and Mr. Brooks recoiled away like her words might hurt him. "That's mine." She looked at him defiantly, grabbed her bag by the handle, and held it close to her side. Mr. Brooks held up his hands, smiled, and nodded his head like he understood.

The house was nice enough, it was a smaller house than the Burke's house was, but it was less cluttered. So, it actually looked quite spacious. Belle was shown to her room, and she quietly marvelled at it from the doorway as the adults entered the space.

It was the biggest bedroom she had ever been in.

There was easily enough space for two people in this room, maybe three. At the one end was a large bed with a sturdy-looking wooden headboard. Beside it, was a nice-looking nightstand that matched the wood of the headboard. On it was a small digital alarm clock, and a small reading lamp. Across from it, at the other end of the room, was a desk and chair that looked brand new. The room was painted light blue that glowed softly with the light coming in from the small window on the far wall.

Belle took a cautious step into the room, still holding her suitcase close by her side, like she was ready to bolt from the room if the need arose.

It's so big, she thought as she took it all in. *This can't all be for me.*

How could such a small person take up so much space? She could easily do a cartwheel in this room, if she wanted to, and not worry about hitting a single piece of furniture. The room was completely bare, save for a single framed picture Belle spied on the dresser by the closet while the adults were talking.

"What do you think, kiddo?" Miss Jones asked with a big smile painted across her face. "Pretty nice, eh?" Belle answered her by nodding absently while looking around the space that was exclusively meant for her. "Why don't you unpack while we talk in the kitchen for a bit?" Again, Belle simply nodded.

Soon after, the adults filed out of the room. Belle watched closely as Mr. Brooks gracefully swiveled his shoulders to exit through the doorway. When she was left alone in the room, quietly it felt even bigger than it did before. She moved towards the bed and laid her suitcase by its end. That's where she liked to keep it when she first arrived at a new house. Belle quickly debated unpacking *The Box* and placing it under the bed. That was the place she felt was always the best place to keep it, so it would be close to her but still hidden safely away. She quickly decided against it. This place was still new. She needed to make sure it was safe before she could risk exposing it to this strange environment.

Instead, she moved towards the dresser and looked at the photo on top of it. It was clearly an older picture of two people, Belle tearfully recognized one of them immediately.

It can't be, she thought as a sob escaped her lips. She rushed towards the picture and reached up to snatch it off the dresser. Belle took one look at her mother's youthful face and felt her eyes start to water. *It is! It's really her!*

Belle held the picture close to her as she rushed to her bedroom door and quickly closed it, sealing herself off from the adults in the kitchen. She went to her bed where she sat with the picture gently cradled in her hands.

In the picture, her mother was an absolute beauty. Belle had never seen her mother look so pretty, and rarely had seen her with such a big, glowing smile on her face. Her long flowing blonde hair was draped gracefully around her shoulders, and her stunning blue dress conformed lovingly to her form.

She looks like a princess, Belle thought as the first tear splashed down on the glass of the frame.

Then something else struck Belle, and it stole her breath away.

Belle first noticed the sparkly banner behind them, the one that had *Grad 2010* written in big, bold letters. The second thing was the eerie resemblance the tall man in the picture had to Mr. Brooks.

That's my dad!

Belle had never before seen a picture of him. She frantically wiped the wetness from her eyes so she could see clearly, and studied every each of his form.

He towered over her mother in her pretty blue dress and pearls, he shared a lot of the same features as Mr. Brooks, but it was clear her father was more handsome.

He looked like a proud knight in his dark suit with a broad smile that showcased his perfect teeth. It was clear to Belle how the two of them felt about each other by the way they clung to each other in the faded picture. They were in love, no doubt about it. More tears fell onto the surface of the picture, so much so Belle grabbed the edge of the blanket on the bed and started to furiously wipe the wetness away. She knew pictures didn't like water, and she couldn't damage this...new piece of her mother, *and* her father.

Then a knock came at the door.

"Isabelle?" Miss Jones's soft voice came a second later.

"Just a minute!" Belle said loudly, stalling for time, and quickly rushed the new picture to her suitcase. Belle unzipped the lid and stowed the framed picture away in record time before she roughly wiped away the wetness on her face.

"Come out when your ready, kiddo. We're going to take off and I wanted to say good-bye before we leave."

"Be right there," she called back and gave her nose a quick blow into the soft material of the blanket. Belle stood for a moment in the center of her impossibly large room, with the soft blue walls, and breathed in deeply. She didn't want the adults to know she had been crying.

When she was ready, she exited the room and turned into the small kitchen. Mr. Mills was already by the door. Miss Jones and Mr. Brooks were in the kitchen. Everyone looked to her when she exited the room. On reflex, Belle shrank away from their gaze. Miss Jones came up to her, bent down, wrapped her lean arms around Belle's small frame and gave her the slightest bit of pressure.

"You're going to be okay," she said when she released her. "You're in good hands, *but*," she paused, reached into her pocket, and produced a small business card. "If you need *anything*, you call me. Even if you just want to talk. My cell number is on the back." She stood up and looked down on her with a warm smile. "Other than that, you won't see me again until our six-month review. Do you have any questions for me before I go?"

Do you have to leave? Belle wanted to ask, but she knew what the answer would be.

"No," she said quietly.

"Okay, sweetie. I'll see you later." Miss Jones smiled broadly and thumbed towards Mr. Brooks. "Take care of this one, he's new to being an adult." Miss Jones winked before she turned to Mr. Brooks and pointed at him sharply. "And you! Don't fuck this up," she said harshly.

Both Belle and Mr. Brooks recoiled away from the comment. Miss Jones's expression softened and she then gently patted Mr. Brooks on his wide chest, right where his heart was, with some affection.

"Good luck," she said looking up at him. "That goes for you too," she said and gestured to the card in Belle's hand. "You need anything, you call me."

Mr. Brooks smiled warmly, nodded his head, and extended his hand to her.

"No chance, big guy. Bring it in," she said with genuine warmth and moved in to embrace the man.

Belle watched as she raised herself up onto her toes to whisper something into Mr. Brooks's ear. Belle probably wasn't supposed to hear it, but she did.

"You hurt that girl in any way, I'll rip out your spine and feed your lifeless corpse to those cows out there." She backed away and smiled at Mr. Brooks's stunned face before she patted him on the shoulders, said her goodbyes, and left.

Belle stood with the giant man in his kitchen and watched the SUV back up and pull out of the yard. Leaving the two of them in the empty, silent house. They both continued to stare out into the lonely yard, but soon enough Belle felt the large man beside her shift. She could feel his gaze upon her like the heat from the sun.

Belle quickly craned her neck to look up at his face.

"Can I go in my room?" she asked quickly. Mr. Brooks gave her a nervous smile and nodded.

Belle pivoted on her feet and hurried towards her new room and promptly closed the door behind herself.

Once safely nestled inside, she let out a breath she didn't even know she was holding.

Outside her door, she could hear Mr. Brooks move into the other room. The dining room, Belle supposed it would be called, although technically it was still connected to the living room. However, though, there was a tiny step you had to descend into the living room, and it did have a banister on each side of it. It was the only thing that separated the two areas, so Belle didn't know which one it should be called.

It didn't matter, the main thing is that Mr. Brooks had moved away from the kitchen.

Mr. Brooks was a scary man. He loomed over her like a mountain. One that threatened to crash down upon her tiny frame at any moment. Mr. Brooks didn't have a warm, welcoming smile like her father did. He had an awkward grin that hinted towards the effort it took to put it on his face. He had crooked teeth too, with one goofy tooth in the front that stuck out more than the others. Like it was trying to escape his mouth.

She moved away from the door and into the center of the room, *her* room. She just stood there and turned a full circle. It was utterly empty, but she didn't mind at the moment. The color of the walls gave the room the illusion of being in the middle of a wide-open space. She didn't know why, but she could breathe a little easier now. Like the world was no longer pushing in on her.

She soon started moving around the room, checking the drawers of her desk, the nightstand. She opened the closet door for the first time, only to find it too was completely empty. She moved to the bed, hopped onto it and sat cross-legged and just took in the serene calmness of her room.

I wonder if Mr. Brooks will let me decorate it? She wondered idly as she scanned over the bare walls.

Belle didn't even have the foggiest idea of what she would put in the room. Part of her was still unsure she wanted to disturb the gentle serenity of this space, while another part strongly debated if she would even be allowed to do such a thing.

I wonder what normal girls put in their rooms?

Belle hadn't been in a lot of other girl's rooms, but she had seen some on television. Those rooms were usually filled with little knick-knacks, trophies, pictures, and girly decorations of all kinds. Not to mention, their closets were always brimming with clothes.

Belle didn't have any of those things.

Some time later, she heard Mr. Brooks approach her door. She saw the shadows of his legs under it, and she reflexively tensed up. Then came a gentle tapping. The floorboards creaked as the shadows under the door shifted, and a cue card came scooting into the room from under it. After that, Mr. Brooks moved away from the door.

Curiosity got the best of her. Belle scampered off the bed, moved over to the spot on the floor where the card was, and picked it up.

Did you want to get some ice cream?

Belle quietly opened her door and peered out into the kitchen. Mr. Brooks was there, sitting at the small table in the kitchen, looking at her with a playful expression.

"I like ice cream."

Mr. Brooks smiled.

They drove for over a half hour in silence, because Mr. Brooks couldn't talk and Belle couldn't think of anything to say. She didn't even know what the point would be if the person next to her couldn't reply in any way. So, she just stared out the window as they cruised across the open landscape.

Belle was quick to spy the welcome sign for Russell, it was rather hard to miss. It prominently featured a cartoonish-looking bull on it, right above the town's name. Belle thought it was a silly name for a town. Russell was a person's name, not a name for a town.

She wondered with some amusement if there was a town out there in Manitoba called Mike.

Shortly after they crossed the town's limit, Mr. Brooks pulled off the highway and into a gas station that shared a parking lot with a large motel. He pulled in beside one of the pumps and retrieved a small notepad from his pocket along with a pen. Belle waited as Mr. Brooks scribbled his message down.

We just have to get some gas, the little note said. Mr. Brooks grinned warmly at her before he exited the truck. Belle figured that meant she was supposed to follow him in, and besides that, she wanted something to snack on for later on tonight when she was alone in her room.

"Hey, Emmett," the older man behind the counter looked up from his customer and gave Mr. Brooks a friendly wave. Mr. Brooks returned the little wave with one of his own before he filed in behind the customer who was already at the till. Belle quickly moved in between the aisles and moved herself into position.

Stealing was a tricky thing. Belle found that she had developed a talent for it. The trick was knowing what you were going to steal, waiting for the right opportunity to slip it into your pocket, and not hesitating. She kept her ears peeled as she moved to the back of the store. She soon spied the larger bags on candies she liked because they fit nicely into the pocket of the grey hoodie she was wearing, and they made little noise once they were in there. Belle's ears told her the man behind the till was finishing up with his customer, so he was distracted.

Her hand subtly shot out, quickly eased the bag of M&M's into her pocket, and quickly continued on down the aisle. Belle forced herself to look normal as she filed in beside Mr. Brooks, who just looked down at her and smiled weirdly.

Don't fidget, she warned herself as her heart pounded away in her chest while she stood there, looking innocent and sweet.

"Hey there, Emmett," the greying man behind the counter said happily as Mr. Brooks stepped up to the counter. The two men exchanged a look before Mr. Brooks started moving his hands slowly.

"You want a fill on pump number two?" the aging clerk asked, with little confidence. To Belle, it sounded more like a question. "Is that right?"

Mr. Brooks gave the man a thumbs up, which pleased him greatly, and then Mr. Brooks went to his notepad before he tore off the page and handed it to the man.

"Well Emmett," the man replied looking confused. "If you want some candies, just go grab it so I can scan it."

Oh no! The suspicion coursed through her like lightning, shattering her careful façade. Belle looked up at Mr. Brooks and the subtle sternness of his expression told Belle her fears were correct. She looked at him wide-eyed and then shot the clerk a look.

"I see," he said with amused disappointment. "Looks like someone has some sticky fingers, eh?" He was looking directly at her when he said it.

No! Belle took a step back on instinct. She would have gone further, but she felt Mr. Brooks's warm palm on her back. Keeping her in place. The clerk gave Mr. Brooks a sorrowful expression.

"I'm going to have to put her on the board, Emmett." He then thumbed behind him towards a small white board Belle didn't notice before he pointed it out.

It was a simple white piece of wood with pictures haphazardly tacked to it. "Russell's Thieves" were painted boldly at the top in large letters. Numerous pictures of people, mostly kids, but Belle spied a few sad-looking adults in there too, hung from their tacks with little fanfare. One picture at the bottom caught Belle's frantic eyes, it showcased a small boy with blonde hair and thick-rimmed black glasses.

In the picture he was red-faced and crying, the perfect picture of shame and misery. Belle saw that face and knew immediately she did not want her picture on that wall.

"No," she squeaked. She hadn't meant to say anything at all.

"I'm sorry little-lady, but if you do the crime, you do the time." Beside her, Mr. Brooks began scribbling again. "I'm sorry Emmett," the man said quickly after he read the note Mr. Brooks gave him.

"Those are the rules. You get caught shoplifting; you go on the wall. It's that simple Emmett. I don't play favorites," the man ended sternly, like the matter was closed.

Mr. Brooks looked down at her with an apologetic expression.

"No."

"I'm going to need the bag in order to scan it," the clerk said coldly.

Mr. Brooks moved towards her, and like she suspected, it felt like a mountain was crashing down on her.

"No! Stop it!" she yelled as Mr. Brooks reached for the pocket of her hoodie with the slight bulge in it. "Don't touch me!"

She cried and bolted for the front door. She had to get away. Even though, she had no idea where she could run to get away from *this*, but she couldn't stay here. That much was clear. Mr. Brooks didn't allow for that though. He held her firm, but that didn't stop her from fighting his grasp like a wild animal that was caught in a trap.

"Let me go! Let me go!" she continued to scream, even after she felt her entire body lift off the ground.

Mr. Brooks forcibly carried her out of the store, and over to his truck. The whole time she was weakly slapping the arms that held her. At the truck, he opened the door and deposited her screaming form into the passenger seat. Belle thrashed around in her seat for a moment once he dropped her into it, and then he held his hands up like he was surrendering.

"I didn't do anything!" she screamed, even though she felt the weight of the evidence in her pocket. Mr. Brooks looked at her severely, waited for her to quiet down before he pointed to his eyes, and then pointed sternly at her. His message was unmistakable.

I saw you.

Belle shrank in her seat. This time she didn't budge as Mr. Brooks eased himself forward and fished the bag of candies from her pocket. With no place to run or hide from what she had done, Belle started to sob.

"I'm sorry." Mr. Brooks gently touched her shoulder, and when Belle looked up, he handed her a message.

Don't worry about it. We'll get through this.

Behind Mr. Brooks, Belle spied a man cautiously approaching the truck. He wore stained, tattered clothes and heavy-looking boots that were unlaced on his feet. His hair was messy and he looked like he hadn't washed it in days. Mr. Brooks must have seen the look of concern on Belle's face, because he quickly turned to see what caught her attention.

"Hey bud," the man said craning his neck to see past Mr. Brooks's large frame to her. Belle just hid away from his looks. "Everything okay here?"

Mr. Brooks scrunched up his face in frustration and used his massive arm to angrily wave the man away. She was happy to see that the man reluctantly got the message and turned to slowly move away. Mr. Brooks then turned back to her, breathed out once, and went back to his notepad.

I'm going back in there to pay for everything, AND give you a minute to relax.

He looked at her with raised eyebrows before he gave her another page.

THEN we're going in there and getting that picture done.

"No," Belle whined after reading the note. "I don't want to be on there. I didn't mean to. I'm sorry." Mr. Brooks silenced her by holding up his hands before he went back to his notepad. This time, he was scribbling for some time.

It's not that big of a deal. I think everybody in the town has been on that wall at one point or another. I've been up there, your dad was up there, and I think your mother was even on that board at one point.

Belle read the note with teary-eyes. When she finished, she looked up at him and Mr. Brooks was grinning.

"I still don't want to be on that board. I'm not a thief," she said defiantly. "I just wanted something to snack on later. I was going to pay for it," she lied, straight to his face. Mr. Brooks just gave her a smirk. He wasn't having any of it.

Just stay here, and calm down while I get this done.

He looked at her again, this time with a heated sort of disappointment as he placed his little notepad on the dash of the truck before he retrieved the bag of candies she stole and marched back into the store. While he was inside the store, Belle sat quietly in her seat and idly looked around her surroundings, trying desperately not to think about what she had just done.

You have to do better, a voice inside her scolded her. *We have no place to go. If you screw this up, that's it. Nobody is going to want you after that.*

Movement caught her eye and snapped her back. Her eyes moved to the man from earlier, the ugly man in the stained clothes that approached Mr. Brooks. He was there at the corner of the gas station, but now he had a friend in a plaid shirt with him. They were talking secretly to each other, and when the man in the dirty clothes noticed Belle was looking in his direction, he waved. She immediately shrank down in her seat, away from the scary man with the dirty hands. For added measure, she even reached out and closed the passenger door.

Mr. Brooks exited the store soon enough. He walked around the front of the truck, and moved towards the fuel pump. Belle watched him the whole time he began filling the truck.

So, Belle immediately noticed the three men approach Mr. Brooks.

She instantly recognized the man in the dirty work clothes, his friend with the plaid shirt, but now there was also an older man with a balding head and a weathered face. All three men approached Mr. Brooks from the rear of the truck. Belle looked on nervously as the older, rounder man called out to Mr. Brooks.

"Hey man," he said sternly. Belle felt anyone who heard those words would know the intent behind them was anything but friendly. "Hey," he said again, and this time, Mr. Brooks looked over to him. "I got a question for you," the weathered man said as his two cohorts circled around to Mr. Brooks's side.

Belle saw Mr. Brooks immediately look in her direction, but he wasn't looking at her. He was looking to his notepad that was on the dash.

"Is that your daughter in there?"

Belle could clearly hear the heated question from the man through the open driver's window. Again, Mr. Brooks tried to wave the men off, but it wasn't working this time. The rounder one held up his hands to look nonthreatening, but Belle was keen to notice the other two were slowly moving closer.

"Look. I don't want any trouble, but we all saw you carrying that little girl out of that store. Maybe you want to explain that?"

Belle could see Mr. Brooks's shoulders visibly slump before he reached for the driver's door handle.

As soon as the door opened, chaos broke loose.

"He's reaching for something!" one of them yelled hoarsely. "Get him!"

All three men rushed forward and swarmed over Mr. Brooks and dragged him to the ground. The driver's door slammed shut and Belle yelped at how violently it happened. She lost sight of the men, but she heard their struggle.

"Hold him!" one of them said.

"Watch out!" another one cried out as the commotion moved to the back of the vehicle. Belle lifted herself up onto her seat and looked out the back window in an attempt to see Mr. Brooks.

At the back of the truck, she saw Mr. Brooks suddenly rise up onto his feet, struggling angrily with each man holding his arms in a death-grip so they were spread out to the sides. His face was distorted with rage as he fought against the men on his arms, and winning by the looks of it.

Then he locked eyes with her, and Belle saw the fight drain from his body. The two men at his sides took their cue and wrestled him down onto one knee by the back corner of the truck.

"I'm calling the cops!" the round man, the one who started this whole terrible interaction, said and moved around from behind the truck with his phone in his meaty digits.

"Get the girl!" the man in the stained work clothes yelled from Mr. Brooks's side. Belle heart sank as she turned to the round one, his glassy eyes locked onto hers as he started towards the passenger door.

Belle screamed.

"Leave me alone!" she cried out and scooted away from the door.

She frantically looked over to Mr. Brooks, and she couldn't believe what she saw.

His massive body just shot up from the ground. With a look of stone-cold determination, he rose up, spread his legs into a wide stance, and fought against the men anchoring him in place. Or at least that's what she thought, but the next instant he swept his mighty arm forward, and the man in the plaid shirt at his arm pitched forward. His legs caught on Mr. Brooks's leg and he was thrown to the ground. With his hand free, Mr. Brooks moved in close to the man on his other arm before he dipped down, twisted at his waist, and tossed the man over his shoulder. The man's body collided loudly with the truck's tailgate before he rebounded off it and settled onto the ground.

Mr. Brooks rushed forward, bodychecking the man in the plaid shirt out of his way as he was rising off the ground, and he pressed forward just as the round man was reaching for the passenger door handle.

Mr. Brooks's large palm descended on top of the other man's hand. Belle could see his meaty digits digging into the flesh of the man's hand. Mr. Brooks then gave the wrist a sharp twist, which caused the man to cry out in pain before he stepped in between him and the passenger door of the truck, and simply pushed the round man away.

Then he quickly held up his hands in surrender, and furiously patted the air in front of him. Mr. Brooks shot her a quick look, to ensure she was unharmed. When he locked his eyes with hers, he nodded slowly before he turned back to his attackers. The three men limped and staggered into place, forming a loose circle around

Mr. Brooks. They looked like injured wolves who were still foolishly attacking a much larger predator.

Then Mr. Brooks looked at the round one, made sure he had his attention before he pointed to the phone that was still in the uninjured hand, and then brought the thumb and pinkie of his other hand up to his face in the universal gesture for *telephone.*

"Oh, I'm calling the cops, asshole. Don't you worry about that," the man said angrily as he awkwardly dialed the call using his one hand.

Mr. Brooks nodded agreeably before he sank down onto his knees and slowly put his hands behind his head, putting himself at the mercies of his attackers.

Belle could only look on anxiously.

"You just stay there, dickhead!" the one in the plaid shirt said with a threatening tone. He then turned to his cohort in the dirty work clothes. "Get the girl," he said and motioned quickly towards the truck.

The man looked at his friend incredulously. He had been the one who had been thrown into the back of the truck. Apparently, he was still feeling the effects of the collision. He was hunched over and winced with each step.

He didn't get far though.

Mr. Brooks froze the man in his tracks with a loud, banshee-call of a whistle. When the man looked to Mr. Brooks, he was holding his keys in his hand. With a press of a button, he locked the doors to the truck, and engaged the alarm. He then used his head to motion for the hunched over man to move away from the truck.

Just like that, the power dynamic of the situation dramatically shifted.

It was no longer the three men keeping Mr. Brooks at bay. Now, it was Mr. Brooks keeping the men from the truck. While on his knees with his hands behind his head, he protected her from the unknown assailants.

Until the police showed up minutes later.

At that point, when the R.C.M.P cars showed up, Belle knew she had ruined everything. She didn't know what was going to happen after this point, but she knew it was all her fault. So, with no options left, and nowhere to escape to, she shrank into the seat and retreated into herself.

That is, until the knock at the window came.

Outside, a middle-aged police officer with a short, neat haircut and a wide smile gave her a curt little wave.

"Could you unlock the door?" he asked lightly and pointed down to the door's controls on the handle.

Belle inched closer to the door and pressed the button before she retreated her hand like the switch hurt her. The officer opened the door and stood there with a stupefied look on his face.

"My god, you look so much like your mother." He said inexplicably. Belle gave him a mildly suspicious look.

"You knew my mom?"

"Oh jeez," the officer said quickly. "Where are my manners? My name is Calvin. Calvin Biggs. I knew your father, *and* your mother." He said it like it was a point of pride for him. "They were good friends of mine. Really good friends. So, believe me when I say how much of a genuine pleasure it is to finally meet you." With that, he extended his hand to her. Belle quickly shook his hand and retreated back to her seat. "You want to tell me what happened here, Isabelle?"

Belle couldn't hold it in any longer. Her internal dam had just folded in on itself and the whole story came out like a raging torrent of water. Tears and snot ran freely down her face, and Belle wiped them on the sleeve of her hoodie as she confessed her sins to the kind-faced police officer.

When she was done, he looked at her for a moment longer before he sucked on his teeth and spoke.

"That's a hell of a first day," he said and looked at her empathetically.

"Am I going to jail?" Belle asked sheepishly. "For stealing." She sat there and prepared for life's next blow.

"What? No," Officer Biggs said quickly and waved his hand in front of himself. "Old Henry back there doesn't charge people for shoplifting. He just takes their picture for his board."

"What about Mr. Brooks?"

"Nobody is going to jail today, sweetheart." He smiled again and shrugged his shoulders. "Those guys got an alert on their phones about some girl in the area who went missing, and saw Emmett carrying you out of the store like that, and they decided they better step in. It was an honest mistake," he said and spread his arm open, as if to say, *what can you do?*

"I think he broke that guy's arm," Belle said looking over to the trio. They were by the corner of the store talking with the other two officers. The larger man was cradling his one arm in by his side. Officer Biggs chuckled warmly.

"Yeah, probably, but what did he expect would happen when he came between a papa bear and his cub?" he asked lightly and gave her a wink. "The video footage from the cameras doesn't paint a flattering picture for those boys. They look like they might be smart enough to realize what they did wrong here, and just move on." Officer Biggs then turned back to look at Mr. Brooks, who was standing idly behind the police officer. "You good?"

Belle saw Mr. Brooks make a complicated series of hand gestures.

"No, you're good to go. I still have to take their statements, but I know where to find you if I have any other questions. This seems pretty cut and dry." Officer Biggs turned back to her and studied her for a bit longer before he finally spoke. "Well, Isabelle, duty calls, but it was a pleasure to meet you and I imagine we will be seeing more of each other."

At that, Belle's expression changed to one of dread.

"*Because* Emmett is a good friend of mine. So, I'll probably see you at the farm or something like that. At least," he said and then gave her a serious look. "That better be where I see you next." He then dropped the serious expression, smiled brightly again, and waved his goodbyes.

After that, Mr. Brooks's frame stood at the door and he slowly waved her out of the truck. Belle bit her lip and scooted back over to the passenger side to exit. He leaned into the truck after she hopped out to retrieve his notepad from the dash before he led her back into the store, where the clerk was practically jumping out of his skin.

"Oh my god, Emmett! I can't believe those guys attacked you like that! I'm so sorry that happened! If I had any idea-." Mr. Brooks silenced the thin, greying man with his hand before passing the man a note. "That's kind of you to say, and I appreciate your understanding in this."

The man put the note aside and fished his smartphone from his pocket. He pulled up the camera app and pointed the phone at them. Belle just stood there, trying to make herself as small as possible.

"Say cheese," the man said.

Mr. Brooks dropped down to her side, pressed his face in close to hers, and brought his hand in an enthusiastic thumbs-up in front of her. Belle shot him a look, and he saw he was looking forward with a giant smile on his face, his crooked teeth were in full display as he looked up at the camera. Belle looked back to the camera numbly, and that's when the flash went off.

Back at the truck, Mr. Brooks handed her a note he quickly wrote.

Let's go get that ice cream.

"We're still getting ice cream?!" she asked quickly and gave him an incredulous look.

She couldn't help it. It was unbelievable to her that she would still get a nice treat after she caused Mr. Brooks all that trouble. Belle also couldn't help the lone tear that drained down her cheek as she looked at him. He looked at her warmly before he returned to his notepad.

I started my day planning to take my niece out for ice cream, and that's exactly what I plan on doing.

"Thank you, Mr. Brooks." She knew it wasn't enough, so she added: "I'm sorry for all the trouble I caused today." Mr. Brooks wrote her a quick note and handed it to her before he started the truck's engine.

Call me Emmett.

CHAPTER 8

Brooke

Today was the department store.

It was Wednesday morning, so it was supposed to be the hardware store, but last night she got a call from her friend Caroline. Her sister had gone into labor. According to Caroline, it hadn't been going well. There was even talk of transferring her sister to Brandon, though no decision had been made.

Brooke could tell by her friend's tone, that she wasn't leaving her sister's side, but it was the start of summer. Her store's peak revenue season, and Caroline couldn't afford to simply close for a family emergency, not if she could help it. Caroline was quick to run down the list of people she tried before calling her, which Brooke didn't find particularly flattering. She also went on to say her mother had spare keys to her store. She lived in Binscarth too, only a few blocks away actually, so that was handy. Brooke basically had to open the store, turn on the lights, and run the till until Caroline's part-timers came in at noon. It should be easy.

How could Brooke say no?

After she hung up the phone, she quickly texted Tim and got him to cover for her at the hardware store the next day.

It was the only plan she had to change.

Brooke couldn't complain. Caroline didn't open the store until nine in the morning, so at least she got to sleep in. When she finally did leave the house, she wore a nice fitting pair of jeans with a white blouse with frills around the neck-line to hide her bosom. She capped the outfit off with her brown leather handbag, and matching sandals. When she entered her car, the day was already quite warm. The sun was shining brightly in the sky, and there was a nice breeze that cooled her skin. She felt it was going to be a good day.

Even *her* stop sign didn't spoil her mood.

She got the spare keys from Caroline's mother, Judy, easy enough. The hardest part was finding the right moment to interrupt Judy to tell her she had to get on the road to open the store. Russell was still a twenty-minute drive away. Brooke took her time on the highway. She pulled off into Henry Johnson's gas station for a quick fill and a cup of his hazelnut coffee that he brewed in the morning, assuming the rig-hands didn't drink it all.

"Hey Henry," she called to him as she walked through the door. He was fussing about with something behind the counter, but quickly looked up when the door's bell chimed to announce her entrance.

"Morning Brooke," he said with his usual nod and friendly smile. "Looks like it's going to be a lovely day today, eh? They say it might rain later on in the week though," he said it like it was just assumed she knew who *they* were.

"How's the coffee today?" she asked lightly as she approached the little counter Henry set up for the collection of labelled coffee warmers.

"Better than that swill Tim Horton's peddles," Henry replied in kind.

Please, please, she playfully pleaded with the universe. *Come on, be there.* She walked up to the warmer with the *Hazelnut* label and placed her pink, metal twenty-ounce travel mug under the spout and pulled on the little lever. *Yes!* She smiled as the warm, fragrant beverage started to fill her cup. She took it as a sign today was going to be a good one, not that it meant much, but a good day was never something to scoff at. Any day she didn't focus on the listless nature of her life, was a welcome one.

"Just the coffee today, Brooke?" Henry asked as he moved towards the till.

"Yeah," Brooke replied absently as she looked over Henry's infamous board for any new offenders. The last one had been little Lucas Adler, and his picture was one of abject shame and humiliation. Lucas looked in that picture how Brooke felt on most days. She was certain in some dark place inside her mind there was a little Brooke Talbot who was crying in the same manner as Lucas Adler was in that picture.

Today, she was greeted with a new arrival.

What the hell?! Brooke leaned forward to get a better look at the new picture. She was surprised to find Emmett Brooks was in the picture. Honestly, his massive frame took up the majority of the background. He was standing awfully close to a small girl Brooke had never seen before. His cheek was almost pressing against the dour-looking girl who was hiding her shameful gaze behind a few tufts of her dark-colored, brown hair. Emmett didn't look shameful, the exact opposite actually. He looked ecstatic; he even had a thumbs-up in the picture.

"Hey, Henry?" she said and the old clerk replied with a small noise. "Is that Emmett Brooks in that picture?" Brooke gracefully pointed to the new photo on the board, and watched with a confused expression as Henry visibly deflated.

"Oh my god, Brooke," he said wiping his remorseful face with his hand. "Did you hear about what happened?" he asked, like it was a particularly juicy bit of gossip. Brooke couldn't help herself.

"What?" She leaned in closer.

"Well," Henry said, diving into the story. A few days ago, Little Miss there had a bag of candy in her pocket, smarties, M&M's, or something like that, it's not important. I didn't even catch her. It was *Emmett* that pointed it out to *me.* So anyways, I go through my little routine and get my camera ready, and the girl *freaks* out. Like a full-on tantrum. Emmett hauls her up and carried her back to his truck so she could calm down. Poor thing. You should have seen her eyes when she got caught. It was like Lucas Adler all over again." Henry thumbed back to the board. "But I told him. I said, '*I don't play favorites, Emmett*'."

"Who is she?"

"I don't know," Henry said and seemed disappointed he didn't ask at the time. "Her name's Isabella. Isabella? Isabelle? No, It's Isabelle. Yep, I'm certain of it now, it was Isabelle."

Oh my god, Brooke thought scandalously as she thought back to the spring when Emmett was fixing up his house for his lady friend. *She must have a daughter, and Emmett caught her shoplifting! Man,* Brooke smiled to herself, *this day just keeps getting better.*

It was a tasty bit of gossip indeed. Brooke had no intentions of sharing any of it, but it was a treat to know it herself. There was no harm in enjoying someone else's drama. It was one of the small pleasures of living in a small town, after all.

"Then Emmett goes back out to gas his truck."

Brooke was hardly even listening at this point. She was busy thinking of the reaction on Emmett's girlfriend's face when they got back to his house and had to break the news to her. Whoever she was.

"And three guys jumped him and dragged him to the ground."

"What?!" Brooke exclaimed, a little louder than she anticipated.

"I know!" Henry mirrored her own shocked expression. "I couldn't believe it either! It happened *right* out there." He pointed out the window to the gas pumps. "I saw the whole thing. Damn near crapped my pants. I tell you, Brooke, I've never dialed the cops so quickly in my life."

"What happened?! Is Emmett okay?!" Brooke asked and looked back to the picture on the board. In it, he looked fine, happy even.

"By the time I got back to the window," Henry said, returning to his story, and completely ignoring Brooke's question. "Two of them had wrestled Emmett to the ground, and the other one was moving towards the truck. Where the little girl was. Isabelle."

"Jesus." It was all Brooke could say. This story had grown far beyond simple gossip, and she was thoroughly invested.

"I'll tell you what else, I've never seen anyone get as riled up as I saw Emmett Brooks get when that fella started towards his truck. I'm sure if Emmett could talk, he would have been screaming bloody murder by the way he threw that guy to the ground. His friend though," Henry let out a low whistle before he continued. "Emmett just up and tossed that guy into the back of his truck, and that guy was walking funny after that. Then Emmett storms up to the fat one walking up to his truck and broke the arm that was reaching for his door. Then the cops showed up," Henry said, like it was the end of the story.

It infuriated Brooke.

"Well?!" she exclaimed. "What happened then?"

"What do you mean?" Henry looked at her confused. "The police sorted it out after that."

"Well, why did they jump Emmett? Was this Isabelle person involved somehow? Did anybody get arrested?" Brooke held her hands wide in a questioning manner. She felt like Henry should have expected those questions, and should have the answers loaded and ready to go.

"Well, Calvin said-."

"Calvin got involved?!"

"Well, of course. There's not much that goes down around here that Calvin doesn't know about," he said it like it was a point of pride for him. "Anyways, Calvin said it was all a big misunderstanding. Apparently, those three guys were rig-hands who were staying at the Inn over yonder." Henry thumbed across the parking lot he shared with the Inn. "One of them got some sort of an alert on their phone, and they thought Emmett was kidnapping the little girl. Bunch of dummies," Henry said sourly. "Calvin said if they read the whole bulletin, they would have known that it was some Indigenous girl way up north. I guess they weren't smart enough to do that, so they ran into Emmett half-cocked, and paid for it. No harm, no foul."

No harm, no foul?!

"Are you kidding?" Brooke gave him a look of playful disbelief. "They *assaulted* Emmett, for no reason."

"Well," Henry countered cautiously. "I don't know about that." Brooke just looked at him, with actual disbelief this time. "All I'm saying is it probably wouldn't have gotten as far as it did if it weren't for Emmett's...you know, *condition*."

"That doesn't give them the right to jump him."

"Yeah, well, I imagine seeing someone as big as Emmett carry some screaming child into his truck might be a cause for alarm." Henry gave her a knowing look.

"I guess," Brooke said as a way to end it.

She liked Henry Johnson, but in that moment, she was having trouble being in his presence. She quietly handed him her debit card and they finished their business. They parted saying friendly goodbyes to each other. Brooke considered that to be a high note considering how her mood had suddenly soured.

Unbelievable! She thought angrily as she entered her car. *No harm, no foul?*

She couldn't believe someone would think that after actually seeing it happen. She only heard about it, and she was pissed. Worse yet, Henry very politely tried to cast part of the blame onto Emmett. Sure, she would admit he was a large, intimidating man, and yes, watching him haul a child into a truck might be alarming. Emmett wasn't a damned animal, though. He might not be the sunniest of characters, Brooke could empathize with that, but he was more than reasonable.

Maybe they tried talking to him? A voice inside her tried to reason with her. If they had, Brooke couldn't imagine it escalating to a full-blown altercation. *Yeah, well, that's the problem isn't it. They can't technically talk to Emmett, can they? When you ask someone a heated question, like, say, 'are you kidnapping that child?', and you don't receive an immediate answer, people tend to assume the worst.*

"Whatever," Brooke said aloud before she started her little car and pulled out of the parking lot.

During the short drive to Russell's Main Street, maybe for the first time, she tried to imagine what it would be like to be Emmett Brooks. To have a part of himself that was always locked away from people, because there was only so much you could write down onto a notepad. She thought back to when Emmett first walked into her life, back at the hardware store. She remembered the meticulous list of supplies he handed her, the one that made her job so incredibly easy. How long did it take him to come up with that list? Did he do that for every interaction he had with people? Brooke didn't know of anyone else in town, other than Calvin Biggs, who knew sign language. So, there was literally only one person Emmett could *really* talk to. She liked Emmett, he was a nice guy, but she didn't know a thing about him.

Well, that's not exactly true. She remembered his little grins at all of Brooke's little quips and jokes. She even got him to laugh once or twice. It sounded a little weird, but at least it meant he had a sense of humor.

He was attentive; when Brooke talked to him, he always watched her with those ultramarine-blue eyes. He did that with everyone. She couldn't speak for the others, but when he did it with her, it made her feel like she had his sole attention. Like his universe only included the two of them.

He was dramatic. Emmett had a multitude of facial expressions, and there was a lot he could convey with just a raise of his eyebrow and a tilt of his head. He had at least a dozen different kinds of smiles, each unique to the message he was trying to convey. Brooke especially liked the little sly smile he gave right before he wrote something funny on his notepad.

She felt there was a real intelligence there too. She couldn't pinpoint what exactly gave her that impression, but with Emmett, she thought he was akin to a deep lake. The kind where you gaze upon its still, serene waters, and never once think about what might be going on within its depths.

I wonder if sign language is hard to learn, she wondered idly as she pulled into The Bargain Barn's employee parking area at the back of the store.

She parked her car in behind the two blue sea-cans Caroline used to store some of her inventory and moved into the store through the employee entrance at the back of the building. She walked past the employee and storage area that took up a portion of the back of the store. It was really just a long, wide hallway filled with boxes, clothing racks, mannequins, and it even had a small kitchenette against the back wall of the store. The main retail area was tightly packed with clothing racks in the center of the store, and shelves that lined the perimeter.

Honestly, for a town with a population that just recently broke two thousand people, it was a nice store. Caroline had a multitude of clothing options for all occasions, for men or women, children or adults. She had a small, yet well stocked shoe section, and Caroline even had a section for small household appliances.

It was like a mini-Wal-Mart.

Brooke turned on the lights before she moved to the front door, where she unlocked the simple deadbolt. In Winnipeg, a store like this would need to have a security alarm, retractable gates on the entrance, bars on the windows, and have at least three different locks on the front door. Not to mention, giant concrete barriers that would prevent thieves from just driving a vehicle through the entrance to create a gaping hole in which to enter through.

Small towns, baby!

The morning was incredibly dull, as Caroline said it would be. She had a few people come in to idly browse around the store. A woman Brooke recognized came in and bought her little girl a bathing suit. Brooke had a minutes long conversation with the woman, the whole time fighting to remember how they knew each other. Brooke thought she might have gone to school with her, but she couldn't put a name to the face that was talking at her.

The rest of the time she searched YouTube videos on her phone for how to learn sign language. American Sign Language, or ASL for short, was actually a pretty popular topic on YouTube. She easily found an introductory series. She was bored, and she thought it might be a pleasant surprise for Emmett. A little something to brighten his day. Though, chances were pretty good she was going to screw it up and probably say something completely different then what she intended. Again, Emmett might get a mild kick out of the attempt.

Turns out, ASL was surprisingly straightforward. Brooke quickly learned the five important features to any sign she might learn. The first video she watched highlighted them early on. Hand shape, palm orientation, movement, location, and non-manual signals. Honestly, Brooke didn't understand the last one yet, it hadn't come up in the lessons she perused so far. She found it easier to remember and categorize the signs she was learning. She sat on her little stool behind the cashier's counter and practised them as she closely watched the videos.

About an hour before lunch, she was surprised when she recognized Emmett's poorly-colored truck pull into one of the parking spots on the street. Brooke was even more surprised when a tiny figure hopped out of the passenger seat. She immediately recognized the little girl from Henry's board.

Oh my god, Brooke thought with delight, *that's her!*

She was tickled when she saw her and thought scandalously when the time would be that she would meet the mother. Emmett's elusive girlfriend.

Brooke quickly closed down her phone, quickly ran her hand through her hair to give it some bounce, and smoothed out the front of her blouse.

"Hey guys," She greeted them with a big smile as Emmett and his little passenger walked through the door.

The little girl, Isabelle, wore a faded yellow t-shirt that showcased several dirt stains. At least, Brooke prayed that was dirt. She wore pants that were too long for her skinny little legs, and Brooke spied what looked like a fresh tear in the material above the knee. Her hair was hidden underneath an orange trucker hat that was far to large for her head. Beneath its large rim, Isabelle's steel blue eyes regarded her cautiously.

Emmett was dressed in his usual manner. Well-worn jeans with a long-sleeved, button-up work shirt. As always, he had the sleeves of the shirt rolled up to his elbows to expose his meaty forearms. He immediately recognized her and spread his hands to the sides, with his palms up and the fingers slightly bent, and he shook them slightly.

What?

Holy shit, Brooke thought suddenly, *I know sign language.*

Brooke didn't pay any attention to his question. She couldn't afford to. She had been practising her greeting for almost an hour, and couldn't risk getting sidetracked. She assumed she would have more time to properly learn this, but she felt confident.

She first brought her right hand to the corner of her forehead, fingers tightly together, and then moved her hand outwards away from her head. She was careful to ensure her palm remained facing her.

Hello.

Immediately, Emmett recognized the sign, and she was rewarded with a quizzical expression that bloomed across his face. His slightly shocked face just spurred Brooke on.

The next one was harder. Brooke made her two hands into a thumb-ups fist, and put them together so they were pointing in different directions, one towards Emmett, and one towards her. Then she switched their positions slowly before she used the index finger of her right hand to point towards Emmett.

How are you?

With a dumbfounded expression, Emmett looked at her and repeated what he said, with even more enthusiasm.

What?!

He quickly recovered, pointed to himself before he changed his hand to the *five-hand.* That's what the ASL people called an open palm with the fingers spread apart. Emmett took his five-hand and touched the thumb to his chest, and ended it by pointing to himself again.

I'm fine.

Brooke was quickly running out of things she could say. She only got through the first video, after all. But she still had an ace up her sleeve. She took her own five-hand and touched her thumb to the spot between her breasts.

Good.

She couldn't help the grin on her face as Emmett looked at her with a challenging expression and sucked loudly on his teeth. As if to say, *ok, let's see how much you really know?* He first made one of the signs she had been studying, *when*, she recognized that one right away. The next sign kind of looked like zombie hands that he slowly shook at his sides; Brooke didn't know that one. Then Emmett slowly pointed towards her before he made the sign for *learn*. Again, it was one of the twenty-five signs she learned in the first lesson. He finished by taking his pointed index fingers on both hands, with the palms out, and waved them in opposing circles to each other in front of himself, *sign*. She didn't understand it all, but she knew enough.

When did you learn to sign?

"When did I learn to sign?"

She eagerly asked to confirm, through a wide smile, and eagerly waited for his reply.

She couldn't help the little laugh she made when he nodded his head. She reached over the counter to excitedly touch his forearm and gave it a friendly squeeze.

"I watched a video this morning and learned a few of the basics," she said lightly as she moved out from behind the counter and walked around so she was standing in front of them. "I thought I'd give it a shot." She gave him a quick wink. "It might be nice to have a secret language with someone I can gossip to." Emmett nodded promptly and pulled out his notepad.

That's why I do it, just to talk smack in front of people without them knowing. They shared a chuckle before Brooke set her friendly gaze upon the little girl.

"Who do we have here?" she asked brightly and gave the defiant-faced girl a cheery smile.

"I'm Isabelle," she said quietly and promptly thrust her hand out in front of her for Brooke to shake.

"That's probably the prettiest name I've ever heard," Brooke stated playfully, hoping to get a rise out of the small child. She was rewarded with the smallest of grins. "I'm Brooke." She leaned out and gave Isabelle's tiny hand a gentle shake.

"Brooke?"

"Yeah." She winked at her. "It's like a stream, only much cuter." Her usual reply was, *only sexier*, but she didn't think that was appropriate for someone Isabelle's age.

Brooke then went back to her scant ASL repertoire and pulled out another gem for Emmett. She wiped her open palms together once before she closed her palm and pointed both index fingers to the sky, and then she brought them together. She ended it by pointing at Isabelle's chest.

"It's nice to meet you."

Isabelle said nothing, she just regarded her earnestly from behind the brim of her hat. When Brooke straightened, Emmett smiled broadly as he handed her a note.

She's my niece. She's going to be staying with me.

Brooke stared at the little note wide-eyed. *What?!* Then she read it again just to make sure.

"For how long?" she asked instinctively.

It was then she noticed Isabelle edging closer to have a look at what the note said. Brooke handed her the note for her to read.

Emmett looked at her with a smile and took the index finger of his right hand and pointed to the sky, and moved it around in a full circle. He then slowly closed his hand into a fist with his thumb and pinkie finger extended, the phone-hand, she called it.

He touched the thumb to his right eye, close to his eye, and moved it down his cheek. Brooke was at a loss, and showed it on her face.

"What does that mean?"

Emmett took out his notepad and quickly scribbled something down and showed it to her and Isabelle.

Forever.

"You're kidding?" she blurted the question at him with what she imagined was a shocked expression. She couldn't help it. "How is Becky? Is she at the farm?"

Immediately, Emmett's expression darkened and he sucked in air loudly through his teeth. Brooke started to suspect she may have said something wrong. It was Isabelle who confirmed it.

"She died," she said quietly and looked up at Brooke with her defiant little face, but she knew better. In her steel-blue eyes, Brooke saw the cracks in the façade. She saw the pain.

"Oh my God," Brooke instinctively brought her hand to her mouth to try and hide her shock. She was doing a poor job of it. "I'm so sorry to hear that."

Brooke lowered herself down so she could look Isabelle in the face, and placed a hand softly onto her shoulder. Brooke could feel her tense up but was pleased she didn't pull away. She wanted to hug the child, to wrap her arms around her and try to take some of that pain away, but didn't feel that would have been appropriate given they had just met.

"Your mother was a pretty amazing person."

"Did you know my parents too?" Isabelle wiped her nose with the back of her hand and looked at her.

"I went to high school with them," Brooke said with a smile, like it was a fond memory. "They were like the *Ross and Rachel* of our school." *Then Clive Adler came along and ruined everything.*

"Who's that?" Isabelle's face scrunched up in confusion as she looked to both of them. Brooke, who was thankful for the distraction, looked at her with mocking disbelief.

"From *Friends*." Isabelle just shrugged her shoulders. "Are you joking?"

Jesus! How old am I?

Brooke looked to Emmett for her rescue and he gave her a remorseful look and shrugged himself. She stood up straight and looked at the two of them.

"So, is there something I can help you with, or did you guys come to see if I can fit *both* my feet into my mouth?"

Isabelle responded perfectly.

"You can put your feet in your mouth?" she asked, like the very idea of it grossed her out.

"Oh, sweetie," Brooke said with playful exasperation. "I do it at least two or three times a day." Emmett chuckled breathlessly and showed her his notepad, with three simple words on it.

We need clothes.

"Oh well," Brooke said and spread her arms and motioned around the empty store. "You came to the right place, *at* the right time. We have the whole place to ourselves. So, what kind of clothes are we looking for?" Emmett shrugged. *Typical.* "Work clothes, pretty clothes, or school clothes?" Brooke ticked them all off her fingers. She could have gone on, but by the look on his face, Emmett got the point. "I'm going to need more to work with here, Emmett."

Work clothes.

"Well," Isabelle cut in quietly after she read the note and craned her neck back to look up at Emmett. "Could I get some pretty clothes, too?" This rugged-looking, stained, trucker-hat wearing child asked so sweetly Emmett was powerless to say no. Brooke wasn't surprised when he quickly nodded. He returned to his notepad and showed her the amended version

And pretty clothes too.

"What's our budget?"

At that both she and Isabelle looked at him expectantly. Emmett looked down at Isabelle and narrowed his eyes playfully before he held up his hand with his fingers spread.

Five.

"Five hundred?!" Brooke and Isabelle asked almost in unison, with matching amounts of surprise. Emmett just nodded proudly.

"Okay," Brooke said. She clapped her hands together loudly and looked down at Isabelle with an excited expression. "You get to go on a bona-fide shopping spree! Are you excited?" To her muted disappointment, Isabelle shrank a bit. "What's wrong?" she asked quietly, leaning in.

"I'm not good at shopping," Isabelle said like she was confessing a sin.

"Don't worry," Brooke said quietly, as if she was about to reveal a dark secret, and reached down and took Isabelle's small hand into her own. "It's practically my superpower."

She stood up and led Isabelle deeper into the store.

CHAPTER 9

Zeke

Zeke was released on July fourth. Their American cousins to the south celebrated that day as their Independence Day, the day they officially separated from the British Empire. It was an auspicious day, and he took it as a good omen for his future endeavors.

The Organization had come through for him, just like he knew they would. Once the ugly business of the shortages was straightened out, and the deliveries got back on track, the mysterious gears of The Organization started to turn in his favor again. Next thing he knew, the Government of Canada took two months off his sentence. For good behavior, they said.

Just in time for summer.

The exit procedure with inmates was painfully tedious. It was the prison's final twist of the screw, to make him sit quietly while he received a thorough physical, one that involved a complete cavity check. So, that was awesome. Then, he was made to stand at the property counter and sign out each individual possession they had confiscated off his person when he first arrived. There was a small change room to the side, which the inmates were supposed to use to change back into their civilian clothes, but Zeke couldn't be bothered with such niceties. He stripped down to his underwear right there in the hallway, in full view of his attending guards and anyone else who happened to be in the corridor.

His slim-fit, black jeans hugged his lower body as it went over his skin. Next, he put on the white and black AC\DC shirt with the Distressed logo on it. Over that, he slipped on his red, long-sleeved, button-up silk shirt. He smiled at the guard as he took his time tying the narrow black tie into place. Then, came the Italian leather shoes. They had been an impulse buy, but never one he regretted. They practically caressed his feet when he eased them on. He tucked his shirt into his pants before he fastened the modest belt buckle that prominently featured a skull on it. Over all of that, Zeke twirled the long black trench coat around his body with a bit of flare and put his arms through the sleeves as if it was a magic trick. When he was done, Zeke Simard breathed out a deep breath.

He was himself again.

"Ere," Zeke said to the property clerk with a bit of a smile. "You can ave dese back." He carelessly bundled his old prison attire into a loose ball and shoved it across the counter. He took the rest of his belongings and stuffed them into the pockets of his coat, gave the clerk a cute wave, and walked tall towards the exit.

Outside, Zeke paused just beyond the front door. He heard his guard escort file in behind him and waited impatiently as he breathed in the afternoon air and rolled up his sleeves of his long coat.

It was rather warm outside after all.

"Get going," one of the guards behind him said quickly. "Let's not make a big thing out of this. Just head to the gate."

"Ah!" Zeke didn't even look back. He just shot up his raised finger. "I am a free man now. Da second I walked trough dose doors back dere. You fuckers can't touch me. Just relax," Zeke said lightly as he looked up at the bright sun in the sky and withdrew the five-year-old pack of cigarettes from his pocket. "Enjoy the beautiful day."

He popped a stale-smelling smoke into his mouth and lit it with the cheap lighter he had when he was arrested. He breathed in the smoke deeply, letting it fill him up, before he craned his neck to the sky and slowly blew it into the wide, blue sky.

Zeke then started to tap his toe.

Music started to bubble up from his core and fill his head. Zeke couldn't help himself as he used his free hand and gently slapped the drumbeat against his thigh. Then his shoulders started to bob forward in time with the tune in his head. He left his smoke in his mouth, and sucked in a deep breath through it as he loudly clapped his hands together before he looped his thumbs into the beltloops at the front of his pants and started off diagonally on the hundred-meter concrete path with a lively step that was reminiscent of a country line dance. He led with a series of half-steps with his heels and jutted his hips dramatically to the side. He took three lively steps forward in this manner, before stopping, taking one step back, and then starting off in the other direction.

He paused, clapped his hands loudly again before he spun in a tight, full circle before he came to rest staring at his stunned escorts. Zeke brought his hands in with flare before he shimmied his shoulders with a dancer's grace. He shot his hands into the classic finger-guns gesture, except instead of fashioning his two hands into pistols, Zeke just flipped them his middle fingers and shot it towards their unimpressed faces. He did this a few times as he rhythmically shuffled backwards. He then brought his middle fingers in for a big kiss before he shot them out to the sides and spun in a grand circle.

By this point, Zeke had maybe travelled ten feet. He channeled his inner Fred Astaire and danced the whole way to the exit gate. Most people practically speed-walked towards that gate, towards freedom, but Zeke wanted to savor this moment. He took almost a full five minutes to traverse the other ninety feet, dancing the whole way.

"Ouvre ce putain de porte, idiot!" *Open the gate, Idiot!* Zeke spoke loudly to the guard manning the tiny shack to the side of the gate when his dance came to an end. The guard slightly frowned as he reached down and pressed the intercom button.

"I speak French, dickhead."

"And yet da gate remains closed," Zeke said, smirking at the man. "Maybe I said it too fast?" he offered lightly and the guard rolled his eyes at him before he hit the buzzer.

A moment later, the inner gate opened, and Zeke strolled through carelessly.

Zeke crossed the road to the visitor's parking lot and felt the breeze blow through his coat like a superhero's cape, fanning it out behind him.

It felt liberating.

He quickly eyed a familiar black Chevrolet Suburban with tinted windows, it stood out like a sore thumb in the amongst the scattering of compact cars that were in the visitor's parking lot. Zeke hunched down as if he was trying to get a better look inside, though it was obviously impossible. He smiled widely when all the doors opened almost in unison.

"*There you are, you suave bastard!*" Remy shouted as he exited the driver's seat of the SUV. His excitement gave his accent a sharp tone.

Zeke could see his whole crew made the trip, just as he had instructed them to. Richard exited from the shotgun seat and smiled and waved as Zeke approached the SUV in a fast strut. Kevin exited from the driver's side rear seat; he waved as well but he clearly looked uncomfortable in the prison's parking lot. He probably felt just being here was bad luck. OJ, was the only member on his crew who wasn't some shade of white. He was Indian. OJ was short for some god-awfully-long name, the likes of which nobody in the crew had been able to remember, much less pronounce correctly. It was something he constantly nags them about.

They all knew his last name was Khan.

They would never forget that, because they had sat down one night and watched Star Trek II: The Wrath of Khan. They all busted a gut when William Shatner dramatically shouted OJ's last name at a particularly tense moment in the movie. They still did it every-now-and-then to get a rise out of him.

"I never though I'd be so happy to see your ugly face," Zeke said with a joyous smile and he stepped up and embraced Remy warmly. When he released him, he turned to Kevin, who was the next closest. "You look like you're about to shit your pants," Zeke chuckled as he embraced the man.

"A prison parking lot isn't my idea of a *fun day out*," Kevin replied lightly and returned the embrace.

"Boss man!" Richard said joyfully the second Kevin released him and quickly swooped in for his own hug. "Fucking awesome to have you back," he said when he released Zeke and held him by the shoulders.

"I shall leave you *just* as you left me," an unmistakable voice said with grim determination from the back of the SUV. Zeke turned and saw OJ rounding the back corner of the vehicle with a murderous look on his face. "*Marooned*, for all *eternity*." He was paraphrasing the movie they had all watched so long ago. Zeke knew his part.

"KHAN!" He clenched his fists and shook them wildly as he screamed his friend's name into the sky.

They all shared a hearty laugh.

God, it was good to be back.

After they got the pleasantries out of the way, they filed back into the SUV. As always, the shotgun seat was exclusively reserved for Zeke. Remy drove, as he often did, and the other three quietly moved into the back.

They settled into their seats for the three-hour-drive back to Toronto. They didn't speed down the road, nor did they pass booze or drugs around the inside of the SUV. They didn't even listen to the radio loudly. They were professionals, after all. They didn't attract needless attention to themselves. Plus, most of them were pushing thirty years old. They were getting too old for that bullshit. That's not to say they didn't enjoy the occasional rager, but there was a time and place for that sort of thing. This was neither of those things.

Zeke kept a close eye on the digital clock on the dash.

At two o'clock, Zeke pulled a cigarette from his pack and slowly popped it into his mouth.

"Uh, boss?" Kevin spoke up cautiously from the back.

Everyone knew there was no smoking inside the vehicle. Especially Zeke. It was his rule, after all. No one else dared question it, but Kevin was probably just wondering if this meant everyone could smoke as well. He probably meant as a way of asking permission.

"It's okay, Kev. I'm just celebrating something. We can bend the rule this one time," Zeke said quietly and lit his cigarette.

"Your freedom?" Kevin asked like it was obvious.

Probably the only nice thing about a short stay in a maximum-security prison, maybe the only one, was that there were plenty of lifers walking around. Zeke appreciated those sad souls like a commodity to be used.

It cost him twenty thousand dollars to arrange the assault of Doug Grimes. *Old Grimey*, his friends called him. He was just another inmate who was in for a long haul on a murder rap. It wasn't a life sentence, but he would be a senior before he left Milhaven. That's probably why The Organization hired Doug to rape him. Zeke often wondered during the last four months how much they paid the man to shove his cock inside Zeke's ass until it bled. In the end, he guessed it didn't really matter.

He was paying two men, both lifers, ten thousand dollars each. Two thousand before, and eight thousand after the job is done, to give Doug a *Molson Enema*.

It was a simple enough procedure. You take a man, stretch him over something before you remove his pants and underwear. Then, when he's naked and exposed, you take a greased-up beer bottle and forcibly jam it up their asshole until the last quarter of the bottle is sticking out. Then you break the end of the bottle off, preferably with a hammer, and immediately afterwards give the recipient a swift kick to propel the broken end of the bottle into the rectum.

Of course, before the bottle was to be broken, Zeke instructed the lifers to whisper a simple message into Doug's ear. *Zeke Simard says hello.* Hopefully it would be the last thing that rat-fuck would ever hear, other than his own pained screams, that is.

It was to happen at two o'clock today, as Doug Grimes was getting off his shift at the laundry.

"Retribution," Zeke said quietly and with a sly smile as the clock ticked over to two-oh-one. "Retribution."

Zeke had a guy on the inside who worked in the infirmary, he would confirm whether or not the job had been done. Twenty thousand was a steep price, but he had to ensure they did the job to his specifications, and in the long run it was a small price to pay for piece of mind. Zeke didn't think he could live with himself knowing someone out there in the world had violated him like that, and he didn't do something about it.

He respected The Barrister's logic when he told him to let it go. Obviously, he would be the first suspect if anything were to happen to Old Grimey. That's part of the reason he waited until he was well and gone from the prison, instead of busting that bottle off in that guy's ass himself and watch him bleed all over the floor like a dying pig. He couldn't prove it, but Zeke suspected he won some favor with the higher-ups by dealing with Grimes the way he had. He believed it said a lot about himself to his handlers. For starters, he could be trusted to follow orders, like a good soldier should. He would have proven he was resourceful, discreet, and above all else, vindictive. All good qualities in an aspiring criminal.

"So, Zeke?" Richard leaned forward and warmly clapped his hand down on his shoulder to get his attention. "What do you want to do on your first day as a free man? Go to the club, get some drinks, maybe find ourselves some loose women." Richard laughed and gave Zeke a knowing squeeze.

It had been years since Zeke felt the tender warmth of a woman, even it was a hooker. Richard's words soured his mood.

That's what started all this bullshit in the first place, you stupid child.

Zeke loved Richard like a brother, but he was an uncompromising womanizer. It was fine when they were younger, but it was starting to cause problems.

"I could use something to eat," OJ spoke up quickly.

"No, Richard," Zeke spoke up after exhaling a lungful of smoke. He reached over and moved the rear-view mirror so he could see the backseat. He narrowed his eyes at Richard. "We ave to deal wit your *porcelets.*" *Piglets.*

"Well," Richard started to say sheepishly while retreating his eyes away from Zeke's. "I just figured you'd want to wait a couple days before we tackled *that.* You know, maybe get checked in with your parole officer first."

"Dumbass," Kevin said quietly, but still loud enough that everyone in the vehicle could hear him, and with obvious distain.

He knows the score, Zeke thought to himself.

"You tought wrong, *mon ami.*" Zeke said casually as he flicked the ash from his cigarette out the window. Four monts," he said and brought up four digits for the people in the back to see. "I've been waiting four-long-monts to fix *your* mistake, Richard. I am not going to wait another day. Dat's da difference between you and me. I don't let my mistakes fester, like you ave." He coldly looked at Richard for another second before his gaze shifted to Kevin. "Are we all set?"

"Yep," Kevin said after giving Richard his own chilly side-eye. "I have everything we need."

Good, Zeke thought and nodded towards the man.

The difference between Richard and Kevin was apparent just by looking at them. Richard was dressed in loud, flamboyant clothes and gold chains. *He's almost thirty years old, and he dresses like he belongs on a reality tv show.*

Whereas Kevin wore simple jeans and a clean button-up shirt and light black coat. Kevin would instantly blend into a crowd of people, which was the point. While Richard dressed like he was trying to attract every eye in the area. Like a goddamn child.

"What are you going to do?" Richard looked up from his shoes and met his viper-like gaze in the rear-view mirror. "Just...I was thinking," Richard said.

That was your first mistake, Zeke quipped inside his head and took another drag off his cigarette.

"Maybe we could just buy them off? Just give them enough money to disappear."

"Dey won't," Zeke shot back, keeping his tone calm. "They are *porcelets,*" he said it like it should explain everything. He could tell by Richard's confused expression, it didn't. "Dey will take all I ave to give dem, and dey will still want more. No," he said firmly and waved his hand dismissively. "Dere is only one way to deal with dese fat, little *porcelets.*" He purposefully let the statement hang inside the interior of the SUV, like a test.

Remy sighed in the driver's seat beside him. In the back, Kevin grinned and nodded his head. OJ was silent, but Richard still looked confused.

He failed.

"What's that?" he asked nervously when no one else spoke.

Zeke turned in his seat so he could look Richard in the face with his bored expression. His cigarette hung bounced precariously from his lips as he spoke.

"We slaughter dem."

***

Zeke sat in the comfortable leather couch his crew had arranged in the back shop area of their headquarters. The Organization had set it all up for them when they hit the big time. They purchased a small building in an industrial park that was north-west from Richview in Toronto. It was a small, indistinct building that had little in the way of fanfare or advertising on the street-facing side. Just a small sign on the tiny patch of grass that read: CRL Construction. He assumed it was some construction business that went tits-up at some point before The Organization swooped in and snatched up the small, unremarkable building.

It was perfect for their needs.

It was long, narrow, and positioned between two much larger properties, so it was easy to miss. The small building had a narrow, paved driveway that led to the fenced-off yard at the rear of the building. As well as a large vehicle door at the back with enough parking inside for their large SUV and the older Ford panel van they used for deliveries. The front quarter of the building of reserved for the small reception area, and a couple of offices. Zeke had a small cot set up in one of them. He planned to sleep here until he found a proper residence. The best part, was the tiny door on the side in the open area that revealed a discreet stairwell the led down into a small storage room. It was a near perfect location for a lab. Remy spent a small fortune setting up a functioning lab down there that had only one purpose.

Methamphetamine production.

The only real problem was ventilation. For that, they cut a sizeable hole into the floor of the shop, straight down to the storage room. They were smart about it, and kept the hole close to the wall. That way, they could wire in an industrial ventilation fan, and attach it to the wall with one duct running down to the lab, and another running up to the roof. Kevin and Richard hooked up an industrial air scrubber to sanitize the exhaust air coming out of the roof. Their building was not two blocks from an industrial scrap yard, so there was plenty of chemical odors lingering in the air, but Zeke wasn't about to take chances.

He was a smart criminal, after all.

He was raised by criminals, tortured and trained by them. He brought himself up from the streets by keeping his head down, his eyes peeled, and his ears open. He had seen all types of criminals come and go during his time. He learned from them all.

He learned that meth had the best profit margin over all the other narcotics out there. Since the esteemed Canadian Government went and legalized marijuana, pot was no longer a viable option. It didn't have a great profit margin, but it was safe.

He couldn't *make* cocaine. He could only sell it, and he didn't like the idea of being someone's bagman, so that was out.

The designer drugs like ecstasy and molly, requires too much equipment and materials to manufacture. Not to mention the market wasn't really there. He did the math.

Meth was his ticket, but only *smart* criminals could manufacture, distribute, and most importantly of all, deal with the vast amount of cash that came in. For that part, Zeke found himself a bookkeeper. Not an actual accountant, because those are trained professionals that had to adhere to a strict code of ethics. That meant they would cost more, and they essentially weren't even needed. A bookkeeper could handle all the necessary paperwork to arrange a Limited Corporation to handle the cash flow as well as set up his crew as registered employees of that corporation. As far as the government was concerned, Zeke ran a very lucrative roofing business and had four extremely well-paid employees. Now, this all took away from their profits, but the money they got in return was completely clean. Which, to a criminal, was like ambrosia. It was like a gift from the gods.

That's how he achieved The Organization's notice, by being a good criminal.

Zeke cleared his mind when he heard the others move through the door to the front offices. All three of them filed through the door, so that could only mean one thing. Kevin confirmed it when he moved into the shop area.

"They're here," he said sternly.

Zeke looked to his crew and eyed each for a full second.

Kevin stood completely still with a blank expression on his face, his automatic pistol was tucked into the waistband of his jeans. Kevin was their enforcer. He wasn't muscle, he was *better* than that. Honestly, Kevin probably would have taken care of this problem if Zeke asked him to, but that wasn't fair. He left Remy in charge, so, it was his call to make. The unfortunate part is, he never made that call. Kevin was cautious. He was a military vet, but Zeke couldn't tell if that was part of it. He didn't think Kevin was chasing some adrenalin rush he learned to crave from combat. He was part of the Bomb Disposal Unit, and spoke of long anxious days defusing various roadside IED's his unit came across. Kevin liked the money, and Zeke suspected whatever fear the man had was washed away in the Afghan desert cutting a wire and hoping he wouldn't be erased in the next second. He was a risk versus reward kind-of-guy.

He looked ready.

Richard and Remy looked liked scared rabbits that were ready to jump out of their skin at any moment. Zeke couldn't blame them, they weren't made for this part, nor was it their role in the crew. Richard was the face, back when they had to worry about distribution. It was him who made the initial contact with the street-level dealers. Everybody liked Richard. Now, that they were under The Organization's purview, he was demoted to delivery driver. He drove the truck and made the drops with Kevin. He really wasn't needed, but he came up with him and Remy, he was basically family. That meant Zeke had to fix his mistakes.

Honestly, Zeke didn't want Remy here for this, but he left him in charge. He probably should have left Kevin in charge, but Remy was his best friend. He trusted Remy. He felt he could handle the responsibility, and for the most part, he did. Remy wasn't good with confrontations though. The three little pigs took advantage of that, all the while Remy knew it was happening, but he didn't do anything about it.

This was his fuck up too.

"Okay," Zeke said lightly, reached down and snatched up his glass of bourbon. He downed it in one swig, breathed in loudly through his teeth, and placed the glass back down. "You know wat to do. Get into your positions." Beside the sofa, he spied Remy's frame begin to file in behind Kevin. "*You stay right there,*" he growled to his friend in their native language and pointed to the spot where he wanted him to stand.

This was a teachable moment, and Zeke didn't want him to miss it.

The trio entered loudly through the back door of the building. Zeke's view of them was blocked by the black SUV, but he could hear them. They were joyously carrying on about something of zero consequence. Until they moved towards the front of the large vehicle that is, then their little giggles and comments came to an abrupt halt.

The tiny woman in front came to a slow stop in front of the SUV, and Zeke saw her face scrunch up in annoyed confusion. Immediately, he didn't like what he saw.

In his humble opinion, she was too thin, bordering on unhealthy, but she covered it up well with the skin tight exercise apparel she had on. It gave her the look of a long-distance runner. She was pretty, no doubt. Zeke could readily see how this one made her way through life. The party girl. She had expensive-looking dark hair with lightly frosted tips, and a streak of bright blue on the side of her temple.

Charlotte, he reminded himself.

Beside her, standing slightly taller and with a fairly athletic build, was her brother, Travis. It was obvious by their looks they were related. Travis cut his dark hair short, wore jeans with holes worn into the knees and a Blue Jays jersey. With a tacky-looking military jacket over that, his whole outfit clashed horribly. He came in with a smile on his face, and Zeke took some pleasure in watching it evaporate.

On the other side of Charlotte, was a true brute of a man. He had olive skin, black hair that was slicked back, with cauliflowered-ears and a crooked nose that bespoke of someone who was comfortable with his fists. He wore jeans with a white t-shirt, and a black leather jacket. A thick gold chain stood out prominently around his neck. It was like he was on his way to a costume party and dressed up as a stereotypical gangster.

In front of them, Zeke sat comfortably in the leather couch behind a wide coffee table. He had cleaned all the junk that littered the top of that coffee table during his crew's extensive cleaning session. Now, the surface of the table housed only a few items that Zeke had carefully laid out on the table, like it was a display. Closest to him, was an expensive bottle of Tennessee bourbon, and an ornamental glass that still held about two fingers of the amber-colored liquid. On the side of the coffee table that was closest to his guests was a large, black shotgun laid across the length of the table. Behind it, placed carefully on their ends, were three brightly-colored, red shells.

Smart criminals would have seen that display and immediately recognized the implied threat.

"Who the fuck is *this* guy?" Charlotte posed the question to Remy, who was standing weakly by the side of the couch, with obvious annoyance.

"Yeah," her brother chimed in with some humor. "What the hell is this? Like, is this guy on his way to prom or something?" He thumbed towards Zeke on the couch and then chuckled at his own joke. The other one, Levi, was silent.

He only stared at the shotgun.

"Where's our shit?" Charlotte looked to Zeke this time and posed the angry question.

Zeke reached into his pocket and pulled out his pack of stale cigarettes. He popped one into his mouth and looked over the flame at Charlotte with cold eyes.

"Hey, I asked you a question? *Where* is our shit?"

"Dat is an apt term for it. *Shit,*" Zeke said pulled the cigarette from his mouth slowly. "It was *removed.* Trown away. It took some time, but we managed to sanitize dis place of you." He included all of them in the statement, but he only pointed at Charlotte.

"You did what?!" Charlotte asked. She looked like she had a lot more to say, but she was cut off by Levi.

"You're him, aren't you? *Simard*?" he asked cautiously, and the other two looked to him before their gaze pivoted back to Zeke. He smiled broadly, spread his arms wide, and bowed slightly.

"In da flesh," he said and settled back into his seat.

"Wha-?" Charlotte looked dumbfounded, again Levi cut her off before she could get the word out.

"You weren't supposed to get out for another two months."

Oh! Clever boy, Zeke thought to himself, thoroughly amused this one was keeping tabs on him. He wouldn't have guessed he was the smart one.

"Correct!" Zeke wagged his cigarette towards the man, like he was impressed with him. Then he snapped his fingers loudly.

"What the hell?" Travis called out when Kevin appeared from the other side of the panel van, with his menacing-looking pistol in his hands, pointing right at Travis's stunned face. "What are you doing?" he whined towards Kevin.

"Shut up, you moron."

Levi looked behind him in time to see Richard move in behind them with a pistol in his hand, and a remorseful look on his face, cutting off any possible escape. The big man slumped his shoulders and looked back to the couch.

"So, what is this?" he asked grimly, like he already suspected what the answer was.

"Downsizing," Zeke said with a flourish of his arms.

"Fuck off," Charlotte said with venom.

The men on her sides didn't share her skepticism. Travis was shifting his focus between Kevin's pistol and Zeke. Levi looked like he was just waiting for something. Zeke had an idea what it was, and he respected the man for that.

"This is just a bunch of bullshit. Do you have any idea how much money we made for your ass?" She gestured angrily to include the men at her sides before she ended it by pointed one of her manicured nails at Zeke in a manner he didn't appreciate.

Not one bit.

"Ah! Yes," he said with little enthusiasm as he reached forward and plucked one of the bright red shotguns shells off the table. "Da trash bags filled wit da crumpled-up twenties we found in da office back dere." Zeke chuckled quietly as he pulled a felt pen from the inside pocket of his jacket. "Wat da fuck am I supposed to do wit dat? I can't pay my rent wit a bunch of crumpled twenties. I can't buy a car. We can't pay our chemical suppliers wit a bag of twenties, can we? Now dat I tink about it, da only ting I could buy wit crumpled-up twenties, that wouldn't raise suspicion, is drugs, alcohol, and cigarettes." Then Zeke eyed her coldly. "Assuming dat money was even *meant* for me." He used the gesture to motion at the trio in front of him. "I'm kind of getting da impression dat money was meant for your pockets, not mine."

"We earned it," Charlotte said defiantly, much to the disappointment of her compatriots.

"Dat you did," Zeke agreed with her while he carefully removed the cap and neatly printed Charlotte's name along the length of the shotgun shell. "Da real question in front of us today *mes amis* is, wat did you cost me?" At this point, he held the newly marked shell in his hand and began to tick off their offences with the fingers of his free hand. "You disrupted my distribution. You stole *my* product. Exposed *my* operation to scrutiny by dealing your silly dime-bags to your filty little street rats." *Not to mention, you cost me my anal virginity.* "You tried to weasel yourself into the wrong operation," he said, held up his left hand for them to see, and wiggled his partial pinkie at them. Levi was the only one who seemed to recognize the significance of it.

Then he reached for the shotgun.

"What the fuck?" Travis visibly tensed up. Kevin kept his distance, and eyed the man over the iron sights of the automatic pistol.

"He's bluffing," Charlotte said as a way to calm her brother. Zeke just eyed her coldly as he loaded the single shell into the shotgun.

"Am I?" he asked darkly and racked the shell into the bore of the shotgun.

"You don't scare me."

He had to admit, this one had balls. *Zero* common sense, and absolutely no ability to read a room, but she *was* feisty.

"*Mon cheri,*" Zeke said slowly. "I was never *trying* to scare you."

He then leveled the shotgun at her chest and pulled the trigger.

BOOM!

At this distance, there was no chance he would miss, not with a shotgun. The buckshot struck Charlotte's tiny body just under her unimpressive bosom. Immediately fabric, tissue, and blood erupted out from the impact points and sprayed the men at her sides. The buckshot tore through tissue, pulverized bone, and launched Charlotte's tiny body backwards. She solidly struck the front of the SUV and then violently rebounded off and fell to the ground, where she laid still as her life's blood leaked out and pooled around her midsection.

"CHAR!"

Travis dropped down by her body and gave her corpse a firm shake. It was then that he looked up at Zeke with furious eyes.

"You fucking killed her!" he howled in utter disbelief, like it was unexpected.

Zeke only smiled and shrugged his shoulders.

"I'll kill you, you bastard!" Travis rose up and moved towards Zeke.

Then Kevin shot him.

Travis only managed one step before Kevin promptly lowered his pistol and shot him in the same leg he had just moved forward. The man's fury evaporated immediately as he cried out and crumpled to the ground, where he rolled around whimpering and clutching his wounded thigh.

Zeke looped his arm around the shotgun, held it in place as he reached down picked up the second shell, and took out the felt pen. Again, he wrote the intended target's name on the shell. He liked to do this because he felt like it gave the shell an added purpose. Like this shell had made its way from the factory to this exact moment, and now it was fulfilling its destiny. Like it had always been meant for Travis, and he was just confirming it by writing his name on it. When he was done, he loaded the shell into the underside, and loudly racked the shotgun again.

"Wat about you, big man?" Zeke asked Levi as he slowly moved in front of him, looking up at him with the shotgun between them.

"What about me?"

"I *do* ave an opening," Zeke offered lightly. "Just one, but it doesn't come cheap." He then held the shotgun out in front of himself for the large man to take.

"Zeke, what are you doing?" Kevin asked sternly while training his pistol on Levi.

"If he soots me, you soot him, and you guys can carry on witout me." Zeke never took his eyes off Levi's. "Dere's only one way out for you now, *mon ami.*"

Levi slowly reached out and took the shotgun from Zeke, much to Travis's horror.

"I never liked you," Levi said to his *friend* on the ground, and pointed the barrel in his direction.

"Oh, fuck you!"

"Ah!" Zeke said sharply to stop Levi. "One second." He held up his finger while he made a show of checking his pockets. "To seal da deal," he said merrily as he fished his new smartphone out of his pocket. Zeke waved his hand and motioned for Richard and Kevin to move out of the shot. "Action!" Zeke cried out like he was a Hollywood director and pressed the record button.

"No! Hold on!" Travis called out and quickly looked to the camera before he pivoted his head to his friend holding the shotgun, just in time to witness him pull the trigger.

BOOM!

Travis took the buckshot in the upper torso in a spray of fabric and gore. He made a weird yelping sound when it hit, and the force sent his body rolling across the floor a few feet. He didn't move again after that.

Zeke stopped recording, and signaled to his crew.

"Alright!" Zeke cheered and stowed his phone away before he clapped his hands a couple times while relieving Levi of the shotgun. "Nice work. I didn't tink you would do it for a second dere."

Zeke handed the shotgun off to Kevin when he stepped up. Kevin quickly removed a cloth from the pocket of his coat, and furiously wiped down every inch of the shotgun.

"Hold this," he said to Levi and presented him with the weapon again.

The large man knew the score, he took the shotgun and held it in the same manner he had when he shot his friend. When he was done getting his fingerprints all over it again, he handed the shotgun back to Kevin. He used the cloth to grab the weapon by the barrel before he moved towards the back of the SUV to stow it in the back.

"You ever heard of a *get-out-of-jail-free-card*? You know, in dat board game wit da rich guy?" Levi looked at him and nodded. "Good. Dis?" Zeke motioned around them, indicating the moment they were currently in. "Dis is your *go-straight-to-jail-for-da-rest of-your-fucking-life-card*." Zeke stepped back, and reached down and plucked the last shell off the coffee table and presented it to the man. "Dis is your lucky day. You came close to da end today, remember dat, and remember who it was dat didn't erase you from this earth."

"Shit! There's blood all over the front of the van." Kevin said when he returned from the back of the SUV. Richard and Remy were visibly shaken.

"Don't worry about it," Zeke replied with a smile. It evaporated when he turned back to Levi. "Okay, your first job is to clean dis mess up. All of it. Da cleaning supplies are in da front office, first door on your left." Zeke checked the man's tasks off on his fingers. "Get rid of da bodies, da car, and fucking sanitize this place. No joke, we will be running a black light over dis place when we get back, and it better be spotless. You want to be da muscle? *Dis* is what da muscle does in my operation. After dat, if you choose, you may walk away from dis ugly affair. No strings. We will wait a month, and I better not see your fucking face until da end of dat time. I will listen to da news reports, and I better not hear about our friends here. Make it like dey never existed." He gestured to the bodies leaking on the floor. "Dis will also give you time to clean yourself up. Were you using my shit?"

"A little," the large man confessed quietly.

"Dat will have to come to an end as well, *if* you want the job." Zeke nodded to the man and slapped his hand gently on the man's shoulder before he turned back to his own crew. "Okay!" he declared. "Let's go get some dinner."

They filed into the SUV and backed out of the building, leaving Levi to clean up the evidence. He would have Kevin follow up on it later, but for right now he believed he deserved to relax a bit and enjoy a nice meal. They all agreed on a nice steak house they had enjoyed before he had been put away. Halfway to the steak house, Zeke turned his head to the back of the vehicle.

"After our meal, Kevin, I'm want you to show me da house where *mon petite Belle* is staying. I know it's late." He added to cut Kevin off before he even mentioned it. "I know I won't get to see er, I just need to see da house, you know? To see wat kind of people are taking care of my little girl." Zeke didn't know why he said that, he didn't need to explain himself. "So, after you'll take us dere, yeah?"

There was a disturbing silence from the back.

"Yeah, about that." Kevin said with trepidation in his voice. "I got bad news, boss."

CHAPTER 10

Belle

Belle woke up with every intention of going right back to sleep. The air inside the room was cool because Emmett had a rule of keeping the windows in the small house open during the night, and closed during the day. Emmett laboriously explained that this was to keep the house cool during the day. Belle wasn't so sure about that. The inside of the house was plenty warm by mid-afternoon. Right now, though, she was perfectly comfortable snuggled into her warm blanket. She felt the cool breeze from her window kiss her exposed cheek. Then she rolled over and made the mistake of opening her eyes.

The alarm clock by her bed was practically staring at her. Its large digital display read eight-thirty-two in the morning. Suddenly, Belle didn't feel like sleeping anymore.

"Shit!" she hissed quietly and threw herself out of bed.

Emmett liked to start earlier in the day, that way they could finish their chores and watch tv in the afternoons, when the day was the hottest. Usually, he was tapping on her door shortly after seven in the morning, and he would have breakfast already cooking on the stove. Belle had to admit, there was nothing better than waking up to the smell of eggs and bacon cooking on the stove. *Why didn't he wake me up?* Belle asked the question in her head with a bit of annoyance. Like, he *should* have woken her up. Something inside Belle started to worry and she quickly opened her door and exited her room.

To an empty house.

"Emmett?" she called out as she walked into the kitchen. Her feet made little slapping sounds against the linoleum as she went. On Emmett's chalkboard she quickly spied his note.

Isabelle,
Got a text from a friend late last night,
He needs help with his combine.
Long, boring work in a field.
You've been a big help lately and I
thought you could take the morning off
and relax at home.
I'll be back around noon.
Breakfast is in the fridge.

Emmett also listed his cell number below that and added: *Call if you need, but don't be mad if I don't feel like talking. Lol!* Belle rolled her eyes at Emmett's little joke.

He always had a joke of some kind to tell at breakfast. He would casually reach over and write the joke on the board, and look at her stone-faced while she read it. Some of them were actually pretty funny, some were real groaners, but each one brought a smile to her face in one way or another. The best ones were the ones that broke him down into laughter as well. Emmett had a weird laugh, it sounded like a dog madly panting. When she first heard it, it was a little unsettling, but she was used to it now. She learned to pay more attention to his expression, that's where the joy was. Sometimes he would snort. *That* was funny.

Belle lazily opened the fridge. *Yay!* A part of her leapt for joy when she saw the plate brimming with large portions of eggs, hashbrowns, and four strips of bacon. All covered lovingly with plastic-wrap. Belle quickly took the plate out, removed the wrapping on it, and popped it into the microwave for a full minute.

Oh man! Belle slapped her forehead gently, *I completely forgot.* Belle padded back to her room, and quickly moved toward the dresser. *Yes!* There on the dresser, in the same spot he always left it, was another picture of her parents.

It had become almost a game between the two of them. That first night, Belle had swiped the first picture off the dresser and hid it away from Emmett. The next morning, she awoke to find a completely different picture of her parents in a different frame, on the dresser. So, she swiped that one too. The following morning, there was yet another framed picture, in the exact same spot. However, this one came with a note.

You can keep the picture, but I only have so many frames.

That's how their little game started.

In this picture, Belle saw her father effortlessly carrying her mother on his wide back. They both wore sunglasses as they looked at the camera with big smiles. Her mother looked like she had been laughing at the time the picture was taken. *This was taken here,* Belle deduced when she recognized the large tree in the background. It was the same tree in the yard a distance from the house. As always, Belle could almost feel the love they shared radiating off the picture.

Bing!

Belle quickly removed the picture from the frame, and stowed it in the drawer of her night stand. She set it with the others she had. They were right beside her collection of all the little notes Emmett had given her so far. Then she placed the empty frame back onto the dresser and ran back into the kitchen.

Her breakfast was glorious, even reheated it still tasted just as good. Belle sat at the kitchen table, and enjoyed the silence of the house. While she ate, she looked over Emmett's note again on the chalkboard. She was a little sad she couldn't keep this one. It was a good one. Belle liked to keep all of Emmett's little notes. She didn't know why, it was like a hobby. She didn't mean to keep the first few.

After that crazy first night, when they got back to the farm, Belle said goodnight and went to hide in her bedroom, she found them in her pocket. She read them over in her bed while she waited for sleep to come, and then she read them over again.

Her favorite note was still the very first one Emmett had ever handed to her. *I'm so happy to meet you.* It wasn't even really a note, because it was written on a cue card, but whatever. In it, Emmett had underlined the *so happy* part of the sentence, and the exclamation point at the end stood out brightly, like he was excited when he wrote it.

Don't worry about it. We'll get through this, was another one she liked to read on occasion. She had maybe about a dozen that she would put amongst her favorite notes. They were all special to her, but some of them just induced a feeling in her that she couldn't readily identify, but she knew it was good.

They will be a nice memento when the time comes for us to leave this place too, a mean-spirited voice inside her jabbed her cruelly. Belle took a forkful of the eggs Emmett had prepared especially for her, and thought about the first sign she ever learned.

Forever.

That's what Emmett signed when the lady at the clothing store, Brooke, asked how long Belle would be staying with him. *Forever.* Belle thought about that moment and used that memory to beat the mean voice into the background of her mind.

Then she read over the note on the chalkboard again. *Relax at home,* it said. Something about that word, *home,* resonated like a bell tone inside her.

She knew why, of course. She held no illusions about her place in this world. She was a stray. Like all strays, she dreamed of a forever home, because home was much more than just a location. Home was a place where you *belonged.* A place where you didn't have to worry about leaving one day. A place where you could make plans for things. Big things, small things, all kinds of things because you would still be there in six months, or a year, or five. Home was a place where you stayed until *you* were ready to leave. Where you were always welcomed back with open arms that gave big hugs. The idea of *home* seemed too good to be a reality, it probably wasn't.

Belle didn't know for sure if this place was her home. That seemed like a lot to ask for. What she did know, was until the time came for to actually leave this nice, quiet place, she was going to pretend like it was.

She finished her breakfast, rinsed off her plate, and put her dishes in the dishwasher with the other dishes waiting to be washed. She moved back to her room, stretched her arms wide in the center of *her* room and did a full circle with her arms open, like she was a princess. Belle looked to her newly stocked closet. It wasn't as jammed-packed as the closets some girls had on tv, but it was certainly more than she could fit into the small suitcase she arrived with. It would be a problem if she ever had to pack that suitcase up again, because she didn't know how she would pick her favorites.

That was a problem for later.

She decided on denim overalls today. She didn't want to fish the pair she had on yesterday from the clothes hamper. They were clean, but why would she do that when she could just wear some of the other new clothes she had? Brooke had picked out three different pairs of overalls for her, each a different color.

"It's important to be able to mix and match," Brooke had said to her at one point when she was picking out the overalls.

Turns out, shopping really was Brooke's superpower. She fondly remembered how the woman led her through the store, pulled down various items of clothes, placing them against Belle's shy frame, and either added it to the cart or the item was placed back on the rack with a quick shake of Brooke's head. The fitting room was the best part. Not at first, though.

"No," Brooke said lightly when she first appeared from the fitting room and strolled out with her arms at her sides and her head down. "Do it like this."

Brooke walked to the door and turned back with a sudden dramatic flare and swung her arms stiffly as she strutted forward a few steps. When she stopped, she popped her hip to the side, placed her hand on it while her other hand swept her dark hair to the side, and held a neutral look on her face. When she was done, Brooke gave her a mischievous expression and motioned for her to try. Belle did her best approximation of Brooke's fiercely graceful movements. She felt she did a good job too.

"Work it, girl!" Brooke clapped, and when Belle looked, she saw Emmett was broadly smiling as well. "Yep," Brooke said proudly. "That one's a keeper. Now, go get the next one on," she said as she shooed Belle back into the change room. With each outfit, Brooke showed her a fun, new way to show it off.

It was easy to like Brooke.

Belle went with the black overalls, and the black-and-white striped shirt Brooke thought was cute. She went to the full-length mirror that Brooke insisted Emmett buy, because *every girl needs a full-length mirror.* She said it with a humorously disappointed face that hinted that Emmett should have known that. She looked at herself in the mirror, turned herself this way and that, admiring her new outfit in the mirror. *I like this,* she decided and smiled at herself. Her hair needed a good brushing, and desperately needed to be cut and styled, but it still looked good in a ponytail. So, that's what she did. With one of the frilly scrunchies Brooke picked out for her.

Then a soft knock came at the front door of the house. At least, Belle assumed that was the front door, it was the only door she had ever used. She knew there was another door that went out onto the porch, but Emmett rarely used that door.

She went to the kitchen and looked out the window. In the front of the house, she saw a large, dark-blue truck that she didn't recognize. In the driver's seat was an older man with a cowboy hat on. Belle had a hard time making out the features of the driver, but she caught his wave when he did it. She weakly waved back before she moved towards the door, and opened it.

Standing outside was a small boy with short blonde hair, and thick, black-rimmed glasses that hung awkwardly from his face. Belle recognized the boy's face from the picture board at the gas station. Mr. Johnson's. In his hands he carried a medium-sized box.

"Oh!" the boy said and looked at her with a bit of a surprised expression. Like he had been expecting someone else. "Hello," he said softly.

"I know you," Belle said quickly and pointed at him.

"You do?" the boy said suddenly confused.

"Yeah," Belle said with a wicked smile. "You're on the *Thieves Board.*" She said the word with scandalous flair. The boy's expression quickly dropped. "You're a thief." She said it lightly, as if to imply a sort of kinship with her.

The boy didn't take it as such.

"No, I'm not!" he said angrily, and then shrank away from his own outburst. "My cousins tricked me. They told me they paid for it. It wasn't my fault." He weakly defended his crime like Belle already knew the ugly details. She didn't, but she felt bad for him.

"I wasn't saying anything," she replied quickly. "I'm on that board too."

"You are?"

"Yeah," she said and nodded solemnly. "Right next to you. It's like we're picture buddies or something." The boy just looked at her with a blank expression.

"Is Mister Brooks home?" he asked, changing gears.

By the fearful look on his face, she could tell he very much hoped he wasn't. She was pleased she could put him at ease, but she let him sweat for a moment longer

"Nope," she replied and watched him look at her like she just made his day.

"Well," he said sheepishly and looked back to the man in the truck. "Maybe I could leave this with you and you could give it to him. Tell him I gave it to you," he said, then quickly realized the two of them never actually exchanged names. "I'm Lucas. Lucas Adler."

"Isabelle," she quickly replied.

"Nice to meet you," Lucas replied almost automatically and gave her a little smile. "Are you Mister Brooks's daughter?" he asked, like he already knew she wasn't. Belle didn't let it phase her.

"His niece," she said proudly, and gestured to the box in his hands. "What's in the box?"

It was then the smallest of whimpers escaped its confines.

"It's a puppy."

"A puppy!" Belle whined with utter surprise and opened the door further for the boy to enter the house. "Oh my god! Lemme see," she said guiding him into the kitchen.

Lucas slowly lowered himself down onto the floor and carefully placed the box in the center of the linoleum. He quickly opened the flaps, and Belle's heart utterly melted.

Inside was the tiniest little dog she had ever seen, with dark black fur covering the majority of its tiny body. Except for his little paws, those were white, and the coloring around his face was streaked with white too. The moment Lucas revealed it to the world, the puppy started yelping wildly and jumping up one of the sides of the box.

"He's so cute," Belle whined, she couldn't help herself. She had never seen anything as adorable as that small puppy was.

"He's a Miniature Schnauzer," he said reaching into the box. "They're super-cute." He said it like he was bragging about it. She didn't care, she just waited eagerly as he slowly handed the dog to her. "Me and my mom raise them. We have a big farm just over there." He pointed towards the kitchen window.

Honestly, Belle wasn't really listening. She cooed and whined as the little creature in her hands furiously wagged its tail and squirmed merrily in her lap. Lucas then reached over and quickly scratched the puppy affectionately behind the ears.

"I named him Max, but I guess you can name him whatever you like," he said with a hint of sadness. Belle locked eyes with him and she could see the sorrow in his eyes. "He was my favorite."

Belle then remembered what the boy said earlier, put the pieces together, and suddenly felt sad for the boy because he was giving up something precious to him.

"Why are you giving him to Emmett?" she asked suddenly intrigued.

"I shot his dog," Lucas said with obvious shame.

"You shot his dog?!" Belle yelped loudly. *No wonder he's scared.*

"I didn't mean to," he said quickly. "It was an accident. I was just shooting cans. I like to do that," he said defensively. "But I wasn't being careful, like my dad taught me. I didn't even know Mister Brooks was in his field. I got into a lot of trouble."

"Does Emmett know this?" she asked rubbing Max's tummy.

"No," Lucas said quietly. Then he dropped a real bomb. "I guess I shot Mister Brooks too."

"What!?" she shrieked. Lucas recoiled away from the shrill sound of it.

"That's what my grandfather said," Lucas offered like he was having trouble believing it too. "He said he saw Mister Brooks later that same day, and he had been shot in the leg. So, I guess that was me." Lucas said and looked like he was trying to hide his gaze behind his glasses.

"Jesus Christ!" Belle looked at him grimly. "Maybe you shouldn't tell him *that* part."

"Well," he said and looked towards the door. "Maybe you could tell him I stopped by." He looked at her with new hope in his eyes. "You could tell him I'm really, *really* sorry. Then maybe when he sees Max he won't be mad anymore." Belle couldn't argue with that logic. Anyone who took one look at this dog couldn't possibly be mad at anything anymore. "Be sure to tell him Max was the best one."

Then Belle remembered something.

"You know what you *should* do," she said with a measure of excitement. "The next time you *do* see Emmett?"

"What?" Lucas responded cautiously.

"This," Belle said and slowly proceeded to show Lucas the same greeting Brooke used on her. She slowly used a motion similar to wiping her palms clean, she was careful to make sure her left palm was facing upwards, like Brooke did it. Then she took her two separated index fingers, and brought them together, before she pointed her right hand towards Lucas's chest. The whole time she slowly said the sign's meaning.

"Nice. To meet. You." She smiled proudly when she was finished. "It's sign language. Emmett likes it when people use sign language."

"He does?"

"Oh yeah," she said with absolute confidence.

"Okay," he said perking up before he repeated the sign back to her. "Nice. To meet. You."

"That's it."

"Cool," he said with new hope, and again, looked towards the door. "Well, I should probably get going. My grandfather is waiting in the truck, he didn't want to come in." Lucas then gestured towards the box. "I put a blanket in there, it's Max's, but under that I got a leash, a container of kibble for him, and a couple pee-pads. Max isn't quite house-trained yet. So, maybe take him out every few hours. I also put a collar in there for you to use. It doesn't have a tag on it, because I didn't know what Mister Brooks was going to name him."

Belle looked down at her new furry friend in her arms, cooed slightly and leaned into touch noses with the little puppy. She was rewarded with a few quick licks.

"I like Max," she said gently holding his advances back. "I think it suits him."

After that, Lucas rose off the floor and headed towards the door. Belle remained cross-legged with Max excitedly hopping up into her hands, trying to steal more licks.

"I'll see you later, Isabelle." Lucas turned and repeated the sign she had taught him. "It was Nice. To meet. You."

"It was nice to meet you too, Lucas." She said lightly as he turned away. "Hey! Maybe, if you want, you could come by sometime, and I don't know, hang out with Max and me."

She wasn't going to lie. Lucas looked younger than she was, but beggars-couldn't-be-choosers. So, she made sure to keep her tone light, unassuming, definitely not desperate, but internally something inside her tighten.

"That would be nice," Lucas said with an uneasy smile. "As long as Mister Brooks is okay with it."

He gave her a small wave, and left.

Belle heard the truck's door outside open and then close before the engine fired up, and the truck slowly drove away. She laid down on the floor, and Max immediately scampered up her chest and started showering her with little licks.

"Did you hear that, little Maxie?" she said, twisting away from the slimy kisses. "I think we just made a friend."

Belle really didn't know how this day could get any better.

Belle played in her room with Max for the rest of the morning. She quickly discovered Max like to play with her socks, so Belle took a dirty sock out of her clothes hamper and folded it into a small ball. She used that and tossed it for Max to fetch. Belle couldn't help but giggle at the awkward way the dog ran after the sock. When he retrieved it, Belle would eagerly slap her thighs and Max would come bounding back towards her. He jumped into her lap with wild abandon, fully trusting her to catch him in her hands. She did every time, without fail. Then she would gently rub down his entire body, much to his furry delight. When Max dropped the sock from his mouth, Belle would quickly scoop it up and toss it again, and their game started all over again.

Soon enough, Max started to slow down, and every-now-and-then he would let out a big yawn. Then, when he returned with the sock in his mouth, Max let out a final yawn, curled up into a small ball on her lap, and fell asleep.

Belle didn't dare move a muscle.

She just sat there on the floor beside her bed, and looked down at the warm, little ball of fur on her lap. She marvelled at the fact this small creature trusted her, and felt safe enough to fall asleep while nestled into her. It was like she was watching a little miracle happen. She knew it wouldn't last, this perfect little moment of serenity and cuteness, but right now she didn't dare do anything that might disturb it.

"I *did* make a friend today," Belle whispered softly into Max's sleeping form. "When I met you, my little Maxie. You're going to be my best friend forever." She wanted to pick Max up and kiss his little head, but she didn't want to wake him. Instead, she took her one finger and gently stroked his head, right between his upright ears.

I will never let anything hurt you. She didn't say it, she didn't know why, but she felt it was something she shouldn't say out loud. Like, just saying it would be tempting the world to prove her wrong. She couldn't risk that. She couldn't let her universal bad luck affect this small, perfect being.

Sometime later, Belle recognized the sound of Emmett's truck as he pulled into the yard outside. She quickly reached up, pulled a pillow off the bed, and used her fist to create an indentation in the center of it. She carefully transferred Max's sleeping form into the divot. He let out a big yawn, threatened to wake up, but then snuggled into the pillow and remained still. She slowly crept out of her room and silently closed the door behind her before she moved into one of the chairs by the small table in the kitchen.

That's where she waited for him.

What if he doesn't want a dog? A nervous voice inside her asked.

Her heart skipped a bit when she realized that was a very real possibility. One she hadn't considered until this very moment. She simply couldn't understand why someone wouldn't want a free dog, especially one as sweet, and adorable as Max. She had some points she could bring up. Right of the top of her head, she could promise Emmett that she would take care of him. Clean up his messes, feed him, bath him, take him for walks, and whatever other dog-related chore she hadn't thought of. She would promise herself to all of it. She could also bring up the fact that Max was a small dog, and he wouldn't take up much space. It was even in the breed's name, *Miniature* Schnauzer. Honestly, Emmett would probably barely notice he was there. *Which could be a problem if Emmett stepped on him. That* was another problem for later. She would do whatever she had to in order to keep Max.

Emmett opened the door, walked into the kitchen with a big smile on his face, and a couple foot-long submarine sandwiches that swung from their clear, plastic bags in his large hand.

"You got subs!" Belle exclaimed excitedly. Emmett looked at her, and used his right fist to nod. That was the sign for *yes.* "Did you get me a pizza?" That was the kind she had the last time, and it was really good.

Emmett moved to the chalkboard and used the eraser to quickly wipe away the message from this morning. Belle watched with some sadness as it disappeared, but watched as Emmett wrote two simple words.

You bet.

Then, as they often did, Emmett showed her the signs for what he wrote. He first pointed at her with his right index finger, *you.* She already knew that one. Next, Emmett put both his hands out to the sides with their palms up, and then levered them towards the center. Like, he was folding a large towel, *bet.*

Emmett laid the subs on the table, retrieved plates and glasses for the two of them, and poured glasses of orange juice from the fridge.

He seems like he is in a good mood, Belle thought as she scanned his face for a reason not to tell him about Max this instant. *No, wait until after lunch,* she thought finally. Emmett was usually in a better mood after he had a good meal.

Halfway through their lunch, as he often did, Emmett picked up his chalk and went to the board.

What do you call a fish in a bowtie?

"What?" Belle finally asked after some thought.

So-fish-ticated

Belle had to read it aloud a few times before she got it.

"*Gawd!*" she groaned loudly, much to Emmett's amusement. "That's the worst one yet."

Then the gentle scratching came from her door.

Emmett immediately heard it. She could tell by the way he froze mid-chew and turned towards her door. He had a look of grave concern on his face as another persistent scratch came from her door. Emmett went to wipe his mouth, and she could tell he was about to get up.

Belle sprang into action. Before Emmett could leave his chair, she bolted up from hers and blocked his path to her bedroom door.

"Don't get mad," she said quickly. "I was going to tell you, but I wanted to wait until after lunch." It was then that Max decided to let out one unmistakable slight whine. "It's a dog."

Emmett just smirked at her because the little whine that came from her room was obviously from a dog. He took his two hands, palms up with his fingers slightly bent, and shook them slightly at his sides.

What?

"This boy stopped by and dropped him off. His name is Max," she said sweetly. "He was giving him to you, for *free*." She gave him a look to emphasize the point.

Emmett took his right index finger that was slightly bent and put it to his chin before he pulled on the digit, like he was squeezing a trigger.

Who?

"Lucas. Lucas Adler. He said he lives right over there," Belle said, pointing towards the kitchen window.

Emmett's expression dropped to one of muted anger. Belle had been around the man enough to know when he was angry, even if he was trying to hide it. He turned to the chalkboard, wiped it cleaned, and Belle could hear him digging the chalk into the board as he quickly wrote. He tapped the board loudly when he wrote the exclamation point at the end.

I know where he lives!

He turned back to her and used his index and middle finger of his free hand and tapped it against his thumb. He should have been using his right hand for that sign, but he was still holding the chalk.

No.

"What?!" Belle's own expression dropped as well. "Why? I promise I'll take care of him. He's so small, he won't get in the way. Please! Please, please, please," Belle said in rapid succession. All her finely tuned points were thrown out the window when she saw the heated look on Emmett's face. She had to do something.

Emmett returned to the chalkboard.

The Adlers are not our friends!

"What?" Belle said taken back by this new information. "What do you mean?" Emmett was already wiping the message away before Belle even got the question out.

He knows Lucas shot his dog.

If he knew that much, then it wasn't a stretch to assume he also knew it was the same person who shot him.

"If this is about Lucas shooting your dog, he said he was *really* sorry. He almost cried," she added because she thought it would help her case.

Emmett shot her a shocked look, huffed angrily, and went back to the board.

He didn't know, Belle thought and felt a pit open up in her stomach when she realized she just made things worse. Emmett backed away from the board and presented her with his message.

We're not taking anything from the Adlers!

It's going back as soon as I'm done lunch!

It's going outside!

I'm sorry.

"No," she said, thinking back to the unspoken promise she made to Max. "You can't." She wanted to say more, but her throat tightened up and the tears started to come. "Please, Emmett! Please, let me keep him! I'll be good."

Emmett moved towards her bedroom door. Behind it, Max was whining more intensely. Part of her feared Max somehow knew what was happening in the kitchen. *No,* Belle thought and she stepped forward and placed her hands on his stomach to try and hold him back. *I promised him,* she said to herself and she pushed against Emmett with all her might to keep him away from Max.

Emmett took one of his arms, gently swept her to the side, and walked right by her. Belle continued to plead with him as he angrily stepped to her bedroom door. When he opened it, Max's little body bounced out of the room, and Emmett scooped him up in his large hand.

Then Max started yelping.

"No!" Belle cried out. "YOU'RE HURTING HIM!" she screamed and balled up her hands into tiny fists and started beating them down on Emmett's back. "LET HIM GO!"

She continued to beat her fists against Emmett, trying desperately to get him to focus his rage on her instead of poor Max. He was wiggling uselessly within Emmett's crushing grasp as he swiftly walked him to the door

"NO!" she yelled again as Emmett simply opened the door and deposited Max outside on the ground. He turned back to her with heated eyes, but Belle had her own heated expression for him. "YOU CAN'T LEAVE HIM OUT THERE! HE'S JUST A PUPPY! WHAT IF SOMETHING HAPPENS TO HIM?!"

Without thinking she moved towards the front door, but Emmett blocked her approach with his impossibly large body. Belle yelled at him and beat her hands against his chest to get him to move.

He just stood there stubbornly, and looked down at her.

With nothing left to do, Belle backed away a step and screamed her fury at him with such intensity it made her ears hurt.

"I HATE YOU!"

She moved to the table, scooped up her plate with her half-eaten sub on it, and threw it across the kitchen. The plate shattered against the corner of the stove, spraying her sub all over the stove and cupboards, and sending bits of plate everywhere.

"I HATE YOU!" she yelled at him again before something inside her told her to escape this whole situation.

Belle ran into her room, and slammed the door shut.

Around her were all the remnants of little Maxie. The blanket he liked to play tug-o-war with, his little container with food that never got opened, the tiny collar she never got to put on him, and the leash she never got to use.

You promised him, she scolded herself. *You promised him you'd take care of him.*

She wept horribly in the center of the room thinking of her unkept promise. She wondered where Max would go after Emmett returned him, but was stung by the knowledge of knowing wherever Max did end up, they would never be able to love him as much as she could. If she was just given the chance.

Belle screamed her frustration at her bedroom door.

CHAPTER 11

Emmett

What are you doing? Emmett asked himself as he stared out the kitchen window in the direction of the Adler's ranch, and idly looked around his yard. *Like, what the actual fuck are you doing?*

Outside, the little dog, Max, was whining and yelping incessantly at the door. Behind him, he could hear Isabelle sobbing loudly in her room. The remnants of her sub *and* plate were strewn about in the corner to his side.

All in all, he had made a real mess of things in an amazingly short amount of time.

That stupid dog! he cursed inside his mind, but after a deep breath he quickly had to admit to himself it wasn't the dog that set him off. It was the *Adlers. If Isabelle knew how those people ruined our lives, she would hate them too.*

Another deep breath came.

Is that what you want? For her to hate them?

The answer came swiftly, and definitively.

Of course not.

He felt like that was one of his jobs, to protect her from those kinds of emotions. Emmett knew he carried his hatred for the Adlers around with him like a cancer. He remembered on some occasions feeling like it was eating him up inside. That was fine for him. He was okay with that, but he didn't want that for Isabelle.

Another breath came and went.

It dawned on him, slowly, that if he wanted to properly shield her from the tragedy that befell her parents, he would also have to shield her from his hatred for the Adlers. She didn't know what Clive Adler did to her mother, and if Emmett had his way, she would never know. If that was the case, he had to try and do the impossible.

He had to let go of his hatred.

At the very least, ease up on it. He knew Lucas Adler represented the new generation. It was hard to admit it, but Lucas wasn't his enemy. *While you're at it, maybe stop thinking of having enemies at all.* He had Isabelle to think about now, he didn't have the luxury of having enemies he could dwell on. He had to focus on her, and what she needed.

She needed better from him.

He felt raw about the interaction they had. His ears still rang from the way she yelled at him. There was nothing more he wanted than to slam his fist down on the countertop as hard as he could. He knew he couldn't do that, because there was a chance it could break. That was always a possibility, but the sudden noise would probably scare Isabelle as well. It would just make things worse.

He had to fix this.

He bent down and started picking the broken pieces of the plate off the floor, along with the remnants of Isabelle's sub, and placed them in the trash. He took a few minutes to clean up the scene until all traces of the mess he caused was wiped away. He then went to the front door, where the screen door was still closed, and looked down at the tiny whimpering dog that was caught in the middle of all this drama.

Jesus! He is *a cute little bugger,* Emmett couldn't help but think when Max looked at him with those beady, little black eyes.

He opened the door.

Max didn't need any more prompting, he clumsily bounded through the door and immediately stumbled on Isabelle's shoes. Max put his paws on the first step that led in the kitchen and tried uselessly to jump onto it.

Why do people even like dogs this small?

Emmett sighed before he picked him up and placed him on the kitchen floor. Max didn't waste a moment, he excitedly skittered across the kitchen to Isabelle's door, before he let out a little yelp, and scratched the door with his little paw.

The door almost immediately opened.

"Max!"

Isabelle dropped to the floor to allow Max to hop into her awaiting lap. She scooped up the dog's tiny form and held him close to herself. The entire time, Max was squirmed against her embrace to try and reach up to lick her chin. Then Isabelle gave him a look that melted Emmett's heart, and made him feel even more shame over how he initially reacted, before she spoke.

"Does this mean we can keep him?"

Yes, he signed with a warm smile, and a soft nod.

Isabelle looked at him with a look of absolute joy before her face tightened up and a fresh batch of tears came. She sobbed horribly as she carefully put Max to the side before she rose up and hurried towards Emmett. She roughly collided with him as she threw her arms around him, sobbing into his abdomen, and squeezed him tightly.

"Thank you," she whimpered, barely able to get the words out. "Thank you so much. I'll love him forever."

It was the first time his niece had ever hugged him.

Emmett's own eyes watered. He quickly wiped the wetness away before he lowered his head and gave Isabelle a little kiss on the top of her scalp. He hadn't planned on it, but it just felt natural to do.

Emmett finished his lunch while Isabelle played with Max in her room, like she was keeping the little dog to herself for the time being. He was okay with that. She was happy, that's all that mattered.

They decided to forego today's chores.

The cows aren't going anywhere, he told her in a note.

They drove for almost an hour and crossed the border heading to Yorkton. Isabelle wanted to go shopping for Max. The first quarter of the drive she went on about all the little things she wanted to get for the dog, all the while Max enjoyed some back scratches on her lap and looked out the window. Emmett kept his responses to what few signs Isabelle understood and tried to mirror her enthusiasm but internally he was doing the hard math.

When his mother died, her life insurance paid for all her funeral expenses, and paid out two hundred thousand to his father. A year and a half after that, he had to put his father into a home. Thankfully, his father didn't touch the insurance money. Emmett remembered he treated the money like it was tainted somehow, and maybe it was, but that didn't stop Emmett from using it after he was granted stewardship over his father and his affairs.

That was just over two years ago now.

Every month, thirty-five hundred dollars comes out of his mother's account to pay his father's room, and various expenses at the nursing home. It was a small comfort to know his mother was still taking care of them. That was forty-two thousand dollars a year, which was insane to him. After two years, he had almost burned through half of his mother's insurance money. Carter Brooks was still a relatively young man. He had plenty of years ahead of him. Unfortunately, they wouldn't be the good years. They wouldn't resemble what he imagined his father's golden years would be like, not even a little. He couldn't help that, but he still had to ensure his father was cared for.

During his funk, the problem of continuing his father's care always seemed like a problem for later. If it came to it, he could always sell the farm. That's what he thought, he could always sell it all and rid himself of the burden. Now, he had Isabelle to think about, and *later* seemed to be rushing towards him like a freight train.

He had taken twenty thousand out of his mother's account to pay for the renovations, and pay off some creditors that he had been neglecting, and used the rest to pad his account for the government people. That was six months of his father's life he just used up. *It's for Isabelle,* a voice would always remind him. *She needs it more than him.*

They were both adrift in the world. Both Isabelle and his father needed people to care for them. The horrible difference Emmett forced himself to admit was that Isabelle had a whole life worth of smiles, laughs, warm hugs, and good memories ahead of her. Carter didn't. He loved his father, he was a hard man, but only because life had been hard on him. If things didn't change, Emmett would have to make a horrible decision that he knew would tear him up on the inside.

So, he had to change things.

He did the math. To make the farm profitable enough to leave his mother's account alone, he would have to board another hundred head of cattle. He had fifty now. Twenty-two of those were his own. With the full section of land he had, he could handle three times that number, but he was only one man. There was only so much he could do. Plus, he didn't want to be working all the time. He needed those cows before Christmas time, or risk dipping into his mother's account again, and costing his father more time.

His business plan was fairly straight-forward. He would approach a few of the smaller farms in the area, the ones who may not have the land available for more cows. Emmett would offer his services as a way to expand their herd without having to upgrade their existing facilities or buying more land. He would charge them a monthly fee that would represent the expenses for their care, plus twenty percent, and when the cows went to sale, Emmett would take fifteen percent off the final sale price. However, if the potential client winced away from that, Emmett would hit them with a promise that he could increase the average weight by at least ten percent using a combination of the best grain feed money could buy. Emmett's high-quality hay, and good old-fashioned wide-open space to roam freely.

Luke Babineau, the man whose combine Emmett helped repair for no charge this morning, read Emmett's entire pitch off a cue card he had prepared beforehand. He could see the man was thinking the proposal over. Emmett suggested he could start by taking the few cows the man did have, and board them over the winter. *Just give me six months, and you'll see how much I can fatten them up,* he wrote after the man read the proposal a second time. They ended the conversation with Luke saying he would think it over, but he kept the card the proposal was written on. Emmett took that as a good sign.

"Emmett?" Isabelle asked quietly, and when he glanced at her, she had a concerned look on her face. "Is everything okay? You're kind of quiet." He quickly turned and smirked at her poor choice of words. "Well," she chuckled sweetly. "You know what I mean. You just look kind of...I don't know, *funny*." There was a slight pause before she spoke again. "I'm sorry about lunch, and I'm sorry about what I said." Emmett responded with a sign he knew Isabelle was familiar with.

It's okay.

"I don't hate you." Isabelle slowly stroked Max, who was laying quietly in her lap. "I shouldn't have said that. I didn't mean it." He looked at her, and gave his warmest smile before he pulled out his notepad. He struggled to write the simple message while driving, but he felt it needed to be said.

I get mad sometimes too.

There was so much more Emmett wanted to tell her. He could've told her about all the times he fought with her father, and recounted for her all the times he had told Tommy he hated him more than anything else in this world. He wanted to tell her about the mistakes he made because of anger, to let her know it was natural, but also to caution her that some mistakes couldn't be fixed with just a simple apology. Like the plate from lunch, some things just stayed broken once you ruined them. He was an expert on anger issues, and sighed heavily knowing he couldn't share those insights with her because she wasn't good enough at sign language yet, and he was driving.

Instead, he smiled and nodded gently after she read his simple note.

The pet store was a beautiful disaster. He had a figure in his mind when he entered the store and told himself they would not exceed that limit, under any circumstance. That didn't last long as Isabelle and Max tore through that store. Emmett laughed on more than one occasion because he wasn't sure who was leading who. Of course, after about two aisles Max promptly squatted down and pooped right on the floor. Isabelle looked up at him with a distressed look as Emmett handed her the note with a big smile.

He's yours. Clean it up.

Emmett held onto the furry-bag-of-energy's leash and they stood guard over the tiny pile of shit while Isabelle ran in search of something to clean up the mess with. Max wildly scouted about the aisle while Emmett watched for Isabelle's return. Seconds stretched on into a full minute before Emmett started to feel his anxieties begin to scratch away at his calm.

She should be back by now, he said to himself and huffed impatiently. *What if something happened?* He asked himself nervously as he started to fidget in place. He took a deep breath and reminded himself that she was a twelve-year-old girl in a fairly well-populated store, who was very capable of screaming if she felt the need. Then he told himself to relax and be patient.

What if she left? What if she just walked out the door and ran away?

He looked down at the tiny dog at the end of the leash madly sniffing about along the bottom of the shelves. *She wouldn't leave Max,* he replied to his anxieties eating at him and wasn't proud of the sudden bit of jealousy he felt. It was easy to love small, cute things that didn't pose a threat to anybody. Big, scary things, like him, had to try harder. It wasn't fair, but life was rarely fair.

Okay! Where the hell IS this girl?

Emmett moved to the end of the aisle, gently pulling the preoccupied puppy along with him, narrowed his eyes, and furiously searched for Isabelle.

Just to have her show up behind him.

"Got it!" she called to him, madly waving a handful of paper towel in one hand, and a spray bottle in the other. He resisted the sudden urge to write a stiffly worded note. "This lady showed me to where they have a station for this sort of thing," she said excitedly as she hurried over to him. "She says it happens all the time," she said giving Emmett a look. "So, we don't have to worry about it. We just have to clean it up." Emmett silently sighed out his relief and continued to hold Max as Isabelle cleaned up his mess. She didn't like it, that much was apparent by the grimace on her face, but she did a thorough job of it.

Two aisles later she had to do it again when Max peed.

Emmett was a little disappointed with himself when they walked out of the store with a loaded cart. *This girl has me wrapped around her little finger,* he said to himself as he started loading their numerous purchases into the back seat of his truck while Isabelle loaded herself and Max into the passenger seat. She insisted on having Max use one of the two dog beds they bought for him to lay in for the way home.

Emmett didn't plan on spending close to five hundred dollars on a tiny dog that was *supposedly* free. *There's no such thing as free,* he remembered his father saying on occasion, usually with little humor.

Isabelle was the picture of happiness on the trip back. Max promptly crashed into his bed and slept the entire time as she went on about all their exciting new toys for him, and genuinely pondered which ones Max would enjoy the most. She rattled off a list of pros and cons for each toy, much to Emmett's amusement.

It was a good afternoon.

"Can I have another sub?" Isabelle asked sheepishly as they approached Russell.

Emmett huffed a bit, and furrowed his brow at her. Again, he struggled to write a message for her. He didn't like to do this when he was driving, but the highway was utterly empty, and he couldn't let this stand.

I bought you a sub already. You didn't want it, remember?

"I know," she said, disheartened after reading the note. Then he quickly scribbled down another one and put his notepad away.

I'll make you lunch when we get home.

"Thank you."

Emmett was half-way through making Isabelle her bologna sandwich just the way she liked it, and with the sandwich cut diagonally. As she explained it, this was so she had a thin end to start from so she could work her way towards the thick part.

His phone buzzed in his pocket. Emmett didn't recognize the number.

Hey! Big man! It's Chaz! I had some dipshit who dropped out last minute. Your vids have been exploding. You up for another round or two? I can pay you a thousand to fill in for this match, win, lose, or draw. Plus, if you win, I'll sweeten the win bonus to another thousand. Plus, I might be able to find another sucka for you to fight if you're up to it. I need your ass here in two hours, though.

Emmett raised an eyebrow at the unexpected opportunity. He quickly started typing his reply.

$1500?

He didn't have to wait long for Chester's response.

I respect what you're doing, my dude, but the only reason I'm offering you a cool grand is BECAUSE your videos are doing so well. I got a whole pack of deadbeats I can feed to this guy for a third of that price.

Clock's ticking...

Emmett slowly shook his head. *That little asshole really IS a good businessman,* he said to himself with a measure of disbelief. *He's not the only one, though.*

Chester's father would probably be hanging out around the exposition grounds. Emmett could steal him away for his pitch.

Rene Dupuis would be a perfect candidate for his boarding operation. It might be a bit of a long shot, but any shot was worth trying at this point.

I'm in.

He would just need a babysitter.

Immediately, he thought of Calvin. He knew his friend would be eager to be able to spend some time with Isabelle, and he would only need a couple hours. Emmett quickly messaged his friend with the request.

Shoot, buddy! No. Sorry. I got plans with my brothers tonight. We're going out.

Emmett quickly racked his brain. He supposed he could leave Isabelle here alone again. She would probably be perfectly content to spend a couple hours just playing with Max. Then another candidate crossed his mind. He checked the clock on the wall, it was getting close to supper time, she might be busy. Emmett pulled her number up from his contact list, and texted the number Brooke had given him.

Hey, It's Emmett. Are you busy?

There was a bit of a pause

Is that a joke? She replied.

He furrowed his brow at the strange question and wondered how he should reply to that. A second later she sent him a picture.

In the picture, she was clearly lounging comfortably on a deck somewhere. He assumed it was her parent's place, in the background he spied the highway. In the foreground, were her two bare legs that were crossed out in front of her, and to the side was a small table with a long-neck beer bottle on it.

I just figured you'd be working...somewhere. Emmett couldn't resist the tiny jab. Brooke Talbot did have a surprising number of jobs around Russell. So far, Emmett had run into her at the hardware store, the clothing store, and the drug store.

Lucky you, this is my one day off. Emmett paused because he saw the three little dots that meant the person on the other end was typing. He waited like this for a full minute. *What's up?* She finally wrote.

I have a job to do in Churchbridge, and I need someone to babysit Isabelle. He sent it away and continued typing. *It should only be a couple hours.*

She's twelve. I'm sure she doesn't need a babysitter. She'll be fine. Emmett breathed in and thought about his day so far.

I left her alone this morning, and I came back and she had a new dog. I can't risk it! He put the exclamation point in as a joke, he was confident Brooke would get it.

She has a dog?!

Emmett quickly scrolled through some of the pictures he had taken of Isabelle and Max, he sent her what he considered to be the cutest picture. It was of Isabelle picking up Max's poop in the pet store with a face of abject horror, while Max looked up at the camera with his tongue out.

OMG! That's adorable! He's so tiny. She must be freaking out.

Yep. Emmett sent it away before he returned to the issue at hand. *Anyways, I got to be there in two hours. Can you do it?* He sent it away before he quickly added. *I don't want her to be alone.*

Emmett worded it differently this time, and hoped Brooke picked up on it. It's not that he was afraid what would happen if Isabelle was alone. That wasn't the issue. He didn't want her to feel lonely. This morning was bad enough. Emmett stared at the three dots as he wondered why he didn't just tell Brooke the truth.

First came the *thinking* emoji.

Can she paint nails? He just looked at the question for a moment. Trying to decide whether there was a joke or some reference hidden in there somewhere he wasn't understanding.

Yes?

Lol, she replied quickly. *I guess we're going to find out. I'm on my way.*

***

Like before, Emmett was led to the ring by one of Chester's crew. He wondered idly if she was related to him somehow or if she just wanted a nice-paying job. She wore form-fitting exercise wear with Chester's production company's logo across the rear of the pants.

Classy, Emmett thought with a grin.

Just like before, he chose to simply wear his work jeans. He removed his boots and socks in the waiting area so he could kick in the match if needed. Thankfully, Chester provided the fighters with flip-flops they could wear to-and-from the outdoor ring. Emmett didn't bother wrapping his hands again, and just wore Chester's MMA gloves over his bare hands.

The first red flag that caught his eye was the size of the crowd, the bleachers around the straw-bale ring were practically filled with a good crowd standing along the outside edging for a good angle to watch the event. Emmett told himself not to worry about it as he approached the ring.

The next red flag, was his opponent.

Who the fuck is this guy?!

Across from him was probably the meanest looking African-American man he had ever laid his eyes upon. This guy wasn't as tall as he was, and by the look of him, that didn't bother him one bit. He had a bald head that was shaved smooth, and he looked at Emmett from behind a furrowed brow of concentration that reminded him of an angry bull who was about to charge. He wasn't dressed in jeans, he wore loose-fitting boxing shorts, and Emmett could see his hands were wrapped underneath his gloves. The other problem was that this guy looked like a well-muscled instrument of destruction. He had little body fat, but Emmett saw his beefy shoulders, trim abdomen, and lean arms that were firing out jabs with surprising speed. He was clearly a trained boxer, which was the third red flag.

Then movement from the crowd caught Emmett's eye.

There in the stands, was Calvin, waving madly at him with a look of concern on his face. Beside him, Emmett saw Calvin's younger brothers waving eagerly at him as well.

What are you doing? Calvin quickly signed. The look of dire concern still painted on his face.

Making money, he signed casually. When the expression remained, he added, *what's wrong?*

Do you know this is a title fight?

That's when the fourth, and final red flag hit home. Emmett just looked at him in the stands with a gaping mouth.

What?! No! He has those?

Yes, you fucking idiot. That guy is nine-and-oh. All by knockout.

Jesus! Emmett cursed to himself as the introductions came. The black man across from him apparently liked to be called The Destroyer, which Emmett took as just another bad sign. Emmett rolled his shoulders a few times when they introduced him. He looked to Calvin again who signed quickly.

Nice jeans, by the way. Emmett could tell by the sour look on his face he was being sarcastic.

He drank from the water bottle that was provided, put in his mouth guard, and walked to the center of the ring to touch gloves. There was little else he could do. At the very least, he would still make a thousand dollars. That would pay for today's shopping trip with a little extra left over for the future. If he won, however, that would be a big boost to his bank account.

First things first, he reminded himself when he saw the grim look of determination on his opponent's face.

Emmett still liked his chances. This guy wasn't the only trained fighter in the ring, but one thing was clear. This was going to hurt.

The whistle blew and the fighters charged towards each other with fire in their eyes, and clenched fists.

For Isabelle.

CHAPTER 12

Brooke

Brooke sat alone and played a farming game, ironically enough, on her phone while Judge Judy played quietly on the television. She sat in the big recliner she assumed was Emmett's. Her father had a similar chair in their living room, placed for the best view of the TV. She had to hand it to him, the living room set looked new, and the soft-leather sofa practically hugged the body.

She was actually impressed with the little house.

When she first arrived, Isabelle insisted on giving her the full tour as soon as Emmett pulled out of the driveway. She eagerly grabbed Brooke's hand and led her through the house. Brooke didn't mind, she had to admit she was curious herself. It was a cute house. The colors she picked out for Emmett really brought some life to the bathroom and kitchen. Though, if she saw the kitchen beforehand, she probably would have gone with a darker color to match the wood of the cupboards a bit better. She nailed the color in the bathroom though, but was a little disappointed with the gawdy light fixture Emmett went with. It was nice enough, and cast a decent amount of light in the right place, but all that polished brass and frosted glass clashed with everything else in the room. Isabelle's room was her favorite.

Again, she nailed the color.

When Brooke entered the space it gave the perfect illusion of a wide-open space around them, the kind she had grown up with.

"And look at this," Isabelle said excitedly before she shooed Max back a bit and did a cartwheel in the middle of her room. "Isn't that *amazing*!"

Brooke agreed, though she wasn't sure what she was supposed to be impressed about. Isabelle's room was a little bare, but it was tidy and gave off a general air of peacefulness that was nice. Isabelle was quick to show Brooke her closet and point out all her favorite items they bought during her shopping spree. After which, Isabelle looked at her with a smiling face.

"So," she said with a twinkle in her eye. "Emmett said we're going to paint our nails."

"Fucking rights, we are," Brooke said excitedly and held up the oversized, brown leather handbag that was hanging from her shoulder. Isabelle recoiled shyly away from the curse word, but then smiled mischievously and giggled a bit.

They painted their nails on the kitchen floor. The bathroom was too cramped, and she didn't want to attempt such a thing on any place with carpet, and definitely not on the beautiful hardwood floor in the dining room. She instructed Isabelle to grab some old towels they could spread out in the center of the room.

Isabelle went with a nice metallic-blue color for her finger and toenails. Brooke decided to try this garnet color that she had had on her shelf at home but had yet to use. They first started with the toes, because Brooke felt if mistakes were going to be made, she preferred them to be done on her toes. First, she expertly colored each of Isabelle's tiny nails and then held Max while her small frame contorted humorously around Brooke's feet in order to apply the nail polish. In the end, she did a passable job. Then, they moved onto the fingers.

They sat on the kitchen floor, talking about unimportant things while Taylor Swift played softly from her phone. At the same time, they tried to keep Max away, since Isabelle didn't want to touch him until her nails were dry. The puppy desperately wanted onto the little island of towels they had made. They made a game of it.

Their nails dried around the time Emmett was due back. When he didn't show, Brooke rolled with it and switched to teaching Isabelle how to braid her hair, but first she had to wash it. Of course, Emmett didn't have any conditioner in the house.

"This is like a spa day," Isabelle said with some awe as Brooke slowly combed her damp hair before she began braiding it.

She told Brooke she wanted long, narrow braids at her temples to frame her face, with the rest pulled back into a low ponytail. Apparently, the style was fashioned after the female lead in some tv show she liked. Brooke had to admit, from what Isabelle described, this Delilah person was quite the badass bitch.

"Do you think Emmett will like it?" Belle asked about her new braids.

"I know he will," Brooke replied confidently and tried not to think about the time.

After a while, when Emmett still didn't show, concern began to creep in. She checked her phone often, usually when Isabelle wasn't looking, to make sure she hadn't missed a text. She hadn't, there was nothing.

So, she made dinner.

She huffed angrily as she prepared the meal in the unfamiliar kitchen, while Isabelle watched TV in the living room.

This wasn't what Brooke had in mind for her evening.

Emmett had said a couple hours, and being the foolish girl she was, Brooke believed him. She had planned to spend those hours doing nails with Isabelle and prettying themselves up for his return. Then, maybe, she would suggest a few beers on the deck to enjoy the summer evening. She was eager to test out all those ASL lessons she had been studying on YouTube. After her initial success with it, she kind of got the bug. If one could even say such a thing about sign language. If she was being honest, she had even contemplated inviting herself for dinner, if the vibe felt good. Possibly, even help Emmett prepare the meal. She didn't plan on cooking. Brooke had fallen out of love with it when she accepted she would be cooking only for herself for the foreseeable future. She could set the table though, and talk to him while Emmett prepared the food. Secretly, she was hoping for barbecue. Cattle farmers always had the best steaks. Afterwards, she would clean up so Emmett could keep his hands free to sign. That's what she really wanted.

She wanted to find out who Emmett Brooks really was. She didn't even know why, but there was something about the man that she felt herself gravitating towards. She liked being around him, she was mature enough to admit that. It wasn't anything that sparked the flame of passion and desire. God, no. Brooke didn't even think she had it in her for such things anymore, but she felt she could be good friends with Emmett. They connected on some level. Like quirky neighbors on a sitcom.

When she finally found the baking pans, Brooke made chicken nuggets and fries.

"Emmett usually makes burgers," Isabelle stated as a-matter-of-fact when she informed her of tonight's meal. Brooke just looked at her with a quizzical expression.

"What? Like every night?" she asked with a bit more surprise than she intended. Isabelle looked at her from the leather sofa and shrugged. "Well, Emmett's not here. So, you're getting chicken nuggets and fries." She said with a playful sternness and turned to walk back to the kitchen.

"Can Max have some?" When she looked back to the sofa, Isabelle was giving her a hopeful look. Even Max, who was sitting beside her on the couch, was looking at her with his cute, little face. Brooke tilted her head and put her hands on her hips.

"No," she said like Isabelle should have already known that. "He has plenty of dog food to eat if he's hungry." Brooke went to turn away but stopped herself. "He can have *one* nugget, and we *both* get to give it to him." She gave Isabelle a hard expression that should have warned the girl not to push her limits, but Isabelle just gave her a little grin that confirmed Brooke's suspicions. She had lost that round.

They ate in the kitchen. Isabelle immediately picked out the largest chicken nugget on her plate for Max, and used her knife to cut the nugget into two pieces. She handed Brooke her piece, and then proceeded to furiously blow on her own piece to cool it. When it was ready, Isabelle quickly passed the treat down to her dog. Brooke ate her food and let the half-nugget cool beside her plate.

When dinner was done, Brooke got the dog's attention with the tasty little morsel of food before she spoke.

"Sit," she commanded the tiny dog.

Of course, he just looked at her, wagging its tail. It took ten minutes of patience on her part. First showing the dog what she wanted by gently pushing his hindquarters down, and then rewarding him with tiny bits of the nugget she tore off, but it worked.

"Sit," Brooke said for what seemed like the hundredth time, and as if guided by some invisible hand, Max promptly plopped his butt onto the kitchen floor. "Good boy." She handed the small dog the treat and scratched him behind his ears and down his neck. Brooke turned back to Isabelle with an amused expression. "I hope you were paying attention, because training men is done in a similar way." She winked at her playfully.

"That's what Delilah says!" Isabelle exclaimed excitedly.

"She's not wrong."

After dinner, they both cleaned up the dishes and tidied up the kitchen. She didn't have to ask Isabelle for her help. Like some automatic response, as soon as the plates were emptied, Isabelle rose up and started collecting the dirty dishes. It was actually more like Brooke was helping Isabelle clean up. It was nice, only spoiled somewhat by the fact Emmett was still nowhere to be seen. She used this time to tell Brooke all about this Delilah character from her Crimson Tides show.

"You really like that show, huh?" Brooke finally asked with some amusement. Secretly praying to change the topic.

"Yeah," she confessed quickly. "All my friends at my old school watch it, they talk about it *all* the time. I only got to watch a bit of the first episode."

Wait, what? Brooke thought back for earlier in their discussion.

"I thought you said your other friend, Latesha, let you watch it on her phone *all the time*." Brooke didn't like the way Isabelle's expression shifted suddenly under her gaze, a guilty little expression flashed across Isabelle's face for a second, and then it was gone.

"Well," she said, quickly recovering. "She was busy a lot. So, she wasn't around much, but when she was, she always let me use it. We were really close, even though she was older than me. She was going to move out to the coast, and she said I could visit her there whenever I wanted."

It sounded to Brooke like she was bragging slightly about how well liked she was in her previous home. It slightly saddened Brooke that Isabelle had to leave those friends behind.

"So, you're telling me you haven't even finished watching the first episode? This show you've been going on about for the last hour, and you haven't even watched the entire first episode yet?" Brooke only realized how harshly she was questioning the girl when Isabelle shrank away from her a bit.

"I guess."

"Well, did you want to watch it?"

Isabelle, looked to her for a time, stunned.

"Are you serious?" She looked at Brooke like it was the craziest idea ever conceived of, and yet in Isabelle's eyes she saw a glimmer of hope.

"Why not?" She shrugged and gestured into the living room. "Emmett's got that big fancy tv in there, I'm sure we could download the app onto it. Easy-peasy."

"Oh my God!" Isabelle's hands shot out and grabbed Brooke's and she started excitedly jumping in place. "Yes, please! That would be amazing!"

"Okay, calm down." She said so Isabelle would stop roughly wagging her hands. "Why don't you go let Max out while I get everything ready." She probably could have asked Isabelle to do anything and she would have agreed in that moment. It was adorable, but Brooke just wanted her not to focus on the fact that they still haven't heard from Emmett. "Use his leash this time," she called to Isabelle as she quickly scooped up Max in her arms. "So, we don't have to chase after him again, please."

"No problem." Isabelle looked back to her. "Can we have popcorn?"

"If you show me where it is, we can."

Brooke downloaded the app, and paid the subscription fee for a full month using her credit card. Emmett could pay her back. That wasn't the issue that was nagging the back of her mind. *He's fine,* she told himself when she went back to the kitchen to make the popcorn.

They watched two episodes of Crimson Tides while snuggled close to each other on the sofa. It wasn't a bad show, luckily there wasn't anything that was inappropriate for Isabelle. With vampire shows, you never knew what you were going to get. It was rated mature, but thankfully that was for the gratuitous use of blood effects, and numerous uses of the F-word, which Brooke figured was fine for someone Isabelle's age. The show centered around the children of the ruling class of the vampire hierarchy, and their many relationship issues.

In the first episode, Malcolm, the son of the vampire ruler, ends his centuries long relationship with his betrothed, Delilah, by attempting to kill her. That got Brooke's attention. Delilah thwarts the attempt by absolutely slaughtering her would-be killers, only to succumb to her wounds. That's when they were introduced to Christian, the human who finds Delilah and tends to her wounds. Honestly, it was basically a vampire soap opera, but it was compelling stuff.

She could see why the kids liked it.

By the second episode, the popcorn and sodas were a distant memory, and Max was curled up into a ball at the other end of the sofa while Isabelle snuggled close to Brooke.

At one point, she even reached over to move Brooke's arm around her shoulders so she could move in even closer.

"Is this okay?" she asked weakly.

"Yep. It's fine," Brooke answered quickly and tried not to think about how natural it felt to have a little person in her arms. She couldn't help herself. She rubbed Isabelle's shoulders reassuringly and pulled her in even closer.

This is fine, she told herself. *Enjoy it while you can, but when the time comes, you have to let her go,* she cautioned herself. It was a gift to have a child respond like this to her, she knew that. She liked Isabelle a lot, but she wasn't hers. Brooke had to remember that.

At the end of the second episode, Brooke rustled Isabelle's sleepy form at her side.

"Okay, kiddo, bedtime."

"Is Emmett home yet?" The clock on the wall said it was nearly ten o'clock. Outside, the summer sunset was finishing up, threatening the darkness to come.

"Not yet, sweetie. He must be working late," Brooke said, making an effort to make it seem like the obvious reason.

"He won't get to see my hair," Isabelle whined sleepily.

"The braids will keep until the morning. Don't worry," she said shooing her off the sofa. "Get going."

Now, as the clock rolled past ten o'clock Brooke was starting to become increasingly more concerned. She wasn't listening to Judge Judy tear into the poor fools in her court, nor was she overly distracted by her farming game, but she heard the clock on the wall. She heard each tick like a muted hammer-strike from the other side of the room.

Screw it, I'm texting him. This is getting ridiculous.

She didn't text him before because she didn't want to interrupt his work, and honestly, everything was fine. It's not like she had plans or anything.

He doesn't know that. I could have gone out tonight with some friends, if I wanted.

She didn't know how true that was, but it felt true. Honestly, she was thrilled to have a chance to spend some time with Isabelle, but she was starting to feel like Emmett was taking advantage of her kindness.

Where are you? I expected you back hours ago.

There was no point beating around the bush with it. She was annoyed and she felt she was justified to convey that in her text with a few sharp words. Brooke was a little disappointed how much she sounded like her mother when she read it again, but she didn't let it phase her. After ten more minutes with no response, Brooke returned to her phone.

Hello?

Ten more minutes went by and Brooke decided it was time to actually call. She didn't exactly trust what she would say once Emmett picked up the phone, but she felt confident he had it coming.

It went straight to the electronic voicemail.

That's not good, she thought to herself and lowered the phone to her lap. She quickly ran through the options ahead of her and tried to determine what the next course of action should be. If she had Calvin's number, she could just call him and get him to look into it. She could probably could get a hold of him through the Russell detachment, but that seemed like an overreaction to her.

Jesus, Brooke! How long are you going to wait?

What if Emmett had struck a deer, ran off the road, and is now on some lonely road in the middle of nowhere bleeding out.

Brooke decided she would make a cup of coffee.

Afterwards, she would think about it some more, and after that cup was done, *then* she would figure out what she would do next. Brooke rose off the overly-comfy recliner and moved into the kitchen. Emmett had one of those pod-type coffeemakers, but he only had one type of pod. *Breakfast roast*. She distracted herself for awhile trying to figure out how it worked but finally managed to get it brewing. She placed a mug in the pour spot and watched the stream of dark liquid begin to fill the cup.

Then it kept going.

"What?! No!" Brooke hissed quietly, so as not to wake of Isabelle in her bedroom. "Stop," she quietly commanded the appliance fruitlessly before she hastily removed her cup, splashing coffee on the counter, and she quickly set it aside in search of a new cup. The entire time the stupid coffee maker kept pouring coffee out onto the counter until Brooke finally got another cup under it. Out of frustration, she angrily pulled the cord out of the wall, when it became clear this cup was going to fill up as well.

That stopped it.

"Goddamn it," she cursed as the coffee on the counter started to spill off the edge and onto the floor. Brooke searched for a towel to soak up the mess, and that's when she noticed the illumination of headlights coming down the lane.

She suddenly forgot all about the coffee draining off the counter as she stared at the spot where the vehicle coming down the lane would pass by the newly-painted Quonset, and silently prayed.

Emmett's truck slowly pulled into the yard and approached the house. She finally let herself breathe when she saw it was him behind the wheel as he pulled in beside her little car. He noticed her as he opened the door, he gave her a wave that looked more like a weird sort of salute, and then he promptly fell out of the truck.

"What the-?" She started to say and abandoned the rest as she rushed towards the door.

The night air still had plenty of warmth to it as Brooke ran to Emmett's side. He was in the middle of picking himself off the ground when she got to him. She reached down and hooked her hands under one of his thick arms and lifted with her feet to help him up. He noted several strained hissing sounds that came from Emmett's form as he rose to his feet. Once standing, he teetered precariously on his feet and reached out to steady himself against the truck.

I'm fine, he signed slowly with his free hand, and looked at her.

Brooke couldn't help the gasp that escaped her lips.

Emmett's face bore numerous little bruises and scrapes, but what really caught her eye was the swelling of the left eye and the nasty-looking cut on Emmett's lower lip. When he looked at her with those blue eyes of his, she was quick to see the left one was badly bloodshot, but she noticed the glassy way they regarded her as well.

What the hell happened? She wondered and thought back to the three men who had jumped him before over some misunderstanding that could have been avoided if Emmett didn't have his handicap.

"Oh, Emmett," she soothed and stepped towards him and placed her hands lovingly on his abdomen. He winced away from the touch, and hissed.

That's when Brooke smelled the booze on his breath.

"Are you drunk?" she asked him, immediately switching gears. The soothing, almost motherly tone had instantly evaporated from her voice, and she leveled him with a hard gaze.

She clenched her jaw when she saw the childish grin that the bloomed across his battered lips. Like she caught him stealing candy or something.

A little, he lazily signed with that same stupid grin on his face. *I was-.* He finished with a sign she didn't recognize.

"You were *what*?!" she snapped back, in a way that didn't invite an answer. None-the-less, Brooke tilted her head to the side like she was waiting for one.

Emmett caught the shift in her mood immediately, and he went to reach for his notepad, Brooke knew he liked to keep in the breast pocket of his shirt, but tonight it wasn't there. He clumsily patted down the rest of his pockets, to no avail.

"Just type it on your phone," she said with increasing annoyance. She felt it wasn't something she should have to tell him to do.

Emmett was quick to pull out his phone, but he quickly held it up to her so she could see it was dead. *Well, that explains the missed texts, at least.* It was a small comfort given her rapidly declining mood. He looked at her with a remorseful face, and she signed angrily at him.

Use sign language. I'm learning more. It wasn't the best English, but it was usable. Emmett regarded her with an expression of surprise, and then thought for a moment.

I had a good day. R-e-n-e D-u-p-u-i-s gave me twenty-five cows for, Emmett motioned around the yard and Brooke just had to assume some business deal went down in his favor. She didn't know who Rene Dupuis was, though. That must have been who Emmett was working for today. *Then I went out with C-a-l-v-i-n to,* he finished with a sign Brooke didn't understand, but she could guess what it was by the joyous way his expression changed for that one sign. *Party.* She waited for him to continue on to the part that explained the mark on his face. She waited for him to tell her about the fight he obviously got into, but it never came.

"I see," she said sweetly and stepped closely to him. "And at no point during this *work* you were doing, or when you were drinking with your buddies, did you think to get a hold of me and let us know you were okay?" She looked at him the exact way her mother had when Brooke was a teenager, but unlike her mother, she wasn't playing around.

Brooke gave him a small punch in the ribs.

On any other occasion, it would almost be considered a playful punch. Given how Emmett winced away from her touch before, though, she doubted he would find it very playful.

Emmett hissed loudly and dropped down to one knee, while clutching his side. Brooke didn't have much sympathy for him. She stepped forward and shoved him over into the gravel. It was surprisingly easy.

"I was *worried* about you, you *asshole*!" She didn't mean to say it. She meant to say *Isabelle* was worried about him, but the mistake just slipped out. Emmett rolled painfully on the ground for a moment before he looked at her again. "I've been dodging Isabelle's questions about you all night." Brooke stood over him and threw her hands up. "I'm quietly *shitting* myself over here, because I didn't know what to tell her. I didn't know what was going on."

Is she okay? Emmett signed from the ground.

"Of course, she is okay. I'm an *amazing* babysitter," she quietly barked at him. "We did each other's nails, I braided her hair, *then* made dinner, and we ended the night by watching some bullshit-teenage drama about vampires, that is actually pretty good! You need to watch the first two episodes to get caught up," Brooke said, thinking back to the look on Isabelle's face when she told her they could watch it. "Because she really likes it, but doesn't have anybody to watch it with!" She shook her head at him. "You're such a goddamn *Malcolm*!" she said in her fury. *Okay, now you're just talking nonsense,* she told herself as she looked down at the confused expression on Emmett's face. "When are you going to tell me about the fight you obviously got into?" she asked quickly, to move on from the silly comment.

I'm sorry, he signed with a cautious face before he hissed some more and picked himself up off the ground. *You're right.*

"I know I'm right," she replied quickly. "I don't need *you* to say it."

I-something-*called.*

"Couldn't you have called, text, or whatever?" she asked him, to confirm her suspicions. Emmett quickly nodded. "Damn right, you should have! *And,* you should have made sure your damn phone was charged." Again, he nodded, but this time it was a lot more reluctantly. Like, he was accepting something he didn't like.

You're right, he signed quickly but then he continued. *Why are you*-something? She could tell by Emmett's expression that he was asking a question. Brooke finally learned what a *non-manual signal* was.

"Why am I so *mad*?" she asked him in a stern tone that dared him to answer.

Emmett looked like he prepared himself for the worst before he slowly nodded. *He's honest, I'll give him that,* she thought as she looked at him like she was shooting lasers at him.

"*Why am I so mad?*" she shot the question back to him like she was disappointed that she even had to explain it to him. "Well, maybe I just thought we were better friends than *this*."

We are friends, Emmett quickly signed sloppily.

"Sure," she said and nodded sarcastically. "The drop-what-you're-doing-and-take-care-of-my-kid kind of friends, but apparently, I'm not good enough to hang out with. Or am I wrong in assuming there was no reason you and Calvin could've come back here for your *party*?" She angrily signed the word back to him the same way he did it. That one caught him off guard. "You don't think I can hang out, talk shit, and drink beers?" she challenged him. "No, I'm not that kind of friend, I'm just the *babysitter*." She said the word with definite venom that Emmett recoiled away from.

I'm sorry, he signed again.

"You know, I'm about filled up with enough apologies for one night, Emmett. I think I should just go," she said turning towards the house.

Emmett staggered after her as she entered the house, and when he did, she turned back to him and sharply brought her finger to her lips, commanding him to be quiet. Then she pointed to Isabelle's room. Brooke moved past the rapidly cooling puddles of coffee on the counter and floor on her way into the living room to collect her handbag, and when she returned to the kitchen, Emmett had a new notepad and pen in his hands. He quickly wrote something down and ripped the page out as soon as she entered the room.

You're right, about everything. I'm sorry. Please, let me explain.

She read the note and looked up at him, unimpressed.

"You don't have to explain anything to me, Emmett," she said with sweet sarcasm. "We're not like *real* friends or anything, I'm just the *babysitter*." Back to the notepad he went and Brooke waited patiently for him to finish.

I don't want you to leave mad.

"Oh, well, I guess we're both going to be a bit disappointed tonight, aren't we?" she said and moved towards the door. "You're just like your brother," she quietly hissed with disdain.

A massive arm shot out, and blocked her path to the door. The suddenness of it shocked Brooke. She was startled by it, and jumped back a bit. She looked up at Emmett with fury only to see him staring right back at her. He gestured for her to wait, and went back to his notepad.

What's that supposed to mean? The word *supposed* was underlined so strongly it left a deep indentation in the page.

"I know you idolized Tommy, Emmett, but he only knew one way to fix his problems, and that was to smash it with his fists. I thought you were better than that, but here you are, doing that exact same shit he used to. Going out, getting shit-faced, and getting into fights. Jesus!" Brooke angrily shook her head. "Have you even considered what would happen to Isabelle if you got arrested? Hmm? Did you?" She could tell by the hurt look on his face, he hadn't.

That's not fair.

Brooke just looked up from the page and chuckled sourly.

"Life's not fair, Emmett." She stepped passed him on her way to the door. "Tomorrow," she said turning back to him at the door. "Isabelle is going to show you her new braids, and no matter what they look like, you better act like they're the best braids you've ever seen." Emmett looked at her with a sad face, and quickly nodded.

I'm sorry, he signed again.

"Get yourself cleaned up. You look like shit. Isabelle is going to lose her shit when she sees you." Emmett sighed deeply and nodded again. He knew. Brooke took a deep breath, and some of the anger inside of herself let go. "I'll talk to you later," she said softly, because she *did* want to talk to him later, but that part was up to Emmett.

CHAPTER 13

Zeke

Zeke pulled into the parking lot of CRL Construction and quickly maneuvered his thirteen-year-old Ford Escape down the lane that ran beside the building to the back lot. The vehicle had well over two hundred thousand kilometers on the odometer and made a screeching noise if he stepped on the gas too hard. The interior was clean at least. Zeke tried not to pay any attention to the cigarette burns in the seats from the previous owner. Kevin insisted on discretion when he got the vehicle for him.

"This is what a parolee would drive," Kevin said as a way of an explanation when he first showed him the shit-box of a vehicle. "Trust me."

Zeke did trust him, so he reluctantly drove the puke-green SUV without any further complaints. Kevin was right, of course. Zeke was paying him to be right about such things, that was his job. He would be on probation for the next year and a half, which meant his life would be subject to heavy scrutiny from law enforcement at any moment. He had to not only be employed during that entire period, but he had to register his employer with the government. His parole officer had to know where Zeke was living, and he had to actually stay there because he was subject to random home inspections. Again, it was Kevin who found him the little rundown townhouse in West Scarborough, right on Pharmacy Ave. Every night, Zeke went to sleep to the sounds of sirens.

It's fucking bullshit I have to go in on my day-off, Zeke mused to himself as he slowly crept alongside the building. He was now an active employee of the same roofing company that employed his crew, except of course, he wasn't getting paid nearly as well. Thankfully the government didn't do their random checks at places of employment, or else he and his crew might actually have to replace someone's shingles.

He rounded the corner of the building and immediately saw Kevin, and his new assistant, standing by the man-door having a smoke. They both gave him a quick wave as he pulled up close to the perimeter fence and parked his ugly little SUV.

"Bonne journee, mes amis!" Zeke said with obvious cheer when he approached them, and he wore the biggest smile he could put on his face. He couldn't help it.

He'd been waiting for this day for a long time.

Honestly, a month and a half wasn't a long time, not really, it just felt like it was. He knew why, of course. Important things, like *truly* important things always weighed the heaviest on the mind. For him, it was the things that were out of his control that were always the most arduous to wait for.

The expansion of his operation, aided by the strict guidance of The Organization, was going like clockwork. Zeke and Richard found a nice spot in an industrial zone that was in decline on the other side of the city that was perfect for a new lab. Remy was training Richard in the cook process so he could take over this operation when the time came for Remy to setup and run the new lab. This operation would be Richard's responsibility once both labs were up and running. There were tonnes of little details that needed to be covered yet, and that took up the bulk of Zeke's time.

So, he left his side project to Kevin and Levi.

Admittedly, when he first learned Ma Belle had gone missing, he had been upset. He might have said a few things he regretted, but he couldn't help it. He assumed Kevin meant Belle had run away. The thought of her being out there wandering the endless cold streets, and sleeping in the infinite dark and forgotten corners of Toronto, was unbearable. She belonged with him. They were kindred spirits. This world was hard to their kind, the children of rape, and she needed him to shelter her from the worst of it. Her junkie mother told him as much. Becky Lamoine was just another junkie-whore he strung along with free packets of meth in exchange for whatever the hell he wanted from them. After that moment, when he learned the tragic truth of her child, he knew what he had to do.

The restraining order came after a botched attempt to relieve Isabelle from her mother's care at her school. It wasn't a good look for him in front of his crew, but he couldn't help that. He couldn't leave that special little angel in the care of that junkie whore, she didn't care about Belle, not really. Only Zeke could keep her safe, only he could give her the type of life she deserved. Becky's drug-addled mind just didn't realize that.

Shortly after that, Zeke got pinched by the Metro Police, during a shipment that he wasn't even supposed to be delivering. Fate got in the way of his plans back then. Then years later, fate also removed an obstacle from him when Isabelle's whore mother kicked the bucket, but he still cried a bit. Without him to keep her safe, Belle would be left to suffer the many cruel blows the world had to offer a child of violence. Kevin kept an eye on her during his incarceration, when he could. Until one day, he couldn't anymore, because Belle wasn't where she was supposed to be.

A problem Zeke would soon rectify.

"Zeke," Kevin said as a way of a greeting and nodded his head towards him. The big guy, Levi, nodded once as he approached them. He took out a cigarette for himself and quickly lit it.

"Is he in dere?" he asked and took a big drag off his cigarette. Kevin nodded.

For the last month, Kevin had been following the man of the foster house Belle was last staying at, Brian Burke. He liked to say he was *surveilling* the man. For the first couple weeks, Kevin learned his routine. These nine-to-five types always had a predictable routine. They had to. The whole basis of their existence was that they were at a particular place at a particular time, for a particular reason. *Home, work, home, repeat.* After that, and when Levi returned to the fold, he handed the job off to him.

Then Kevin followed Levi. To keep an eye on him.

Levi must have passed the test, because he was still breathing.

"Yep," Kevin said with little emotion. "He's all prepped for you."

Zeke smiled because he knew it meant that humble, mild-mannered Brian Burke was blindfolded, stripped of every ounce of clothing the man had on, and was tied firmly to a solid steel chair. Zeke insisted upon this. He empathized with Kevin and Levi, because nobody wants to strip another man down and have their cock swinging in their face as they tied his ankles to the chair, but it was important for the psychological element. Earlier on in his life, Zeke learned that when you strip a person down, you remove a lot more than just their clothes. You take away their perceived identity, and all the little psychological protections that went with it. Suddenly their carefully manicured persona was ripped away and your victim was left with their core being blindly exposed for the world to see. Like a babe in the woods, that's when the fear starts to creep in.

"Ow'd it go?" Zeke inquired breathing out a thick cloud of smoke.

"No problems. We nabbed him at the grocery store. *Clean.*" He dragged the last word out, and smiled proudly when he said it. *Clean,* meant everything went as planned, no witnesses, and the subject didn't see their faces.

"You see?" Zeke playfully slapped Levi across his wide chest, and pointed towards Kevin. "Dat is ow a professional does it." He nodded and said nothing.

"Yeah, there's something else. Like I said, we nabbed him at the grocery store, which he seems to do pretty consistently every second Saturday. He does this little shopping trip alone. *Always.* When he's there, he always stops at the post office, where he owns a PO box, and always picks up this little packet. It's inside on the sofa. It's from an anonymous PO box on the other side of the country," Kevin said with an air of dread, like he was listing off the red flags in the man's behavior that he noticed.

"Did you open it?" Zeke asked with an excited grin.

"It's a felony to open other people's mail," Levi said, cutting in suddenly. Both Zeke and Kevin gave the man an incredulous look. Levi looked nervously at the two of them. "That was a joke."

Only Zeke chuckled a bit.

"Shit! You ad me going dere," Zeke said and lightly slapped the man on his expansive chest before he turned back to Kevin. "So, wat was in it?"

"A thumb drive," Kevin answered and raised his eyebrow. "Before you ask, no, I didn't look at see what's on it. I'm not putting *that* into anything I own, and I would recommend you do the same."

"Wat are we tinking ere? Kiddie porn?" Zeke asked casually and saw Levi's face scrunch up in disdain.

"Almost definitely." Kevin stamped out his smoke with his boot. "Like I said, I'm not checking it to find out. Do with it what you will," he said waving the matter away. "I just thought you should know."

"Do you ave is phone?"

"Right here," Levi said, retrieved it from his jacket pocket and passed it to him. "We can't open it with the facial recognition with the blindfold on."

"Naturally." He expected as much. "Not to worry, I will take care of dat."

"You're going in there?!" Levi looked at him with a questioning expression Zeke didn't like. "*You're* going to talk to him?"

"Dere a problem I'm not aware of?" Zeke looked up at him with cold eyes.

"No," Levi replied quickly and held up his hands. "No, problem here. I was just thinking with your accent..." He let his words trail off but Zeke just gave him a look that challenged him to finish his sentence.

"Yes? Wat about my accent?"

"It's just that its...*pretty distinct.*" By his expression, the words seemed to cause Levi physical pain to say.

"He's not wrong," Kevin added quietly.

"You tink I'm da only Frenchman in the GTA? Eh?" Levi immediately shrank away from the question. Kevin, on the other hand.

"You're the only Frenchman who currently has a restraining order put out on him by Rebecca Lamoine."

"She's dead," Zeke snapped back and then sucked in a lungful of his cigarette while giving Kevin wild eyes. *The nerve of this guy bringing that shit up to me!*

"Yeah, but that order included her daughter, so I'm pretty sure its still active, and even if its not, there's still a record of it," Kevin said with a casual ease, but his words still stung because he was right. There would be a record of it somewhere. "I know you don't want to hear this, but you're the *last* person who should be talking to him. *Assuming* the plan is still to release him when we're done." It was Kevin's turn to level him with a challenging expression.

"You worry too much," Zeke said lightly with an air of casualness, but Kevin knew better.

"Suit yourself," he said and shrugged his shoulder, like he could care either way, and waved Zeke towards the door. "We'll be waiting out here if you need anything."

Zeke confidently walked into the rear of the building alongside the black panel van they used for deliveries. *Some pick-ups as well,* Zeke joked to himself as he approached the rear of the van. The heels of his Italian shoes clicked loudly on the floor and echoed ominously with each step.

There, zip-tied to an old steel chair, blindfolded with a thick piece of cloth, and naked as the day he was born, was Brian Burke. He was a small man. By the look of him, he wasn't the over-achieving type. He had medium-length, light brown hair that did little to hide the bald patch in the back. Zeke would have put him a bit closer to fifty-years old, a little past his prime, when the body starts to droop slightly.

"Who's there!" Brian called out nervously and jerked his head from side to side.

"Ello, Mister Burke. It is a pleasure to meet you," Zeke let his accent add flare to the otherwise dull English words.

He walked over to the other steel chair that was in the room, and slowly dragged it across the floor. The subsequent loud metal screeching noise of the bare metal legs digging into the smooth concrete floor reverberated loudly around them. He took great pleasure in the way Brian squirmed against his restraints when the loud sounds started buzzing around the bay. By the way those same restraints were digging into the meat of his forearms, Zeke guessed they hurt. Kevin used thick, industrial zip-ties. There was no way this flabby stick of a man was going to pull free of them. He'd have better luck chewing off his own arm. When the chair was in place, Zeke walked loudly back to the large coffee table where the few items he needed were meticulously placed. He quickly picked up the knife and the thumb drive before he walked back and sat himself down into the chair.

"Do you know why you're ere, Brian?" Zeke asked softly.

Behind the blindfold, Brian Burke started to gently weep.

"You got the wrong guy," he whined between sobs. "Whatever this is, I *swear* to you, you have the wrong guy. Please, you have to believe me."

"Shhhh, Brian."

Zeke reached up and gently caressed the man's chin, which caused Brian to stiffly recoil away from his touch like it was burning him, and breath in wild gasps.

"It's okay," he said in a soothing voice. "Calm down."

"Please."

"I know. Get it out."

"I'm not the person you think I am," Brian said weakly and wept some more.

"Shhh," he said again like he was trying to comfort him. "It's okay. You're among friends ere. Dis is a safe place for you, *mon ami*. Ere, you can be wo you truly are. No judgement from me. Besides dat, I need you to be onest wit me, because as dey say, da trut shall set you free."

Brian didn't say anything else, so Zeke took that as his cue to proceed. He took the Ka-bar knife and pressed the flat of the blade against Brian's forearm.

"You feel dat, *mon ami?*" he asked seductively and just held the flat part of it against his skin.

Brian tensed up like electricity was running through him.

"Yes," he yelped finally. "I feel it."

"What do you think it is?"

Before he could answer Zeke started to slowly move the blade up his arm to his elbow before he lovingly moved it up his saggy little bicep. At the shoulder, Zeke moved the knife so it was no longer the flat of the blade that traveled across his skin, it was the tip. Zeke spied the little, angry red line the tip scratched across the man's chest.

"Come on, Brian," he teased softly. "You know what that is. Just say it."

He turned the blade in his hand and gently ran the sharpened edge of the blade over his meager path of chest hair. Brian just whimpered horribly as Zeke delicately shaved away a patch of it.

"It's a knife!" the words finally burst forth from his mouth.

"*Tres bien!*" Zeke said and removed the knife from his skin. Brian visibly exhaled like he was coming up from the depths of the ocean. "Correct. It's important you know dat if I feel you are not being trutful wit me, I'm going to cut you. Is it going to urt? Yes, of course, but you'll survive. I can make you urt all night, Brian. If you make me. It is also important that you remember dere is a way out for you ere, Brian. Just tell me wat I want to know, everyting, and afterwards, you can go back to your little pretend family. Dat's wat you want, isn't it Brian? To leave dis place, and *never* look back?"

"Yes!" Brian shot back obediently.

"Den just answer all my questions." Zeke brought out the thumb-drive that Kevin found in his envelop. "Open your right hand, please." When he did as he was told, Zeke slowly placed the drive in the man's hand, and let him feel it.

Brian started to weep with a renewed vigor.

"Please," he whimpered between sobs.

"Dis isn't about dat, Brian. I want you to know dat," Zeke said firmly and waited for his words to sink in, and Brian to regain some of his composure.

"What?"

"Dis is not about whatever is on dat ting in your and. Like I said Brian, you're among *friends*. I just need some questions answered, and you can take dat drive and go on your merry way."

Zeke clapped his free hand down onto Brian's exposed thigh and he jumped against his restraints again.

"Believe me, I take no pleasure in dis. Just answer my questions, Brian." Zeke leaned in close and whispered into Brian's side. "Spread your legs a bit, would you?" Brian snivelled horribly as he struggled to move his shaking legs apart, but he did it. "Now," Zeke cautioned smoothly. "I'm going to need you to old *real* still."

"Oh, Jesus!" Brian cried out when he felt the cold steel of the knife blade on his withered cock, and bucked in the chair before some inner voice must have reminded him there was no place for him to go.

The thumb-drive in his hand flew to the side as it shot open in his white-hot panic. After that, he settled and breathed out quick, ragged breaths in an attempt to control the inner turmoil as Zeke carefully scooped up his cock onto the flat edge of the knife, and balanced it there.

"Are you ready for my questions, Brian?" Zeke asked calmly, keeping the knife still. When no reply came, he jiggled the knife and the man's penis danced a bit on the blade. Brian's answer leapt from his throat.

"Yes!"

"What's the unlock code for your phone?"

"Seven-five-one zero," Brian said with little hesitation.

Zeke quickly pulled out the phone and punched in the code. He was pleased to see the phone's home screen pop up. Zeke smiled.

"Where's Isabelle Lamoine?"

"Isabelle?" Brian tilted his head, like he was genuinely surprised to hear his angel's name. Again, Zeke jiggled the knife, and Brian tensed up like a mild shock coursed through his body.

"Ah!" Zeke sucked on his teeth, and made a disappointed groan. "I was oping you were smart enough to realize you're not in a position to be asking *me* questions, *Brian*." He said his name with obvious disdain. "Do I need to cut you? Because, if I'm being onest, dere's not a lot ere you can afford to lose, Brian." Zeke didn't bother to jiggle the knife again. Brian's body was already rigid with abject terror.

"No! *Please*! I'm sorry! Jesus! Sh-she's in M-Manitoba. T-that's where they t-took her. She's got an uncle there. That's all I know."

"Oh, well, let's ope not Brian, because dat's not enough. Not yet," he cautioned the man playfully as he pulled up Brian's picture folder from his phone.

"What's da uncle's name?"

"They n-never told us."

"Who is da government worker in charge of er case?"

"Jones. Nicole Jones," he gave up the woman's name so fast, it was frankly a bit pathetic. Zeke idly shook his head as he slowly thumbed through the various pictures of the man's mundane life.

Until Zeke came upon a batch of photos that weren't so mundane.

The first picture that caught his eye was of a young black woman with a lean, athletic build posing with her back-side to the camera and looking back with a smile that was bordering on seductive. She was wearing plain-looking grey sweats and a form-fitting white tee.

What do we have here, Zeke thought to himself wickedly as he kept scrolling.

There were maybe four more pictures of the black girl posing in a kitchen in her sweats and shirt, they all were disturbingly inappropriate for a man to have on his phone. After that, there were another six that featured the same young woman in a scant-looking robe in a bathroom, it was obviously just after a shower. There were another ten that showed the same girl posing merrily on her bed in satiny pajamas.

Why Mister Burke, Zeke thought with some amusement. *Are you dipping your fingers into the dark chocolate?*

Zeke then scrolled to the next picture and his amusement ended immediately.

There she is!

Zeke was lost in the excitement of seeing his little angel again, he had momentary tunnel-vision. He could only focus on her sweet ivory-skinned face, free of any blemish that would taint her absolute perfection. He marveled over how much she had grown in the short time it had been since they were last together.

My angel!

He was stunned, so he didn't notice the true context of the picture until the shock of seeing Belle wore off.

When it finally did, Zeke felt his grip on the knife holding the man's dick tighten dangerously.

The picture was obviously taken without Belle's knowledge. She was in the bathroom with the door partially open, and it looked like Brian was peeking his phone around a corner in order to snap the photo. She stood in front of the mirror with only an over-sized towel wrapped around her. Zeke spied her bare legs sticking out from the bottom. Belle appeared to be combing her silken hair in the mirror.

Zeke squeezed the phone in his hand so tightly, the screen cracked.

"Okay, Brian," Zeke said after he regained his composure. He felt the white-hot rage inside him, but Brian didn't need to know that. Not yet, anyway. "Last question. You ready?"

"Y-yes."

Zeke dropped the phone from his hand and let it clatter to the ground. His newly-freed hand shot out, wrapped around Brian's narrow neck, and he squeezed until his fingers were digging into his flesh. He let Brian gasp out a few ragged breaths before he leaned in close to the man again and growled the next question with restrained rage.

"Did you *touch* Isabelle!? Did you lay your filty-fucking-hands on *my girl*?" He didn't wait for an answer, he squeezed his hand until Brian gagged.

"N-no," he wheezed hoarsely. "I s-swear to you, I-I didn't." Brian spoke the words like they may be his last as his face took on an unhealthy shade of red.

Zeke released his grip on the man's throat, and let his weak-looking cock slide from the knife blade back onto the seat's decades-old cushion.

Brian gasped for breath and raggedly coughed out for a moment before he regained his composure. Zeke waited until the man was settled before he clapped his free hand onto the back of the man's neck, then he leaned in and kissed Brian once on the cheek.

"I believe you," he said to the blindfolded man and softly patted him on the back of his neck. Like they were comrades who survived an impossible ordeal. In a way, they had. "I believe you, Brian." He said again to reassure the man the worst of it was behind them.

Zeke rose up and put the knife back onto the coffee table before he returned to stand over Brian's shaking form.

"You did it, Brian. We're done. I'm going to go outside and talk to my associates out dere. It'll maybe be another fifteen minutes before dey come back in ere, and cut you out of dat chair. Then you can get dressed. You ave to keep the blindfold on, of course."

"I u-understand completely." Brian said almost apologetically.

Zeke could tell he could see the light at the end of the tunnel. In his mind, he was probably imagining himself walking through the front door of his cozy little home.

"Thank you. Jesus, God! Thank you so much. I swear, I swear on my mother's life I won't tell anyone about this."

"Dat's nice of you," Zeke chuckled coldly. "In return, I promise not to tell anyone about whatever is on that thumb-drive of yours. Ang in dere, buddy. It won't be long now." Zeke slapped him gently on the cheek.

Brian winced away from it.

Zeke walked loudly to the back door and exited into the afternoon sun. Kevin and Levi both eyed him expectantly. He waited until the door closed behind him before he spoke. Zeke used that time to light a cigarette.

"Kill him," he said to Levi as he breathed out his first drag of the smoke.

Levi looked to Kevin for direction.

"Snap his neck," Kevin said quickly. "We'll dump his body at the bottom of a concrete staircase somewhere." Levi nodded once before he turned his bulk towards the door. "You know how to do that, right?" he called after him before Levi made it to the door. Zeke watched as he pivoted his large face around and gave Kevin a dumb expression.

"I figure you just twist his head around until it's facing backward."

Zeke and Kevin exchanged amused expressions.

"Yep," Zeke said with a smile. "Dat should do it."

CHAPTER 14

Belle

Emmett pulled the truck in front of the small school and parked. Belle looked out the window and saw dozens of strange children slowly filing into the modest-looking school. There was a bus service but Emmett insisted on driving her on the first day of school. He'd been acting weird all week.

He's probably just happy to be rid of you, a familiar voice spoke up from her depths.

Beside her, on the bench seat of the pick-up, was her school bag which Emmett meticulously assembled the night before. She'd shared Emmett's giddy sort of excitement this morning, but now, seeing all those other kids file into the school, she felt something flutter around dangerously within the pits of her stomach.

"Do I have to go?" she asked quietly still watching the children. When she did look at him, she gave Emmett a distressed look. "Maybe we could tell them I wasn't feeling well," she began, and Emmett smiled warmly, like he was entertaining the idea. "I could stay with you today. There's so much work to do back at the farm," she said looking at him seriously. "Way too much work for you to do alone." Emmett raised his eyebrow at her, but she persisted. "You *need* my help to fix the fence. Who's going to hold the thing so you can nail the wire to the post-thing? Besides, somebody has to watch Max to make sure he doesn't get in the way. You wouldn't want to drive over him or something, would you?" Emmett lowered his gaze at her and signed.

He'll be fine. He tilted his head to the side and regarded her closely before he signed again. *What's wrong?* Belle wasn't good at sign language, but Emmett was really good at sticking to the few signs she did know. *What's wrong?* He signed again and Belle looked down at her lap.

"What if they don't like me?" she asked quietly, like it was a certainty she was preparing both of them for. Belle felt her bottom lip quiver and a sting in her eyes. She was sure she was going to cry. That is, until she felt a large, and impossibly warm hand gently rub her back. She looked at him and saw his calming expression regarding her earnestly. He then slid her a cue card from the pocket of his work shirt.

The first day is always hard. Just go in there, be yourself, and try to have fun.

"But I'm not good at making friends," She confessed softly.

Me too, he signed quickly.

"Really?" She looked at him incredulously just to have him reflect her expression back to her.

You can talk, he signed with a small grin before he went to his notepad. Belle waited patiently while he wrote his note. When he was done, he ripped the page off and gave it to her. *I think the trick is not to try and make friends. Just go in there and treat everyone like they are a good friend, and see who is friendly back.*

"Did you have a lot of friends in school, Emmett?" Belle saw his expression sadden slightly.

No, he signed slowly. Emmett held up his finger for her to wait and returned to his notepad. *I couldn't talk and nobody knew sign language. You're not me, though. You are so much more. Don't worry about making friends. I have no doubt they will like you.*

"But what if they don't."

Then, you do as Taylor Swift says, Emmett's note said. When she looked up at him from it, Emmett hopped a bit in his seat as he performed the TikTok dance she showed him that was done to the popular song.

"Shake it off?" Belle asked and giggled a bit at his antics. Emmett nodded and smiled again. She huffed at bit in her seat and looked out towards the school again.

Maybe this won't be like last time, she told herself as she spied a girl about her age walk towards the school. She was wearing a pretty blue dress with a floral pattern on it with a jean jacket over top. The girl looked old enough to be in Belle's class. She looked down to her tan coveralls, which she had really grown fond of over the last month, but now, seemed wholly inadequate for this new situation. She also had on the light-blue, long-sleeved top Brooke had picked out for her. Belle thought she looked cute when she looked at herself in the mirror this morning, but seeing that girl stride confidently towards the school's entrance made her rethink her whole look. At the sides of her vision, Belle could see the two little braids of hair Emmett had painstakingly prepared for her. They still weren't as good as when Brooke did it, but he was getting better at it. The rest of her hair was swept back and collected into a tight ponytail that sat low on her head so her hair could flow down her back.

Just like Delilah.

You already have one friend, Emmett's next note read and Belle looked to him to explain.

Emmett pointed to the large black truck that pulled in front of them. She looked at the truck curiously for a moment until the passenger door opened and a familiar figure carefully climbed out of the passenger seat, and then adjusted the thick-rimmed glasses on his face.

"Lucas goes to this school?!" Belle exclaimed and looked to Emmett who nodded his confirmation. *I can't wait to tell him about Max,* she thought excitedly and waved at him furiously when he looked in her direction. She was thrilled to see he gave her a big smile and waved back quickly. "I'm going to go say hi," Belle said, reached for the door handle, and hopped out of the truck.

Completely oblivious to the sour expression that bloomed across Emmett's face when the driver exited the truck in front of them.

"Hi, Isabelle!" Lucas called to her and awkwardly ran over, his heavy backpack throwing off his balance. "How's Max doing?" he asked eagerly.

"So good!" Belle said with a big smile that soon faltered with her next words. "Emmett wouldn't let me bring him."

"Yeah, my dad won't let me bring any of our dogs either. He says I'll never get out of the truck if we bring them."

Just then Belle saw a man in a checkered shirt and blue jeans move around the front of the dark pickup Lucas exited. His dark hair poked out from a baseball hat that had a logo on it Belle didn't recognize. He had a clean shaven, narrow face with a hawkish-looking nose and serious eyes that narrowed when his gaze landed onto Emmett, who was still sitting in the truck.

"Who do we have here, son? One of your little friends?" the man asked, placed his hand on Lucas's shoulder and grinned down at her.

"Dad, this is my new friend, Isabelle Brooks." Lucas gestured to her.

"Lamoine."

"Huh?" Lucas looked at her confused.

"My last name is Lamoine," Belle softly corrected her friend. *My new friend,* a voice inside her repeated the words, eagerly testing them out. She found she liked the sound of it, just like she knew she would.

"Oh," Lucas replied with a muted shock. "I'm sorry. This is my new friend, Isabelle *Lamoine.*" Lucas gestured to her again, just like he had before she interrupted him.

Belle was quick to notice something about her last name caused the man to slightly frown. "Isabelle," Lucas said and then gestured to the man with the hawkish nose. "This is my dad, Owen. Owen Adler."

"Lamoine, you say?" Mr. Adler asked her with a friendly interest as he rubbed the back of his neck. "So, your mom is...?" He let the question hang strangely between the two of them.

"Rebecca," she said quickly and eyed the man closely. "Do you know her too?"

Mr. Adler sucked on his bottom lip briefly, and looked at her as if he was trying to search for the right words to answer the question.

"Yeah. I knew her." He looked at her for a moment, Belle felt his gaze upon her as he studied her face for a moment before he continued. "Well, it's a pleasure to meet you." He extended his hand towards her.

Belle reached out for it but the sound of a vehicle's door closing startled the man, and he quickly withdrew his hand before he turned back to Emmett's truck.

"Emmett," he said in a cautious greeting as Emmett moved around the front of the truck and positioned himself behind Belle. "I was just meeting your niece here. Anyways," he turned back to her and gave her a nervous grin. "It's a pleasure to finally meet you, Isabelle." He slowly extended his hand towards her again.

He glanced towards Emmett as he did, as if he was asking permission. Belle quickly shook it before he retreated the hand again.

"Lucas here as been talking about you ever since he dropped off little Max."

"*Dad*," Lucas complained quietly and gave his father a quick slap against his arm.

"Lucas," Belle said to draw the boy's attention back before she stepped aside and presented Emmett's large form to him. "This is my uncle, Emmett Brooks." She said and smiled inwardly as Lucas had to crane his neck upwards to look Emmett in the face. When he did, Lucas took a step back. Belle quickly leaned in towards Lucas. "Do what I showed you," she quietly instructed him with a sly grin.

"It's. Nice to. Meet you," Lucas said nervously and awkwardly did the signs Belle had shown him when she first met the boy. She couldn't help but to smile when Lucas did them. He didn't do them with any sort of confidence, but he did them correctly. That's what was important.

Emmett just let out a long sigh and looked down at the small boy.

It's nice to meet you, Emmett signed slowly.

"Son? Is there something you wanted to tell Mr. Brooks?" Mr. Adler asked the way adults sometimes do, and looked down at Lucas's stunned face.

"*Now*?!"

"He's standing right there, there's no better time." Mr. Adler placed his hands on Lucas's shoulders and leaned down at softly spoke into his ear. "Don't be afraid, son. Just tell him. Go on." He said and gave Lucas the smallest of nudges forward.

"Um, Mr. Brooks?" Lucas began and reluctantly looked up Emmett's looming form again to look him in the face. "I have something to tell you, something that's going to make you mad."

Emmett looked over to Belle and raised his eyebrow at her. She returned it with a look and then quickly signed.

Be good, she signed from the side when she was sure Lucas wouldn't notice. Emmett just grinned a bit before he winked at her. Belle didn't know if that was good or bad for Lucas, but she was about to find out.

"In the spring," Lucas began, shifting his gaze between his shoes as he did, like the words he was looking for were printed on the tops of them. "When your dog was shot, and died." Lucas paused, and Belle could hear him sniffling slightly.

She felt for him. It wasn't easy to stand in front of Emmett's mountainous shape and apologize for something.

"It...it...it was," poor Lucas stammered horribly trying to get the words out.

Emmett quickly dropped down onto one knee, so he could look him in the eye, but the sudden motion only startled Lucas and he yelped a bit and jumped back.

"Hey now, Emmett." Mr. Adler stepped forward and raised his one hand slowly.

Emmett looked at him with a calm expression and softly patted the air in front of himself.

Emmett reached out and placed his hand gently on Lucas's shoulder. His wide palm completely enveloped the boy's tiny shoulder and his fingers wrapped around to the back. Emmett softly clicked his tongue to get Lucas's attention, and when he slowly lifted his head to look into Emmett's soft blue eyes. When he did, Emmett removed his hand from his shoulder and slowly pointed to his own eyes in a gestured that gently said, *look at me.*

Lucas swallowed hard, but he did it.

"It...it was me. I shot your dog," Lucas said quickly, and after that the words seemed to leap from his mouth. "It was an accident. I didn't mean to. I was shooting at some cans, but I wasn't supposed to. I didn't know you were in the field Mr. Brooks, *honest.* I didn't know bullets went that far. My dad is always telling me to look *downrange* when I'm shooting, but I didn't really know what that meant. I do now." Emmett wore an empathetic expression as he listened to Lucas's confession, and nodded slowly at each point. "I'm really sorry I didn't tell you sooner. I was scared."

Emmett stopped him by slowly patting the air again, and then gestured for Lucas to wait while he went to his notepad. He scribbled a bit before he tore the note off and handed it to him. Both Belle and Mr. Adler leaned in to get a look at the note.

I really appreciate you telling me that. I was really upset when King died.

We all make mistakes.

I forgive you.

You're a brave kid.

Belle hardly had enough time to read the note before Lucas rushed forward and pressed himself into Emmett.

"Thank you, Mr. Brooks." Lucas could only get his arms around the front of Emmett's wide chest. Emmett softly patted Lucas on the back.

"Okay, son." Mr. Adler stepped forward and eased Lucas away from Emmett. "That's good. Give Mr. Brooks some room to breathe."

Lucas allowed himself to be pulled back and Emmett rose to his feet again. This time looking to Mr. Adler, who just returned the gaze for a moment before speaking.

"That was good of you Emmett. I appreciate it, given everything that has...well...you know." Mr. Adler finished with a weird sort of grin and extended his hand to him.

Emmett frowned at the hand that was being offered to him, like he didn't know what to do with it. *Just shake it,* Belle said inside her head. That's what adults were supposed to do when someone wants to shake their hand. She softly nudged Emmett's side to prompt him to accepting the small gesture, but to her surprise, this time Emmett nudged her back.

No, he signed sharply when she looked up at him, never taking his eyes off Mr. Adler.

"No? That's fine," Mr. Adler said lightly and withdrew his hand. "No problem." He quickly turned back to Lucas. "Well, son, you're all set. You have a great day today, okay? Be good." Belle and Emmett looked at the two as Mr. Adler bent down to hug his son, like the two of them had done this same ritual a thousand times.

"I will dad. I love you."

"I love you too."

When the Adlers finished, Belle looked to Emmett and wondered if maybe they should hug too. *Does he want me to hug him?* She asked herself and studied Emmett's face for the answer. A part of her secretly hoped he did. She saw what the Adlers had, and some forgotten piece of herself longed for that too.

Emmett looked at her briefly as well.

Have a good day, he signed. At least, she was pretty sure that's what he said. Belle didn't know the sign for *day* yet. When he was done, Emmett extended his closed fist towards her.

"I will," she said and quickly bumped the fist. Part of her was happy the awkwardness was behind them. "You have a good day too, Emmett."

She walked away with Lucas, leaving Emmett and Mr. Adler on the sidewalk.

It's not enough, the thought popped into her head and nagged her with each step she took away from Emmett.

She wouldn't mind it if they said *I love you* when they parted. She knew it had only been two months, which wasn't a lot of time for such strong feelings to manifest.

What if he doesn't say it back? She wouldn't blame him if he didn't, but she still felt what they had required more than just a casual good-bye. Emmett was more than just another foster parent to her, and she wanted to be more to him than just...

She turned back.

"Emmett!" she called back to him just as he was moving around the front of his truck. He quickly shot his look back to her. Belle stood and slowly did the sign Emmett showed her in the clothing store. It wasn't much, but it neatly simplified the complexity of what she felt inside herself for him.

Forever.

Emmett stopped, and looked at her with a stunned sort of expression that made her wonder if she did the sign correctly. Maybe she had just said something completely different than what she intended. Then he smiled, and she knew by the expression on his face she had done it right. Even better, he slowly repeated the sign back to her.

Forever.

They waved their good-byes , Belle turned back and approached her new school with a sense of optimism she wasn't accustomed to.

CHAPTER 15

Emmett

The call came shortly after lunch. Emmett figured Isabelle should be filing back into the school after the afternoon bell that signaled the end of the lunch recess.

He was continuing his work expanding the animal shelter to house the livestock he was planning on boarding. His father's enclosure housed fifty cows in a heated shelter with a concrete floor that made manure clean-up easy. Emmett's shelter wouldn't be as nice, but it would be just as functional.

His plan was to build his open-air shelter onto the back of the animal shed his father had built back in the day. Emmett drew out a rough plan on a sheet of grid-paper one night while he was catching up on Crimson Tides, much to Isabelle's annoyance. He planned four post-lines extending fifty meters from the shed, creating two wide corrals for the cattle. At his numbers, it would be a tight squeeze, but it would work. Besides, he only had to worry about the late winter months, when the temperature drops and the bitter winds blast them from the east. If he could provide his livestock with a nice, relatively warm place to rest during those months he could save a small fortune on feeding costs.

Emmett was placing one of the giant fifteen-foot-tall posts into the hole he had drilled into the hard dirt when his phone buzzed angrily away in his pocket. He wiped the sweat from his brow before he retrieved his phone.

The call display read: Ecole St. Lazare.

That can't be good, he thought as he opened the app that allowed him to talk on the phone via an electronic voice. The app was meant for deaf people.

"*Hello,*" an unflattering, and obviously robotic voice spoke over the line. Emmett hated using the app.

Mr. Brooks? He read the words scroll across the dialogue box of the app as the person on the other end spoke them. *This is Glenda Tanguay, the principal at Ecole St-Lazare. Listen, Mr. Brooks we've had an incident here at the school and we were hoping you could come in for a meeting with Isabelle and myself.*

Emmett cursed inside his head as he read the message. *That's really not good,* he said to himself as he typed his reply in.

"*What happened? Is Isabelle okay?*" the cold robotic voice droned over the line.

Isabelle is fine. She got into an altercation with another student over the lunch hour. Given the nature of it, I thought it was best to address it immediately. Nip it in the bud, as they say. Could you come in?

"*I'll be right there,*"

Fabulous. We'll talk more when you get here. After that, the line went dead.

Shit!

Emmett solidly punched the post he just planted in the hole by his feet. Brooke's parting words from weeks ago flashed through his mind after he did it. *You're just like your brother.* She wasn't wrong, that was the problem.

Emmett loved his brother. He protected him when no one else would, but even Emmett had to admit his brother had a problem with violence. There were a lot of times Tommy should have just walked away.

He should have walked away from Clive Adler.

As hard as it was to admit, given the hatred he carried around with him for the Adlers, everyone in Tommy's circle would have been better off if he never walked into Maggie's bar that night. Emmett knew if he'd been there, he would have stopped his brother from leaving. He knew how his brother got when he saw red. *Focus on Becky,* he would have told him if he had the chance. *She needs you more.* Like Brooke said, when Tommy was faced with a problem, his first instinct was to smash through it. Growing up, Emmett convinced himself it was noble how his brother bravely stood up to everyone, just like their father had in all his stories about the old days. These days, he was starting to see it was a strange kind of sickness his family had.

He wasn't any better.

He was currently fixing his money problems by fighting. Hell, the building supplies for this shelter were paid for by the money he made fighting in Chaz's little cringe-worthy internet spectacle.

It's just temporary, he thought on reflex but then immediately doubted his own thought because at the core of it he had the same sickness Tommy had.

He liked fighting.

When he fought, it was the only time he didn't feel like some defective person who was silently struggling along, trying to keep up with the other *normal* people, while at the same time, desperately hiding his disability away from others. Isolating himself from them so his defect didn't stick out like a sore thumb.

He didn't feel like that when his hands were raised.

When he was fighting, he felt whole. After his argument with Brooke, he was starting to wonder if that wholeness was part of the sickness his family carried with them. The sickness of violence, when you only felt whole when you were hurting someone else. His father had it, Tommy had it, and he had it too.

Now, he was worried Isabelle had it as well.

Focus!

Emmett had been pacing around the post staring at the phone in his hands as he lost himself in his panicked thoughts. He stopped abruptly and pulled up his contact list. Calvin would be working, or sleeping at this time of day. He didn't want to bother him. That left one other person who could translate for him, and he didn't even know if Brooke was still talking to him. Emmett didn't want this to be the thing that broke the silence between them, but he *really* didn't want to sit in front of the principal, and hand her little notes he ripped out of his little flip-book during the entire duration of this meeting.

Shit!

Emmett opened his message chain with Brooke. The last entries were the numerous texts she sent the night she babysat that went unanswered.

Hey, I know we haven't spoken in a while, but I need your help with something.

Emmett wasn't thrilled he was contacting her just to ask for her help again. He had been meaning to stop in and try to smooth things over a bit with her, but days have a funny way of turning into weeks.

I'm working, Brooke replied quickly. Emmett took that as a good sign. After all, she didn't have to reply at all.

Is there any way you can take an hour off or something? It's about Isabelle. Emmett stared at the three dots until Brook's next message came through.

I'm listening.

She got into a fight at school. He wrote quickly. There was no use in beating around the bush with it.

Oh, wow. I wonder where she gets that from? Brooke wrote back just as quick.

Ouch! Emmett thought to himself as the words cut him deeply. So much so he was reconsidering this idea. He took a breath and returned to his phone.

I deserve that. He sent the message away, and thought carefully on what to write next. *How's your sign language lessons coming?* He hoped that was a cute way to indicate what he needed her for.

Good enough. I'm studying up for when the time comes for you to kiss my ass a bit. I wanted to be prepared for all the nice things you were going to say to me. There was a pause while the three dots flashed along the bottom. *I didn't think I'd have to wait this long, though.*

I'm sorry about that night. He wrote, at a bit of a loss at what else he could say.

You said that already.

Emmett sighed.

You were right. I shouldn't have left you hanging like that. That wasn't fair to you.

Getting warmer. Brooke wrote back, and Emmett waited briefly to see if she was going to write anything else. She didn't.

And you're not JUST a babysitter.

Emmett paused there, not sure how he should continue. He liked Brooke, she was special. He met other women like her, ones he really felt a connection with, but like those other women, he doubted she had a place in her life for him. He left the message as is and sent it off.

Getting warmer.

And you deserve to be treated better than that.

Getting warmer.

Emmett smirked at his screen. *Ok, now's she's fucking with me,* he thought with some amusement. He had a smile on his face as he started typing.

And your super smart, and the prettiest girl at the hardware store, or pharmacy, or clothing store, or wherever the hell else you might be working today. Just tell me what you need me to say, I'm drowning here.

I like where you're coming from here. I respond well to compliments and desperation. Maybe cap it off with a comment or two on how stupid you were.

OMG! So stupid! Emmett wrote hoping that would do the trick.

LOL! Ok. I'm in. When do you need me there? St-Lazare, I assume?

Emmett breathed out a deep breath and smiled. He was actually looking forward to seeing her again.

Yes. Thank you! Did you want me to pick you up?

No. I will meet you there in twenty minutes. I'm leaving my house now.

Emmett frowned at the screen before he sent his next text.

I thought you were working. There was a pause and Emmett smiled to himself at the possibility that he had caught Brooke in a little fib.

I lied. Sue me. See you soon.

Emmett put his phone away and whistled loudly while he looked around his surroundings for Max. Soon enough, he heard the bell-like sound of his tags rattling on his collar as he appeared around the corner of the fence and came scampering to his side. When he reached Emmett's side, Max promptly plopped his furry bottom onto the hard-packed dirt and looked up at Emmett expectantly. As part of his training, Emmett reached into his pocket and pulled out a small treat, he bent down and offered it to Max, who eagerly snapped it up off his palm. Emmett was sure to click his tongue loudly twice when he did, it was his way of saying *good dog.* That was part of his training too.

With little Max in tow, Emmett left his project and walked back to the house to clean up a bit before he headed out to face his latest failure head-on.

Emmett pulled up to the front of the school, close to the spot he dropped Isabelle off in the morning, and immediately saw Brooke leaning against her car in front of him in a sleeveless blue blouse and faded blue jeans that hugged her hips wonderfully. Her dark hair hung in gentle curls and flowed down past her shoulders. *Wow.* Emmett couldn't help but to look at her dumbly for a moment before her cute little wave broke him out of his spell.

He quickly exited the truck.

If the girls from high school could see you now, they would be jealous as shit. You look amazing, he signed quickly, more for himself because he doubted Brooke understood what he said. It wasn't beginner stuff.

"What?!" she asked with some surprise, just like he expected her too. "Why thank you! That is so nice of you to say, Emmett. I thought it was a pretty nice outfit myself, but I didn't think I would make *all* the girls from my *high school jealous* over it."

That, he wasn't expecting, not one bit. Emmett's expression dropped and he felt the blood rush to his cheeks as Brooke threw his words back at him. Her smile told him she picked up on his surprise.

"I told you. I was studying up for when you kissed my ass, and you didn't disappoint," she said with a big smile and then winked at him.

How much have you been studying?! Emmett looked at her incredulously, secretly hoping to move on from what he had signed earlier. It was true, but it wasn't for her, not really. Though, he guessed there was no harm in her actually knowing it.

Brooke just gave him a look, and then answered with sign language.

A lot. I felt bad after our last talk. I came on hard, and I think if I was better at signing then, maybe we could have talked better. So, I've been watching F-r-i-e-n-d-s episodes and translating them into sign language. Which sucked, because I had to look up many words on the internet. Plus, they talk really fast on that show.

It had been almost a month since they last spoke, and Emmett couldn't believe how deftly she was doing some of the signs. There were obviously some she had to think over, her speech had a few pauses where she struggled to remember the correct sign, but her progress was nothing short of incredible.

Emmett regarded her with an expression of great interest before he responded.

You did all this for me?

Brooke smiled and moved her fingers into the two-finger pointing hand, and touched her thumbs together before she pointed at him.

Fuck you. Emmett reacted to the signs meaning like an actual physical blow. Brooke chuckled slightly at his reaction. "I learned that one too. You know, in case this reunion of ours didn't go as well as I hoped. I learned all the good curse words, some of them might even surprise *you*," she said with an air of intrigue, while completely avoiding his question.

You're such a goddamn child, he signed shaking his head with amusement, testing her.

"Yep," she replied grinning wickedly. "That one too."

Hopefully, we won't need your extensive repertoire of curse words here.

"Whoa, there big guy. What's this one?" she asked and repeated the sign for *repertoire.*

R-e-p-e-r-t-o-i-r-e.

"Jesus, *Mr. Fancy-pants* over here. Let's try to keep it simple in this meeting, shall we?" she said with a mock look of annoyance as she moved between their vehicles and onto the sidewalk. "So, what's the plan here?" she asked looking back at him as he followed behind her.

I just want to smooth this over however we have to. Let's just go in there, make whatever apologies we have to, and get out of there as quickly as we can.

Emmett didn't want this to be a problem with the government people when the six-month review came due. He didn't know if schools kept records of things like this, but he knew that this didn't look good on paper, not at all. The first day of school and Isabelle is called in the principal's office for fighting with another student. He didn't know for sure, but he was pretty sure that sort of thing was severely frowned upon by social workers.

They walked into the school, and Emmett knew from his time here exactly where the office was, and led Brooke to the glass paned office. There, they saw Isabelle sitting with her head hung low on one of the chairs along the wall. She quickly looked up when she noticed their approach, dropped her gaze just as quickly, and promptly started sobbing once they entered the office.

Emmett rushed to her, dropped down in front of her and softly clicked his tongue to get her attention. When he did, he looked at her empathetically and signed softly.

What happened?

"It wasn't my fault, Emmett. I swear to God. This time, it wasn't my fault," Isabelle said quickly. Emmett just nodded and repeated his sign.

What happened?

"We were playing tag on the playground, me and Lucas. Some of the other kids from his class were playing too. Then the bell rang and we all headed back inside, but there were these two guys who started picking on Lucas. They wouldn't let him into the school. They said '*this door isn't for dorks*' and told him to use another door. They were being *assholes*," she whined the word like it explained everything, and maybe it did. Beside him, Brooke suppressed a slight chuckle while Emmett winced away from the word. "They took his glasses. He was crying, Emmett."

"Did you tell them to stop, sweetie?" Brooke spoke up from his side, Emmett shot her a glance before he nodded and looked back to Isabelle.

"I did. I was yelling at them to leave him alone, but they wouldn't listen. I didn't know what else to do." Isabelle dropped her gaze to her shoes. "So, I kicked him in the balls."

Emmett wiped his face with his palm in an attempt to hide his disappointment, beside him Brooke spoke up again. Perfectly putting words to what he felt.

"Oh no," she said softly. "Who are these guys?"

"Paul and Charlie Fullerton," Isabelle said the names like they meant something to her.

"Who?" Brooke asked and Emmett turned back to her.

L-u-c-a-s's cousins, he signed to her but she saw her attention was focused on something else.

"Isabelle?" Brooke asked before she stepped forward and touched a red patch on the right-side of Isabelle's scalp, right where her braid should have been. "Where's your braid?" Isabelle looked up at her with tears slowly streaming down her face and opened her hand to relieve the coiled remains of her braid in her palm. "Motherfuckers!" Brooke growled loudly. Both Emmett and Isabelle flinched away from the comment. "Those little *shits* tore your braid off?"

Keep your voice down! Emmett signed sharply to her and looked over to the receptionist and smiled reassuringly.

"I couldn't stop them," Isabelle weakly confessed. Emmett reached out and gave her shoulder a squeeze.

It's okay, he signed when she looked up to him. He saw the hurt in her eyes.

"I tried, Emmett. You have to believe me," She pleaded with her bottom lip quivering and a fresh batch of tears collecting in her eyes. "I was *trying* to be good. I tried *so* hard. When Lucas started crying, I didn't know what else to do. I *had* to do something. They wouldn't leave him alone." Emmett nodded.

He knew.

It's okay, he signed quickly because he was more than sure Isabelle knew those signs. *You did the right thing.*

"What?" Isabelle asked weakly, confused about what he had said at the end. *I really have to get her on whatever lessons Brooke is doing,* he thought as he looked at her, smiled and reached for his notepad.

"He said you did the right thing, sweetie." Brooke said before he could. Isabelle looked at him wide-eyed.

"But I got in trouble," Isabelle said like the concept of getting in trouble for doing the right thing was new to her. "The teacher said I could be *suspended,*" Isabelle said with a rising sense of panic, Emmett could see it on her face.

He held his hands out in front of her in a gesture that she recognized as *slow down*, and he took in a deep breath and encouraged her to do the same. When she finally did, he slowly continued to sign, and to his utter delight Brooke softly translated.

"You can't fight with the other students.," Brooke said.

"But you just said I did the right thing," Isabelle whined to him.

"You did, but you broke the rules doing it. Now, you have to face your punishment, whatever it might be."

"I don't wanna. I'm scared." Isabelle looked to him, and then to Brooke before her gaze fell to her shoes and she sobbed softly. "What if they make me leave again? I...I don't want to leave. I like it here."

Emmett didn't even have to do the signs. Brooke just knew what to say.

"Oh sweetie," she said with a gentle firmness as she leaned in closer. "You're not going anywhere. No matter what happens in there." Brooke gestured back into the office's interior. "You are staying right where you are. Your uncle would never let anyone take you away from him."

It worked. Isabelle looked up at him. Her steel blue eyes reminded him of Tommy's.

Forever, he signed slowly.

Isabelle leapt out of her chair and wrapped her arms around him. Inside, Emmett's heart threatened to jump out of his chest.

"I'm so sorry, Emmett." Isabelle sobbed weakly into his ear. He couldn't help but feel a sting of disappointment because he was sure she was going to say something else, but he quickly brushed it aside and gently squeezed the impossibly small girl in his arms.

The new center of his universe. The one thing that everything else in his life revolved around.

He held Isabelle for a time and when they parted, they both looked up to Brooke, who was quickly wiping some wetness from her eyes.

Are you crying? Emmett signed, teasing her.

No. She signed sharply. *Shut up. Mind your own business.*

"Brooke, are you crying?" Isabelle asked with near perfect timing a second later. Brooke just growled with amused frustration.

"No," she huffed. "I'm just allergic to heartwarming shit, okay?"

"Mr. Brooks?" a voice called to them from behind.

Emmett turned and saw an older woman with a stout frame. Her greying hair formed a tight bun at the back of her head and she wore an unappealing olive-green pant suit, with a blue frilly blouse underneath her suit jacket. By her look of distain, Brooke was not impressed by the woman.

I immediately don't like her, she signed quickly.

Be good, he signed before he waved to the rapidly approaching woman. *We need her on our side.*

"Hi, Mr. Brooks." The woman in the olive-green pant suit extended her hand towards him. Emmett eagerly, but gently, shook the woman's petite hand. "I'm sure we've met before," she said quickly. "I've met all the parents but it's impossible to remember all of their names, so let me introduce myself again. *Thank God,* Emmett thought. He had forgotten the woman's name. "I'm Glenda Tanguay," she said with a big smile and gave his hand a small pump before retreating her hand back. "And you are?" she asked with a hint of confusion as she extended her hand towards Brooke.

"Brooke. Brooke Talbot." She reached out and shook Glenda's hand lightly. "Translator," Brooke said quickly, answering the unspoken question that hung in the air between the two women.

"Ah! Excellent. Well, we don't normally allow anyone but parents or guardians in the meetings, but I suppose this is a special case. Please," she said gesturing towards her office. "Let's have a quick chat and get this all sorted out. Oh, Isabelle, honey," Glenda spoke up when she noticed Isabelle moving in beside him. "This is just for the grown-ups. If you wouldn't mind waiting out here for a bit while we get this all cleared up."

"Okay," Isabelle gave him a worried look.

It's fine, Emmett signed to her quickly. *Don't worry.*

Emmett left her in the waiting area and fell in beside Brooke.

Is it a good thing or a bad thing that she wanted her to stay behind? Brooke had an amused expression on her face when she signed the words. Emmett looked at her coldly.

It means she is going to say something she doesn't want her to hear. He saw how her expression dropped and her jaw slightly tightened. He just made a calming gesture before he quickly signed. *Be cool.*

I just hope she isn't going to be a bitch about this, Brooke replied deftly before she took her seat in front of Glenda's cluttered desk.

"I'm sorry," Glenda asked with some interest when she noticed Brooke signed at him.

"Hmm?" Brook answered innocently.

"Well, I just noticed you said something to Mr. Brooks, and I was just curious what it was."

Emmett clicked his teeth to draw Brooke's attention to him. *Easy on the smack talk. You're supposed to translate, remember? Turn your chair a bit so you can see me better, and talk as if it's me saying the words, because that's how an actual translator does it.* Brooke looked a little annoyed at his directions, but thankfully she just nodded at the end and scooted her chair to the side so it faced him more than Glenda.

"And that was?" Glenda asked with some tension in her voice. Probably because Brooke wasn't actually translating anything yet.

"Oh, sorry. He was just telling me how to do my job. You know, typical *mansplaining* stuff," Brooke said lightly and waved the question off before she settled herself into her seat. "Okay, I'm ready."

Emmett looked at her, and slowly rolled his eyes so only she could see before he turned back to Glenda and flashed his biggest smile.

"Thank you for coming in, Mr. Brooks, I know this time of year is hectic for a lot of people and I appreciate you taking the time."

Emmett signed slowly, giving Brooke plenty of time to translate.

"Please, Call me Emmett. It's no problem at all," Brooke said, easily translating his signs.

"I assume Isabelle got you up to speed as to the nature of the incident?"

"She did."

"Well, just in case she left out any details," Glenda began cautiously before she ran over the events again.

Emmett noted all the main bullet points were basically the same as the story Isabelle had told him. Except apparently, Isabelle had bitten Paul Fullerton hard enough he had to go to the nurse's office. By the way Glenda explained it, that fact bothered her the most.

"I'm sure you can see why we would view this kind of behavior as concerning. Now, I understand Isabelle is from...*unfortunate circumstances,*" she said dancing around the truth of what she wanted to say. *A foster child.* "But I feel it's important to reinforce that this kind of thing is not to be tolerated in our school."

"I completely understand, and I want you to know I don't-. I'm sorry Emmett," Brooke quietly interrupted. "What was the last sign?" Emmett quickly spelt it out for her. "*Condone* fighting of any kind. Isabelle understands this, and is very sorry for her actions. I promise you, this won't happen again."

"I should hope not," Glenda said with some indignation. Emmett could feel sweat starting to form on his brow. "Violence against another student is a serious matter. That's why we feel it's appropriate to suspend her for three days."

Fuck, Emmett signed reflexively. Thankfully, Brooke caught the mistake.

"What?!" she exclaimed with no less shock than what Emmett felt.

"I know it sounds extreme, but the punishment *must* fit the crime."

Glenda leveled Emmett with a hard stare like he should have already known that, and if he did, maybe they wouldn't be in this situation. That stare made Emmett wish he could shrink away to nothing in the small chair he was in.

Beside him, Brooke clicked her tongue softly, just like he did when he wanted someone's attention.

Permission to speak freely here, boss.

Please, I'm fucking dying over here.

You still need to sign though, Brooke quickly signed and turned her attention to the principal. "Sorry, Glenda, I was just asking Emmett for clarification on something," Brooke said absently before her demeanor hardened. "Anyway, Emmett was wondering why we didn't see the boys involved in *the incident* out in the waiting room as well? Did you already have a meeting with their parents, or were you going to do that later on today?"

Glenda sighed deeply.

"I did already have a long talk with the Fullerton twins, and they expressed a lot of regret over the incident. I felt that was sufficient enough for the time being." The subtle shift in the expression on Glenda's face told a different story though. Emmett caught it, and he was sure Brooke did as well.

That's a good point. I didn't think of that. Keep going, he signed. Brooke nodded to him and played her part perfectly.

"Isabelle feels a ton of regret as well. Yet, you want to suspend her for three days. Emmett's a little confused over the disparity between the two punishments."

"I'm sorry to say that the sad fact of the matter is that Isabelle instigated the altercation. Our policy is to-,"

Bullshit, Emmett signed angrily.

"Bullshit." Brooke said confidently almost at the same time. Emmett flinched slightly away from the comment and look towards her.

You weren't supposed to say that.

"Don't look at me like that, Glenda. He said that," Brooke said and quickly pointed in his direction, throwing him under the bus. "What we're trying to say is, Isabelle is not only new to this school, she's new to the whole area. She spent her entire summer locked up in a farmhouse with this big galoot."

Brooke absently thumbed over towards Emmett. All he could do was give her a slightly hurt look, which she didn't pay any attention to. Brooke was solely focused on Glenda.

"In that time, she made one friend." Brooke held up her index finger in the space between her and the principal to emphasize her point. "Lucas Adler. So, when she saw her *one* friend being bullied, what did you expect her to do? Was what she did right? Of course not. Nobody here disputes that, but you can't suspend her for three days. That's not what she needs. She needs to be around kids her age. She needs friends. If you take her out of school, you take that chance away. You'll make it harder for her to socialize." Brooke leaned forward in her seat a bit, and at this point it was obvious to the woman across from them that Brooke was no longer translating for anyone. "So, here's what we're going to do, *Glenda*. We're going to take Isabelle home for today, and Emmett will make sure Isabelle understands this can not happen again going forward. Then, tomorrow, we can start fresh." Brooke dramatically made a wiping motion with her hands. "Clean slate." Brooke paused to look over to Emmett.

You're amazing, he signed.

It was like Brooke was taking all his anxieties and giving them a voice. Emmett was a little ashamed to admit he locked up when Glenda started talking about a three-day suspension. That would crush Isabelle, but he didn't know what he could do to avoid it.

Brooke just nodded, like she already knew.

"I think that would be acceptable," Glenda said with a slow nod. "When you explain it like that, I can see how that would be more beneficial for her in the long run. We all want what's best for Isabelle, after all." She finished by displaying an affable smile.

"Of course," Brooke replied quickly and flashed a pleasant smile of her own.

"Well," Glenda brought her hands together in a gentle clap. "I think that about does it. Again, I appreciate you taking the time to come in, Emmett." She rose up from her seat and extended her hand over the desk towards Emmett, who shot up and shook her hand. Emmett was just happy to leave. Glenda gave Brooke a suspicious look. "And Miss Talbot, I appreciate you lending us your *translating services* for the day." Brooke shook her offered hand.

"I'm sure it won't be the last time you see me," she said lightly. Though to him, it sounded like a mild threat.

"Well, hopefully the next time the circumstances will be different," Glenda said as Emmett and Brooke were turning towards the door to her office. "We'll look forward to seeing Isabelle in the morning. *Fresh start*, like you said. Biting someone isn't very lady-like, after all." Glenda said absently, but the comment resonated inside him like an evil bell tone.

But it was Brooke who abruptly turned.

"*Excuse me*?!" By her harsh tone, and the expression of contained rage on her face, Emmett knew the meeting was about to take a turn for the worst.

Emmett softly placed his hand on Brooke's shoulder to silence her. She looked back at him with a questioning frown. He simply smiled and patted the air between them. Brooke sighed heavily, but she remained silent as Emmett reached into his breast pocket for his notepad. He wrote a quick note that nicely summed up what he was feeling in that moment.

Don't worry. I promise you, Isabelle won't bite the next bully who messes with her.

He showed the note to Brooke, who chuckled slightly before she looked up at him, nodded her head before she opened the door and walked out of the office.

Emmett folded the note and placed it on the principal's desk before he too walked out of the office without giving her a chance to read his message.

"Let's go," Brooke said forcefully to Isabelle when she approached. "We're leaving." She held her hand out for Isabelle to take.

"What happened?" Isabelle asked with a worried look as she rose off her seat and took the offered hand.

Don't worry, Emmett signed quickly with a warm smile. *It's fine.*

"Your uncle is taking us out for lunch, and you're having a milkshake," Brooke declared as she led Isabelle out of the front office with Emmett following quickly behind.

"I am?" Isabelle asked with obvious confusion.

"Yep, we both are. We *earned* it."

CHAPTER 16

Brooke

Brooke was restocking the bulbs in the lighting department when she heard Tim's sneakers squeak on the tile floor at the mouth of the aisle.

"Brooke!" he said excitedly. "There you are."

She barely heard him.

She was listening to a true-crime podcast in her ear. She liked to do that while she did the busy-work of the early morning before the customers started filing in. Now that the summer was officially over, and the countdown to Christmas began, the hardware store was now in its slow season.

All hopes of a full-time position had evaporated months ago when Bruce explained the full-time position was going to Scott. He said it was because the man had been there longer, but Brooke secretly suspected it was because Scott and his new wife just had a baby girl in the summer. She couldn't argue with that logic. She didn't really need the position, after all. She just wanted it for herself. A silly little goal she could focus herself on, and she couldn't even make *that* happen.

So, now, she listened to podcasts while she did the mindless work, and reflected on how easily some people ruined their lives. She heard their sad tales of desperation, greed, jealousy, and hatred. When she did, she felt better about herself. Like her life wasn't a giant ball of shit rolling downhill, growing increasingly larger with each turd it picked up along the way.

"Here I am," Brooke agreed throwing her hands up, because she didn't know what had Tim so excited.

"Jesus, Brooke, you've got to see this." He said rushing down the aisle towards her. "I think this is *R-two*." Brooke flinched away from the term, dropped her head and shook it slowly disapprovingly.

"I swear to God, Tim, if you call Emmett that name one more time, I'm going to slap the shit out of you," she said sternly as she looked up at him again. "Or worse yet, I'll tell him what you said and let *him* do it," she joked.

"You wouldn't," he said, stopping in his tracks with his phone in his hand, suddenly concerned about something completely different. The shift in his expression made Brooke chuckle shamefully.

"No," she reluctantly agreed. "I wouldn't." Mostly, because Emmett wouldn't care one-bit what Tim called him behind his back. "But I'll still slap the shit out of you, so cut that shit out."

"Yeah, fine. Whatever. Take a look at this," he said handing her his phone. "A friend of mine sent me this link last night. There's some kid in Churchbridge who has this backyard MMA-thing going. It's a big deal around there apparently. He posts the fights online every week. He sent me this because this one guy just destroys this other guy in the second round with one punch. I couldn't believe it."

"Okay, so? What does this have to do with Emmett?" she asked innocently, not seeing the connection.

"Well, I think he's the guy fighting," Tim said, sounding a bit surprised he even had to say it. "It's all queued up and ready to go, you just have to press the play button on the screen," Tim explained quickly, like she didn't know how to use a video app on a smartphone.

She rolled her eyes and press the play button like he instructed.

"Doubtful," she said as the muted video began. "I'm pretty sure Emmett has better things to do than beat up some guy in somebody's backyard," she said dismissively.

The video focused in on one of the fighters. *The Beast,* looked like a college athlete of some kind, like a football player or maybe a wrestler. Something that required a large, lean frame. In the video, he suddenly waved to the crowd. Brooke assumed his name had been announced. The video panned around, and Brooke saw a ring that was outlined with hay bales that had several bleachers around it.

Who has that in their back yard? Brooke wondered idly.

"Don't assume just because Emmett is big and intimidating, that he-," she halted as the camera stopped on the other fighter, *King.* "What the fuck?! That's Emmett!" she cried out dumbly as the video played on.

"That's what I thought," Tim agreed as he moved in behind her so he could watch the phone in her hands as well. "It kind of looks like he gets his ass kicked a bit in this first round, but he comes out in the second round and absolutely *erases* the guy."

Brooke watched on numbly as the two men flew at each other in the beginning of the round. True to Tim's words, it did look like Emmett was getting beaten up a bit. The other, younger man started throwing punches at him with wild abandon, backing him up to the hay bales. When the round ended, Emmett shook himself off a bit before he walked back to his corner and had a drink of water like nothing had happened. She watched as he took notice of something off camera, like somebody had said something to him. Emmett quickly waved it off before he took another drink.

The second round was over before it really had a chance to begin. Brooke yelped a bit when Emmett stepped forward and thrust his elbow into the man's chest in a way Brooke had never seen before. The blow sent the other man flying into the dirt where he stayed until some attendants came to his aid.

Emmett had won the match.

"Pretty incredible, huh?" Tim asked excitedly behind her, Brooke barely noticed. She was still staring at the screen as the video played on, until she finally stopped the playback.

I have a job in Churchbridge, she remembered him telling her when he asked her to babysit Isabelle. The same night he mysteriously disappeared for hours. When Emmett did finally show up that night, he was drunk, bloodied, and bruised. Brooke's jaw tightened as she made the connection.

"Yeah," she sneered. "That's pretty *fucking* unbelievable, alright." *He lied to me,* she thought venomously.

Then she noticed the timestamp on the video's post. It was months before that night happened. Then she scrolled down on the page, and saw King's/Emmett's other fights.

"Jesus Christ, how many of these are there?"

"Like seven," Tim said cautiously, probably sensing her hostile reaction to the news, even though Brooke was trying to play it cool for him. "In the last one, he beats the heavy-weight champion. Some dude named Destroyer."

Brooke quickly found the posted video, and immediately the timestamp struck her like a cold fist. It was the same night Emmett asked her to babysit. That night, when he finally showed up, Emmett had signed that he and Calvin were *celebrating*, which she mistook for *partying*. The lost pieces of that night were coming together, and with it came the familiar feeling of betrayal.

He should have told me. The thought echoed annoyingly inside her head.

"*Asshole*!" Brooke cursed under her breath as she handed Tim his phone back.

"What's that?" Tim asked lightly, intently scrolling through his phone, possibly looking for another video to show her. If he did, she wouldn't watch it. She had seen enough.

"Excuse me for one second, Tim." Brooke rose up from her task. "I have to ask Dale something," she said and sternly walked out of the aisle.

If Tim said anything in response, she didn't hear it.

Dale quickly agreed to cover for her over the lunch hour, just like she knew he would. He gave her a little grief, the way older folks sometimes like to do, but in the end he relented. She just had to suffer through his bit of pageantry before he did.

When the clock hit twelve, Brooke stiffly walked to the staff room to retrieve her coat. She exited the store soon after, turned right and walked straight to the diner. It was two blocks away, but when she turned, she was greeted with the sight of Calvin's cruiser parked in front of it.

Perfect, she thought as she hurried down the sidewalk.

She entered the diner, and walked straight to the back booth where she knew Calvin liked to eat his lunch.

"Did you know Emmett is fighting in some backyard fighting ring out at Churchbridge?!" she asked rather loudly as soon as she approached the table.

Calvin was in full uniform. The table he was sitting at was empty except for a clipboard that had some form he was meticulously filling out with information from the little flipbook he liked to carry around with him. He looked up from his work with a quirky sort of smile.

"Oh, hello," he said with mock surprise. "Nice to see you too, Brooke. You're looking good. Nice weather we've been having lately, eh?" he asked sarcastically with his little smile never leaving his face. Brooke relaxed her stance and gave Calvin a shameful expression of muted regret. She was good at those. "Would you like to sit down?" he chuckled and gestured towards the bench seat across from him.

"I would," she quickly confessed and slid into the seat. "So? Did you?" she persisted.

Calvin sighed deeply, closed his flipbook and placed it on top of the clipboard before he placed both items on the seat beside him. He then looked at her while he took a deep breath, like he was quietly preparing himself for something.

"I do, yes." He folded his hands together on the table and gave her a thoughtful look. "I know all about it," he said quietly. "I was actually the one who suggested it to him." Calvin gave her a mildly challenging look.

"What?!" Brooke barked out the question. She couldn't help herself. Some part of her expected that Calvin knew. She suspected he might even condone the behavior, but she never imagined he was the one who suggested it to him. "Why the hell would you do that?"

"I don't think that's for me to say," Calvin said with a raised eyebrow, like he was thinking the matter over.

"Why not?"

"Well, because you two are...you know...*an item*, or whatever you want to call it," he said awkwardly.

"What?!" Brooke was taken back a bit by the comment. She recovered quickly, though. "No, we're not. It's not like we're dating or anything."

"Well, not yet, but I assume you're going to ask him out at some point."

What? Brooke couldn't help but be thrown off by where Calvin was steering this conversation. It was heading towards dangerous territory. She didn't want to think about that stuff, because she didn't want to admit there was some part of herself that wanted it to happen.

"Why would *I* ask *him* out?" she asked defensively.

"I just thought that's why you are learning sign language," he said like it was more of a statement of fact. Calvin's smile widened as he suddenly cracked his knuckles and began to sign. *Or do you not like him in that way?* He looked at her with a challenging expression.

Is this a test? She quickly replied in kind, speaking of their sign language, but apparently Calvin had something else in mind.

Maybe. Maybe I'm just curious what your intentions are exactly towards my friend.

Are you being serious right now? Brooke signed and gave him a look.

Deadly serious. E-m-m-e-t-t doesn't need his heart broken again. Not now, not with everything else that's going on.

Brooke quickly, but softly, waved her hands in front of her to stop Calvin from signing anything else.

What are you talking about? We're just friends.

Really? Calvin signed and suddenly looked at her with a sad expression. *That's too bad. You two make a cute couple. He talks about you all the time, and you two sure seem like you're more than just friends.* Brooke silenced him with a hurt expression.

If I was so important to him, he would have told me the truth about the fighting. I wouldn't have to find out from somebody at work.

Calvin sighed deeply, paused for a moment like he was considering something, and then signed his reply.

He probably just doesn't want you to know how poor he is. He's proud like that.

The news struck her like a gut punch. She wasn't expecting this. Her mind instantly fought against the idea.

How poor can he be? He just spent a small fortune renovating his house, she signed and gave him a challenging look, which Calvin smirked at.

Where do you think that small fortune came from? Calvin sighed briefly. Brooke could tell he was uncomfortable talking about this behind Emmett's back. His next signs confirmed her suspicions. *I really think this is something you should talk to him about, if you want to know.* Brooke just looked at him, exasperated.

He won't tell me, not all of it. He's too proud, remember? Brooke gave him a knowing look as she threw Calvin's words back at him. His expression told her he reluctantly agreed with that statement. So, she continued. *If it affects him, I want to know. Tell me.*

Calvin smiled at her.

Careful. That sounds like girlfriend-talk to me.

Don't be an asshole, Brooke quickly signed with some frustration. She wasn't here for Calvin to play matchmaker. That, and she only had so much time before she had to get back. Calvin's little chuckle only added to her already increasing frustration level.

I'm surprised you know that one, Calvin signed with some amusement. She assumed he was referring to the curse word.

You better believe I have a vast repertoire of swear words I can draw from.

Brooke slowly signed the new word Emmett taught her before their meeting with the principal a few days ago. It was her turn to test Calvin. She couldn't help the little grin that bloomed across her face when Calvin's confused expression looked back at her.

What's this one? Calvin finally signed with some shame and repeated the sign for *repertoire* back to her.

"Repertoire," Brooke said aloud. "So, did I pass?" she asked as the waitress brought Calvin his lunch. A cheeseburger with a side order of French fries.

"Thank you so much, Margie," he said to the waitress as she set the food down on the table and quietly walked away. "Yeah, I'd say you passed," Calvin said looking back to her, obviously impressed. "Emmett said you got *freakishly* good at sign language. I just thought he was exaggerating, but Jesus! How long have you been doing it?"

"Since July. I practise a few hours every night," Brooke bragged casually. She didn't think her progress was that monumental, but she wasn't about to shy away from a compliment. "Once I got the basics down, I started translating tv shows and filling in the blanks." Calvin nodded appreciatively.

"I did that," Calvin said excitedly before he took a big bite out of his burger.

He then looked at her with an embarrassed expression and pointed to his food. Brooke couldn't tell if he was asking permission to eat his lunch in front of her, or whether he was offering her some of it. Either way, she quickly waved it off.

"So?" she asked expectantly. "Are you going to tell me what's going on with Emmett?" She further inquired, impatiently and then had to wait until he was done chewing his food for his reply.

"No," he finally said, to her utter disappointment, and frustration. "Not all of it, anyway. Like I said before, I don't feel it's my place to say. If you really want to know, you should talk to him. What

I *will* tell you, though, is that he has been in a bad place for a long time." Calvin said it like it was a sad fact he had been burdened with. "Like a *real* bad place. It was hard to watch at times. I was sure, at some point, I was going to have to arrest him or..." Calvin paused, like he didn't even want to say it. "Well, I don't know what, but I knew it wouldn't be good. Then news of Isabelle came, and it was like someone had switched something inside the man's head. Suddenly, he wanted more than to just drink himself into oblivion and hide away on that farm of his. Problem was, he dug himself into a bit of a hole, and if he wanted a life with Isabelle, he was going to have to fight for it. *Literally*." Calvin held up his hand when he noticed she was eager to jump in. "Before you ask, he had already sold everything of value, and he didn't want to touch his scant little herd, or his mother's life insurance money. *That*, is for his father's care." Brooke nodded thoughtfully.

She knew about Carter's Alzheimer's, though she didn't hear it from Emmett.

"That didn't leave him with many options. I suggested it because his back was against the wall, and it was something he could do." Calvin now sounded like he was explaining why he set Emmett down this path, like he needed her to understand. "Hell, it's what he's been training for his entire life."

Calvin paused to take another bite of his burger. Brooke waited patiently as he did, quietly mulling over what she had learned thus far.

"Also, I think he likes it," he said, and Brooke couldn't help thinking he sounded a bit remorseful when he did. She had a nagging suspicion as to why.

"So, he *is* just like Tommy."

"No," Calvin said immediately, and shook his head profusely. "Nope. Not even a little bit."

Calvin took a big bite out of his burger before he set it back down on his plate, quickly wiped off his hands, and began to sign again.

I will never say this out loud, because T-o-m-m-y was my best-friend growing up, and I loved him dearly, but I like E-m-m-e-t-t more. Calvin looked genuinely hurt by what he was signing.

"Tommy was a great friend. He was always a lot of fun to hang out with, and when you were with him, you knew he had your back. No matter what." Calvin's hurt expression stayed in place as he continued. "But being Tommy's friend meant you were the one who had to hold him back when he lost it, or worse yet, you had to be the one who pulled him off some guy he was beating to a pulp. It was *exhausting*," he confessed quietly. To her surprise, when Calvin next looked at her, he had tears in his eyes. "If I had been there, that bullshit with Clive Adler would never have happened. I could've talked him down." Brooke reached for him in a comforting gesture, but Calvin smiled and waved it off. "I'm fine. What's done is done. I'm just telling you this because you need to understand that Emmett isn't anything like Tommy was. Tommy just liked hurting people, I'm sure of it, and he just waited for somebody to give him a reason to hurt them. Emmett's not like that. He likes winning. I think that's what he likes the most. You know, *other* than the money. Just having people cheer for him, he's never had that." Calvin gave her a quizzical expression. "Have you seen the fights?"

"One," she admitted quickly. "The one where he elbows the guy in the chest."

"Ew, that's a good one. That was the first. If you watch them, look at how he reacts when the crowd cheers for him. It's like he doesn't know what to do with that kind of attention. He looks embarrassed most of the time."

She did recall at the end of the video, just before she abruptly paused it, and she remembered the confused sort of bewilderment on Emmett's face as he looked around himself at the end of the fight.

"So, this is all legal?" Brooke switched gears. "He's not going to get in trouble for what he's doing?"

"As far as I can tell, it's a hundred percent legit. A little trashy for my liking, but it's legal."

"And what happens when he gets hurt?" Calvin smiled at her again.

"For someone who is *just a friend*, you sure seem to be concerned about the big guy." Brooke crossed her arms in front of herself, unimpressed. "*Fine*," he said giving up his nonsense, and got back to answering her question. "If he gets hurt, well I imagine he'll quit. You're still confusing Emmett for Tommy. Emmett doesn't love fighting the way Tommy did. Don't get me wrong, he's amazing at it, but it's more of a means to an end for Emmett. Like a job. A job he is really good at, and enjoys, but he doesn't love it," Calvin said with an air of finality. "He loves Isabelle." Calvin then locked his eyes on her in a hard glance. "I think he's falling in love with you, as well."

Brooke knew she didn't react to the news well. Most women would swoon with emotion when they found out someone like Emmett was developing feelings for them. Brooke just worried.

"Yeah, exactly," Calvin said, seeing her reaction. "So, you keep that in mind going forward. Also, keep in mind, you could do a lot worse than Emmett."

"Jesus! Pick a lane, guy. You can't tell me to stay away from him in one breath, and in the next tell me how perfect he is for me."

"I never said *stay away from him*. I'm rooting for you guys. You're like my Ross and Rachel," he said and took another bite from his burger. As much as he infuriated her, she appreciated the reference.

"You know about me, right?" Brooke asked him with a serious expression as he chewed. "Like what happened to me and Graeme. Why he left me? All of it."

He looked at him as his chewing slowly came to a stop and he regarded her with an empathetic expression she didn't like. He nodded slowly.

"I'm *broken*," her voice cracked from the tension in it when she said the word.

She wanted to say more, but she didn't trust herself. Instead, the two of them just looked at each other for an awkward moment, like they were both mulling over what had been said.

"Why would Emmett want anything to do with this *mess*?" she asked and swept her hands down herself. Afterwards, she looked at Calvin in a way she wasn't proud of. She looked at him with hope, and tears, in her eyes.

Calvin didn't disappoint.

"Because you make him happy," Calvin said warmly with that little knowing grin of his. "That's what I figure, anyways. If you really are curious, though, you should find out for yourself."

"Maybe I will," Brooke said quietly, while a small idea popped into her head. "Will you tell me when Emmett is going to fight again?" she asked quickly.

"Why?"

"Because I want to see it, for myself. I want to see him fight."

"I suppose I can do that," Calvin said cautiously, like he didn't really want to, but he couldn't see a way around the request.

"Thanks. I appreciate that. I promise, I'm not going there to start any sort of shit with him. I just want to see. In and out. Emmett won't even know I'm there."

"I get it. At least, I think I do. You'll probably know when he's going to fight anyway, because he's probably going to ask *you* to watch Isabelle," Calvin said, sounding a bit hurt.

"That's true." Brooke then looked at the clock on the wall behind the counter. "Shit! I have to get back. I only get a half hour for lunch, and I'm late."

"Well, you'd better get going then," Calvin said, like he was shooing her playfully out of the booth. "Hey, thanks for coming in for the talk." Brooke gave Calvin a weird look.

"That's what I was going to say," she said as a joke.

"I'm serious. It's nice having someone else who's looking out for the big guy."

They said their good-byes, and Brooke left the diner feeling better about things than she had when she entered. Though, she thought about the conversation she had with Calvin for the rest of her day.

***

"Sweetie?"

Her mother softly touched Brooke's arm as she washed the few items that either wouldn't fit into the dishwasher, or weren't meant for it. Like her mother's wooden salad bowls. Before that gentle touch, Brooke was staring off into the distance and watched the cars zipping past on the highway. That, and she was thinking about Emmett.

"Is everything okay?"her mother asked in her trademark *Mom*-voice. The one that was practically dripping with concern. "You were quiet at dinner. You look like something is on your mind." Brooke couldn't deny that.

"I do."

"Did you want to talk about it?" she asked and moved in towards the tea kettle that was simmering on the counter by the stove. It was then Brooke saw the empty coffee cup in her mother's hand.

"Wait. Are you here because you were worried, or to get another cup of tea?" Her mother flashed Brooke a guilty grin as she began to refill her cup.

"It can be both things," she said quickly and playfully slapped Brooke on the forearm. She then turned, leaned against the counter, and brought the cup to her lips. "So, talk." Brooke raised her eyebrow at her mother, but she decided not to fight it.

"I found out somebody I trusted is keeping secrets from me," Brooke said, completely confident she could talk about what was really bugging her without giving her mother any of the pertinent details.

"Oh," her mother said with sudden interest. "Is this about Emmett?"

"What the fuck?" Brooke blurted out and watched as her mother winced away from the word. She didn't care for swear words. She wasn't bothered by her mother's distaste, though. "How could you possibly know that?" Brooke's question slipped out. "I mean, *why* would you think that?" Her mother's cute little laugh told Brooke everything she needed to know.

"A mother knows."

"No, seriously. How?" Brooke challenged.

"Well, for starters, you learned an entirely new language just so you could talk to him." Her mother took another sip of her tea, the entire time she looked at Brooke with her amused expression.

"I don't know why everyone is making such a big deal about that. I just thought it would be nice to learn something new, *and* it would give him somebody he could talk to."

"Uh-huh," her mother shot back quickly, utterly unconvinced. "What about all the nice little outfits you've been wearing lately. The low-cut blouses, the tight-fitting jeans, the *heels.*"

"I like to look nice," Brooke shot back.

"And the push-up bras?" her mother asked with a raised eyebrow.

"Gravity is a cruel mistress," Brooke joked, sounding hurt. "You should know that." She nodded to her mother's own bosom. Her mother responded with a mock-hurt expression and slapped Brooke's arm again.

"Not to mention the fact that he's practically all you talk about anymore."

"That's not true," Brooke snapped back. "I talk about a lot of people."

"You *complain* about a lot of people, dear. It's not the same thing." Her mother gave her a knowing look and took a sip of her tea. Brooke couldn't argue with that, but she was still going to try. Her mother spoke again before she got the chance, though. "Plus, you drop whatever you're doing whenever he texts you."

"Yeah," Brooke shot back sarcastically. "Because I'm *so* busy all the time."

"Well, you seem to be busier now that he's in your life."

"I'm not in his life," Brooke quickly said, feeling like she and her were treading dangerously close to an argument.

"Okay, so you don't like him?" her mother asked innocently.

"I never said that."

"So, you *do* like him?"

"Yeah," Brooke said like it was the obvious answer. "What's *not* to like?"

"So, it's Isabelle you don't like then?"

"What?! No. She's the cutest thing in the world. Why would you even suggest that?"

"So, you like him, and you like his niece. So, what's the problem here, Brooke?" Her mother looked at her with those eyes of hers. Like, she could see right through her. "Seems to me, everything you want in life is right in front of you. The only question I have is, why are you not taking it?" Her mother dropped her bomb of a question, and then tilted her head towards her. She did like when she thought she had the upper hand in a discussion.

"Because," Brooke started to say loudly, with obvious indignation. "Because...well...it's just that..." *Think goddammit!* She screamed inside her head when she couldn't think of another reason why she shouldn't investigate what she and Emmett had, other than the obvious one. The one she held close to her heart. That way, nobody could see it, and they wouldn't know what it had done to her.

"Oh, *Brooksie*." Her mother quietly said her pet-name for her, and gently caressed her cheek with her free hand. Like she did when she was a kid. "That *prick* really hurt you, didn't he?" she said the curse word with such venom, Brooke was caught off guard by it.

After all, her mother *never* swore.

When the shock wore off, the question hung between them until Brooke's defences came down, just like her mother knew they would. She had left her there, raw and exposed. For the first time, in a long while, Brooke allowed herself to touch the scar on her heart. Her bottom lip quivered dangerously for a small second before the tears welled up in her eyes, and the first sobs came.

"Yeah," she chuckled cruelly through the tears. "He kind of did." With that out of the way, there was nothing left but to fall into her mother's waiting arms and just let the tears flow. "He left me like I was *nothing*," she whimpered into her mother's shoulder. "Everything we had been through, all that time, and he just treated me *like...like...like* some *goddamn* broken appliance he had to replace with a better model. I thought he *loved* me, mom. I *really* did." Brooke's words were barely intelligible by this point, so she just gave up on explaining it further and cried in her mother's arms.

"Shhhh," her mother cooed lovingly into her ear as Brooke openly sobbed into her shoulder like a wounded child. "Let it out, baby. It's okay."

Damn her! A part of Brooke cursed her mother because she made it so easy to just give in to what she was feeling, and cry her eyes out.

"I can't...I can't go through that again," she blubbered her confession into her mother's shoulder. "Never again," Brooke hissed.

It was at that point her mother switched gears.

"Hey!" she said and roughly pulled Brooke away and held her by the arms. "Don't say that!" Her mother then gave her a little shake to emphasize her point. "Love and faith are on the same coin, sweetie. You have to take a chance if you want to be happy, and you *deserve* to be happy. Everybody does, but it's not just going to fall into your lap." Her mother looked at Brooke sternly, like she should already know all this, and maybe she did, but it was still nice to hear. "You've got to go out there and get it for yourself." Brooke sniffled a bit, and wiped the remaining wetness from her face.

"But what if he hurts me like Graeme did?" It was the only question in her mind.

"Do you think he will? Hurt you like Graeme did?"

"I don't think so. I think he *really* likes me, mom." Brooke smiled weakly at her mother, because part of her was proud of the possibility a man like Emmett Brooks could love her.

"What's not to like? You're a strong, capable, beautiful woman." She gave Brooke's shoulder another little shake. "You're *my* daughter."

"I'm scared, though."

"That's how you know it's real, dear." Her mother smiled warmly and rubbed Brooke's shoulders. "You go out and get your happiness, sweetie. You deserve it. Don't be afraid, be fearless. That's the *Brooksie* I always knew. Graeme may have hurt you, that's fine, it's part of life, but don't let that stop you from finding happiness, because then he wins, *and* we can't let that *cocksucker* win."

"*Mom!*" Brooke looked at her mother with a mock expression of shock, but she just shrugged, smiled, and took another sip of her tea.

"*Sorry, not sorry.* That's what the kids say these days, isn't it?"

"It is," Brooke said gently and stepped towards her mother and hugged her again, just as her father walked into the kitchen with his own empty cup. "Thanks, mom."

"What's all this now?" her father called out with some humor from behind her. "Nobody told me there was a hugging party going on in here. There'd better be room for me in there," he said with that goofy voice he liked to use sometimes.

"Get in here, you old fool," her mother called out with a hint of annoyance and quickly waved him over. A heartbeat later Brooke felt her father move in behind her and wrap his arms lovingly around both her and her mother. Then he applied the slightest amount of pressure.

"What are we hugging out here?" he asked softly.

"Brooke is having man troubles," her mother replied, and offered nothing further.

"Oh baby," her father cooed softly into her ear. "You let me know which boy is causing you problems and I'll beat them up for you." Brooke smiled at his comment. He didn't mean it, of course, but it still felt nice to hear.

"It's Emmet Brooks, dear." Her mother quickly informed him. Brooke suspected she enjoyed the awkward pause that followed before her father cleared his throat nervously.

"In that case, maybe we'll let your mother deal with it."

CHAPTER 17

Nicole Jones

Her date for the evening, Dale Petersen, pulled up to the one empty parking spot on the street, and expertly backed his vehicle into the spot. He was a good driver. It was one of the numerous things she found appealing about the man.

She lived right on the border of Riverdale and Blake-Jones neighborhoods, only a few delightful blocks from Withrow Park. It was a pricey neighborhood. Normally, owning a house here was something a civil servant like herself could only dream of affording. She had her first husband and his secretary to thank for giving her the opportunity to live in such a nice place. She'd been here for ten years now, living on her own, turning her quiet, little three-bedroom house into a little sanctuary for herself. She found it was vital for her mental health to have someplace where she could escape *The City.*

"I had a *really* nice time tonight," she said warmly once Dale put his sedan into park.

He had insisted on driving tonight. It was an unexpected treat to be chauffeured around during their date. He took her to a nice Italian restaurant, where they dined on the most amazing fettuccini she had ever consumed in her entire life, and she drank a bit too much wine. Afterwards, they went for a walk around Old Toronto. At night, the city was alive with lights, sounds, and people that were oblivious to the concrete and glass giants around them as they made their way down the streets. They found a table at Yonge-Dundas Square and drank a few cups of coffee to keep the slight chill in the air at bay, enjoying each other's company.

Dale worked in finance. They met at a coffee shop they both liked downtown. The first time she saw him, she was quick to note he wasn't wearing a wedding ring. Over the course of the summer and early fall, they had bumped into each other a few times. At first, they exchanged nods, then smiles that were followed by cute little waves, and when they finally said hello to each other, she decided to introduce herself. She waited until the leaves started to turn before she decided to ask him out.

"Me too. I had an amazing time, Nic. It's nice to get out of the house," he said with a shy little grin.

Dale had a fourteen-year-old daughter, and he shared custody of her with his ex-wife. At Nicole's age, it was nearly impossible to date a man without some form of attachments. Dale took custody on weekends, which is why they went out on a Thursday.

"I'm glad you suggested the walk afterwards. I liked having a chance to just talk, you know?"

She did. There was something about this dark-skinned man with the quirky, awkward smile, and round, thin-rimmed glasses that intrigued her. She wanted to know more about him. Turns out, he was just as advertised. A lovable dork with a handsome face, and a bit of a *dad-bod*.

"Me too," she quickly agreed. She then reached over and gently placed her hand on his forearm. "I also really appreciate you driving. I *seriously* didn't mind meeting you at the restaurant." Dale lived in North Toronto, which was a forty-five-minute drive away, if traffic was good.

"Every princess deserves a chariot," he said sweetly, and only partially ruined it when he followed it up with, "M'lady." He then bowed his head towards her and did a small flourish with his hand.

God, why do I always fall for the nerds? She mused inside her head as she watched Dale's little spectacle.

When Dale lifted his head, Nicole quickly leaned in and kissed him, mostly to just get it out of the way. She liked him, and she was too old for screwing around like bashful teenagers. She was also concerned he might say something stupid and ruin the moment between them. In her experience, men rarely handled these awkward moments well.

To her delight, Dale was an excellent kisser.

His soft, warm lips gently caressed hers lovingly in a way that sent tingles down her spine. When they parted, she knew she wanted more, and poor Dale looked like he had come up for air. He sucked in a deep gasp and looked at her with a boyish excitement.

"Wow," he said. She took that as a compliment.

"Agreed," she said seductively and stared deeply into his chestnut eyes. "Did you want to come in for a drink?" She looked at him with eyes that told him it wasn't a beverage she was offering him. However, Dale apparently didn't get that message.

"Oh," he said suddenly embarrassed. "I don't actually drink." His expression showed his sudden awkwardness. "I mentioned that back at the restaurant." Nicole rolled her eyes in full view of him.

"Dale," she advised him slowly. "I wasn't *actually* offering you a drink." She then raised her eyebrow at him. If he didn't understand it this time, maybe it was for the best.

"*Ohhh!*" Dale exclaimed quietly in a way that showed he finally understood what was on the line. "You mean *sex*." The giddiness of his tone made Nicole chuckle.

"Yes, Dale. I mean sex," she confirmed with some humor.

"Well...it's just...You know...This is our first date and all...I didn't really expect to," Dale stammered adorably.

"Hit a home run?" she offered gently.

"Well, yeah." He looked at her with a mixture of shyness and embarrassment. Which she found endearing. She touched his forearm again and gave it a gentle squeeze.

"Well, technically, it's more like I'm letting you walk the bases." She smiled seductively at Dale, who apparently didn't get the joke. She forgot he wasn't a sports guy. "Listen, Dale." She looked empathetically at him and spoke softly. "I'm old enough to have sex with whoever I want, and I don't really feel the need to beat around the bush about it, if I don't want to. I like you. You're a sweet guy. So, I just thought it would be nice to have a little fun after our date. Maybe start the weekend off on a high-note. So, going back to our sports analogy, home base is yours," she said looking at him expectantly. "If you want it."

"Yes," Dale said almost immediately after she finished, and like the lovable dork he was, he couldn't leave it at that. "Please, and thank you, I guess. It's been a *really* long time-."

She silenced him with another long, passionate kiss. To her delight, his tongue gently tickled hers.

"So, let's go then," she whispered into his ear when they parted.

He didn't need any further convincing.

Dale quickly shut off his car, exited and walked hurriedly over to open her door. Like a real gentleman.

"M'lady." He used the same silly flourish of his hand to gesture her out of the car.

"Please stop saying that," she said softly as she exited the car, she smiled at him and patted his chest reassuringly.

"Yep," he replied quickly as he closed the door and fell in behind her as she led the way towards her quaint little getaway for what she hoped would be amazing lovemaking.

They entered through the front door, and to her pleasant surprise, Dale pulled her in close and kissed her passionately. Nicole couldn't help the soft moan that escaped her as she felt his lips on hers.

"Mmmm," she purred when they parted. "That's more like it." They smiled at each other seductively as they removed their coats and placed them on the hooks by the door. "I'm going to grab a quick glass of wine for myself, and I'll meet you on the couch." She raised an eyebrow at him before she added, "Or would you prefer to go straight to the bedroom?" She didn't love the expression she got back.

"I was actually wondering if I could use your bathroom?" He looked at her sheepishly.

Please, God, let it be indigestion and not Viagra, she thought to herself and tried not to let her wild assumptions spoil the mood.

"Of course," she said lightly. "Upstairs to the right, it's the door on the left. The door to the right leads to my bedroom."

"Meet you there?" he asked smoothly and grabbed her hips to pull her into another kiss.

"I'm looking forward to it." She was sure to bite her lower lip before she winked at him.

Dorks loved girlie-bullshit like that.

Nicole walked in to her cozy kitchen and dining room, and headed straight to the cupboard to retrieve a wineglass. She grabbed the bottle of white she had been working on this week and poured herself three fingers of wine. She took a quick sip and it warmed her insides as she thought of the naughty things she was going to do to Dale tonight.

That's when she noticed the red light on her alarm panel.

Nicole picked up her glass and walked over to the panel by the back door to inspect it further. To her disappointment, the alarm had been disengaged, and if memory serves that red light meant there was some disruption with the phone line.

Are they working on the lines? This late? Nicole wondered if she should check her landline, but then something else caught her eye.

The back door was unlocked.

Nicole quickly reached out and turned the deadbolt to engage it before she cautiously peered out the window into the darkness of her narrow little backyard. Nothing moved out in the blackness. She quickly thought back to before Dale arrived for their date.

What had she been doing? Did she go outside and simply forget to lock the door?

Maybe, she thought as she looked back at her kitchen with new eyes, *but what are the chances I forget to lock the door on the same day the alarm goes out?* She placed her glass on the table and stalked back into her living room and surveyed the space.

Everything looks in order, she thought to herself when she finished. She had a lot of nice, easily profitable items in her living room. First and foremost, would be the large flat-screen television. That was a hot-ticket item in the crime world, and yet stood unmolested in the same spot it had always been.

Maybe you're just being paranoid, she told herself as she scanned the room again.

But then a loud *thump* came from upstairs.

Nicole swiftly moved to her jacket and reached into the pockets for her phone and the steel, retractable baton from her police days before she quietly moved up the stairs, keeping her ears peeled.

"Dale?" she asked cautiously and she was answered with the sounds of dry heaving, at least that's what she first thought, but then the truth came crashing down.

He's choking! A voice screamed inside her skull and Nicole rushed up the stairs with the steel baton in one hand, while her other hand hit the emergency dial button on her phone. *He's having an allergic reaction,* a hopeful voice inside her called out. She even entertained the notion by trying to remember what Dale had ordered at dinner.

When she reached the top of the stairs, Nicole's cynical side suddenly gave her the finger. *See? I was right!* It said.

To the right, at the end of the hall was Dale, and he was being held in a rear-naked choke by a sturdy-looking male dressed in all black. Black jeans, black hoodie, with a black balaclava mask. Not a ski mask, like she would have expected to see, but a military-style balaclava. Dale was staring at her with wildly pleading eyes as he fought uselessly against his attacker.

"Let him go!" Nicole bellowed and widened her stance before she flicked the baton to the side, extending it out to its full length with a metallic *snick*. "Now!" she growled in a way that implied dire implications if the man didn't do as she commanded.

To her disappointment, the man just tilted his head towards her before he spoke.

"In a minute," he said calmly while looking right at her. He then looked at her quizzically. "Were you going to do something or...?" He left the question open ended.

"Oh, *sugar*," Nicole said with eager anticipation as she looked quickly down to her phone. "Just give me a moment, and I'll show you just what I plan on doing." The call had yet to be picked up when Nicole noticed movement come from her side.

Apparently, the man in black hadn't been talking to her.

Out of the darkness of her office, came a massive shape that exploded through the door and collided right into her with a brutal shoulder check. Nicole bounced off his rampaging bulk and flew into the opposite direction, straight into the door of her spare room. The door had been closed at the time. If it wasn't, she would have flown clear across the room.

As it was, she impacted the hollow door, heard a loud crack, and felt it slightly give against her weight. Nicole was sure the entire side of her body that hit the door was going to have a prominent bruise, but she couldn't worry about that now.

Nicole quickly recovered off the ground after the big man stomped his foot down onto the screen of her smartphone where it laid on the floor. It immediately shattered and went black. Undeterred, Nicole rose herself up onto one knee before the dark-covered giant descended upon her next. She took the steel butt end of the baton that poked out slightly from the bottom of her fist, and slammed it into the inside of the knee on the leg that just smashed her phone.

The guttural cry that the man let out was very satisfying.

Nicole was quick to follow it up with a shot to his exposed groin that stole his breath away. The big man sank down to the ground just as Nicole was rising off of it, and she expertly kneed the man in the face on her way up. It was a decent hit, the impact rattled her joint a bit, but it also stunned the giant long enough for Nicole to reach her free hand around the side of his head and pull his skull forcibly into the corner of the wall by the door. The man's large, covered head violently rebounded off the wall and it left his center exposed. Nicole didn't waste a moment and sent her ankle-length, two-inch heeled boot into his sternum, and growled viciously as she kicked the man down the staircase she had just climbed.

Nicole took great pleasure in the thunderous way the large man went ass-over-teakettle down the stairs. He let out a pained grunt with each and every impact he made on the way down to the ground floor. She then flashed an evil grin to the other, smaller man at the end of the hall.

"Just you and me now, *sunshine*!" Nicole sneered at the man holding Dale. He wasn't looking good, all the fight had left him, and his arms weakly slapped against the man holding him. Dale's eyes were open but he wasn't looking at anything, his eyes just rolled lazily around in their sockets as the last bit of consciousness drained from him.

She couldn't wait any longer.

Nicole rushed forward, and tried not to pay any attention to the numerous sharp pains that erupted from her injured side. Those heated barbs were only partially muted by the sudden spike of adrenalin in her bloodstream as she stepped forward.

The smaller man in the black balaclava frowned at her as he tossed Dale's limp body into her bedroom, the very same place she was supposed to meet him for some playful sex. Nicole could tell by the way his body fell to the floor, Dale wasn't getting up any time soon.

She didn't have the luxury of thinking about him right now, Nicole had her own life to worry about.

She rushed forward, after Dale was clear, and quickly closed the distance between her and the man in black. He moved with surprising speed. Normally, she would have expected typical thieves to flinch away from such aggression, but this guy just held his ground and shot out his front leg in a front kick that caught her in her mid-section. All forward momentum was halted, and the impact briefly stole her breath away.

He didn't stop there.

The man in black threw a series of quick, measured punches that hinted towards a professional fighter who was probing her defences. Looking for an opening. She couldn't let him find one.

Nicole quickly leaned back away from the first punch, used the steel baton in her right hand to jam up the second punch before it got any real steam behind it, and viciously chopped the third punch away with the baton. She slapped it down on his arm, right above the wrist. The man quickly yanked his hand back, and when he did, Nicole flicked the baton out and struck the man in his throat. Nicole smiled as the man crumpled slightly and gagged. She pressed her advantage by holding her free arm in front of her and charged into the man, pushing him back against the closet at the end of the hall.

He offered little resistance as he crashed loudly into the flimsy folding doors. She pressed him further into the door with her free arm and held him there before she proceeded to beat his side with the baton in her other hand. She quickly found her targets and hit them all. Outside of the knee, the outer thigh, and when it came time to hit the ribs, she turned the baton in her hand and savagely stabbed the hard butt-end into the man's side over and over again. A childish voice inside her screamed, *I'm winning.*

Then, she wasn't.

The man cursed something under his breath and shoved against her forearm. When she returned the force, the man quickly hooked his hand onto the back of her elbow and pulled her to the side. With that done, the man quickly drove his fist deep into Nicole's ribs. She yelped painfully as the impact drove the air from her lungs.

She wasn't going to lie, it hurt. It hurt bad.

It was the kind of pain that could derail a person's fury, because that's exactly what happened to her. Maybe it was her age, maybe she had let herself go too much, but that one punch caused her to pause and reconsider her approach.

That's all her attacker needed.

She didn't even see the punch that hit her, she only felt it. It crashed into her cheek like the hammer of God, and everything dimmed for a moment as she recoiled away from it. When her senses returned a heartbeat later, her brain quickly informed her that the baton was no longer in her hands. Unfortunately, that wasn't the most pertinent problem she had. Somewhere in the fog of her mind, something was screaming at her to bring her right arm up. Nicole didn't bother to question it, she just acted. Her hand shot out, caught the follow up attack close to the forearm, and solidly blocked it.

"Don't get greedy," she said quickly. It was something she had said in the past to sparring partners who were too aggressive for their own good. She didn't know why she said it. It just slipped out.

Nicole's hands reached out, grabbed a fistful of the man's jacket, and she quickly pulled herself into him. At the right moment, she lowered her forehead and headbutted the man, hopefully across the bridge of his nose, but it was impossible to tell. The impact rattled her as well, but she had been ready for it. They recoiled away from each other, but she held on tightly to the man's jacket. Nicole did what came naturally to her, she took a small step forward, and kicked the man in the groin like she was kicking a soccer ball. The man cried out painfully and pitched forward. Nicole dropped down to the ground and used her falling weight to pull the man forward into the closet door. It was one of the few times being short worked to her advantage. The man in black crashed head-first into the door overhead and when he rebounded back, she used that opportunity for a double-leg takedown.

She wrapped her arms around both his legs, just above the knees, and used her legs to pull the man off his feet. Something popped painfully in Nicole's back a second before she dumped his ass onto the hallway floor with a loud thump. She staggered for a moment, feeling the room spin around her, and she was forced down to one knee to steady herself.

Find the baton! A voice screamed inside her, and she madly scanned her surroundings as the smaller man on the ground struggled with his injuries.

"What the hell?" She heard her attacker ask the universe with bitter surprise, and mild frustration.

She didn't have much time, she knew that. Even with the baton, she was a poor match for these two assailants. Fear advised her to take refuge in her bedroom. She could lock the door, and call the police using the landline from the phone on her nightstand.

The landline is down, remember? A cruel voice reminded her. *At best, running away now would buy you another minute.* Experience, and all those hard lessons her father had taught her, advised her to take a different, more direct course of action.

Don't run, finish it!

Her eyes locked onto the baton.

She knew what she had to do. Nicole scooped up the baton from its spot on the floor, raised it up over her head, and brought it crashing down across the man in black's shin bone.

"Ow! Fuck!" he cursed and quickly crab-walked away from her. She knew she didn't break the bone. She just wanted him to *hurt.*

She wanted to taunt him as he retreated, but she instead used the precious time to get to her feet. As she did, her legs shook in a way she didn't appreciate. She used her free hand to touch the spot on her cheek the man had hit. When she touched it, pain flared up immediately from the gnarled flesh of the cut. The blood on her hand confirmed it.

Most women probably would have wilted like a dying flower in the afternoon heat at the sight of their own blood. However, they didn't have Chief Warrant Officer Nick Jones, of the Canadian Joint Task Force Two, as a father. *We don't run away from our problems dear,* he said to her on numerous occasions. So, when she saw the crimson on her hand, and felt the fresh adrenalin dump in her bloodstream, she only had one answer for that age-old question, *fight or flight?*

Nicole tightly gripped the baton in her hand and stalked after her assailant, who was still on the ground. She neared the man cautiously, because she didn't want to press her attack and get pulled into a wrestling match with the man. At that point, he would probably just overpower her and that would be the end of it. She wanted him to attempt to stand. Then, she would rush him and batter him to a pulp with the baton. It was only a matter of time before she hit something vital.

She stepped menacingly towards the man on the ground, who was watching her closely and slowly retreating away, with the baton raised and ready to strike over her head. As soon as she stepped past the opening of the stairwell, the giant reappeared.

She felt his massive hand wrap around her ankle with a painful grip that threatened to crush the bones in her leg. Nicole didn't wait for the man to try and pull her off her feet before she struck. She brought the baton down hard on the man's exposed wrist like she was trying to chop right through it. That time, she was fairly certain she broke something by the way the man cried out.

"Mother-!" he began to say but she cut him off when she kicked him in the face and smiled inwardly when the man stumbled down the stairs again.

However, the giant distracted her long enough for the smaller one to get back onto his feet. She turned back just in time to catch another fist across her cheek a second before his weight crashed into her. The blow dazed her long enough for the man to pivot inside her arm and slide her right underneath his own. When he was done, he had his back to her holding her right arm, with the baton, trapped snuggly in his armpit. She knew exactly what her attacker was doing. He wanted the baton, pure and simple. She couldn't let that happen, not under any circumstance.

Nicole sent two sharp uppercuts into his lower back, right where she guessed his kidneys would be, and she turned her fist inwards slightly to really dig her little knuckles into the meat of his back. *That worked,* she thought when he yelped a bit and his body tightened up with each blow.

Her attacker responded by elbowing her in the face with his free hand. Nicole winced away from the sharp pain, and her vision briefly filled with multi-colored stars that danced across her vision, tearing her attention from the here-and-now. She shook it off, and realized with some disappointment that this was only going to end one way, with her giving up that baton. In another second, his free hand would simply chop down his arm and free it from her grasp. She knew there was nothing she could do. After all, she'd done that move herself, many times in fact.

So, she released the baton from her grasp and let it clatter to a rest on the hardwood floors. With it gone, and practically forgotten, Nicole planted her boots on the floor and shoved the man forward into the already battered closet door with all of her might. Right before the point of impact, Nicole yanked her right arm out from the man's armpit. The man collided awkwardly into the closet. She didn't waste a second and savagely booted the back of the man's leg forcing him to his knees.

Now you're in trouble, she thought.

Leverage was no longer on this guy's side. His height and weight advantage had simply evaporated. She had him on his knees, pressed against the closet door. There was nowhere for him to go, and no way for him to maneuver out of this.

Behind him, she towered over him like a vengeful God

She grabbed the back of his collar with both hands, yanked it back hard, before reversing her direction and ramming him uselessly into the closet door, just to keep him off balance, as she lined up her knee. She pulled him back again, thrust her knee hard into the meat of his back, and when he tightened up, she gave him a quick elbow into the side of his head. The man in her grasp yelped painfully and tried to strike back at her, but when he did, she simply shoved him back into the closet door and pressed her weight into him. Then she started the process all over again, this time she hit the other side.

"You broke into the wrong goddamn house, idiot!" she taunted him as she bounced his head off the closet door again.

The man in her grasp was flailing weakly now, he didn't have much left to give towards his defence. She felt for him, she was running pretty much on rage alone herself. She knew she was leaking blood everywhere, she could feel it running freely down her chin as she slammed her idiot attacker into the door one more time. She snarled at him as she rammed her knee into his spine.

Then she felt it.

A tremor tickled the bottom of her feet as it vibrated up from the floorboards. Nicole knew immediately what it was, and for some reason, thought of Jurassic Park when she felt it. Before she could react, the giant's massive arm hooked around her chest, and simply hoisted her off her feet, like a parent who was separating their aggressive child from another.

Just like that, Nicole was flying.

The strange calm that came with the feeling of weightlessness only lasted long enough for her to appreciate it. Then it was ripped from her when her body crashed into the wall at the other end of the hallway, and gravity pulled her roughly down to the floor.

Get up, something inside her screamed. In that moment, she knew it was probably the worse thing she could do for herself. God only knows what she broke when she hit that wall, but her survival instinct told her that was a problem for later. Right now, she was still in danger. She had to deal with that first. She could worry about what's bleeding or broken later. She grunted hoarsely as she fought to rise herself up to her hands and knees, fully intending to stand, but before she could get any further, she felt the thunderous tremors in her gut again.

Then the kick came.

It felt like someone had hit her in the ribs with a large log. Her whole chest compressed painfully before her body was lifted up into the air again, and the force of the blow rebounded her off the wall a second time. Nicole was sure she felt something crack, a few things actually. Again, gravity cruelly pulled her to the floor. Nicole laid there face down, and just struggled to breathe. Something inside her was broken, she felt it. This was the end for her. She had put up a good fight, and lost. It happens. All that was left was for her to decide how she would spend her last few moments before the darkness at the edges of her vision finally claimed her.

Nicole growled savagely and bit back the pain in her ribs as she got her shaking limbs underneath herself and lifted herself off the ground.

That's my girl, her father said from the blackness that was slowly creeping in.

"You broke my fucking arm!" the giant yelled at her indignantly, like an angry child would, from somewhere above her.

Nicole painfully craned her neck to look the man in the face. Her vision swam dangerously and she had trouble focusing on him, but she still managed to flash her bloodied teeth in a satisfied smile.

"Fuck...you," she said breathlessly and then inexplicably chuckled a bit.

She saw the giant's impossibly large boot come up, and watched helplessly as it came down.

Bringing the darkness with it.

***

"Nic?" she heard a voice softly call her name from the entrance to her hospital room. "Nic? Are you awake?"

She was. She had been awake all morning, but there was little else to do but watch episodes of Judge Judy on the shitty little television that was mounted to the wall by her head, or sleep. Either way, no matter what she was doing, she would be doing it with the constant fiery aches from her injuries. Until the afternoon, that is. That's when the nurse came around with her pain medication. After that point, she could let herself fall into the pain-free stupor of the medication.

Nicole opened her eyes, and tilted her head towards the door. Her left eye was still horribly swollen, but at least she could still see out of it.

She should have recognized the voice. When she looked, she immediately recognized Matthew Lapointe, a colleague from her days in the Toronto Police Service. Like her, he was working his way towards fifty, and was starting a bit of a paunch around his mid-section. His dark hair had a bit of salt that started to accumulate around the sides of his head.

"Hey, Matt." She weakly waved her friend into the room.

She watched as a younger man she didn't recognize followed Matt into her room. She was also quick to note the young man had his duty-book out and ready.

"I'm assuming this isn't a social call," she said with her raspy voice as she motioned to the book in the junior detective's hand. The look of anguish on his face confirmed that she still looked just as bad as she felt.

"I wish it was," Matt said remorsefully. "The captain is on my ass to get ahead of this thing as soon as I can. If you're not up to be interviewed right now, Nic, just say it and I'll kick junior to the curb here, grab us some coffees, and we can bullshit about the *good ole days*." Nicole just chuckled dryly, and the pain from her ribs seized her body up. By the sheepish look that was on his face, Nicole could see he wanted to get the details of her assault, what few still remained inside her head, but he loathed to push her on it too much.

"No, It's fine." She quickly waved him off. "I understand. Tell you what, you hand me that cup of water over there," she said and gestured weakly to the trolley off to the side with the plain white plastic cup with the straw poking out of the top of it. "And I'll answer any questions you have," she said, but then quickly added, "What I can remember of it anyway. Everything is still kind of... foggy."

"No, I completely understand." Matt hurried over to the cup to retrieve it. "I don't want to rush you, but any details you could give us right now would be a huge help. We have the patrol guys canvassing the neighborhood. We might be able to pull a few usable leads from that, but you know as well as I do." Matt continued as he took the cup into the bathroom to refill it with fresh water. He even let the cold water run for a bit before he refilled her cup. "Anything of real value is going to come from the victims." Nicole winced slightly at the word, *victim*. It left a bad taste in her mouth. It wasn't Matt's fault, though. "So, anything you can tell us, at this point, would be very helpful."

He was always a good guy, Nicole thought warmly of him as he brought her a fresh cup of cool water.

"If you don't mind?"

"Of course," she agreed quickly and took the offered cup from Matt. She eased the straw into her lips and took a couple big sips to rinse out her mouth, and cool her sore throat. "Shit, that's good. Thank you." She noisily cleared her throat before she took another sip. "To be honest, Matt." She looked at him with a teasing expression. "I'm surprised it's you interviewing me, I didn't peg you for Robbery Division." Anyone who knew Matt Lapointe would have gotten the joke, but the two officers in front of her didn't crack a single smile.

"What?" she asked cautiously.

"This has been bumped up to Major Crimes, Nic." Matt regarded her with a saddened face. "Your male friend, Dale Petersen," Matt read his name off dispassionately from memory, and Nicole feared the worst. "He suffered a heart attack at some point during the assault." Matt must have seen her expression drop, because he was quick to add, "He's not dead, but the doctors say his brain was starved of oxygen for a time." Matt took a deep breath and ripped the band-aid off for her. "They think there might be some brain damage, but they won't know the extent of it until he wakes up. He's still in a coma," Matt explained slowly, giving her time to soak in the implications of what he was saying. His last words unintentionally added salt to her numerous wounds. "I'm sorry, Nic."

CHAPTER 18

Zeke

Zeke got the message from Kevin shortly after midnight. He had been waiting for it for the last two hours. He spent that time sitting in a darkened room in his shitty little townhouse with the stereo softly playing in the background, while the noises of the city were sounding off in the foreground. So, when the text came through, he didn't miss it.

The job's done. We had problems.

It was a simple message that exemplified Kevin's nature.

The plan was to meet at the office in the morning and go over what Kevin, Levi, and Khan had found in the social worker's house. The woman the Burke fellow gave up, Nicole Jones, worked in the social services building downtown, which was unfortunate. There were three ways they could retrieve that information. Breaking into the woman's house had been Kevin's idea, and represented the lesser of the three evils.

Breaking into a government office downtown was impractical, to say the least. Kidnapping the woman, and getting the information from her directly was, by far, the quickest and easiest way Zeke could see to solving the problem. Even he couldn't deny a missing social worker would raise questions though, and there weren't many degrees of separation between him and Nicole Jones. It wouldn't take a Sherlock Holmes to connect those dots.

Break-ins, however, happen all the time within the Greater Toronto Area. Kevin advised they would toss the place, take what they needed, and disguise it as a sloppy burglary. He made it seem simple, but the problem with Kevin's approach, as always, was that it would take time. It was infuriating. Any other time, he probably would have easily agreed to Kevin's approach, but when it came to his precious little Belle, Zeke felt like he had already wasted a lifetime just finding her the first time. Each day without knowing her whereabouts felt like a knife slowly sliding into his flesh.

He had to relent though, because Kevin was right.

However, that didn't mean he had to idly wait in his noisy little townhouse until tomorrow to find out exactly what *problems* occurred during the heist.

Before he even entered the building through the rear entrance, Zeke knew something was wrong. He could hear the three men bickering at each other like old women.

"Just hold still, you big dummy!" he heard Kevin hoarsely command.

"Fuck you, man! I'm in a lot of pain here," Levi replied angrily.

Zeke stepped out from behind the large SUV that was parked in its usual spot. Khan was the first to see him arrive, and Zeke didn't like the nervous way he was smoking his cigarette, nor did he like the shocked look he gave Zeke before he quickly returned his gaze to whatever he was looking at.

"Okay, here we go. One, two, thr-," Kevin said loudly just as Zeke came around the back corner of the SUV in time to hear the sickeningly wet sound reminiscent of knuckles cracking. Except this time, it was Kevin forcibly readjusting Levi's broken nose.

Kevin stood over the man's large form as he flinched from the sudden jolt of pain.

When he was done, Kevin limped back painfully while Levi promptly brought the towel that was in his hand up to his nose and blew out a thick wad of dark, clotted blood. He winced painfully when he did too. The whole scene in front of him looked like the triage from a war movie, bloodied towels littered the top of the coffee table, along with a first-aid kit that had been torn into like a wild animal had gotten into it.

"Wat da fuck?" Zeke called out loudly, and spread his arms around the area with equal parts distain and surprise.

Kevin turned around like he was having trouble just standing up, and when he finally managed to turn to face him, Zeke could see he wasn't doing too great himself. By the swelling, and the two black-eyes, Zeke guessed Kevin had his nose broken as well, but if he did, it wasn't nearly as bad as Levi's. The big man just looked at Zeke with an sunken expression but remained silent as he reached out and grabbed an emergency icepack off the table. It was the kind paramedics used. Levi pulled it out of the wrapper, sharply compressed it, and placed the pack tenderly on his face as he leaned back in his chair. It didn't escape Zeke's attention the large man did the entire thing with his left hand, while his right was nestled tightly to his side.

Zeke looked at Kevin expectantly.

"We had problems."

"Yeah, I can see dat. Were you going to tell me a *social worker* did this? To da two of you?" Zeke quickly looked to Khan again, and as he suspected, the man was unharmed. Though, at the moment, that fact didn't seem to give him any satisfaction.

"That *bitch* was no social worker!" Levi said defiantly from underneath the icepack that was covering his bruised, swollen, and bloodied face. "Stop calling her that." Then he continued to mutter loudly. "Some *psycho-commando-ninja bitch*, or something, but she wasn't a damned *social worker*. I've never seen a *social worker* that could fight like that. Fuck me, it was like Bruce Lee came back from the dead and grew tits. She broke my goddamn arm!" he said bitterly to remind them.

Zeke looked back to Kevin with an unimpressed expression and a raised eyebrow.

"We were interrupted," he said calmly before tilting his head towards Khan, because apparently turning right to face the man wasn't an option for him right now. "Because *some fucking-idiot* had to take a piss!"

"It wasn't *my* fault! I had been holding it for over an hour," Khan whined loudly and took another deep drag off his cigarette. "What the hell was I supposed to do?" Kevin painfully readjusted himself so he could glare at Khan.

"You were *supposed* to fucking wait until we got back. You were *supposed* to signal us if she returned, *which she did*, so we could hustle our asses out of there, instead of being caught with our *dicks* out."

"I was only gone for five minutes," Khan shot back. Zeke could only shake his head at the man's stubbornness.

"Yeah, *you raging asshole*! That's all the time it took for things to go to shit." Kevin angrily chopped his hand in the man's direction. "All because you couldn't do your fucking job. So, do yourself a favor and just shut-the-fuck-up, please." Kevin turned back to Zeke and went to pinch the bridge of his nose in frustration, but then remembered his injuries. Instead, he gently ran his thumb and forefinger up and down the bridge of his nose before he gave him a quizzical expression. "How is it? Is it straight?" he asked inquiring about his nose. Zeke leaned in and peered at the swollen, discolored flesh around the affected area.

"I tink so," he said unconvincingly. "As far as I can tell, anyway." He leaned back and switched gears. "Was it just er?"

"She had a date with her." Kevin probably read the expression on Zeke's face, because he slowly shook his head. "He wasn't the problem. I had him taken care of almost immediately when he came upstairs. No," Kevin sighed. "This was all the social worker." Kevin gestured over his hunched over, pained frame with obvious frustration, and maybe even a little shame mixed in.

"No goddamn *social worker* fights like that," Levi muttered quietly to himself underneath his icepack.

"Apparently, Dis one does, eh?" Zeke posed the question to Kevin with some amusement. Kevin only snorted.

"She had a steel baton with her, the same kind the cops use, and she knew how to use it, too." Kevin was dangerously close to sounding impressed with the woman. "Levi slammed her ass into a door, and she thanked him by throwing him down the stairs. I did marginally better, but between the two of us, we eventually wore her down." Zeke shot him an incredulous look and threw the man's words back at him.

"*Eventually wore her down?* Sounds to me like I sould be putting er on da payroll. Jesus Christ, guys." Zeke said with muted disappointment. They were supposed to be professionals, after all.

"If you can afford her, it probably wouldn't be a bad idea," Kevin joked bitterly.

"Great," Zeke replied sarcastically. "But we *did* get wat we went dere for in da first place, correct?" Thankfully, to that, Kevin nodded slowly and gestured back to the SUV.

"We got her laptop, the desktop computer from her office, as well as a shit-ton of files I thought might be relevant that I found in a file cabinet she had in her office." Kevin then nodded towards the SUV behind Zeke. "There's also a bag of shit we stole as well in the back."

He said it dismissively because Zeke knew the stolen goods were destined for disposal. Whatever items Kevin snatched were inevitably worthless to them. They were a ruse, a red-herring to draw the police's attention away from their true target, and served little purpose now, other than to connect him and his crew to the crime.

He then leveled Kevin with a hard look.

"Did you leave anyting behind?"

"Pessimistically," He began slowly, and Zeke could tell by his distant expression that Kevin was thinking back to the altercation with the social worker, this Jones woman. "Probably some DNA.

Like, the balaclavas should have soaked up most of it, but let's be real here. There's no way we could have a dust-up like that and *not* leave a little DNA somewhere. It's the little things that get you," he said, like Zeke needed to be reminded of that.

"Ow did you leave dem?" Zeke asked Kevin cautiously, meaning the Jones woman and her date, and he watched as Kevin's expression shifted, like he knew exactly why he wanted to know.

"I called the ambulance from my burner, for the guy." Kevin looked at him with an expression of suppressed regret. "He didn't look too hot, and his pulse was a little weak for my liking. The woman is going to spend a day or three in the hospital, I'm sure, but she'll pull through."

Zeke just nodded thoughtfully, and considered the problem in front of him.

"Hey," He called out to the bruised giant lumbering in the chair off to the side. "Is your DNA in the system?"

"Naw," Levi said quickly, and eased the icepack off his swollen face. "I've been printed, but never swabbed. Before you ask, yes, I was wearing my gloves the whole time I was in the house. So, we're good there."

"The military has my prints and DNA, but there's no way the feds will let the cops see those without a real good reason," Kevin said to reassure him. Though, Zeke didn't find it very reassuring.

"Ow about a retired cop-turned-social worker who was beaten witin an inch of er life, in er own ome? Is dat a good enough reason?" Zeke studied Kevin's face closely as he sheepishly considered his words.

"You think she was a cop?" Zeke just shrugged at the question.

"You tell me. You're da one wo said she had a police baton, and he's da one wo insists she wasn't just a *social worker*." Zeke gestured to the wounded giant in the chair. "Me? I don't know, for sure, but if it turns out dat she is, dat could be a problem for us."

He wasn't so worried about the police, they would investigate as best they could, and if Kevin was correct, there wouldn't be anything they could do with the scant evidence they may find. The

Organization, on the other hand, was a different beast entirely. The Organization tolerated the side-projects of its numerous members. What they didn't tolerate were disruptions to the supply chain, and unwanted attention from the law. This little episode reeked of amateurish bullshit, and it made him look bad.

Zeke had a meeting with The Barrister in a couple days to sign the purchase agreement of the site for the new lab. It was in Scarborough, which was farther away than he wanted, but it was just off the 401 Expressway that ran straight through the city, so that helped with the travel time for deliveries. Richard's training was coming along nicely. The last two cooks had been his from beginning to end. He was closely supervised by Remy, of course, but he had been in charge during the entire process. Things were falling into place for him, tonight's mess was a hiccup for sure, but he couldn't let this mishap affect their expansion.

"Okay," Zeke said quietly, thinking the problem over in his head. "So, it was a big fucking mess, dat is true, but it was a successful mess, correct?"

"Yes," Kevin said definitively. "Tomorrow, Khan can take the hard drives from the computers to our tech guy. We should have the files by the end of the day. After that, hopefully it's as simple as searching for the Lamoine girl's name and seeing what pops up. Keep in mind, Zeke." Kevin said softly, like he was breaking bad news to him. "This is a marathon, not a sprint. It might take some time to sift through all of it before we come up with an address."

Zeke raised an eyebrow at him.

"You tink I don't know dat?" he chuckled humorlessly at the man.

"It's just," Kevin started to say, but then reconsidered his words for a moment before he started up again. "I know how *important* this is to you." Zeke nodded slowly, both agreeing to the statement, and giving Kevin permission to continue. His eyes, however, told him to tread carefully. "I'll get you that address, boss, I swear. I just need a little more time." Zeke smiled at him, and gently placed his hand reassuringly on Kevin's shoulder.

"I know you will," he said darkly. "Because you're da one who lost my little angel in da first place." Zeke gave him a little grin before he removed his hand. "You're *motivated*." He paused and let the threat hang subtly in the air between them. Kevin signaled his understanding by nodding his head almost imperceivably. Only then did Zeke continue on to other, more pressing matters. "Do we need Da Doctor?" he asked with some disdain after he gave his injured men another assessing glance.

The Doctor, was a divorced veterinarian with a gambling problem. If you talked to the man, he would insist his only problem is that he was unlucky. Zeke knew the type. As long as their vice was manageable, they could delude themselves they had some measure of control over it. It was an addict's fantasy. As far as Zeke was concerned, any vice that was bad enough to lead you to him, was bad enough to be concerned about. He didn't operate in half-measures, people like Dr. Craig Willison were either in his pocket, or they weren't. The people in his pocket, Zeke owned. Body and soul. They might not know the true extent. Like Willison, the opportunity to educate them on their circumstances may not have presented itself, and as long as they continued to stay in line, that day need never arrive.

"Please," Kevin said quickly and with some relief. "We're going to need x-rays. Levi's going to need a cast on his arm, and I got something broken in here." Kevin gestured to his abdomen. "Probably a rib or something. Plus, that bitch kneed me in the lower back pretty good. It fucking hurts to just stand, and I don't even want to imagine what this is going to feel like tomorrow."

"Well, look on da bright side, chiropractors are cheap. Khan!" Zeke waited until the man looked in his direction before he fished the keys for his little shitbox and tossed them to him. "Load up *Free Willy* dere, and pull up to da back door."

Khan didn't need to be told twice. By the way he hurried towards the lumbering, injured giant, Zeke suspected that Khan was more than eager to be leaving. As he should, he fucked up large tonight. Luckily for Khan, Levi didn't need much assistance, or motivation, to leave either. Zeke maintained his cold stare on Kevin the entire time the other two made their way to the rear exit, he waited until the door closed before he spoke.

"I want to say good job, Kevin, but I'm finding it ard. Dis was supposed to be quiet, and clean." Zeke ran his gaze over the plethora of bloodied rags strewn about the coffee table with muted frustration. "*Dis?* Dis isn't clean."

"I know. I know this is bad." Kevin weakly patted the air between them, and briefly lost his balance. He caught himself, but Zeke could see it cost him a bit of pain. He sighed.

"Well, I don't know if I would go as far as to say it's *bad*. It's not good, but it's not dat bad eiter. It's manageable." Zeke sighed again loudly, and held up a single digit between himself and Kevin. "You have one month," he said gravely. "I ave a ton of bullshit to contend wit over our new acquisition."

Meaning the new lab site in Scarborough. There were a ton of details that had to be finalized, equipment that had to be setup, and supplies that had to be acquired. Zeke had a timeline in mind.

"Before dat mont is up, I want your eyes on my angel. I want you to fucking *see* er wit your *own* goddamn eyes." Zeke's finger shook slightly as he hissed the words out. He couldn't help it; he needed Kevin to understand. "Do dat, and all will be forgiven. Do you understand?" he asked him slowly while looking down his nose at the man.

The paradox of muscle in a criminal organization was that you needed people who did the dirty work, amoral individuals who didn't shy away from violence like regular people. But how do you control such people? After all, these are the same people you hired to keep other people in line, how do you keep those same people from straying towards their own ambitions? In the criminal world, there were negative control measures, and positive ones. It's easy to lean towards the negative side of things. To just beat down and threaten your muscle into line. That worked, to a point, but it only worked on weak-minded idiots. Some lean towards the positive side of things, and showered their muscle with money, drugs, or women. Zeke liked to play both sides of the field. With Kevin, he paid him extremely well, with clean money, but he also was sure to inform the man that he knew where every living member of his immediate family was. Every year, each of them received a fifty-dollar gift card in the mail from *Uncle Zeke* for Christmas.

Zeke was sure Kevin was thinking of them before he spoke.

"Yes." He could tell by Kevin's dour expression that he meant it.

"Good," Zeke said with a sudden lightness in his voice, like the unfortunate matter between them had been settled. "Get going." He stepped aside and gestured towards the exit. "I'll call da doc, He'll be waiting for you when you get dere. He'll get you fixed up. Den you two should lay low for a couple of days to eal up."

"We're going to stay here tonight," Kevin said, like the decision was made long ago, and hobbled towards the door. Zeke fell in close behind him. "We can heal up here, and then at least we can get a jump start on the files in the morning."

"Good man. I'll clean up the mess around here," Zeke said reassuringly and kept pace with Kevin towards the rear door. "I'll set up the cots in the offices for you guys too." He scooted in front of Kevin to open and hold the door for Kevin to walk through.

"Sounds good," Kevin said as he passed by him and his way to the idling vehicle. "See you soon."

With that Zeke let the door close on its own accord, walked back to the couch and chairs, and started to absently tidy up the area. He did this with a little grin on his face because a little voice in the back of his mind kept singing the same phrase over and over in his mind as he worked.

I'm going to get my angel back for Christmas.
I'm going to get my angel back for Christmas.
I'm going to get my angel back!

CHAPTER 19

Belle

Belle followed Brooke into the Russell convenience store. It was mid-October, and the east wind cooled her damp head in the short walk from the car to the door. There was no sign of snow yet, and Belle prayed it would hold off until after Halloween. Brooke said she would take her and Lucas trick-or-treating around Binscarth. Belle was thinking of asking another girl from her class if she would like to come as well.

She was still on the fence.

"Hey, Brooke!" Mr. Johnson said with some surprise in his voice, like he wasn't expecting her or something.

She gave the aging man a quick wave as she moved with a definite purpose towards the small coffee counter.

"And who do we have here?" he asked with a measure of concern when he spotted her coming through the door. "Another of Russell's youth, coming to rob me blind. Oh, I got my eye on you, little missy."

"Jesus Christ, Hank. Give a girl a break, it's been months." Brooke didn't even look back as she spoke with a bored cadence. "The only thing that girl steals now are hearts and minds."

"Hello, Mr. Johnson." She smirked, trying to sound polite.

"Hello, Isabelle." He looked down at her and gave her a friendly grin. "I'm just giving you a hard time," he said with a quick wink. "I know you're a good kid. Hey, why's your hair wet?" Mr. Johnson pointed to her damp hair that still hung close to her scalp and neck.

"Swimming lessons," Belle said and promptly shrugged.

"You don't know how to swim?" he asked softly and scratched his clean-shaven chin. Mr. Johnson wore the same tan-colored slacks, white button-up shirt, and nametag he always wore when he was working. Belle had also never seen the man with even a hint of stubble on his face.

"Nope," Belle replied absently. She was looking at her picture on Mr. Johnson's board.

Her eyes were attracted to it every time she came here. She felt the familiar sting of shame, but lately she started to wish that she could add that picture to her growing collection of photos Emmett had given her. She had so many, Emmett bought her a flowery-covered photo album to put them all in. She had other pictures of Emmett, but she wanted *that* one. That was the first picture they took together. Sure, it wasn't a great picture, but it was still special.

"Hmm. Do you like it?"

Belle shrugged and looked at him with a sly grin.

"I like it better than drowning," she said as a joke. From her side, Brooke let out a sharp laugh before she approached the counter.

"She's got you there, Hank." Brooke chuckled a bit more as she put her coffee cup down.

"I see you've been hanging out with *this one* too much," Mr. Johnson said to her with some humor and thumbed towards Brooke.

"What? Nonsense!" she said dramatically. "I'm a delight. I just have to use the washroom; I'll be right back." Brooke turned quickly and left her and Mr. Johnson staring at her coffee. Again, Belle's eyes drifted to her photo.

"Say," she began nervously. "Say I wanted to get that picture over there," she said and pointed towards her picture on the board. Mr. Johnson followed her finger, smiled and then looked back to her with a renewed interest in the conversation. "How would I go about getting it?" She shifted on her feet a bit before she looked the man in the eye.

"Well now, I suppose I could be convinced to sell it? Given the price was right, mind you." He suddenly looked at the picture with a thoughtful expression, like he was coming up with a price in his head. Belle figured she better ask the next obvious question before he thought about it too much.

"How much?" she asked. She didn't like the way Mr. Johnson chuckled.

"You tell me. You're the one who wants to buy it. What's it *worth* to you?" Belle looked at him with a stunned expression. She knew it was a trick. It was easy to tell by the keen way he was looking at her.

"It's worth *a lot* to me," she said simply. Mr. Johnson nodded his head.

"Tell you what," Mr. Johnson said lightly and pointed a friendly finger at her. "And this is only because I like you so much, but if you want, and are able, I suppose I could be convinced to hire you on. Part-time, of course." He then crossed his arms in front of his skinny chest and looked down his nose at her. "I'll pay you a penny a minute."

Wow, that is not a lot. Belle gave him a look, even she knew people make much more than that.

"That's sixty cents an hour. That bag of candy cost two-fifty-nine, but because I like you, I'll round that down to an even two-forty. At sixty cents an hour, that means you would have to work how long before you paid off your debt?" He snapped his finger and pointed to her to answer the question.

"Four hours," she answered quickly and narrowed her eyes at him.

"Clever girl," he said, nodding appreciatively.

"What would I even do?"

"I got a whole parking lot out there that needs cleaning. You could probably spend all four hours just picking up cigarette butts. Plus, I got a bathroom that needs cleaning. Ugh, it *always* needs cleaning. Maybe do some sweeping. You let me worry about what you'll do. I don't have to look very far around here to find something to do, believe me." By the exasperated look on his face when he said it, she believed it. "You just worry about how you're going to get here and back." To that, Belle had the perfect solution.

"I have swimming lessons Mondays and Fridays, I could come here after for a bit. Will that work?"

She knew she would have to clear it with Brooke, but she couldn't see it being a problem. She could work after her lessons for a bit, and then Brooke could drive her home for dinner. If she played her cards right, she could do this without Emmett ever knowing.

"Works for me. Make sure to clear it with Emmett, of course, but if you're willing to put in the effort, I think we can come to an arrangement," Mr. Johnson said with a proud smile before he reached across the counter and offered his hand to her.

Belle returned the smile and quickly shook the offered hand.

"Yikes, I don't think I like the looks of this," Brooke said lightly, as a joke, when she approached.

"I got a job," Belle turned and said excitedly.

"What!? How did you manage to get a job in the time it took for me to pee?" she asked with an impressed look of shock on her face that made Belle giggle a bit.

"As long as it passes muster with Emmett," he cut in and cautioned gently. "Don't forget that part." The two girls both gave the man a look, but only Brooke spoke.

"*Passes muster*? Jeez, Hank, you're really showing your age with *that* one." Brooke gave him a friendly smile and a quick wink before she turned back to Belle. "So, how much are you making?" Brooke asked her lightly.

"Sixty cents an hour."

Brooke snorted loudly.

"Oof! We need to work on your negotiating skills, girlie." Brooke looked to Mr. Johnson who nodded towards the picture board. "Ah! I see. You're working to get your picture off the board. Good for you."

"I thought so too," Mr. Johnson quickly agreed. He then flashed a wide grin at Brooke. "Apparently, some girls have better sense than to just snatch their picture off my board and run out the door when I'm not looking." He leveled a knowing look at Brooke. Belle let out a loud gasp and looked to Brooke with an amused expression.

"Wow," Brooke said with comical disbelief. "Just wow, Hank. Way to throw a girl under the bus."

"You did that?!" Belle chirped.

"In my defence," Brooke replied quickly and looked at her. "I didn't think I would get caught."

"*That's* your defence," Mr. Johnson chuckled. "I have cameras, you know."

"Yeah," Brooke answered as she turned back to him and waved off the comment. "But I didn't think you actually checked them."

"You're the *reason* I started checking them."

"Well, now you're just being dramatic. *Anyways*," Brooke said quickly to change the topic. Belle wasn't sure, but she thought Brooke might be blushing. "I need fifty dollars of regular on pump two, as well as my coffee. Unless, of course, there's some more embarrassing fun-facts from my childhood you'd like to reveal?" Mr. Johnson let out a little chuckle and smiled warmly.

'No, I think I'll save some for next time."

They finished their business and each of them said their good-byes before she and Brooke filed out of the store. On the way home, Belle explained her plan to her.

"Is it okay if we don't tell Emmett. I want to surprise him." She looked hopefully to Brooke as she drove her little car down the highway.

"Yeah, I think we can keep this on the down-low."

At first, Belle thought it would take a long time to work off her debt with Mr. Johnson, but it only took two weeks. As planned, after her swimming lessons, Brooke would drop Belle off at the store and retire to the lounge at the Russell Inn to play the VLT's until Belle's shift was up. Mr. Johnson had originally thought she would only work a half hour each day, it was Belle who decided to lengthen her shift to a full hour. That way, she could work off her debt in half the time. Mr. Johnson didn't mind, and there was definitely enough work to fill the hour.

She usually spent the first half hour concentrating on the chores outside. She walked the parking lot and the perimeter of the store with a little broom and a dustpan. She scoured the area in search of cigarette butts and various pieces of trash. Everything she came across went into the dustpan. When the dustpan was full, she would empty it into the trash can at the front of the store. When that was done, she went around and emptied all the trash bins that were more than half-full. The bags went into the dumpster at the rear of the store. When that was completed, she was to refill the washer buckets by the gas pumps.

Inside the store, there were the bathrooms that always needed to be cleaned. Belle liked that job the least ever since she went into the men's bathroom and found a fresh turd waiting for her in the toilet bowl.

Boys are so gross, she thought when she flushed the turd down.

To her disappointment, women weren't much better. Belle usually finished her shift by taking the large mat by the front door and hauling it to the back for a good shaking before she quickly swept the entire tiled floor of the store. Brooke usually came to retrieve her just as she was finishing up with the floors.

Some days, Mr. Johnson would let her take a small slushie home. Belle quickly found out the kindly old man was a pretty good boss. Every shift, before she went home, Belle always stole a glance towards the picture she was working towards. Each time she did, her eyes would drift to the one beside hers, to Lucas's.

She knew the story of how he came to be on that board. Lucas's asshole cousins, Paul and Charlie, the same two jerks who bullied Lucas at school and pulled out her braid, were the same two boys who tricked Lucas into taking something without paying for it. It wasn't even stealing, not really. She should know because she was an actual thief, and that fact burned her when she looked upon Lucas's horribly weeping visage in that picture.

On her expected last day, Brooke arrived after Belle replaced the broom and dustpan back into the storage room, Mr. Johnson looked almost proud as he watched her approach the counter.

"Well, little Miss Lamoine," he said his nickname for her with some affection from behind his counter. "I guess today is the big day, eh?"

"Yep," Belle said proudly.

"I'm not going to lie; it's been kind of nice having the help around here. God knows the Missus is going to miss having you around. She's taken a bit of a liking to you." He genuinely looked sad as Mr. Johnson turned to his picture board and reached for her picture.

"I wouldn't worry too much about that," Isabelle said slyly. "Oh, not that one Mr. Johnson." She gently corrected the man when he unpinned her picture from the board.

"Huh?" He looked at the picture to confirm he had picked the right one, and then looked at her confused.

Belle just smiled.

"I want Lucas's picture," she said and pointed to the weeping picture of her good friend.

"Am I missing something here?" He looked to the picture again, then to her, and then he finally shifted his confused expression to Brooke.

"Don't look at me," Brooke quickly said and retreated away a small step. "I don't know what's going on either."

"You said if I worked four hours, I could buy one of the pictures off the board."

"Well, sure, but that was for *your* picture." He wagged her picture in front of her.

"Yeah, but now I want Lucas's picture. You *don't play favorites*, right? So, one picture should be the same as all the others. So, it shouldn't really matter which picture I choose." It was at this point Belle looked at him with a mildly challenging expression as she explained her logic. "So, I choose Lucas's."

"But why, sweetie?" Brooke broke in and placed a hand on her shoulder. "I think that's the part we're having trouble with."

With that, Belle gave both Brooke and Mr. Johnson a serious look, one that hopefully conveyed she wasn't just being silly or something.

"Because Lucas isn't a thief," she said defiantly. "He never was. Me? I stole that candy, and if I didn't get caught..." She paused because this next part was harder to admit. "I would probably have done it again," she said with obvious shame. "Lucas doesn't deserve to be up there, I do. At least, for a little while longer." Belle softened her tone, and shifted herself nervously on her feet as she spoke next. "I was kind of hoping I could keep working here for another four hours for mine."

"Huh," Mr. Johnson sighed and idly slapped her picture against his free hand a few times as he looked at her incredulously. It didn't last, though. He soon nodded to himself and returned her picture to the board, and instead, he removed Lucas's picture and slowly handed it to her. "I think that is a wonderful idea." After Belle took the picture from him, he added, "You be sure to give young Mr. Adler my best when you give this to him."

"I will," Belle said, smiled, and then looked down at the tiny treasure in her hand. *Lucas is going to freak when he sees this,* she thought warmly to herself. "Thanks."

"You know, I may not *play favorites*," Mr. Johnson said, gently mocking his own saying. "But you keep this up," he said almost like he was warning her of something. "And you may just become my favorite little person."

"So, I can have a small slushie to go?"

Brooke chuckled beside her.

"That's my girl," she said and Mr. Johnson let a mild laugh escape him as well.

"Fine!" he said with mock exasperation, like she had worn him down. "Get going." He chuckled again and waved her towards the slushie machine.

Isabelle didn't have to be told twice.

On the way home, Belle occupied herself by nestling Lucas's picture in her small hands, and imagining how he will react when she gave it too him at school on Monday. That is, until Brooke reached over and playfully punched her in the arm.

"Ow!" she said dramatically, even though it really didn't hurt at all, and looked in Brooke's direction, taken aback. "What was *that* for?"

"You did a good thing back there," she said softly with a weird little grin on her face. "I'm proud of you."

"So, you punched me in the arm?!"

"Yeah, well, I can't hug you while I'm *driving*, can I?" Brooke gave her a quick look and flashed her a smile. "So, I did the next best thing." Isabelle gave her a dumbfounded expression and held it until Brooke looked at her again. "What? I'm not good at expressing affection, sue me."

Belle briefly looked at her warmly as Brooke peered out at the road ahead of them, before she tore her gaze away. She knew Brooke liked her, but this was the first time she ever admitted to being proud of her. Belle liked the feeling the knowledge manifested inside of her.

So, Belle leaned over and lightly punched Brooke in the arm.

"Neither am I," she said quietly.

CHAPTER 20

Brooke

Calvin was right, Emmett did tell her first about the *job* he had to do in Churchbridge, and just like he predicted, Emmett asked her to babysit. Brooke was quick to agree. She had three days to plan.

Brooke showed up at Emmett's place, and waited anxiously for fifteen minutes after he left to pack Isabelle into her car and drive her to Binscarth. Brooke had arranged for Isabelle to spend the afternoon baking cookies with her mother. Chocolate chip, of course. She made sure of that, no point having her bake cookies if they weren't going to be her favorite kind. Isabelle didn't care, she was just excited to be baking.

Her mother practically burst at the seams when they arrived. By the way her mother was fussing over her, Brooke almost felt bad for leaving Isabelle alone with her for the whole afternoon.

She had a plan though.

A mission, and she was going to see it through to the end. She was going to drive all the way to Churchbridge, find this CDA Productions place, and watch a bunch of hillbillies fight for money.

She didn't want to, but she had to know what was so important Emmett had to hide it from her and Isabelle. From how Calvin described it, Emmett had grown up in a fighting family. Carter was some sort of washed-up champion who passed his knowledge, and his insecurities by the looks of it, down to his children. She knew Calvin wanted to describe it as being noble, but Brooke had a hard time seeing it as anything but sad. Emmett was trapped in the same cycle of violence that ruined both his father, *and* his brother.

She didn't know if she could be with someone like that.

Her heart wouldn't be able to handle something like that. Since meeting Emmett, she felt the urge to give her heart to the man, but inside, she knew it was still a small, fragile thing, like a wounded bird that wasn't ready for the skies yet. She had to protect it from further injury. No matter how much her heart weakly cried out Emmett's name, she couldn't give it to him if he was just going to hurt it, and her, more. She knew what she needed. She needed safe, and Emmett wasn't safe. He felt right to her, *so incredibly right*, but he was still a gamble.

That's why she had to see what he was hiding from her.

Thanks to the map app on her phone, she found the place easy enough. Brooke gawked at the operation as she drove up to it. It was both exactly what she expected, but nothing like what she imagined it would be. She expected there to be a lot of pick-up trucks in the parking lot. She never imagined there would be parking attendants, who were carefully lining the vehicles up into neat little rows. She expected to pay an entrance fee, but she never imagined to see a well-constructed, heated, admissions booth. Nor did she expect the attendant to pull out the wireless Point-Of-Service machine so Brooke could pay the admission fee with her credit card.

Due to the frigid weather, the fights were being held inside a large Quonset that had several radiant heaters on the roof that were aimed towards the bleachers. Brooke made sure she changed her clothes at her parents' house when she dropped off Isabelle. She went with a simple pair of jeans, white sneakers, and a grey hoodie with an old jean jacket over top. Brooke tucked her hair into the back of the hoodie and pulled the hood over her head to further add to her weak little disguise.

She filed into the Quonset and immediately saw the raised, circular platform that had a large, black chain-link fence around it. The Ring. It stood out menacingly above the throng of people that were milling about idly, waiting for the festivities to begin. The air inside the building was thick with moisture and had the sticky-sweet scent of musk in it that tickled her nose a bit. Feeling like a stranger in a strange land, Brooke quickly made her way to one of the metal bleachers that were set up around the raised cage. She climbed to the very top and found an empty seat near the edge.

Brook was pleased to see all the steel posts inside the cage had a good amount of padding on them, as did the cross bar at the top. *It actually looks kind of professional,* Brooke thought to herself as she scanned the fenced-off fighting arena. From her position, Brooke spied several camera pods that were placed around the Quonset in elevated positions, aimed towards the center of the ring. Behind the people meandering around the ring was a curtained off section. Brooke couldn't help but think about the Wizard of Oz when she saw that thick velvet curtain that concealed the back portion of the building.

Why would anyone want to do this? Brooke wondered sourly as she watched the people walking the inside of the building with the food and drinks they purchased from the food truck that was prominently parked within the grounds. She watched them stuff their faces, and belch merrily with abandon. These were the people Emmett was risking his well-being to entertain. Brooke suddenly worried about how she would react if someone near her were to cheer when the boy she liked got punched in the face.

This is a mistake, she concluded suddenly and felt a strong urge to stand up, walk back to her car, and pretend this stupid idea never entered her head. Calvin's words kept her there. *A means to an end,* he had said. *He doesn't love it like Tommy did.* It wasn't just the words, but also the *way* he said it. Like Calvin didn't like it anymore than she did, but he knew the reality of Emmett's situation better than she did. He knew *Emmett* better than she did. She was mature enough to suspect maybe that played a part in this little venture, as well. She had always been a tad possessive over the boys she had liked in the past. Apparently, a horrible heart break hadn't change that.

She had to know.

If asked, she knew she wouldn't be able to explain what she was looking for exactly, but she felt in her gut she would recognize what she *didn't* want to see.

She had seen Tommy fight once. It was at a bush party before the end of grade eleven, and a group of people from her school hid themselves away in Russell Thibadeau's back field for a big fire, and a little drinking. Brooke had been there with Graeme, they were socializing with his friends when it happened. She never saw what caused it, she just heard the gasp from the crowd. When she turned, Tommy's opponent was already falling towards the ground. By the stiff way the boy fell to the ground, everyone knew that the fight was over. That didn't stop Tommy though. He leapt on top of the punch-drunk kid like a jungle cat and started raining blows down upon his face. Brooke would never forget the look of wicked glee on Tommy's face as he beat the kid to a pulp. True to his word, it had been Calvin who finally pulled Tommy off the poor kid. By then, people groaned in horror at the kids broken and bloodied face. Rumor had it, that kid spent the rest of the summer recovering from his injuries.

Brooke knew if she saw *that* look on Emmett's face, it would crush her, because that would be the end of *them*. She didn't want that, *but* she had to know.

A three-minute warning blared over the loudspeakers signalling to the spectators that it was time for them to find their seats.

The first couple of fights were pretty much what she expected to see. Lean farmer kids in jeans and bare feet attacking each other like nervous cats. They would slowly edge closer to each other, fire off a flurry of blows at each other, and then hop back away to safety. Sometimes, those wild attacks would actually connect, and the crowd would groan collectively, as if they all felt the blow. After the first couple of warm-up fights, the fighters started to get larger, bulkier, and more aggressive. These pudgy contestants still wore jeans and were bare foot, but these men were more accustomed to violence, and stood in the middle of the ring battering each other with hard blows that were meant to do damage.

Brooke cringed when one man leaned into a vicious swinging blow and the other man's fist connected solidly with the front of his face. Blood erupted from his nose as the man stumbled to the ground. Thankfully, that fight promptly ended after it became clear the man could no longer defend himself. Brooke watched as the man's friends helped him back to the curtained section at the end.

Each fight had a five-minute intermission that preceded it. Brooke suspected this was so the management could prepare for the next bout, but she also felt it was so the spectators could refill their drinks and buy more snacks. She only left her seat after the fourth intermission to pee. Other than that, Brooke remained in her seat. She didn't want to risk running into somebody she knew; it was always a possibility in rural communities. Worse yet, she couldn't risk running into Emmett for whatever reason.

Emmett's fight was the last fight of the day.

When the invisible announcer called out the coming main event, the crowd cheered uproariously. Brooke sat up in her seat when the first man was announced, Emmett's opponent.

Like the others, they didn't call out the competitor's real name, but rather some pseudonym that fighter came up with. This man liked to refer to himself as *The Mauler*. To Brooke, the name sounded a bit too rapey for her liking. Apparently, this person had travelled all the way from Brandon to fight Emmett. She watched with great interest as the big, burley man stepped up the stairs into the ring, and merrily trotted around it, waving his arms like he had already won the fight. He wore silky blue trunks with white trim, and nothing else except the padded gloves on his hands. The crowd then grew silent as the announcer called out the next fighter. Emmett.

"You know him! You love him! He's the man you all came to see! THE ONE! THE ONLY! THE-UNSTOPPABLE-KIIINNNNNGGGGG!!!!!"

The crowd's response was immediate, and deafening. Everyone in the bleachers rose to their feet, and the incredible noise inside the small building caused her ears to ring for a short period.

This is for Emmett, she thought to herself, dumbstruck by the sheer magnitude of the response. *All this, was for him.*

She could see how this could be intoxicating. How all this could be hard to walk away from. Outside this place, he was kind, unassuming, and often misunderstood Emmett Brooks. Here, in this place, he was apparently so much more to these people who now screamed his fake name with wild admiration. Here, he was a king.

Brooke rose up and even stood on her seat in order to see over the men in front of her.

There he is, she said to herself when she first saw him. *Oh Jesus!* She then thought a little bashfully. *There he is!*

She couldn't help the heated flush that blossomed in her cheeks when she saw Emmett approach the ring, shirtless, with an unassuming pair of grey sweats. Emmett was a large man, she knew that, but she had no idea how beautifully shaped that body was underneath all those clothes he usually wears. He was incredibly muscular, and all those big muscles had just enough fat to softened the hard edges of them. She watched keenly as Emmett walked slowly to the ring, and climb the small staircase to enter. He quickly made his way over to his corner, marked with a colored semi-circle on one side of the mat. She leered at him as he stood on the circle and stretched out his wide shoulders. She bit her lip when she saw the muscles on his arms and shoulders flex in a way that she found *very* appealing. Brooke had to remind herself why she was here to refocus her mind, as the roar from the crowd died down and people sat back in their seats again.

When she did, she noticed that Emmett didn't trot around the ring. He didn't wave to the crowd with wild swings of his arms. Hell, he didn't even seem to notice the crowd, or the all-encompassing noise at all as he stood on his assigned spot, sipping water from his bottle while the announcer finished his spiel.

When that passed, the fighters were called to the center of the ring. Words were said, and when it was over, the two men touched gloves and parted to their separate corners. Inside her chest, Brooke's heart quickened as her brain quickly imagined all her worst fears coming to fruition right in the short time before the bell rang, signalling the start of the round.

Here we go, Brooke said to herself nervously and balled her hands into little fists that sat on her lap, like she was holding onto her anxieties.

The burly man in the blue trunks raced forward to the center of the ring, but he stopped advancing further when Emmett calmly stepped forward to meet him. Emmett's opponent threw a hard series of punches that made Brooke gasp at the suddenness of it. Emmett held his ground against the large man. He simply reached out his arms, deftly blocked the first couple straight punches before he dropped down underneath a wild swinging attack while also moving to the man's side. Emmett came up with a strong uppercut that caught his opponent in the side before he turned and struck him across the face with his other hand. The man in the blue trunks staggered to the side, and Brooke's anxieties spiked, but Emmett didn't move further towards him.

Instead, he waited for the man to turn back to him, and then he saw something she didn't expect. Something she didn't see in any of the other matches. Emmett extended his fist, offering it to his opponent to bump, like he was asking permission to continue, or maybe he was ensuring his opponent was ready before he continued. Whatever it was, the burly man in the blue trunks paused a bit when he saw the gesture as well. He stepped forward cautiously, bumped the fist, and then the fight continued.

Emmett stepped forward this time and launched two straight punches, they glanced harmlessly off the other man's guard. Brooke then saw Emmett coil his body slightly before he threw a hard hook at the man's head. His opponent raised his arm up and easily blocked the attack, but he wasn't quick enough to stop the round kick that came up and hit the man in the ribs on the same side. The whole crowd winced away from the slapping sound that exploded from the ring when Emmett's shin made contact with the man's side. He followed the blow up with another hard punch from the other side, but the burly man ducked to the side and moved away from Emmett as he pressed his elbow into his injured side, like he was protecting it. Emmett studied the man for a moment before he slowly advanced towards him.

Brooke thought the man in the blue trunks didn't look nearly as confident anymore, as he quickly threw a couple jabs at Emmett. She thought those punches did little else than to keep Emmett from getting too close, and for the most part, it worked. Emmett patiently hung back and tested the man's defences with a series of punches that battered the burly man's arms as he tried to keep up with Emmett's attacks. Then the man in the blue trunks shot out his leg, and chopped Emmett's leg in the mid-thigh that tilted him a bit, and then the burly man rushed forward and wrapped his hands around the back of Emmett's neck and pulled him down. He roughly pulled Emmett to the side before he sent a knee into Emmett's gut. She saw that he got his arms on the attack to jam it up before the knee reached its target.

The next instant Emmett gave the man a quick uppercut to the gut, and when the man's hold on his neck slightly loosened, Emmett sent another uppercut between the man's arms and struck him soundly under the chin. His opponent's head recoiled away from the blow, and Emmett used that moment to slap away one of the hands holding him before Emmett ducked underneath his arm and moved in behind the man. It all happened so quickly, Brooke almost missed the way Emmett's one arm snaked under and across his opponent's chest before it popped up by his shoulder. He grabbed his own hand, twisted at the waist while he dropped his weight down, and Emmett threw the man to the ground.

Again, the crowd visibly winced away from the way the man in the blue trunks flopped angrily to the mat. *This is it!* Something inside Brooke tightened as she saw Emmett's opponent recovering slowly on the ground while he just stood over him with a blank expression on his face.

"Get him!" she heard some people around her shout towards the ring, and Brooke tightened her fists on her lap, but she couldn't look away. No matter how much she wished she could.

Emmett stepped forward, dropped his hands, and reached down to offer his opponent a hand up.

Brooke had to stifle the weak sob that escaped her lips, and held back the water collecting in her eyes as she watched Emmett help his opponent back onto his feet. Some people in the crowd booed the display, while others clapped for Emmett's sportsmanship. Brooke saw it and felt something inside herself loosen wonderfully because Calvin had been right about something else.

Emmett wasn't like Tommy.

Shortly after that, the first round ended. The two men shook hands in the middle of the ring amicably and parted to their designated spots.

Brooke let out a breath she didn't even know she was holding within her, and forced her fists to unclench. A part of her wondered if she was being silly while a weird sort of giddiness spread inside her like a strange warmth. She knew she should continue to be wary of Emmett Brooks. There were still a million ways he could hurt her. Her heart remained a weak and injured thing that beat away inexplicably inside her chest for reasons she couldn't even fathom, but now it felt like her heart was uselessly trying to work its way out of her chest to get to Emmett. Like it wanted to be with him. She could empathize with that, she wanted to be with him too.

She peered down into the ring, and watched as someone from outside it passed Emmett a water bottle through the links in the fence. A part of her wanted to stand up and wave her arms until he saw her, like she needed him to know she was there with him. He wasn't alone down there. Some childish part of herself that she thought had died long ago wanted him to know she was with him, now and always.

She didn't though; she still didn't trust her feelings. Just like someone doesn't trust matching lotto numbers when they first see them, it was just too much to hope for. She just enjoyed the knowledge that she *could* love someone like Emmett Brooks. She was too old to believe they would have a fairy tale romance. Hell, she was too old to even *want* some whirlwind romance that would sweep her off her feet, like the movies. She wanted something akin to a warm blanket. A romance where she could retreat from the world. A place where she was safe and cared for, a place where she could unabashedly be the broken person she was. She didn't need to be fixed, after all. She needed to be accepted.

That's why she liked how Emmett looked at her. When he saw her, he didn't see something that needed to be fixed. Even though, if she was being honest, maybe she was, but that's not what Emmett saw. He looked at her like she was already the perfect version of herself.

Ding!

The metallic bell rang loudly and broke Brooke out of her spell.

Round two had started.

Like before, the man in the shorts raced out to the center of the ring, and waited until Emmett got within his range before they started to exchange blows. For every blow the burly man landed on Emmett, he received three in return as neither man gave up any ground to the other. Unlike the last round, the man in the blue shorts didn't attempt to grab Emmett again. Brooke figured some part of the man knew that he was outmatched in that category, and just didn't bother with any further attempts to wrestle Emmett to the ground. Not that he fared any better standing up. It was clear to Brooke, and probably everyone in the building, that the burly man in the blue trunks wasn't going to win. She suspected he knew it as well. Blood ran down his face from a small cut Emmett had opened up on his cheek, and he was moving slower than he had at the beginning of the round. He was running out of steam. The man in the blue shorts started throwing wild punches, throwing technique to the wind and running headlong towards the finish line. Desperately hoping one of his punches would find their mark.

They didn't.

The match ended when Emmett blocked one wild hook, and then another. With his opponent's mid-section exposed, Emmett thrust his leg forward and kicked the man in the abdomen. Brooke watched as the man was briefly lifted off his feet, and stumbled back when his weight precariously came back down. Then the man in the blue shorts slowly sank to his knees. One hand held his stomach while the other weakly waved Emmett off.

The whistle blew. The fight was over.

"Fucking *yeah*!" Brooke screamed as she rose off her seat and cheered with the others in the building as the ref lifted Emmett's hand into the air.

Brooke waited by the front of the food truck, that was now closed up tight. The fights were over, and it was time for the people to go home. The plan was for Brooke to slip away, like a thief in the night, with her questions answered, and for Emmett to never know she was here.

She couldn't do that anymore.

Her breath caught in her throat when he saw him exit the building. He was no longer King, master of the fighting ring. He was *her* Emmett again. Quietly waving to the few people who still remained that recognized him as he made his way to the parking lot.

"Hey!" she called out to him and the childish part of her melted when their eyes met. They regarded each other like long-lost loves who were suddenly reunited. They stared at each other with a restrained longing.

Then Emmett remembered where he was.

I can explain, he signed quickly.

"Oh yeah?" she inquired with sarcastic amusement. "What are we paying for this time? Lumber? Paint? Maybe some new furniture?" she asked softly. She wanted to be mad, maybe a better woman would have had it in her, but she didn't. Not anymore.

Christmas gifts, Emmett signed with a guilty expression. *A smartphone for Isabelle.*

"Are you going to get me anything?" Brooke asked mischievously as she neared.

What do you want?

It was then that Brooke lifted herself up onto her toes, and kissed Emmett fully on the mouth.

It felt like she was falling. A crazy sort of exhilaration blossomed inside her and spread to her entire being, but before the feelings could overwhelm her entirely, she felt Emmett's strong arms wrap around her. Then, they were falling together, maybe falling into each other. She didn't know, but she liked it. That long forgotten part of herself suddenly yearned for it, and she never wanted this moment to end.

But it had to.

She pulled herself away from his warm embrace and looked deeply into his eyes before she spoke.

"I *like* you," she said simply, never breaking eye contact. "Do you like me?" Emmett smiled and nodded softly. "I want to be your girlfriend," she confessed weakly and looked up at him with hopeful eyes. "Do you want to be my boyfriend?"

It sounded silly, like two teenagers confessing they wanted to make out in the hallway at lunch, but it was simple. That's all she could handle right now. The rest would have to come with time.

Again, Emmett quickly nodded and flashed his crooked teeth in an uninhibited smile. Of all his different kinds of smiles, this one was her favorite.

She kissed him again. She leapt up and wrapped herself in him, breathed in his scent, and tenderly explored his lips with her own.

"Okay," she declared when they finally parted. "Let's go." She stepped towards the parking lot and gestured for him to follow.

Where?

"My parents are watching Isabelle. I called them and told them we were going to be a few hours late." She tilted her head slightly to the side. "Churchbridge *does* have a good restaurant, I thought it would be nice if we sat down for our first *official* date and had a nice meal."

That sounds great. Brooke smiled wickedly at him.

"Churchbridge *also* has a motel," she offered quietly with a raised eyebrow.

I want to play it cool here, Emmett signed quickly, *but this is quickly becoming the best day ever.*

Brooke reached out for Emmett's free hand, and let it envelop hers as she led him playfully to the parking lot.

"Okay," Brooke said with an amused tone. "But *technically*, we're calling the motel part our second date, because I don't sleep with guys on the first date. What kind of woman do you think I am?" she asked playfully.

Emmett didn't miss a beat.

The best kind, he signed before he opened the passenger door of his truck for her.

CHAPTER 21

Emmett

It was the week of the Russell Beef and Barley festival. A week-long celebration that signified the end of another harvest. It also coincided with the end of the calving season for the cattle farmers. So, with the new calves born, and this year's crops off the fields and ready for market, it was time for the rural folk to kick back and relax.

On Wednesday afternoon, Emmett and Isabelle went to the hardware store to pick up Brooke after her shift, and they went to the Thrift Sale at the local Elks chapter. All the proceeds went to the Russell Playground Committee. That was the excuse Brooke used after she attacked the clothing section with Isabelle, like someone had hidden a large sum of money somewhere amongst the clothes. Emmett just stood by, he held the possible purchases for the girls, and watched them merrily work their way through the section with a stupid little grin on his face.

He couldn't help it.

Emmett's mind drifted back to the time he and Brooke spent at the Churchbridge Motel. It was a shitty little motel, but they weren't there to sleep. They were pretty sure the clerk behind the counter knew it too, but they didn't care. He thought back to how the sweet scent of her filled his nostrils, the soft warmth of her skin, and decadent wetness of her kisses. Emmett had to admit he was nervous at first.

He wasn't any sort of Casanova or anything.

In his life, he had accumulated a whopping total of three sexual partners. He knew that wasn't a lot, but he wasn't good with women. Hell, he wasn't good with people, but he was especially bad with women. When he was with Brooke, however, none of that mattered. They moved together like it was natural, like they had known each other for their whole lives. They climaxed together, and stared deeply into each other's eyes with a gentle sort of vulnerability when it ended. He remembered his breath caught in his throat by the vision of her lying there naked, because she was beautiful. There were no other words for her. Just a perfect woman.

Well, he thought with some humor, *maybe not perfect.* His smile widened when he looked over to Brooke as she excitedly handed Isabelle a jean jacket she had found in a folded pile of clothes. *She's perfect for us, though.*

Friday night was the K-6 dance at Major Pratt Elementary School. Isabelle had wanted to go because Lucas, as well as some girls from her school, were going to go. One girl from her school, Pressley, had personally invited her. By the gentle, pleading look on her face, there wasn't a chance Emmett could muster the will to say no to her. So, he didn't bother to fight it.

Instead, he leaned into it.

Brooke came to the house to help Isabelle pick out a nice outfit, and do her hair. Emmett retired to his room and changed into a pair of black dress slacks, a white long-sleeved shirt, and he capped it off by including the only tie he could find. He decided to also add a black vest to the ensemble. When he looked at himself in the mirror, he was briefly saddened when he remembered that the last time he wore this outfit was to his mother's funeral.

"Holy shit!" Brooke exclaimed, obviously impressed by his outfit. It felt more like a costume to him, though. "You sure clean up good, don't you?"

How do I look? Emmett signed with a smug look and spun in a small circle with his arms held out to his sides. *Like James Bond?*

"You look like the guy who *ate* James Bond," Brooke said and smiled affectionately. Emmett panted out a small chuckle. "You look amazing," she approached him lovingly and placed her hands on his broad chest before she reached up and kissed him quickly on the lips. "But if this is a beauty contest, I'm afraid you're going to be disappointed." Brooke turned back to Isabelle's room. "You can come out now."

Isabelle nervously walked out of her room wearing a long summer dress, with a pastel purple and green floral print that flowed softly down to her ankles. She had a small black button-up sweater on underneath the jean jacket Brooke bought for her at the thrift sale. Isabelle's dark hair was tied into a thick braid that flowed down the back of her neck, but she still had her two pencil-thin braids that hung down at the sides of her forehead, just the way she liked it. Emmett was quick to notice the scant amount of make-up that Brooke had applied to Isabelle's face. Just a little blush on the cheeks, a bit of lip gloss, and Emmett thought he even saw some glitter on her face.

Brooke was right. If it was a beauty contest between him and Isabelle, then it wasn't much of a contest at all.

Emmett dramatically swooned and slowly sank to one knee, as if he was struck down by the very sight of her. Isabelle giggled at the display.

"Do you like it?" Isabelle asked sheepishly and grabbed the sides of her dress and fanned it out a bit. "I never wore a dress like *this* before."

You look beautiful, he signed and then touched his hand to his heart before he raised himself back up.

"Do you think the other girls will like it?" she asked quickly. Emmett tensed up because part of him worried she was going to ask if Lucas would like it.

If they don't, they're stupid.

Brooke gently slapped his chest.

"Don't listen to him," she scoffed lightly. "They'll love it."

He drove Brooke's car to the dance, because neither woman wanted to show up in his truck. He couldn't blame them, but he also couldn't help feeling a bit hurt. It was a good truck. Reliable. Sure, maybe it wasn't the best shade of brown, and maybe it was a little beat up, but it's never let him down.

He quickly forgot all about his truck when Brooke slowly reached across and scooped up his hand in hers.

It was then Isabelle dropped the bomb on them from the back seat.

"You know you guys can't get married, right?" she said sternly from the back.

If he was capable of making sounds, Emmett was sure he would have made one at that moment. Luckily, Brooke made a slight choking sound that was loud enough for the both of them, and quickly retreated her hand.

"Not that it's any of *your* business," Brooke started to say and turned back to give Isabelle a playfully sour expression. "But say I was to entertain this whole notion of *marriage*," she said the word with some disdain that didn't escape Emmett's ears. "And I'm not saying I am, but I'm just curious why you *think* we can't get married? If we *chose* to."

"Because then your name would be *Brooke Brooks*," Isabelle said it like it was the punchline to a dirty joke, and by how Brooke's expression dropped, it might as well have been.

"Shit!" Brooke exclaimed sadly. "I didn't think of that."

Isabelle laughed merrily in the back, and Emmett couldn't help himself. He added his dry, panting laughter to the mix.

"You two are the worst," Brooke pouted from the passenger seat, but soon enough she reached over for his hand again, and gave it a little squeeze.

At the dance, Emmett quickly found that he was clearly overdressed for the occasion. All the other dads wore jeans and work shirts, while they danced with their children, who wore their Sunday best for the most part. Isabelle quickly led him onto the dance floor, fueled by giddy excitement when the DJ played her favorite Taylor Swift song. When Emmet recognized 'Shake It Off', he immediately knew what was expected of him. None-the-less, Isabelle nodded towards him before their cue came. Emmett simply nodded his acknowledgement, and when their moment came, he fell in beside Isabelle and followed her move-for-move through the TikTok dance she taught him months ago. He even tried to match Isabelle's dramatic flare for the moves. Emmett was more than certain he looked absolutely ridiculous on that dance floor. He probably looked like an angry gorilla swatting flies. It didn't matter, though.

Isabelle was smiling ear-to-ear.

By the end of the first verse, Emmett found that he and Isabelle were in the middle of a line of about a dozen other girls of various ages who followed along as they repeated the dance for the next bit. Towards the end of the song, the number of participants swelled enough for them to need a second line. He quickly recognized Lucas clumsily following along in the second line as best he could, even though it was obvious he didn't know the moves. Beside him was his mother, Lisa Adler. Emmett blushed when he looked up and saw a number of people with their phones out, recording the spontaneous performance.

Brooke was one of them.

She saw him looking in her direction and she gave him a quick thumbs-up without looking away from her phone.

When the song thankfully ended, Emmett found himself surrounded by squealing girls who were excitedly hopping around the dance floor, cheering their own impromptu dance routine. At the sides, the parents clapped for their children. Emmett was looking for a way off the dance floor but the clamoring children around him made it difficult.

He looked over to Isabelle and saw a number of girls had swarmed around her with a happy sort of energy.

"Oh my God! That was amazing!" one of the girls cheered.

"You're a really good dancer, Isabelle!" another one said.

"I love your hair!"

They grabbed her and excitedly led her away. Isabelle looked back with a nervous excitement that shifted to one of remorse as she left him standing there on the dance floor.

Go, he signed quickly with a reassuring smile. *Have fun. I'll be over there if you need somebody to dance with.* He gestured over to where Brooke was standing, with Lisa Adler. Isabelle smiled and turned back to her little friends.

"Yes, please. I'd love to have that video," Lisa Adler said to Brooke when he approached the duo. Lisa noticed his approach. She turned and regarded him like he was holding a puppy in his hands. "Oh my god, Emmett. That was the cutest thing ever. I can't believe that happened. Who knew that song was so popular with the kids?" She then smiled and turned to Brooke with some interest. "Did you know about that dance?"

"No," Brooke said quickly, and with obvious amusement as she gave him the side-eye. "I had no idea." She wrapped her arm in his, pulled herself closer to him and looked up at him adoringly. "This was my first time seeing it as well."

As much as he liked having Brooke wrapped up in him as she was, he had to pull himself away so he could sign.

We practise the routine every morning before school. It's something Isabelle likes to do.

Brooke made a soft cooing noise and Lisa looked at her expectantly.

"He said they practice every day before school because she likes to."

Then it was Lisa's turn to make the noise. Emmett smiled weakly and prayed they couldn't see his flush cheeks in the darkened gymnasium.

Then, Lisa regarded him with a gentle, yet serious expression.

"Can I just say?" Lisa asked and reached out and gently touched his arm. "I know there's a lot between our two families, believe me, I get it. I do. I'm not trying to comment on any of that...*mess.*"

It was at this point Emmett noticed the water collecting in Lisa's eyes. The woman promptly reached up and dabbed the wetness away with her knuckle.

"It's not easy being an *Adler.* The other parents won't even *talk* to me," she said bitterly as she looked around the room, as if she was going to point them out. "I know it's been hard on Lucas. None of the other kids from his school ever come to our house, and he never gets invited to anything. No birthdays, no sleepovers, *nothing*!" Lisa barked. The frustration she apparently had been carrying inside was boiling to the top. "Even his own cousins are assholes to him. It's not fair!"

He could tell she wanted to say more, that there was more she maybe needed to say, but Lisa abruptly stopped and took a deep breath.

"I guess what I *wanted* to say is, I'm just so thankful for Isabelle." A tear escaped her one eye, but Lisa was quick to wipe it away. "They're *so* cute together, and Isabelle is *such* a good friend to him, and he *needs* that. He *really* does. Hell, the only reason he finally agreed to take swimming lessons was because Isabelle went." She looked at him with her sad eyes. "And he was terrified of going to school this year. *Terrified,*" she said the word again to emphasize it. "Now, he's not, and I think that's because of Isabelle."

A little sob escaped Lisa's lips as her defences were crumbling in front of them. She took a breath and struggled to smile at him.

"Can I give you a hug?" she asked weakly.

Emmett was taken back by her display of emotion. He didn't expect there would ever be a time he felt sorry for an Adler, but he did. Before, he was aware of the stain on the Adler name in the area, and quite frankly, he thought it was entirely justified. As far as he was concerned, they deserved everything that came with that stain. Then Isabelle came into his life, and he started to rethink things. He began to see the damage that stain did, and not just to him. He realized that Lucas didn't deserve to be punished for something that was done before he was even born. However, he hadn't realized until this very moment, that maybe he wasn't the only one who didn't.

Emmett put on his warmest smile, and slowly opened his arms to Lisa.

"Thank you," she wept softly as she wrapped her arms around him. "Thank you for letting Isabelle be Lucas's friend. It means the world to him, and me too."

Emmett patted her softly on the back, and looked to Brooke. She placed her hand on her heart and looked at him like she might start crying as well.

"I can't thank you enough." She pulled herself away and brushed off her tears with an embarrassed little laugh. "Jesus, I'm a wreck. Look at me, blubbering all over you. I just wanted you to know that. I'm sorry to bother you."

You're not bothering me.

"You're not a bother, Lisa." Brooke reached over and touched Lisa's arm affectionately. "We're really happy you came over to talk to us." Brooke nudged Emmett's arm. "Right, Emmett?"

He quickly nodded and flashed her a quick smile before he started to sign.

Our kids are good friends, so we should be friends too. To his delight, Brooke translated his words exactly as he signed them.

"I would like that," Lisa said warmly and looked right at him. Then she let out a quick laugh, and fanned her watering eyes with her hands. "Argh! I should go clean myself up, and then I should go and find my kid. Paul and Charles are here somewhere, and I swear to God if they pull any shit I'm going to snap. Thanks again, guys."

"I'll send you that video as soon as I get some decent WIFI."

"Thanks," Lisa said with a definite cheer in her voice that she didn't have when he first arrived. She gave them both a quick wave and turned to walk away, only to quickly turn back to them. "You guys are a really *cute* couple. I just *had* to say that. Okay, bye." She smiled, waved to both of them again, and turned to walk away.

"So," Brooke said playfully, moved in front of him before she grabbed his sides, and pulled herself in close to him. "When do *I* get to go dancing, *Twinkletoes*?"

***

Saturday was the Beef and Barley Cabaret, which was basically the dance that was exclusively for adults. Last-minute tickets costed more. Emmett wasn't really keen to go dancing for a second night in a row, but when a woman like Brooke wants to go dancing, you go dancing.

He wore the same outfit as he did to Isabelle's dance, except he put on a fresh shirt. Isabelle also insisted he wore some cologne.

"Girls like nice smelling things," she said solemnly, like she was handing down some ancient wisdom.

He couldn't argue with that.

Against his better judgement, Brooke arranged for Isabelle to spend the night at Lucas's. Honestly, Lisa was thrilled when she suggested it. Emmett just kept his hands to himself, and let Brooke do all the talking. The kids were even more excited than Lisa was when the grown-ups informed them of their plans.

The drive to the Adler ranch took less than five minutes. It was just two right turns and then a half kilometer drive before their approach. The Adler ranch was the pinnacle farm in the area. Emmett was sure every other farmer would pay a fair sum of money to take a walking tour of their operation. The front of the property was heavily wooded, so much so you couldn't see any of the buildings until you made your way up the approach a bit.

"Whoa," Isabelle said with an awe that hit Emmett like a gut punch as the Adler's yard suddenly opened up in front of them.

The first thing they saw was John Adler Sr's large two-storey house. It was painted a calming blue color and was beautifully contrasted by the white trim. It had a large porch that wrapped around the entire house. Not even Emmett could deny it was a beautiful house. The yard was covered uniformly with a grey decorative rock instead of plain gravel, and no matter how hard Emmett looked, he couldn't see a single weed poking out of it.

He snorted loudly when he saw the brightly colored red barn that was off to the side, but not because the large wooden barn looked absolutely immaculate and stood out like a jewel in the yard. No, it was how John Sr had parked every piece of farm equipment next to each other and arranged by size, starting with a small riding lawn mower, and ending with a large New Holland combine. Each piece of equipment was spotless. It looked like a damned showroom. Emmett marvelled at the row of farm equipment and tried to imagine how much money the Adlers had parked in that line.

Thankfully, Emmett quickly spotted the sign Lisa mentioned that pointed towards the neat little road that led to Owen and Lisa's house. Each of the Adler children had their own house, except for Robbie, he lived with Bill. Owen and Lisa's home was to the west of the main house, and Bill's path led off to the East.

Owen's house was a modest-looking green ranch house, with white trim that was set upon a wide-open field a stone's throw from the main house. It had an attached two-car garage, and in the driveway was a brand-new Chevrolet truck that practically sparkled in the waning light of the evening. Emmett pulled in beside it and shut the truck down.

Without a word spoken, Isabelle grabbed her overnight bag, collected Max into her arms and exited the vehicle. Emmett took a deep breath before exiting, and followed Isabelle up to the front door. Before he could even reach for the doorbell, the front door open sharply, and Owen Adler was blocking the entrance to the house. He looked strangely apologetic.

"Sorry," he said quickly. "I didn't want you to ring the bell because Lisa's *nursery*," he said with air quotes. "Is downstairs, and those little terrors kick up a horrible fuss when someone rings the doorbell. Anyways, welcome!" He smiled broadly at Isabelle, but Owen's happy expression quickly evaporated when he turned his gaze to him. "Emmett," he said simply, and with little enthusiasm.

Let's get this over with, he thought to himself as he brought his hands up to stop Owen from saying anything further. He sighed a bit before he put on a friendly smile and extended his hand to Owen, just like he had at Isabelle's school. He had rejected the gesture at the time, but he was hoping Owen was a better man than he suspected. He worried slightly when Owen looked at his offered hand with confusion.

Then he smiled as well.

"Yeah," he said finally. "Sure. Why not?" he asked no one in particular, grasped Emmett's large hand and gave it a firm shake.

It was then the sounds of loud footfalls bounding towards them came from somewhere deeper into the house.

"Isabelle!" Lucas yelped excitedly as he came hustling around the corner, slipping precariously on the linoleum. Owen winced nervously at the display, but Lucas kept his footing and came running up to them, stopping just short of Isabelle, who was hopping in place beside him.

"Hi, Lucas!"

"Come on!" Lucas reached out and pulled Isabelle, somewhat roughly, into the house. Not that Isabelle minded one bit. "We can take Max and go play with the other puppies, and then my mom said we could make a blanket fort in the living room, and we can watch movies *all* night!"

"Son!" Owen said somewhat sternly, and gently pulled Lucas's hand away from Isabelle. "You're a little *too* excited. Calm down," he said lowering his hand, like Lucas had an invisible lever that controlled his energy level, and his father was lowering it. "Sorry," he said to Emmett, slightly embarrassed before he leaned into him. "It's his first sleepover."

The two adults shared a knowing look and nodded to each other. Owen then returned his attention to his boy.

"Why don't you take Isabelle's bag, and show her to where you guys will be sleeping. You know, get her settled and all that. *Then* you guys can play with the dogs."

"Okay dad," Lucas said lightly, almost completely unaffected by his father's words. Lucas then put his hand out towards Isabelle, who unshouldered her knapsack and handed it to him. "Come on," he quickly gestured for her to follow him, and Isabelle kicked off her shoes at the door before she hurried after him.

Emmett warmed when she turned back at the end of the hall and signed at him.

Forever.

He quickly returned the gesture, and then waved.

"Did...you want to come in for a beer or something?" Owen offered slowly. "I'm watching the end of the game. You a Leafs fan?" He smiled, pulled his notepad out of his pants' pocket and quickly wrote a short note before he showed it to Owen, and prayed he appreciated the joke.

Thanks, but I prefer teams that actually win. Lol.

I have to get going.

Owen barked out a quick laugh, like he didn't expect the joke, and appreciated the slight bit of teasing.

"Yeah," he said slyly. "That's not the first time I've heard that one."

They said their good-byes, and someone who had watched the display might have even thought they were friends when he departed Owen's house.

He drove to Brooke's parents' house, parked in the driveway beside her little car, and walked up to the front door. He knew Brooke had her own entrance to her little basement suite. It was just through the entrance to the garage, and then down a short flight of stairs that was on the left side, but he wanted to do this right.

He rang the door bell, fished the cue card he had prepared out of his vest pocket, and smoothed it out nervously while he waited at the door. Soon enough, the door opened and revealed Lester Talbot's lean form.

"Oh, hey Emmett. Brooke's got her own-," he started to say but Emmett held up his hands to cut him off. He then presented Lester with the card he had been holding.

Good evening Mr. and/or Mrs. Talbot.

My name is Emmett Brooks. I'm here to pick up your daughter for the dance. I want you to know I only have the best of intentions for Brooke. I like her very much. I hope I can have your blessing to date your daughter.

Lester read the note and before he finished, a quizzical expression leapt onto his face. Emmett didn't exactly love the look he had. It was like he couldn't understand the note, like he had written it in an unknown language.

"Mary!" he called back into the house. "Come take a look at this."

A moment later Brooke's mother strolled into the living room behind Lester and walked up to the door.

"Hello, Emmett." She smiled genuinely at him as she approached her husband's side. "What do we have here?" she asked lightly and looked down at Emmett's note that Lester was holding for her. Emmett started to get nervous but then she looked up from the note and smiled warmly at him.

"Would you like to come in for a cup of coffee?"

Fifteen minutes later, while sitting at the kitchen table perusing old photo albums with Mary, and sipping his second cup of coffee, Brooke's text came through.

Where ARE you? Your truck's out front.

Emmett smiled broadly as he replied.

I'm upstairs. Having coffee with your parents.

Emmett couldn't help the dry, panting laugh that he made when he heard Brooke's noisy footsteps storming up the stairs from the basement. Two angry steps later Brooke appeared from around the far corner of the kitchen.

Brooke wore a long dark skirt that fell down to her knees. She had a button-up jean shirt that had the top three buttons undone, which displayed her cleavage in a way he found very appealing, and over that she wore a short leather jacket. Brooke topped off the whole outfit with a cute, black cowboy hat. However, it was the look on her face that made him smile.

"*MOM!*" Brooke cried out with shocked horror at the scene in front of her. She then looked at him with a gaping mouth. "What are you *doing*?" she asked to the entire room.

"What?" her mother asked innocently from her place beside him.

They invited me in for coffee, he signed innocently and shrugged. *How could I say no?*

"Yeah," she said dryly. "That's how they *get* you." Brooke then turned to her mother. "You brought out the photo albums? Really?!"

I especially liked the figure skating pictures, Emmett signed and grinned wickedly. Brooke's eyes widened and she looked to her mother with renewed outrage.

"You showed him the figure skating pictures!? *Mom*!" Brooke whined and threw her arms wide.

"What? You looked so cute in your little outfit," her mother said defensively.

"I look like a boy."

"That's because you insisted I give you that *pixie*-cut," her mother said the word with some disdain.

"Yeah, that's not what a pixie-cut is supposed to look like," Brooke replied with some frustration.

"We called her *Bro* for that entire year," Lester chimed in with a chuckle.

"You know what? Nope," Brooke said dismissively. "We're not doing this." She walked forward, grabbed Emmett's arm, and gently lifted him out of his chair. "We're leaving. He's taking me dancing, and we have to *go*." Brooke lovingly led him towards the front door.

"Well, we wouldn't want to waste that push-up bra," Her mother replied and then sipped her coffee while looking sweetly at Brooke.

"Jesus! Mom!" Brooke called back to her mother from the door. Lester giggled unabashedly beside her.

I like the push-up bra, Emmett signed outside the house before he opened the door of his truck for Brooke.

"Say one more word about my *supposed* push-up bra, and you won't get to see what's underneath later."

Emmett just smiled, and didn't sign another word until they got to the cabaret.

They got to the cabaret soon after they opened the doors to the George P Buleziuk Community Center, which everyone in the area affectionately referred to as simply *The GPB*. The parking lot had several cars and trucks in it already and a steady stream of vehicles were arriving by the minute. The event promised to be quite lucrative for the local Elks Club.

When Brooke led him by the hand into the building, the band wasn't even playing yet. They were just playing random golden country hits over the sound system. People were mingling by the edges of the dance floor in small clumps by the cash bar. Brooke didn't care about any of that as she walked him straight to the dance floor by the hand. She smiled at him as she slipped her other hand over his shoulder and they danced to The Nitty Gritty Dirt Band's, 'Fishing in the Dark' like they were the only two people on earth. Honestly, Brooke was a fabulous dancer, and for the first little bit it took Emmett everything he had to not step on her toes as she quickly led them through the dance.

They found their rhythm though. Soon, he looked into her joyous eyes as she stepped them in circles on the dance floor, and he couldn't help returning the joyous expression as they moved across the dance floor like one being. When the song ended, they released their hold on each other and looked at each other adoringly and breathless, not unlike their first time together in Churchbridge, until the next song started up.

Then they did it all over again, just like in Churchbridge.

They only took a break from the dance floor when the band started to set up. They had a few drinks and wandered through the crowd, signing smack about people they saw, and laughing at each other's jokes.

Soon after, the band took to the stage and when the music started up with renewed vigor, Brooke shot him a mischievous look with a raised eyebrow, and Emmett didn't need anything else.

Let's go, he signed quickly after he tossed his drink into the nearest wastebin. He then grabbed her hand and led her gently onto the dance floor.

They danced.

Brooke laughed uproariously when he spun her playfully around during their dance before pulling her back. Brooke took her cue and spun gracefully into his arms, and he easily dipped her lovingly towards the floor. When he brought her back up, they kissed briefly before Brooke led them back into the dance.

They danced.

When the music was fast, Brooke shuffled and spun them around the floor in merry circles around the other dancers. Never taking her eyes off him, and neither one losing the smile on their faces. When the music was slow, they held each other close and swayed lovingly on the floor like blades of grass in the gentle wind.

They danced.

When the band played a pop song, they danced across from each other. Emmett mimicked some moves he saw on television, poorly, and he was sure he looked like a fool. He didn't care though. Across from him was the picture of beauty's perfection as she moved seductively in tune with the music. He couldn't take his eyes off her. *My god,* he thought as he watched her with undying admiration, *how did I ever get so lucky?*

They danced.

"Goose," Brooke inexplicably whispered into his ear during a slow song some time later. "Take me to bed, or lose me forever." She pulled herself away and looked at him alluringly.

He looked at her with a quizzical expression as he held onto her sides.

Who the hell is Goose? He wondered and thought back to try to remember how much she had to drink.

"Have you not seen Top Gun?" she asked him with some disappointment. Emmett smiled.

No, but I'm not willing to lose you forever. Emmett reached down for her hand and slowly led her towards the exit.

She clung to him lovingly as they walked back to the parking lot. The night looked like it was going to end on a high note.

That is, until he saw Big Bill Adler leaning against the hood of his truck with his massive arms crossed across his broad chest.

"This *fucking* guy," Brooke muttered drunkenly beside him as they approached the dour-looking giant.

"About goddamn time, I've been waiting out here for over an hour," he said venomously and uncrossed his arms.

This isn't good, Emmett thought to himself when he saw the furious look on Bill's face.

"So, come inside then." Brooke chirped beside him.

"Fuck that. Nobody in there wants to see me," he said definitively. "Besides, I'm not here to dance."

Emmett signed quickly, and Brooke loosely translated beside him.

"Yeah, what *are* you here for then?" Brooke asked suspiciously and pointed an angry finger at him. She was clearly a bit tipsy, and didn't appreciate being cock-blocked one bit.

"I got business with this one," Bill answered sternly and gestured towards Emmett. "My father wants to board fifty head at your little *rinky-dink* operation."

What!? Emmett did the math and that would easily put him over his threshold. With those fifty head, his farm would make a profit each month, instead of costing him money.

"He forgets those are *my* cows now, though. I decide what happens to them and where they go, and I'll shovel snow in hell before I see them in *your* field. Not after what your brother did."

Emmett didn't need to say anything, Brooke spoke up and said what was on both their minds.

"What *his* brother did?! Oh, that's fucking rich coming from the brother of a *rapist*." Brooke hissed beside him, and Emmett gave her a quick frown and slowly shook his head.

Some words shouldn't be said, no matter how true they felt.

"Yeah?" Bill shot off the hood of his truck and took a slow, challenging step forward. "I don't fucking remember there being any trial. Hell, Clive wasn't even arrested," Bill said loudly.

Emmett took a half step in front of Brooke. He didn't know what Bill's intentions were, but he wasn't going to risk Brooke. If someone was going to get hurt, it was going to be him.

"Because this *fucknut's* brother decided to take matters into his own hands. If I had been there when that psycho-brother of his attacked Clive, I would have stopped him. I would have *ripped* him into pieces, but I wouldn't have *KILLED HIM*!" Emmett signed nothing, not because he didn't want to, but because Bill was right. "Maybe Clive deserved to go to jail for what he did, maybe a long time, but he didn't deserve to *die*. Not like that. We had to have a closed casket funeral. I couldn't even see his face!" Bill shouted, and Brooke tensed up behind him. Emmett stood against Bill's fury and noticed the water collecting in the man's eyes. "So, I say fuck *that*, and fuck *you*." Bill angrily shook his finger at him. "If you want those fucking cows, you're going to have to fight me for them."

Emmett didn't expect that. Apparently, neither did Brooke.

"What!?" She suddenly barked. "No!" She released Emmett's hand and waved her hands in front of herself. "To hell with that idea. Why do you men always solve your problems by punching them?" Brooke asked no one in particular, but it was Bill who answered.

"Shut up," he snapped back, and Emmett took a small step towards him with a heated expression.

He looked at him with fiery eyes for a moment before he slowly shook his head. Bill smiled proudly, like he was pleased he hit a nerve.

"I know all about your little matches at Chester's sideshow. I'll set it up so it's just *you and me.* No distractions or interruptions. I'll even sweeten the pot for you, *Loverboy.* I'll give you five grand, *cash,* just for showing up, *and* I'll give you a certified bull to stud out for a month in the spring." Bill cocked his eyebrow at him.

Emmett didn't blame him for the arrogant look, it was a sweetheart of a deal.

Okay, he signed. He knew full well Brooke would understand the sign before Bill did.

"What?!" she blurted out and pulled him roughly so he was looking at her. "No," she said pleadingly.

If I do this, I'll be set. The farm will make money, and I won't have to fight again. Don't you see, this is my way towards a better life for me and Isabelle, and you.

"Oh, screw you," Brooke hissed with some annoyance. "Don't make me part of this. I have my own money, I don't need you to do this for me, and neither does Isabelle."

Yes, Emmett started to sign and dropped his expression. *She does. So does my father. I don't want to do this any more than you want me to, but the good outweighs the bad here.* She looked at him remorsefully.

"It doesn't feel that way."

"What's it going to be, *Loverboy*?" Bill sneered at him. "Because I feel we can make this deal and have it out at Chester's, or...I can just call your girlfriend there the C-word, and we can do this right here for free." Bill smiled smugly and pointed at Brooke. "Your choice."

Emmett looked at her, paying no attention to the threat in the air, and smiled.

I won't do it if you tell me not to, he signed slowly and gently held her chin in his hand. Brooke returned his deep gaze, reached up and gave his forearm a squeeze. Then she sighed deeply.

"I'm with you," she said quietly and gave him a small smile. "If you *need* to do this, and if it means you don't have to fight anymore, I'm with you." She looked at him sweetly. "Kick his ass."

Emmett turned back to Big Bill's large form just in time to see him roll his eyes at them. He paid no attention to it. Emmett extended his hand and offered it to Bill with a challenging smirk on his face.

The offer was accepted.

CHAPTER 22

Kevin

They got into Russell late last night. They first went to St-Lazare, and after about a five-minute drive through the tiny town they found the only motel. Kevin didn't have to look at it for long before he decided to go to the nearest thing that resembled a large center in hopes they could find a decent room. Which brought them to this place.

The Russell Inn.

It was actually surprisingly nice. There was a restaurant, which oddly enough doubled as a Pizza Hut, and a nice, comfortable lounge with VLT's for Levi. They were a vice of his. Kevin suspected it was all the bright lights and bells that attracted the big idiot to them, like a child. It even had a pool. Kevin didn't really care about any of that, he just wanted a bed.

The drive out had been brutal. Fourteen hours locked in the rental car with that towering dummy was more taxing than he expected it would be. Honestly, Levi Mitchell was a nice enough guy, but he was tragically dim. Five hours into the drive he started talking about flat-earth theory.

"I'm not saying I agree with it, but you have to admit it's pretty compelling stuff," he said after he listed off the best points.

"No, I don't." Kevin knew he should have left it at that, and tried to change the subject, but he couldn't help himself. The words just flew out, as if powered by his annoyance. "According to this *bullshit*-theory of yours, I could go on top of a tall building with a telescope and see France." He said slowly, praying that internally Levi took a second to actually think about what he was saying.

It was a big ask.

"Well, have you ever tried it?" Levi said as if he thought it might actually work.

Kevin sighed deeply.

The entire car ride had been like that.

They agreed to get a fresh start early in the morning. They had an address, but wasn't like an address he had ever seen. Kevin had only lived in Toronto, though. He learned that what he had was a Legal Land Description. Luckily, they had also stumbled upon the mailing address for the property, which is what led them to St-Lazare. Their original plan was to stakeout the post office in that dinky little town until someone came to pick up the mail for that property. Kevin also considered the possibility of sweet talking the clerk behind the counter to maybe giving them the name of the owner of a particular PO box.

On the long drive down, Kevin thought of another possibility.

Once in his room, and finally free of Levi's endless chatter, Kevin took out his laptop and got onto the internet. A quick google search brought him to a website that took legal land descriptions and converted it into longitude and latitude coordinates. Kevin smiled as he typed in the information he had. This would be wildly easier, and infinitely more discreet than parking their premium-class rental car, because a certain someone needed the leg room, on the street for hours on end. People in small towns tend to take notice of foreign cars. Kevin smiled widely as the website also pulled up a map of the area for the legal land description. His target lived on Highway 42, right where Highway 41 teed into it. After checking the map app on his phone, Kevin quickly saw his target just lived up the hill to the east from St-Lazare. Not even ten minutes away from the town.

"Perfect," Kevin said into the empty room, and decided to call it a night.

The next morning, he and Levi walked across the parking lot to the small convenience store that shared a parking lot with the Inn. Once they entered the store, they both waved a friendly greeting to the elderly, small-framed man behind the counter and made a bee-line straight for the store's little coffee counter.

"Oh," Levi said excitedly. "They have hazelnut." He reached for the largest cup, placed it under the warmer's nozzle, and began to fill it.

Kevin went with a cup of straight black coffee, and capped the cup off with a lid. They both grabbed a muffin from the display case beside the line of coffee warmers, and made their way back to the counter.

"Found everything you were looking for, boys?" the clerk asked with way too much cheer for seven in the morning, as they placed their items on the counter.

"You bet," Kevins said absently, and reached for his wallet.

Beside him, Levi used his elbow to slightly nudge Kevin's side to get his attention. When he looked to the large man, Levi discreetly nodded to the white display to the left side of the counter. It had *Russell's Thieves* printed in bold letters along the top. It took Kevin a second to see what was so important about the board before his eyes drifted to an empty spot along the bottom where a picture had been removed. Right next to that empty space, was Isabelle Lamoine's picture.

In the picture, the child he had been watching for the last five years, looked like she was on the edge of tears as she meekly stood for the picture. The background was entirely taken up with the massive form of a man who had moved in beside Isabelle. He didn't share the sour look of Isabelle's face, quite the opposite, the large man was grinning foolishly in the picture, and even flashed a thumbs-up, like he and Isabelle had just gotten off a carnival ride or something.

Kevin furrowed his brow when he saw the man.

That's the uncle, he thought with absolute certainty, and idly wondered how much of a problem the beefy man might present.

"That's quite the board you have there." Kevin said with a friendly casualness while he held his wallet in his hand. Kevin made a show of leaning in to look at Isabelle's picture before he smiled and wagged his finger at it. "That guy kinda looks like one of my cousins."

"I didn't know you were from around here," Levi said with some surprise. Internally, Kevin rolled his eyes at the man.

"Oh yeah. Are you a *Brooks*?" the man behind the till asked with genuine curiosity.

"No. Amundson," Kevin lied quickly.

"Well, Emmett's dad, Carter, was from out east. Might be a distant cousin?" the clerk offered, like the problem was his to solve.

Emmett Brooks. Yep, that's our guy.

"Unlikely. He just *looks* like a cousin I have. I don't think it's actually him. The resemblance is incredible though. I think we're good to go here," Kevin said finally and gestured to their items.

"I'll get a pack of DuMaurier Extra Mild, too. Please," Levi added quickly, and Kevin frowned somewhat at the ask.

Levi had plenty of smokes.

Kevin had a sneaking suspicion he knew what the big giant was thinking, and like the big dummy he was, he was apparently completely oblivious to the two small camera pods that were pointed directly at them. So, when Levi's massive arm reached out for the picture, Kevin was quick to slap his hand back down before it even crossed the counter. When Levi gave him a questioning expression, Kevin just frowned at him and quickly shook his head twice.

The clerk turned back with Levi's pack of cigarettes in his hand, and added it to their other items. Kevin quickly paid and they said their good-byes.

He left the store in a black mood.

"Were you born stupid, or did you just get hit in the head too much?" Kevin asked venomously as they walked back to their rental.

"What? What's the big deal? I thought the boss would probably want the picture," Levi shrugged with muted confusion.

"You realize we're here to kidnap a small girl, and probably murder her uncle, right? Like, you get that part of it, right?"

"Yeah. So?" Levi replied with a dispassionate easiness only Zeke would appreciate.

"So, we don't want to give the cops anything to investigate, moron."

"You're the one who started talking to him," Levi snapped back defensively.

"Yeah, to get information. That guy back there probably talks to a hundred people every day. Two weeks from now he won't even remember we were here, but he'd definitely remember someone who stole a picture off his board."

Kevin pinched the bridge of his nose and slowly shook his head as he moved to the passenger side of their rental. He looked over the hood of the car and continued.

"And who's picture would it have been. Well, the very same as the person who went missing. Don't you *see*?" he asked as he tried to educate Levi a bit. "It connects us to the crime, dummy. From there they'll move to the Inn, and then they have our credit card records, which yes, might be bogus, but they'll keep fucking digging. Our faces have been recorded by half a dozen cameras, *today!*" Kevin took a deep breath. Levi looked at him with a remorseful expression as his words sunk in, which just angered him more. "The smart thing to do would have been just take a picture of it with your phone." Kevin calmed a bit after that, because that was a good point, and he didn't think of it either at the time.

"You're right," Levi offered as a surrender. "That was stupid. I just thought-."

"No!" Kevin interrupted him like he was punishing a pet. "Don't think. Just do what I tell you. Now, let's go. I want to be at the house before eight."

"Why?" Levi asked as he opened the door to the driver's side. Kevin entered on his side before he answered.

"Because that's when the kid will leave for school."

***

Kevin instructed Levi to keep driving straight as they approached the turnoff for St-Lazare off Highway 42. On the left, as they approached the intersection was a small electrical station, and across the road from that, was the start of Emmett Brook's property. Kevin had Levi drive a full loop around the property. On the south-west corner of the section of land, was a densely wooded area that followed the highway around the bend to the north. He had Levi stop the luxury sedan on the side of the road around the bend, so their flashing hazard lights wouldn't be visible from the intersection. They parked across the road from their target's property, and they both exited the vehicle. The morning sun was just beginning to show itself on the eastern horizon, and the rest of the landscape was covered in the early morning grey with black shadows.

They didn't have much time.

"Okay, I'm going to go have a look." He casually pointed towards the wooded area of the target's property before he looked back to Levi. "I want you to take the jack out of the trunk and jack up the back corner of the car," he instructed him quickly and pointed to the back passenger side of the car.

Levi looked at him dumbly.

"Why?"

"So, people who drive by think you're just fixing a flat," he replied sharply, because Kevin felt it was the obvious answer.

"So, you want me to change the tire?"

"No," Kevin shot back with disappointed frustration, and pinched the bridge of his nose for what felt like the thousandth time since they started this journey. "Don't *actually* change the tire, just *pretend* to change it."

"Gotcha," Levi snapped his fingers and nodded obediently. Thinking that was the end of it, Kevin turned to cross the highway. He didn't even make it a step. "What do I do if somebody stops to help?"

"Do you *really* need me to answer that?" Kevin said sternly when he looked back.

"Hey, you're the one who said I shouldn't think, remember?" Levi said with a stupid grin and a shrug of his wide shoulders.

"Well, just in case you actually *do* need me to tell you. If that happens, thank them for their consideration, and tell them you have everything under control."

"But Kevin," Levi said and suddenly took on a worried expression that didn't suit his face. "What if they don't leave?"

Okay, he's fucking with me, Kevin thought to himself when he saw the stupid look of concern on the man's face.

"Figure it out, Levi."

He punctuated the statement by giving the man the finger before he turned and scurried across the darkened, empty highway. He nimbly stepped through the barbed-wire fence, and disappeared into the trees.

In the wooden area, he ran through the thick tangle of grass that was covered by a light frosting of snow. He would have preferred not to leave tracks behind, but there was little he could do about that now. Afterall, given it was Manitoba in November, it was a miracle the ground wasn't covered with a foot of snow. He headed towards the light of the morning. He knew from Google Maps that the farm house and other buildings were roughly to the north-west of where he and Levi had parked that car.

The wooded area opened up to a fenced-off field. Kevin followed the treeline to the north towards the fence line. Once he got there, he hunkered down below the level of the posts and quickly made his way towards the house, closely hugging the fence line as he went. When he came to the far corner of the field, he spied a vehicle gate that was built into the fence. Kevin immediately followed the tire tracks that led from the field back towards the opening in another, smaller wooden area where he could see the roof of the house poking up from the tops of the bare trees.

Once he got to the new section of trees, Kevin jumped off the tire tracks and followed the edge of the trees to the north. If he remembered correctly, there was a path through the trees up ahead that was big enough to drive a school bus through. He stayed close to the trees when the house came into view, he could see the lights were on through the windows.

Kevin stayed close as he crossed the space between the treeline and the corner of the house in a blink of an eye. Once there, he moved in beneath the lighted window, and just listened.

They were home. He could hear them moving around inside. Kevin moved slowly towards the corner of the house, feeling his heart beating madly inside his chest. He had officially entered dangerous territory. At the corner, he could see the front door, and parked out front was an old looking, shit-brown truck with more dents and spots of rust then he could probably count. There were no other vehicles in the yard. Kevin moved back underneath the wall and considered his options.

He flinched away from a deep thumping sound that suddenly came from inside the house, like someone was pounding on the floor with an impossibly large hammer. *Whump, whump, whump.* A second later he heard Isabelle Lamoine's voice ring out from the room on the other side of the wall he was crouched next to.

"Alright!" Isabelle shouted with some annoyance. "I'm coming! I just have to grab my bag."

This is it!

Kevin took a deep breath to steady his nerves, and he heard people moving around inside. He quickly remembered Zeke's words; *I want you to see dem wit your own eyes.* More than that, he remembered the *way* he had said it. Like the, *or else,* part was simply implied.

Kevin liked to think he was a professional. He liked to think that after two tours in Afghanistan disarming road-side IED's, seeing three of his good friends reduced to a fine mist, and shooting a good number of people dead would have given him a hardened resolve. However, he was a little ashamed to admit to himself that he thought of his kid sister in that moment, when he pulled out his phone and opened up the camera app.

He quietly scurried back to the corner of the house, leaving maybe twenty-five feet between him and the truck. He was facing the passenger side of the truck, the side Isabelle would enter from. If he poked the camera lens of his phone past the corner of the house, he could take a few quick pictures and get out of sight the next second. Hopefully, unnoticed.

Kevin leaned against the house, well away from the corner, and carefully watched the screen on his phone as he poked the top corner of it around the edge of the house. On the screen, he made some slight adjustments to center the shot on the passenger door, and waited for his targets to leave the house. Even though he was expecting it, the sound of the house door opening a few moments later still kicked his heart rate up a notch.

On the tiny screen, he saw the pair exit the house at the far corner of the shot with their back turned to him. They moved closer towards the truck, towards his shot, when Isabelle inexplicably stopped in her tracks.

"Did you remember to bring the permission slip for the hay ride?"

Kevin heard the sound of fingers snapping, but no other response than that. On the screen, the big man moved out of the frame, and the door to the house opened. Kevin slowed his breathing as Belle absently wandered towards the passenger side of the truck.

There!

Kevin rapidly hit the shutter button on the side of the phone, quickly glanced at the photos he was taking as they flashed on the screen. He took numerous photos of Isabelle's side profile before the sound of the front door opening and closing again pulled his hand back. Kevin hustled silently in behind the house, and out of sight of the retreating truck. Once there, he leaned his back against the house and waited for the sound of the truck's engine to slowly die away as they drove down the approach towards the gravel road.

Only when he could no longer hear the truck did Kevin risk looking at the photos. He took a total of ten photos in the short time he had, each of them you could clearly see it was Isabelle Lamoine in the picture.

Perfect. Mission accomplished.

Kevin moved back to the corner of the house to take some additional photos of the yard, and the house for later, before he carefully, and slowly retraced his steps in the snow all the way back to the tire tracks. From there, he made his way quickly back to the car.

"We good?" Levi asked as soon as he crossed back across the highway to the car. To Levi's credit, the trunk was open, the spare tire was placed in clear view behind the car, and the back corner of the sedan was raised up.

"Yeah," Kevin said with a smug smile. "We're golden."

They spent the rest of the day gathering intel on their target.

They quickly packed up the jack and tire back into the trunk and drove their car down the hill to St-Lazare. They found the school easy enough. Kevin instructed Levi to park their fancy car in a church's parking lot that was nearby. Levi stopped the car close to the back corner of the long, narrow building without being told. Here, they were partially concealed from the street, and it gave him a perfect vantage point to the front of the school and the surrounding area. Kevin didn't even need the binoculars to see Isabelle merrily playing with a group of kids by the playground, waiting for the first bell to ring. He didn't see the uncle's truck anywhere, and they had a good position. So, Kevin felt safe watching the little girl for a while longer.

Are we really going to do this? A familiar voice spoke up from inside him. *This is big-time shit. Kidnapping a girl from her family and holding her against her will isn't just a crime, old buddy. It's downright EVIL. You're prepared for that?*

Kevin furrowed his brow again, watching his target. The voice wasn't wrong, but the morality ship had sailed for him a long time ago. He was already going to hell, that much was clear, and he was fine with dying. Cause and effect. You couldn't live this life without accepting the possibility that it could be your downfall. Fine. Whatever. He was still making almost a hundred grand a year, *after taxes*. How else was a veteran with aggression problems supposed to make that kind of money in the *real* world? No, this was the life he chose for himself and he had to accept the pitfalls that came with it. Besides, he was just following orders.

Inside him, the voice laughed wickedly.

Oh, Buddy! You're not a soldier anymore. Zeke Simard is NOT your commanding officer. You don't get to hide behind THAT particular excuse anymore.

Be that as it may, Zeke would make his family pay for his disobedience before he ever dared raised a hand against him. Kevin probably wouldn't even know about it until he got the call from someone in his family. Zeke was like the devil because it felt like he could just make a call and someone, somewhere in the world that you cared about would die. That was part of the deal he made. The Army had the threat of court martial and imprisonment for disobeying orders, The Organization was more discreet, but infinitely crueller in their punishments.

You're smarter than that. You don't have to exactly disobey, but there are a thousand ways you could fuck this operation up for him.

Kevin subtly shook his head as he looked out his window at Isabelle. Never. He came too far in this shithole life, seen too much, lived through too much, just to spend the rest of his life in a box.

No, this was a one-way trip for him.

"Let's go," he said quietly, when the school's bell rang loudly.

He had seen enough.

The uncle was easy enough to watch, he spent the entirety of the day loading large wrapped bales that dotted his fields onto a trailer that was parked nearby. Once the trailer was full, the uncle hooked it up to the tractor he was using for the bales, and slowly towed it back to the yard. After that, he was out of sight for about an hour before he slowly came back with an empty trailer to start the process all over.

Isabelle's lunch hour was from noon until one in the afternoon. Kevin imagined the kids ate their lunches in their classrooms, and then ran for the doors to spend the rest of the hour outside. The sun was out, it was a fairly warm day for November. It was only twelve-fifteen before the first group of children started filing out of the school. Isabelle came out at twenty minutes past noon, and the afternoon bell rang at quarter-to-two sharp to signal the afternoon recess, which lasted for a half hour. After that, Levi drove them to a concealed spot where they could see the east road into St-Lazare from a safe distance. Using his binoculars from his seat he watched the uncle's beat-up truck drive down the winding hill towards the town at five minutes past three, and fifteen minutes later it was amongst a group of vehicles that made the trip back up the hill.

That was enough for the day.

He and Levi ate together in the lounge. They ate small pizzas from the Pizza Hut menu, ordered a couple of beers for themselves, and ate quietly while idly watching the hockey game that was playing on the big screen. Afterwards, they retired to their rooms.

Kevin felt it was best for Levi's well-being if they had separate rooms.

About an hour later, he was half-way through a movie that was playing on a local channel when he heard a quick knock at his door. Through the peephole he spied Levi's lumbering form and sighed quietly before he opened the door.

"You're not going to believe this," he said when Kevin opened the door for him. Levi was wagging his phone in his hand.

He wasn't lying.

They watched the uncle's second fight video on Kevin's laptop in his room. He even took the time to hook the laptop up to the fancy television so they could see it on the bigger screen for a better look. There was no doubt about it, that was Emmett Brooks on the screen beating the shit out of some shirtless guy with a dark farmer's tan on his hairy upper body.

"Fuck me!" Levi winced away from a powerful hook that crashed the uncle's opponent to the ground. "That fucking guy can hit! Did you see that?!" he asked excitedly.

"Yeah," Kevin confirmed with substantially less enthusiasm. "I saw it."

Kevin wasn't exactly thrilled to find out the uncle was about the same size as Levi, if not bigger, and now, he *really* wasn't happy to find out the man had no problem smashing people with his fists and moved like a goddamn jungle cat in the ring.

However, after Kevin checked the dates on the other video, an idea came to his mind.

It took a little digging on the *Hillbilly fight*'s website to find a contact number for the operation. It was still early enough in the night so Kevin pulled out his burner phone and punched in the number.

"Hello," a bored female voice came on over the line. "CDA Productions. Are you signing up for the next fight, or looking for the date of the next event?" the voice said with little real interest, like those were the only two possibilities anyone would call for.

Kevin was quick to answer.

"Neither, actually. I'm a promoter out of Winnipeg, and I'm looking at one of your fighters on your website. I'm interested in signing him for an event I have coming up. He would be perfect for a heavyweight I have scheduled to fight."

The voice just sighed.

"One second." Kevin was put on hold for over two minutes, and it was a man's voice that came on the line.

"Yo, Chaz speaking. Who dis?"

"My name's Ronald Acherson. I'm a fight promoter in Winnipeg. I had a cancellation for an upcoming event that has left me a bit scrambling to find a replacement."

"Uh-huh," the man said agreeably. "I feel you there, bro. That shit happens to me *all* the time. How can I help you?"

"I was looking through the videos on your website, and I think your man, King, would be perfect for my fighter."

"King? Fuck yeah, he's my new champion. A real crowd pleaser!"

"Is there any way you could tell me when his next fight is? I'd like to come down and have a look with my own eyes."

"Shit! That's a long drive down, my dude. Everything you need to know about King is on the website."

Kevin was undeterred.

"True, but I was hoping to have a chat with the man. Plus, if he was agreeable to fight for me, there would be some paperwork I would need him to fill out. I was hoping to get that all taken care of in one trip," Kevin said calmly, before adding, "I'm sure you understand."

"Totally. Two-birds-one-stone kind of shit, I feel you." The man chuckled briefly afterwards. "A thousand bucks."

"Excuse me?"

"That's my usual *finder's fee* for lending my fighters out to other operations. *Cash.*" It suddenly became very clear to Kevin why they didn't use the fighter's real names on the website. Kevin grinned slightly. It wasn't a bad angle.

"Of course," he said like he had been expecting it. "That's no problem at all. I can bring the money with me when I come."

"Sweet," the man on the other end said merrily. "Sweet. Now, there's a bit of a problem with seeing his next fight though."

"Oh?" Kevin asked with genuine interest.

"Yeah, it's a private event. A dude paid me a good sum of money to make it that way, I have to abide. But, my dude, that doesn't mean you can't wait in the parking lot for the event to end to talk to him."

"When is this private event?" Kevin asked cautiously.

"A couple days. Saturday the twenty-first," he said like he was reading it off a piece of paper. "In the afternoon, fight starts at one-thirty, probably will have everything wrapped up in less than an hour. Emmett's...er...I mean...*King's* fight is the only one scheduled for that day. So, if I was you, my dude, I would aim to be here at quarter after one, and maybe we can convince my guy to let you watch the fight. Sound good?"

It was Tuesday. That gave him three days to organize the next phase of the plan. It wasn't a lot of time, but Kevin felt as though all the pieces were falling in line. It was like the universe *wanted* Isabelle Lamoine to be taken from her uncle. Three days wasn't a lot of time, but it could work.

"I think that would be perfect. I look forward to it," Kevin said and gave Levi a thumbs-up gesture.

"Just don't forget my grand, yo."

They said their good-byes and Kevin disconnected the call.

Kevin then went to his smartphone, pulled up the pictures he had taken of Isabelle at the farmhouse and sent them all off to Zeke with a simple text.

We have a window. Can you be here before Saturday?

"A window?" Levi asked confused. "What window? What are you talking about?" Kevin looked at him and smiled.

"The uncle has a fight on Saturday," he said contently.

"Yeah? So?" Levi said and looked at him like he was really trying to understand.

"*So,*" Kevin repeated the man's word back to him mockingly. "He's not going to take the kid *with* him. They'll be separated. That's when we'll take her." Levi nodded numbly like he understood the logic, but Kevin doubted it.

Then, Zeke's reply came through.

We're on our way.

CHAPTER 23

Emmett

"I *did* say I thought this was a bad idea, right?" Calvin asked sarcastically as he exited the driver's side. He had insisted on driving today.

Honestly, Emmett didn't want him here. This felt like something between him and Bill. Brooks versus Adler. But Calvin was a peacemaker at heart, and Emmett knew he couldn't keep him away. Emmett knew, by the way he sometimes spoke about that fateful night, that Calvin carried some guilt with him too. Emmett was sure that's why he was here: to keep the past from repeating itself by making sure things didn't go too far.

He was a good friend.

You did, Emmett signed with a grin. *A few times, actually.*

"That's because I really think this was a bad idea. Say the word, and we'll drive back to your farm and spend the afternoon with the girls. You don't need this."

Except I do, Emmett signed with a sad expression. He could tell by the look on Calvin's face that he knew it was the truth. *It's a sweetheart deal, you know that. He literally gave me an offer I can't refuse.*

"That's the part I don't like, Emmett." He looked at him with sudden concern and scratched his head. "He's *using* your situation to *manipulate* you into this fight."

I know.

"Yeah, well, that's even more of a reason *not* to do it. Emmett," Calvin said incredulously and changed his expression to one of fatherly concern. "You don't need to start up this goddamn feud again. Like, Jesus Christ, just walk away, man! You've got Isabelle now, *and* Brooke. You don't need this as much as you think you do. We can find another way."

You're right, he signed slowly. *I'm not here to start anything. I'm mostly here for the money. As far as I'm concerned, it's over. All of it,* he signed sharply. *I'm tired of carrying it around.* He looked to Calvin, silently praying his friend understood what he meant, because he wasn't sure he could explain it much better. Luckily, Calvin nodded solemnly. *I can't do it anymore. I won't.*

"Then let's just leave. Nothing good can come from this." To that, Emmett just looked at him for a moment.

I'm not so sure about that.

"What's *that* supposed to mean?"

It's just that, Emmett started to sign, but he paused. Unable to quite explain the complexity of what he felt to be true. He had to try though. *It's like what happened between Clive, Tommy, and Becky was this giant disaster that swallowed them up and destroyed them all. You know, maybe not all at once, but that one event led to each of their deaths. Like a black hole of shit that eventually sucked them into it, because they couldn't escape. But I don't think they were the only ones, Calvin. I think we were all sucked into it in one way or another, and we've been swirling around in the shit ever since.*

Emmett couldn't help the tears that formed in his eyes, nor did he feel the need to wipe them away. He still needed his hands to talk. *You got out, or maybe you haven't, but I know you've been trying to get me out of it. I didn't realize that until Isabelle came along and finally got me out, and I think, in some way, maybe I got her out too.*

Emmett thought back to the nightmares that would cause Isabelle to call out in the dead of night. They had eventually slowed to a point that the bad dreams stopped entirely.

I don't know. I know one thing, though. I don't want to go back, Calvin. I don't want to feel like that anymore, or ever again.

"Oh, I get it," Calvin said with a slight chuckle, like they had a inside joke. "Better than you know. That's why I don't get why we're here. You said you got out, but I feel like you're risking being sucked into this blackhole of yours all over again by doing this."

That's not what I'm doing.

"Oh?" Calvin sounded less than convinced. "You don't think so?"

No, Emmett signed quickly. *I think this might help Bill get out.*

"How so?" Calvin asked across the hood of the truck with a renewed interest. Emmett smirked as he thought back to the cabaret.

It was something he said, or how he said it, maybe both, when he confronted me at The G-P-B. Emmett looked at Calvin with some remorse because he had trouble finding the words to describe the feeling he had. *I just feel like he NEEDS this.*

In the parking lot on the night of the cabaret, Bill reminded him of a wolf caught in a trap. Full of anger and pain, but with no idea how he could escape it. Emmett had to admit, he felt a little silly thinking simply fighting the man would change everything in his life. Life was never so cut and dry. He knew one thing, Bill needed to hit something. So, Emmett would give him something to hit. He wasn't going to *let* the man beat him, that was madness. Emmett fully planned to defend himself, but at the same time, he also decided he wasn't here to *fight* him. He tasked himself to walk the razor's edge to winning a fight by not injuring his opponent. He would stand against the tidal wave of Bill's anger and aggression until it ebbed enough for him to see a way forward, or until Bill knocked him to the ground. Emmett told himself if Bill knocked him to the ground fairly, even once, he wouldn't get up. After all, he wasn't here to fight with the man. Emmett knew what it was like to lose a brother. For him, this was closer to shared grieving than it was to an actual fight. After all, you can't expect to free a trapped animal without getting bit. They were in this together, with a secret shared goal. Even though it seemed like they're at odds with each other, they both wanted the same thing.

"What?" Calvin's face scrunched up in confusion. "So, you're saying, you *have* to win, but Bill *needs* to win?" Emmett could only shrug and nod.

Calvin must have understood how impossible the situation was because he groaned loudly and flopped onto the hood of his truck like all the life had left his body. There, he shook his head as it was cradled in his arms before he looked up to Emmett with an exasperated expression.

"Shit's never easy with you, is it?"

I like to keep it interesting, Emmett signed and smiled.

"Tommy would be proud of you for what you're trying to do here," Calvin offered weakly.

Emmett could only smirk at him.

No, he wouldn't. Tommy would want me to smash his face in, Emmett signed with a gentle sorrow.

"Well, *I'm* proud of you," Calvin said almost reluctantly as he picked himself up off his truck's hood, like it was a consolation prize.

If that was the case, he couldn't have been more wrong.

"*Because* a *lesser* man probably would go in there and do just that. *You* plan to go in there and somehow make a friend." Calvin chuckled a bit at the very prospect of it.

I don't know what I'm going to do in there, Emmett signed quickly. *I only know what I'm not going to do.*

Calvin breathed in deeply and looked around the almost vacant parking lot. The only other vehicle was Bill's diesel three-quarter ton truck. Calvin sucked on his teeth loudly as he looked over the empty lot before he finally allowed his gaze to fall back onto Emmett. He had been stalling this whole time, but he had come to the end of the line. With nothing left to say, the two of them faced the ugly task ahead,

"I guess, we should get to it." It was easy to tell that Calvin wasn't happy about it. "We don't want to keep them waiting."

Emmett only nodded, and with his bag in hand, he fell in beside Calvin as they made their way into the grounds. When they passed the ticket booth, Calvin reached up and gently patted him on the back before he chuckled quietly. He looked to his friend, but he didn't comment on it. Calvin just looked ahead with a weird grin on his face. Emmett breathed deeply and let the matter drop between them.

It didn't matter.

He *was* glad his friend was with him.

CHAPTER 24

Brooke

Brooke sat in Emmett's chair and nestled herself into the groove his large frame had already worn into the cushion. When she got here, Lucas was already here, playing with Belle and Max in the yard by the large tree. When Emmett left with Calvin, she called the kids in to watch their movie in the living room. Lucas had introduced Isabelle to the first two Avengers movies when she slept over at his house, and now she was hooked. The plan was for them to watch the third movie while Emmett had his fight with Lucas's uncle. Brooke tried not to think about what Emmett was doing as she made the kids a couple bologna sandwiches, with a small side of potato chips for them to snack on while the movie started.

Brooke didn't like the deal. She understood why Emmett felt he couldn't decline the offer, and she told him what she thought of it. It felt like a trap to her. She couldn't explain the exact rationale, but it stunk to high-heaven. On more than one occasion when she was growing up, her father advised her not to let business get personal. She always thought that was good advice. A little vague and unhelpful at the time, but most good advice was. She saw the wisdom of it here, though. Bill was using a very lucrative deal to pull Emmett into a personal dispute, the *most* personal dispute that Brooke could ever imagine. To her, there was just a *wrongness* to it. Like a strange shadow that was cast upon the whole thing, that promised only disaster and disarray, and neither Emmett nor Bill could see it.

She trusted Emmett, though.

I'm not going to start shit with the Adlers, I'm going there to end it. Emmett had signed to her that night after their lovemaking, when she brought up her concern to him as they laid next to each other. He must have sensed how utterly unconvincing that statement was, because he followed it up with, *I'm not going to do anything that would jeopardize what I have with Isabelle, and you.* He paused to lovingly caress her cheek. *You two are everything to me.*

She still didn't like it, but she believed him.

Brooke distracted herself from her pestering anxieties by scrolling through her pictures from the week of the Beef and Barley festival. She watched how Emmett and Isabelle's performance at the kid's dance had grown into an impromptu dance mob when the other kids filtered in from the surrounding crowd. She grinned at the muted look of concern on Emmett's face when the dance ended and all the kids hopped excitedly around him, as if they might attack him at any second. Luckily, Brooke had kept filming a moment longer, so she caught the moment the two of them exchanged *their* sign. *Forever.* Brooke's heart practically melted every time she saw it.

Those two are so freaking cute together, she thought adoringly about the pair.

Then she scrolled through the photos from the cabaret.

The first one was the best, and the one she lingered on the longest. It was taken by a friend of hers they ran into on the sidelines. It was the only one they posed for, an official photo that commemorated their relationship. They stood by the back wall. The painted cinderblock stood out prominently behind them, but that's not what caught her eye.

In the photo, Emmett stood like a proud giant. She moved into his side and pressed her body against his, and laid her hand lovingly against his chest as the photo was taken. She looked forward and flashed her best smile for the camera. Emmett, however, smiled down towards her when she nestled herself into his arms, forgetting all about the camera in front of them. He was solely focused on her in that moment, and the gentle warmth of his expression made her eyes water.

Graeme used to look at her like that.

The rest of the pictures were clearly taken after she had started drinking.

Emmett had to abstain himself after the first hour, because he was driving that night. There were a couple of photos she took that were of the two of them sharing a few shots before the band started. A photo she remembered taking during the last dance that played over the sound system before the band took the stage. It was Friends in Low Places, a popular country song that always brought people onto the dance floor. In the photo, they pressed their faces together and Brooke flashed her best alluring smile, like a sultry temptress. Emmett had a goofy smile on his face, but she didn't mind. It was genuine. That's what she liked about it.

She had a picture of them both doing a *kissy-face* towards the camera. In another one she took while she gave him a quick kiss on the cheek. There were others she secretly snapped while Emmett wasn't looking.

In one, Brooke snapped a quick picture of him as he was coming back from the washroom. Undoubtedly a little pervy, but the exact circumstances of this picture were a tad fuzzy. So, she cut herself a break. In the picture, Emmett looked like an impossibly large investment banker in his shirt and tie, with his dress vest hugging his body beautifully. He still had his dark tie snugged tightly against his neck, but at this point in the night, he had rolled up the sleeves on his shirt and exposed his meaty forearms. All the rest of the men at the dance wore jeans, and work shirts. Some pushed their comfort zone by wearing golf shirts and slacks. Only Emmett looked like a modern, warrior prince as he stalked out of that bathroom. Brooke chuckled softly when she zoomed in only to notice the looks of shocked awe on some of the other men who were entering the bathroom.

That's MY man, she swooned inside her own head.

"Did anybody want anything from the kitchen?" Isabelle's question stirred Brooke from her daydreaming. When she looked up from her phone, Isabelle was collecting her and Lucas's empty dishes to take them back to the sink.

"No, thank you." Lucas didn't even look away from the tv when he answered.

"No thanks, sweetie." She smiled at Isabelle as she passed her the dishes in her hand.

"Hurry back," Lucas pleaded softly. "Captain America shows up soon."

"I'll be quick," Isabelle answered reassuringly before she disappeared through the rounded archway into the kitchen.

A few seconds later, a crash came from the kitchen that Brooke almost immediately recognized as plates crashing to the ground.

"You okay in there?" Brooke asked quickly after the sound had ebbed, and she expected a quick answer.

When she didn't get one, Brooke shifted in her seat to look back to the kitchen.

"Isabelle?"

Through the archway, she saw Isabelle standing motionless, in front of the sink. The small plates she had been carrying were in broken fragments by the girl's feet, but Isabelle made no move to clean up the mess. She didn't move at all.

Isabelle just stared at something outside the kitchen window.

Something's wrong, a nervous voice inside her spoke up.

It forced Brooke to forget all about her phone and lift herself out of Emmett's chair to investigate a bit further. She lightly climbed the two small steps into the dining room, and quickly spied the brightly colored box that stood between the two metal urns in the china cabinet. Brooke furrowed her brow at it the first time she had seen it. She knew there was a story there, and maybe someday she would hear it.

Something else was concerning her at the moment.

"Everything okay, kiddo?" Brooke paused at the archway for the question, but what she saw pressed her forward.

Isabelle stood in her socked feet surrounded by the broken fragments of the plate she had been carrying, and inexplicably dropped. She was trembling. She wasn't cold, Isabelle wasn't shivering. Brooke's brain instinctively knew the difference.

Then her ears picked up on Isabelle's subtle whispers as she cautiously moved closer.

"*He can't be here. He can't be here. How? How is he here? He can't be here.*" It was like she was stuck in a loop or something.

Through the window a large, black SUV slowly approached the house. Brooke could see the inside of the vehicle, and the numerous bodies within. One caught her eye immediately. The one in the passenger seat. The man in the dark coat with a dark red button-up shirt underneath and a black, narrow tie that hung ominously from his neck. Her gaze lingered on the slick-looking individual a moment longer before she reached Isabelle. Brooke gently placed her hand on the girl's shoulder.

"What's wr-." Brooke was about to ask what was wrong, but before she could get the words out, Isabelle turned to her, white as a ghost.

"We *have* to get out of here!" she quickly said with panic in her voice as she reached up and latched onto Brooke's arm. "We have to go! Right now! Come on!" Isabelle started tugging wildly on her arms to lead her away from the window and back into the living room.

"What?!" Brooke shot back, confused at her sudden, and inexplicable fear. "What do you mean?!" Brooke asked quickly and looked back to the SUV as it came to a slow stop in front of the house. "Who *is* that?!" she asked, somehow already knowing that Isabelle would have the answer. By the sharp way Isabelle yanked on her arms and the wide-eyed look of sheer terror on her face, she knew him.

Suddenly, Brooke wished Emmett was here.

"He's a *bad* man," Isabelle hissed quietly, like she didn't want to be heard. "A *really* bad man." Isabelle paused her yanking and looked at her with pleading eyes that leaked tears down her face. "He *hurt* my mom."

Becky?!

Brooke's mind raced to try and keep up. Her world spun out of control, filling with urgent questions. *How did this guy know Becky? Had he hurt her? Becky lived in Toronto. Did this man travel all the way from there? Why?*

Brooke's mind hit a brick wall when she looked down at Isabelle terror-stricken face and realized none of that mattered now. Her brain told her that if those men had brought doom to her doorstep, for whatever reason, she had maybe a minute to act.

"Get Lucas," Brooke said quickly, and sternly.

She reached up and gave Isabelle's shoulder a slight shake to jolt her out of her terror. She didn't need Isabelle to be afraid, she *needed* her to listen.

"And get into Emmett's room! Go!" she commanded in a *mom*-voice she didn't even know she had, and roughly pushed Isabelle through the archway.

Brooke dared a quick peek outside, just in time to see all the doors of the black SUV open and the men begin to file out. Brooke didn't bother to look at them, she had to move. Some part of her prayed that this was some childish misunderstanding on Isabelle's part. Maybe later she would recount her ridiculous response to Emmett and they would both laugh over how she overreacted to the situation. The growing feeling of dread in her gut told her a different story, though.

Brooke moved to the front door in a mad dash. Thankfully, the heavy wooden door was closed, and locked. She had lived in the city, and found locking the doors when she was home a hard habit to break. She quickly snatched up the kids' coats and shoes before she rushed back into the kitchen, keeping herself low to avoid the window, and moved quickly through the dining room to Emmett's room.

"Put these on!" she commanded to the children the moment she entered the bedroom, and tossed the items in her hands onto the bed.

"What's happening?!" Lucas whined nervously as he scooped up his parka from the bed.

"We're in trouble, Lucas!" Isabelle quickly said. Lucas shrank into himself at the news.

"Hush!" Brooke hissed loudly. "We're fine." She prayed she wasn't lying when she said that. It needed to be said because she needed them to have a clear head. *Do you have a clear head?!* Brooke asked herself as she moved to the west-facing window. "You guys are going to sneak your way back to Lucas's house, and once you're there, you're going to get someone to call the police." She made it sound easy, but she knew it wasn't. Even to her, it sounded like she was asking a lot of the kids.

"The police!?" Lucas yelped as Brooke removed the screen from the window.

"Yes, Lucas, the police. You're going to do that as quickly as you can, okay?" Brooke didn't even look at them as she opened the window out as far as it would go.

"You can't fit through there," Isabelle sobbed weakly.

"I'm not going. You are! Come on! Get your shoes on!" she called out to them sternly when she turned back.

What are you doing? Brooke silenced the voice with a muted growl as she moved in towards Lucas and helped him with his last shoe.

"Okay! Lucas, you're first." She dragged the poor, fearful boy towards the window. "I'm going to hoist you up, and you're going to slide your feet out the window and I'm going to lower you down. Okay, ready?" She pulled on the boy's arm before he replied. Thankfully, Lucas complied and did as she instructed.

She braced herself as best she could, but as small as Lucas was, he still weighed too much for her to gently lower the boy's weight from the window. Emmett could probably easily accomplish that feat. Brooke, however, had to let the boy drop to the snow-covered ground when his weight threatened to pull her out the window. She didn't even wait to see if Lucas landed safely, she turned back to Isabelle and sharply gestured for her to follow.

"I'm not leaving you," Isabelle said through cascading tears.

Dammit!

Brooke angrily rushed towards her but before she could grab Isabelle by the shoulder and haul her towards the window, she rushed forward and latched her arms around Brooke and squeezed.

"I *won't* leave you." Brooke couldn't help herself.

She embraced the small child she had grown so close to over the past few months.

"I love you, kiddo."

The words slipped easily from her mouth, and she bent down and quickly kissed Isabelle on the top of her head before she roughly pushed her back and held her at arm's length.

"Now get your *ass* out that window!"

She didn't wait for another word from Isabelle. Brooke grabbed her and hauled her in front of the window. Isabelle wept horribly as she stepped up on the sill and slipped her legs out the window.

A second later, Isabelle dropped and landed nimbly beside Lucas. She exchanged a look with Isabelle that spoke volumes. There was so much she wanted to say, but there was no time. Brooke had another job to do. She quickly cranked the window closed and replaced the screen.

What are you doing? The voice cried out again.

She left the bedroom and grabbed her phone from beside the big leather chair. She unlocked it, pulled up the messaging app, and opened her conversation with Calvin. He was the best choice to try and reach as Emmett probably wouldn't have his phone with him. Brooke quickly typed the only thing she could think of that would accurately describe their situation before she sent it off.

She had a plan, though not a great one. She would play dumb and try to convince them they had the wrong farm. Some part of her still hoped it was just a tragic misunderstanding. As she entered the kitchen, she convinced herself that talking to the men in the SUV was the best way to straighten things out.

She didn't look out the window as she approached the front door, fully expecting to open it to confront the strange men outside Emmett's house.

That's not what happened though.

As she reached the steps leading down to the entrance, an ear-splitting crack shot through the kitchen like a gunshot as the heavy wooden door flew inwards with wild abandon.

Brooke shrieked loudly and jumped away from the steps as the door ricocheted off the coats hung by the door.

What are you doing?!

The voice screamed in her head, urging her to run, hide, or do anything other than stand and face what was coming through the door.

No, Brooke calmly replied to the voice, even as her heart pounded madly inside her chest.

She knew what she was doing. She was sacrificing herself so Isabelle could escape whatever was going to step through the freshly broken doorway in front of her. She was facing it head-on, so Isabelle wouldn't have to. She was going to do what she always wanted to do.

She was doing what a mother would do.

A few heartbeats later, a hand extended from the outside and eased the door ajar so a man could step into the house. She immediately recognized the man from the passenger seat of the SUV. He delicately stepped inside with his long, black wool coat hanging heavily down his sides.

"Ello, *mon cher,*" he said almost musically and flashed a bright smile at her.

CHAPTER 25

Calvin

The call came through on his phone shortly before the round was due to end.

It wasn't going great for Emmett. To his credit, he was putting on a masterclass on how to block punches, coverup openings, and mitigate damage, but he was still getting hit. Bill unleashed a brutal combo after he pushed Emmett back against the cage, and with nowhere to go, he unloaded on Emmett. Most of the blows were blocked, but a crushing rib shot slipped through Emmett's guard, and Bill quickly followed it up with a straight punch that probably would have cost Emmett his front teeth, if he hadn't been wearing his mouthguard. Bill snuck in a solid hook before Emmett was able to circle out of the corner and put some distance between them. Calvin's heart sank a bit when he spied a trickle of blood running down Emmett's left cheek.

"Hello?" he said into his phone after he accepted the call, his voice showcasing his growing unease. He couldn't help that.

"Calvin?" a voice he was fairly certain he recognized spoke up, and a second later the voice on the other end confirmed what he suspected. "It's Henry Johnson, over at *the store*."

Calvin grinned slightly because of how he referred to the Russell Gas and Convenience Store like it was the only actual store in the town.

"Yeah, Henry. How are you?" Calvin said absently as he flinched away from another body shot Emmett absorbed into his gut.

"Fine. Fine." Henry said quickly to dispense with the pleasantries. 'Look, Calvin, I know I'm *old and paranoid*," he said it like he was mocking himself from something Calvin may have said to him in the past. "But I'm going to tell you a story, and afterwards, I'll let you decide what you're going to do with it." Henry then paused for a reply.

"Okay," Calvin said, forcing his attention away from the fight. Something in Henry's voice piqued his interest. "I'm listening."

"Around the beginning of the week, Monday or Tuesday, I don't remember which. Anyways, these two fellas walk in, dressed in real nice clothes. You know, *city folk*. They stuck out to me because the one guy, a real big dude, like *Emmett Brooks-big*, had a cast on his one arm."

Calvin listened intently to Henry's story as he watched Emmett step forward and kicked Bill in the meat of his thigh. The angry Adler staggered slightly and Emmett used the opening to punch Bill in the mouth.

"Anyways, we talked a bit, they commented on my board, like most people do, and I didn't think anything of it at the time. Just shooting the shit a bit with the customers, you know."

"Yeah," Calvin agreed. "Small talk, I get it."

"So, they leave, and I don't think about them again. Until a couple days later," Henry said in a conspiratorial tone. "I'm watching the surveillance feed for the week to see if there were any shoplifters I might have missed. Anyways, I get to the point where it's the two city-guys, and I watched when I turned to get a pack of smokes for the big guy, and he reaches over for the board when my back's turned."

"For what?" Calvin asked quickly, wondering where this story would eventually lead.

"One of the pictures, I think. Before he could get it, the other guy slapped his hand away."

"Okay," Calvin said with a bit of impatience. Below him, the bell rang to signified the end of the round. Bill growled angrily and spit a gob of red spittle to the mat before he turned and stormed to his corner.

"Again, I didn't think anything of it. No harm, no foul. Then something happened after lunch and it *hits* me. The whole conversation I had with the smaller guy, about the picture he was interested in." Calvin sensed the shift in the man's tone. Henry was worried. "It was Isabelle's."

Calvin instinctively looked to Emmett when he heard the girl's name. He was down in the ring, casually sipping water, looking at nothing in particular and waiting for the next round.

"He was going on about how he thought Emmett was some cousin of his or something, but the whole time he's talking about Emmett, he was *looking* at Isabelle. Like, he knows her." Henry said and let the statement hang in the air. Calvin's mind raced back to something Henry had said earlier, covering all the angles.

"What happened today, Hank?" he asked slowly.

"I see the same two guys, over in the Inn's side of the parking lot, and they're with four other guys. All of them dressed like city folk, and they all pile into a big, black SUV and turn onto the highway, going *towards* St-Lazare. Now, I don't know why a bunch of city-slickers would be heading out *that* way, but the more I thought about it, the worse the feeling in my gut got. So, I called you."

It was then a text message buzzed through on his phone.

First things first, he thought and considered Hank's story.

Something about it didn't feel right to him, either. Calvin was more than sure Mr. Johnson was just being overly cautious, but once Isabelle's name came into the mix, Calvin had to agree with his concern. *Better safe than sorry.*

"Hank, I'm going to call the detachment and have an officer come out and get a statement from you."

"Do you think something is going on?" he asked nervously.

"I'm sure it's nothing, but if it's enough for you to be concerned, it's enough for me to get it down on paper. Do me a favor, transfer the footage of the two men onto a thumb-drive or something? Might as well add that to the statement." Calvin said and perked up when the start of the second round began.

"I already did," Henry said excitedly. "It will be ready for the officer when they get here."

"It should be sometime today," Calvin said as a way to end the call.

"Okay. I'll be here until they come. Thanks, Calvin."

"Have a good day, Henry." Calvin ended the call.

Down in the ring, Emmett met Bill in the center. Bill was clearly moving slower. His mad aggression from the round before was catching up to him. Emmett was bloodied, but he still looked fresh. He clenched the phone in his hand tightly as he watched Bill try to batter Emmett into submission again. After a short moment, a voice inside his head reminded him about something, *the text.*

Calvin opened up his phone and read the short text from Brooke.

911!

Without even knowing he was doing it, like his legs had a mind of their own, Calvin shot out of his seat. He briefly stared at Brooke's simple message that had caused a lightning storm of thought inside his head. He quickly ran through Henry Johnson's story.

Did he mention a time when he saw the group of men?

Calvin quickly ran through the conversation. *After lunch,* that's what he had said. Henry said he was spooked by something that happened *after lunch.*

Calvin quickly thought back to when he picked up Emmett, it was shortly after twelve-thirty. The fight was scheduled for one-thirty that afternoon, and it was a forty-minute drive. *Maybe they waited until they were sure Emmett would be in Churchbridge.*

Calvin thought for a minute about who *they* could be. *City-slickers,* Henry had said. He had also commented numerous times on how well they were dressed. Calvin knew there were a thousand reasons businessmen might need to travel through the area. *Businessmen don't travel in groups of six. They usually travel in pairs, three max.* Six people sounded more like a *crew* to him.

A crew that was interested in Isabelle. He looked incredulously at Brooke's text, and felt a deepening sense of dread.

How? How the fuck would they know to go now? Possibly the only time Emmett wasn't with Isabelle.

It was the one thing he couldn't figure out, the one thing that still allowed him to think that he was maybe overreacting to an old man's story and a bunch of dire-looking coincidences. Nobody knew about this fight. Bill paid Chester extra to keep it off the books. Unless...

Calvin madly stepped down the metal bleachers. He was the only spectator in the building. So, when he descended down the row of metal benches, the booming sounds of his steps resonated around the space. He hurried up to Chester, who was seated ringside at a little table with a metal bell affixed to it. He was closely watching the stopwatch in his hand.

"Chester!" he called out as he fell in beside the kid. "Did you tell anyone about this fight?!" he asked quickly and leaned into him for the answer.

"Hey, man!" Chester waved him off. "Stop crowding me! Look at the stands, *bro*. Does it *look* like I told anybody? Biggest-damned-fight I could ever book and I can't show it to nobody. Fucking Bill," Chester said absently but with definite disdain. "*Motherfucker* went over my head to arrange this bullshit. He made *my dad* force me into it. Can you believe *that* shit?!"

Calvin waved his hands, as if to disperse with the useless information he was getting.

"So, nobody knows about this fight? Nobody knows we would be *here*, at this *time*?" He emphasized the words to try to convey the importance of the information to this dimwit.

"No," he said definitively and Calvin breathed a little easier for a brief heartbeat. Then Chester turned back to him, and wagged his finger, like he suddenly remembered something. "Oh, except for that *promoter-guy* from Winnipeg," he said lightly.

Calvin had reached the end of his patience with the kid.

He roughly grabbed two fistfuls of Chester's thick hoodie before he hauled the small-framed kid out of the chair he was sitting in. Calvin spun him around and pushed him over the table.

"What *promoter-guy?!*" Calvin screamed the question at him. "Tell me!"

"Calvin!" Bill's annoyed voice called out from the ring. "What the hell?!" He could see in his periphery, that Emmett and Bill had paused their fight to watch the commotion.

"What the fuck, bro! What's your deal?!" Chester whined and fought uselessly in Calvin's steel grasp. "Get off me!"

He shook the kid savagely and repeated his question.

"Who the fuck did you *tell* about this fight, you little shit?!" Calvin shook him again.

"Some guy from Winnipeg," Chester spoke up indignantly. "He called me a couple days ago; said he had seen some of Emmett's fights and wanted to sign him! He wanted to *meet* him!" Chester said like he was defending himself. Like he was doing Emmett a favor. "So, I told him he could wait in the parking lot until the fight's over. Shit, man! Go have a look, I bet you he's waiting out there right now!"

Calvin angrily shoved the kid into the table and quickly ran to the window on the man-door of the Quonset to check the parking lot.

A growing part of him wasn't surprised to find only his and Bill's vehicles were in the parking lot.

"Open the cage!" Calvin yelled back to Chester in his *cop*-voice, the one that hinted towards dire consequences if he was disobeyed, and angrily pointed to the cage with the two confused fighters inside of it. When Chester hesitated, Calvin added, "NOW!"

"What do you think you're doing, Calvin?" Bill asked heatedly as Chester moved towards the back of the cage. "We're not done yet!"

Calvin didn't pay him any attention.

"Emmett!" he called up to his friend, and waved him towards the ring's exit. "We're *leaving*."

Why? Emmett signed quickly and looked at him with dire concern on his face. He was always good at reading a room. *What's wrong?*

"I don't know for sure," Calvin admitted quickly. "Something is going on at the farm. The girls are in trouble." Emmett didn't need to hear another word.

"Where the hell do you think you're going?" Bill shouted to Emmett's back. He rushed forward and reached out to grab Emmett's shoulder to stop him from leaving. "We're not done."

Emmett was though, and a half second later, so was Bill.

A strange, choking sound erupted from Emmett's throat as he sharply turned back towards Bill. Calvin recognized it, though. That's what Emmett sounded like when he screamed. Bill didn't even see the blow that ended the fight. Calvin did, a split second before his balled-up fist struck Bill in the mouth. He saw it on Emmett's face.

He was done playing around.

Emmett's mighty fist made a loud slapping sound when it connected that reverberated throughout the building. Calvin instinctively flinched away from the suddenness of the blow, but didn't miss the impossible way Bill's face contorted from the force of it. Big Bill spun completely around, as if God himself had simply reached down and turned him around. He teetered there drunkenly for a breath before slowly wilting to the mat.

Emmett didn't even notice his opponent fall. He was already angrily rattling the cage door for Chester to remove the small lock on the latch.

"Alright! Fuck! I'm getting it!" Chester complained as he fidgeted with the small carabiner as Emmett continued to rattle the door like a raging animal.

Calvin ran to the fighter's area. He burst through the thick curtain, straight to Emmett's things. He madly scooped up his friend's belongings into his arms and hurried back through the curtain. Emmett was free and quickly descending the steps to meet him. The two of them sprinted to the exit of the building. Outside, Emmett ran towards the truck in only the dark sweat pants he had been wearing in the ring. If the light dusting of snow on the ground bothered his bare feet, he made no show of it.

"Put these on," Calvin said.

He opened his door and threw his friend's belongings into the cab before he hopped into the driver's seat. Emmett was a second behind him getting into the truck. By the time he had his door closed, Calvin was already throwing the transmission into reverse.

"Hold on!"

Calvin stomped on the gas and the truck shot backwards with surprising speed. Calvin spun the wheel hard. The truck spit gravel forward as the gravity inside shifted violently. He hit the brakes, shifted the transmission into drive and stomped on the gas pedal like he was trying to hurt it.

The truck exploded forward as the engine roared like a wild predator in pursuit of its prey. He didn't even slow down at the entrance into the parking lot, he eased off the gas as he approached the turn. When his weight started to shift in his seat, Calvin gunned the throttle. The back wheel spun on the loose gravel, just as Calvin expected, and the truck precariously drifted around the corner. He eased off the gas once more to stabilize the pick-up on the road before he stepped down on it again and they rocketed towards Churchbridge.

Calvin's heart raced as a tiny voice inside him reminded him that it was still mid-afternoon on a Saturday. He quickly reached down, turned on his headlights, the emergency flashers, and madly cycled the high beams on and off as he approached the turnoff onto the busy highway. He wasn't in a cruiser, but he could still try to make his truck as visible as possible to the other drivers on the road.

"Watch your side!" he shouted to Emmett as the turnoff approached ahead.

Calvin looked down his side, and his heart sank when he saw a trio of cars. He could make it. Beside him, Emmett snapped his fingers in quick succession to get his attention. When he looked to Emmett's side, he saw a large tractor-trailer unit moving in. His truck fishtailed precariously on the gravel road as Calvin tried to push the gas pedal through the floorboard in order to beat that tractor-trailer unit to the intersection. His heart raced as he flashed the high beams, honked the horn, and fought to keep the wildly accelerating truck on the road.

He risked a glance to the trio of cars on his side. Calvin was tickled to see the lead vehicle must have seen the light display his truck was putting on and slowed down their approach. The tractor-trailer unit, however, didn't slow down one bit. Truckers were like that. He didn't blame the driver. For all he knew, it was some farmer kid racing to his girlfriend's house for a quick screw. Plus, Calvin had the stop sign. Unfortunately, he wasn't going to lose this battle of wills with the truck driver.

He couldn't.

At the intersection, Calvin thanked God for the mild start to the winter season. Ahead of them, they were blessed with bare asphalt on the highway. He couldn't imagine doing this on snow covered roads, that would be suicide. He eased off the gas and took the turn wide. Again, when he felt his weight shift on his seat, he gunned the engine. The horn of the tractor-trailer unit blared loudly inside the cab of the truck, but was soon overridden by the sound of squealing tires as the wheels hit the highway's asphalt. He expertly drifted the truck onto the highway, dangerously close to the large transport truck that was practically kissing Calvin's rear bumper and angrily blaring his horn behind them. He eased up on the gas only enough to stabilize the truck on the road, then when they were pointed firmly down the highway Calvin slammed down on the gas pedal again.

Calvin fished his phone out of his pocket as he watched the speedometer rapidly climb. One hundred kilometers, one-ten, one-twenty, one-thirty...

He placed his phone into its holder on the dash as the speedometer passed one-fifty, and didn't look at it again as he pressed the button on the side of the phone. When the dreamy little icon popped up onto the screen indicating that his phone was actively listening, Calvin spoke loudly and clearly.

"Call work," he said and watch the road in front of him intensely.

The phone rang twice over the truck's speakers before it was picked up. On the other end, a familiar voice spoke up.

"Dispatch," she answered quickly.

"Marcie!" Calvin practically shouted in order to speak over the sound of the raging engine. "Where are our people?"

"Brock is finishing up with an MVA over by Birtle," the dispatcher said dispassionately, wasting no time in her response. "And Jessica is doing radar out by Rossburn."

"Wake up the night shift," he said quickly. "And get them into cruisers. *Full gear.* I want Brock on Highway Forty-One between Birtle and St-Lazare, as soon as he's able to tear away. Jessica needs to be on Highway Sixteen, patrolling from Russell all the way up to Shoal Lake. Send one of the night shift over to Henry's to get a full statement, and get the other one patrolling Highway Forty-One south of St-Lazare. We are looking for a Black SUV with six, adult males inside."

"Got it," the dispatcher said the moment she had a chance.

"Whoever goes to Henry's will have to update us on the vehicle's description when he gets it, until then we pull over every Black SUV that fits our description. I don't care why. Tell them to find a reason. I want vehicle tags, and ID's from everyone inside the vehicle before we kick them loose."

"What are we looking for, boss?"

Calvin sighed quietly as he passed a small sedan on the highway like it was standing still. He didn't want Emmett to hear this part, but he had to cover all the bases.

"Henry will have the descriptions of the men we're looking for, but also be on the lookout for an *Isabelle Lamoine.*" Beside him, Emmett kicked up at the mention of his girl's name. Calvin quickly listed off a description of her to the dispatcher. "Now, I'm heading to the Brooks' farm, that's the site of our unknown emergency. Keep our people on the lookout until you hear from me. Now, I'm going to hang up, and when I do, I want you to call Langenburg's detachment and advise them I'm traveling in my personal vehicle on Highway Sixteen at a *high rate of speed*. I don't want them to try and stop me because I'm *not* stopping. If they could clear a path for me to Russell, that would be amazing, but if not, tell them to watch Sixteen for our SUV and relay everything I told you to them."

"Got it. I'm on it."

Calvin reached up and ended the call. Beside him, Emmett signed quickly.

What's happening?

Calvin didn't want to tell his friend the situation. As far as Calvin was concerned, this was a police matter now. Standard procedure, as unflattering as it sounded, was to treat family members in an active crisis like *mushrooms*. 'Keep them in the dark, and feed them bullshit'. *To keep them calm.* Emotional people complicated things. He couldn't do that with Emmett, though. He was right there beside him. They were in this together.

So, Calvin told him everything as Emmett finished putting on his clothes. He quickly recapped Henry's story and mentioned the cryptic text from Brooke. He took the time to explain the timeline of events in his head that had him so concerned, and finished it off with Chester's mysterious *promoter* that never showed.

"I don't *know* what's going on," Calvin said at the end. Breaking one of his own rules, and telling his friend the truth as he knew it. "But we're going to find out."

Ahead of them was the town limit of Langenburg, and the sign that advised drivers of the upcoming *reduced* speed limit. Calvin started flashing the high beams again, and honking the horn as he approached the town like an angry cruise missile.

CHAPTER 26

Zeke

"Ello, *Mon Cher.*" Zeke stepped up into the quaint little kitchen, and the attractive, middle-aged woman with the long dark hair stepped back away from him with a look of abject terror. He watched with some amusement as the look quickly shifted to one of cautious indignation before she spoke.

"I don't know what you guys think you're doing, but-," she started to say but Zeke didn't let her finish. He wasn't here to talk.

Zeke struck her across the face.

It was clear by the violent way she recoiled away from the blow that the dark-haired woman had never been *really* struck before. Zeke knew prostitutes who could take a blow like that without flinching. This one spun away, lost her footing, and crumpled to the ground. He didn't even strike her with his fist. He was smarter than that. You hit someone with your fist when you wish to injure them. You slapped someone when you wanted them to feel pain.

A good slap was an important tool to any experienced criminal.

Zeke dispassionately walked up to the woman as his men entered the house behind him. He grabbed her under the arms and roughly pulled her onto feet her before he shoved her towards nearest chair by the table. The dark-haired woman let out a small yelp as she crashed into the small table.

"Ave a seat," Zeke growled at her and watched with some satisfaction when she quietly obeyed.

The woman used her whole hand to brush a tangle of hair away from her face. At the corner of her mouth, Zeke delighted at the sight of a small trickle of blood. After all, nothing gets people talking like the taste of their own blood. He turned his head slightly towards his men, but he kept a cold glare on the bleeding woman.

"Search da ouse," he said quietly.

Immediately, Kevin and Khan moved into action. As a pair, they first headed to the stairs that led down into the darkened basement. It was the most obvious hiding spot. They *knew* Belle was here. It was only a matter of time, which he was in short supply of, because of Kevin's supposed timeline.

Zeke pulled out his smartphone, opened his picture folder and scrolled through until he came upon the picture Kevin had sent him a couple days ago. He stepped closer to the woman, savored the way she flinched away from him, and slowly showed her the picture of Isabelle at the front of the house.

"I know she's ere," he said like he was disappointed in her. "It's only a matter of time before I find er."

Zeke pulled his phone away, and then slowly eased out the other empty chair at the table and moved it in front of the woman. He then calmly sat himself down across from her. He reached for her hands, almost lovingly, but that didn't stop the woman from inching away from his grasp. He paid no attention to her as he clasped her shaking hands and held them as he looked remorsefully at her.

"We're in a moment right now, you and I." He looked at her chestnut eyes and gave her a friendly grin as her lower lip quivered uncontrollably. "A *crossroads*, of sorts. In a moment, I'm going to ask you a question. A *very* important question. If you answer da question trutfully, I will let you leave." He smiled at her like he was showing the woman her golden ticket. "You can go back to your life. You can leave all dis misery and suffering behind you. For da rest of your life, you can be proud because you were one of da few people in dis cruel world who survived da tragedy dat fell upon dem." Zeke spoke softly, but with some excitement, like he was listing off all the prizes she had just won. *"Or,"* Zeke said, taking on a cautionary tone while looking expectantly into her eyes and rubbing the backs of her hands with his fingers. "You could be *stubborn*, but you should know, every time you refuse to answer dis question, or give me some bullsit, *tings* will get worse for you. *Exponentially* worse."

He leveled her with a hard gaze as a way of a warning. He knew she understood when she breathed in sharper at the prospect. Zeke then removed his hands from hers to show her three upheld fingers.

"I will ask only tree times. After dat, or if my men find er before you answer..."

Zeke let the unfinished threat hang in the air between them as he fished out his automatic pistol from his waistband. He held it in front of her, with his finger off the trigger, so she could gaze upon its cold, black exterior. He could tell by her eyes, this dark-haired woman did not like the sight of it. With practised ease, he pulled back the slide and ejected a round from the breech into his palm. He then showed her the tiny, golden 9mm cartridge for a moment before he placed it on the table.

"Dat is for you. Dat's yours now. If you want to be stubborn, dat will be your only reward." Zeke pointed to the ominous-looking cartridge standing upright on the table. "What's your name, *mon cheri?*" he asked softly while still holding the gun

"My name?" the woman looked to him and asked weakly. Zeke smiled warmly and nodded to her, like he was giving her his permission to continue. "My name is *fuck-you-you-french-cocksucker*, but my friends call me *fuck you!*" She tilted her head to the side, almost like a challenge.

Zeke just laughed and looked back to Remy, who was standing in the corner of the kitchen by the entrance, shaking like a leaf.

"I tink she's ready, no?" he chuckled to him.

It was then that Kevin and Khan emerged from the basement. Kevin looked at him and stiffly shook his head before he and Khan spread out through the main level. Kevin disappeared through the archway into the dining room, while Khan took the doors at the other end of the kitchen.

"Okay den, ere we go," he said lightly, like the two of them were about to play a game, and leveled the woman with a hard look. "Where is she?" he asked her slowly. He tried to stress the importance of her cooperation, but Zeke had learned from experience that the first question rarely gets answered truthfully. By the weak look of determination on the woman's face, he could see that she wouldn't be any different.

"Look, you obviously don't know Isabelle, *or me,* very well if you think I'm just going to give her up to you. So, go fuc-."

Zeke hit her again.

He used the butt of the gun in his hand, and gave no outward warning of his intention. He just snapped his arm forward and smacked her in the cheek with the gun in a savage blow. The pretty, dark-haired woman had no idea it was coming. One second, she was talking, the next she was rebounding away from the blow and sailing towards the linoleum floor once again. She crashed awkwardly and writhed in pain while holding her wounded face. She managed to turn over, and partially rise up to her knees. She was still hunched over, supporting herself on one hand while the other cradled her cheek. Zeke could see her blood slip between the fingers on her face and fall delicately to the floor.

Zeke rose, and stood over her bleeding form.

"Exponentially worse," he reminded her a breath before he stepped forward, to gain momentum, and launched his leg into her abdomen like he was trying to kick a field goal.

The woman's body jumped up with a sharp, guttural cry that barked out from her throat as her body was thrown partially through the archway from the force of the kick. The loud cry quickly devolved into a pained wheeze as her body slumped to the ground. There she folded into herself, like she was trying to wrap her body around the pain she felt, and she struggled wildly just to breathe in tiny ragged gasps.

Zeke looked down at her with disdain as he ejected the magazine from his pistol and ejected the round from the chamber into his hand. He hit the slide release button on the pistol and stowed the empty weapon into his waistband. The stray bullet he ejected went back into the magazine, then he stowed the magazine into the pocket of his slacks. With that done, he reached down and painfully clamped his hand onto the wheezing woman's ankle. Zeke roughly pulled the woman back into the kitchen. When she was beside her chair again, Zeke reached down to grab her, he yanked her back onto her feet, and mercilessly deposited her back into her chair. The woman remained hunched over, holding her sides, and whimpering quietly behind her shroud of hair.

"Don't do dis to yourself," he softly pleaded with her. "You're still young, and *fairly* attractive. I ate to see people needlessly suffer like dis." Zeke sighed heavily before he turned and moved towards the kitchen counter.

He started idly going through the drawers, because he was looking for something.

"Just tell me wat I want to know. You don't need to go trough dis."

Zeke found one drawer with an assortment of large knives of all kinds. He first pulled out a large butcher's knife, and tested its weight in his hands.

No, he thought, *not heavy enough.*

"Wat are you even to *Ma Belle*? Da *babysitter*?!" Zeke chuckled wickedly at the idea and turned back to the hunched over woman. She lifted her head a bit so she could stare at him through her veil of hair. Zeke could see she still had plenty of fight left in her.

"I'm not *just* the babysitter, asshole." Zeke briefly grinned at her tenacity before he turned back to the drawer. "I'm whatever that little girl needs me to be," the woman whimpered behind him, but with no less conviction than if she had shouted it.

Zeke let her talk. He found what he was looking for. He grinned softly as he reached down and wrapped his hand around its handle and pulled it out of the drawer. Behind him, the woman spoke up again.

"So, you might as well ask your questions. Let's get this over with." Her voice betrayed her when it cracked under the weight of her statement.

"Are you sure about dat?" Zeke asked cheerfully before he turned and showed the woman the large meat cleaver he found in the drawer. "Put your hand on the table," he dared her as he turned the cleaver menacingly in his hand.

The woman slapped her right arm down loudly onto the table. "I'm sure," she said on the edge of tears.

Zeke moved towards her with the cleaver in front of him. He stood over her as he placed his free hand over hers, and held it as he placed the cleaver's blade at her wrist. The woman shuddered behind her veil of dark hair as the heavy blade touched her skin. Zeke looked past her hair to her eyes, and flashed her a big smile before he moved the blade half-way up her forearm.

Then he applied the smallest amount of pressure as he slowly dragged the blade across her skin.

The woman cried out and slapped her free hand against her thigh as the blade easily parted her flesh, but to her credit, she didn't try to pull her arm back. Zeke was pleased to find the blade was sharp enough that he could've probably flayed the woman's skin right off her arm if he wanted to. Her blood drained onto the wood of the table and collected in small pools at the sides of her forearm. When he was done, there was a neat crimson line across the woman's arm, indicating the portion he planned to take if she failed to answer his question a second time.

"Oof! Dat's a lot to lose, *mon cheri.*"

Zeke taunted her by running the cold steel of the cleaver over the lower part of her forearm before he looked at her. Inexplicably, she used her free hand to sweep her hair away from her face. Blood covered the left side of her face from where it was slowly draining down from the small cut on her cheek, the top of her blue sweater was soaking up the blood as it ran down her neck. The rest of her face was covered in a fine sheen of sweat, her hair was slick with it, but there was no denying those eyes.

"Ask your damned question," she whispered to him. "You don't think I'm willing to give up that small bit of myself for *her? Fucking try me!*" she hissed. "Ask me!"

Zeke waved the cleaver playfully over his head before he looked at her dead in the eyes with an unbridled excitement.

"You want me to!" he yelled in her face, waving the cleaver overhead. He looked at her with a strange mixture of frustration and admiration. A lot of stone-cold criminals would have cracked a long time ago, and given him *something*. This seemingly-average woman in the mom-jeans, and plain blue sweater, still held strong against him. Something inside him wanted to break this woman. Belle was important to this one. So, the natural inference was that this woman was important to Belle.

Becky's replacement, maybe? He wondered, looking down into those fierce eyes.

Suddenly, he *wanted* her to betray Belle. So, he could show *Ma Belle* how these people will always inevitably disappoint her.

"You willing to lose an arm over some girl you don't even know, *chienne*!"

"Ask your fucking question, and we'll find out!" she challenged loudly.

"You tink er fater is dis Brooks guy? No, no, no, no." Zeke wagged the cleaver gleefully overhead. "Dat *Adler* guy his er *true* daddy, did you know that? You didn't, *did* you?" He could see by the way her fierce eyes momentarily faltered that she didn't. "Er ore of a moter told me dat."

"Ask me! See if I care who you *think* her father is! I know who she is, who she *really* is. You piece of shit!" She spit a bloody gob onto his fine leather shoes. "And I already *know* who her *real* father is."

"WHERE IS SHE!?" Zeke screamed at the top of his lungs and pulled back the cleaver to strike.

"I got something!" Kevin called from deeper in the house.

"FUCK YOU!!" the woman screamed a heartbeat later. Zeke pulled back on the cleaver, focused on the spot where he wanted to hit. "FUCKING *DO IT*!" she screamed hoarsely.

Zeke brought the cleaver down.

The woman let out a guttural, animalistic roar that filled the room as the cleaver descended, and it only died away when he planted the cleaver into the wood of the table. Beside the woman's arm.

"Saved by da bell, *mon cheri.*" Zeke chuckled and left the cleaver planted in the table, so she could look at it. The woman whimpered and wheezed as she looked disbelievingly at her still intact arm. "So to speak."

Zeke quickly pulled out his pistol from his waistband, pulled the slide back, and let it lock into the open position. He wasted no time scooping the bullet off the table and loading it into the chamber.

"Time to go, *mon cheri.*" Zeke hit the release button and savored the loud metallic sound of the slide locking into place. When the sound died away, Zeke stepped back and raised the pistol towards the trembling woman.

Only to have Remy's hand descend upon it.

"*Zeke! Stop! Don't do this,*" he said quickly, in their native tongue, and softly pushed the pistol back down to Zeke's side. "*We might still need her.*"

Zeke looked at him suspiciously and roughly pulled his hand away from Remy's grasp.

"*What the fuck do you think you're doing?*" Zeke looked at him indignantly.

It was then Kevin came rushing into the room, a second before Khan sheepishly stepped out from the girl's room, like he'd been hiding in there.

"I think they went out the back window," Kevin informed the room, and thumbed back to the living room. "I can see tracks in the snow leading to the trees."

"Okay," Zeke said lightly.

He suddenly perked up, feeling like he was one step closer to his goal, his little beauty. It didn't completely remove the sour taste in his mouth from Remy's interference. He knew how he would deal with him.

"Khan! You're with me." He pointed to the man, and he quickly fell in beside him. "Kevin, you stay with Remy. Tie up *Ma Petite Chienne,* and toss her into the back bedroom."

He turned towards Remy, and took a challenging step towards him. As expected, the small-framed man flinched away from him.

"*When I get back with my little beauty, you're going to be the one who shoots the woman.*" Zeke ejected the round in his pistol and planted it into Remy's reluctant hand. *"In front of her! Or I'll put that bullet into your head."* He nodded down to the round in his hand.

Remy nodded like a remorseful child. He looked down at the tiny bullet in his hand as Zeke retrieved the pistol's magazine from his pocket, and slapped it home into the gun. He chambered a round by hitting the slide release, and he clicked the safety on before he stowed the pistol back into his waistband.

"Let's go," he said to Khan before he turned towards the steps leading down to the front door. "I'll see you soon, *mon cheri.* To finish what we started," he teased the woman's shaking form a bit more before he finally exited the house.

In pursuit of his little beauty. To fulfill their shared destiny.

CHAPTER 27

Belle

Belle's boots slapped down onto the snow-covered ground and she immediately looked backed to the window she'd just slid from. She wanted to see Brooke one last time, to see her warm smile and a reassuring wave. When she did, Brooke was already madly cranking the window closed before she replaced the screen and disappeared into the bedroom.

I did this, Belle thought mercilessly as she looked around herself for a way out, even though no part of her wanted to leave Brooke behind with *that man. He's here, because of me.*

"Isabelle," Lucas whined quietly, tugging at her sleeve. "What's going on?! Why did we have to go out the window?!" he asked with fear in his voice, like he didn't understand why they were driven out the window, but still understood that whatever it was, it was bad. Really bad.

Inside the house, Lucas's questions were answered with a loud *thump* that came from the front. They both jumped at the unexpected sound, but only Belle knew what it signified. *He* was inside the house, *with* Brooke, and it was all because of her.

"Shhhh!" she angrily shushed him before she grabbed a handful of his parka and pulled him after her. "Come on!" she quietly commanded his trembling body into motion.

Her mind raced, filled with white noise that made holding a thought impossible. Part of her wanted to crumple to the ground and cry, certain it was the last time she'd see Brooke alive. It made each step away from the house harder than the one before. Belle forced herself, through the weak sobs that slipped from her lips and the tears that blurred her vision, to pull Lucas towards the tiny path in the grove of trees to the west.

They didn't get far.

After a few steps, the trees enveloped them completely, hiding the house from view. Belle's hurried steps slowed, as if the strength had been drained from her body, and after a few more steps, she slumped to the ground.

She cried.

"It's all my fault," she whimpered, rubbing her thighs as tears streamed down her face. "I did this."

"Isabelle," Lucas spoke up between his own sobs. "What's wrong? What's going on? What was that noise?" he sniffled unabashedly before he spoke again. "I'm *scared*."

You should be scared, she wanted to bark, because there was nothing she could say to capture the danger they were in. *Well,* a wicked voice reminded her, *I'm not in danger. HE wouldn't hurt me. He just hurts the people I care about.*

"He shouldn't be here," she confessed quietly and shook her head in disbelief. A thousand miles away Lucas spoke up again.

"*Who*?"

Belle heard the question, knew what the answer was, but instead of answering it she was bombarded with an entire landscape of buried memories she'd tried to hide away deep inside her psyche.

He was the black shape that sat motionless at the other end of her darkened room when she was younger. His wicked features were only visible when the ember of his cigarette flared. In that split second, his weird grin burned into her vision. He was the man who once punched her mother so hard she had to spend the night in the hospital. That had been Belle's fault too, because she had woken up to find the man was laying beside her in her bed, and she screamed. When her mother staggered into the room, she attacked the man like a savage animal. She had been sick, though. The man easily overpowered her. Belle tried to stop him, but he was so large. All she could do was hide herself away and watch the calamity she had caused. The same kind of calamity Brooke was now facing.

"His name is *Zeke,*" Isabelle growled the name with a burning hatred, before her voice broke back into sobs. "He's here because of *me.*"

Isabelle sobbed with renewed vigor when she thought of how she had betrayed Brooke by bringing the man from her nightmares into their happy, little lives. She inexplicably knew it was she who had brought him here with the same certainty she had that the sun would rise in the east. Only now did she realize how foolish she had been this whole time to try and forget about the man. That realization stung, but not nearly as much as the regret she felt from not telling Brooke she loved her when she had the chance.

She knew she felt those feelings, but she was afraid if she ever told someone how she felt about them, something terrible would happen to them.

So, she kept it all to herself, and it happened anyway.

Stupid, stupid, stupid, Belle cursed herself and beat her fists against her thighs in frustration over her powerlessness.

"What?!" Lucas's sobs lessened with his confusion. "Why? What did you do?" It was an innocent enough question, but it felt like a gut punch to her because she could only think of one answer.

"I was born." She looked back to him with an expression that begged for his forgiveness.

He was her curse.

The black cloud that followed her around everywhere she went. After he was gone from her and her mother's lives, she tried to pretend like he never was. When her mother got her diagnosis though, Belle felt him in the kitchen when her mother gently told her the news. Like a wicked spectre only she could see, sitting in the shadows of the room, his cigarette flaring rhythmically, like a heartbeat, to reveal his black grin. He was there with her at the memorial service, quietly whispering in her ear, reminding her how she only had *him* now. He waited for her in her dreams, quietly stalking her from the shadows. Now, he was here, threatening the life and the people she loved so much.

All that's over now. You know that, right?

She did.

"*Sors, sors, ma petite belle!" a* voice called out merrily from the far side of the house that filled her veins with ice.

It's him!

And he was coming closer.

Belle shot a terrified look to Lucas, her first friend in her new home. She remembered the day she had first met him, the same day he brought Max into her life. The little bundle of furry joy that showered her with licks at every opportunity. She left him behind too. Lucas was here though, right here in front of her.

"I love you, Lucas."

She tried to smile at him, but the expression seemed impossible to conjure up at the moment. He looked down at her with red, puffy cheeks and tears streaming down his face, like it was the last thing he expected her to say. Belle jumped off the ground and threw her arms around him.

"I'm not going to let him hurt you," she whispered in his ear.

Belle knew what she had to do.

She released herself from him and then grabbed Lucas by the shoulder and led him further down the path. She knew *he* would find their tracks and follow them, because of course he would. He followed her to this place, her little sanctuary. So, she was fairly sure there wasn't a place on this earth she could go to escape him.

So, she would stop trying.

Soon enough, Lucas got his legs beneath them and the two of them trotted as silently as they could through the grove of trees. They popped out on the other side into a small clearing before the western hay field. To their left, at the end of the grove of trees, before it opened up into the yard of the farm, were two long lines of hay bales. The large round, wrapped bales were placed end to end so it all looked like two long white tubes. These were the extras that wouldn't fit in with the stacks Emmett formed near the animal shelter.

"There!" she whispered excitedly and pulled Lucas towards the hay bales. Once there, Belle quickly pushed Lucas to the small crawl space underneath where the two tubes touched. "Hide in there, Lucas. Don't come out until they come after me, then run home and do as Brooke told us." Belle's heart ached when she said her... friend's name. "Get your parents to call the police."

"But what about you?!" he whined as he reluctantly moved towards the space. Luckily, the entire area around the bales were littered with tire tracks and their small footprints were hardly noticeable amongst them.

"He won't hurt me," she assured him bitterly. "I'm going to lead him away from you, and when he follows me, that's when you leave. Don't run through the yard, cut through the pasture." Belle quickly gestured to the small pasture to the south. She knew from experience a small person like Lucas could easily move between the barbed wire to cross into the field. "Okay?"

Lucas hunkered down onto his hands and knees and backed into the crawl space.

"No," he pleaded with her and reached for her arm. "Hide *with* me. We'll be safe in here." She just swatted his arm away and gently shoved him deeper in the crawlspace.

"No! He's *after* me. I'm not going to let anyone else get hurt. *I won't!*" Isabelle waved the idea off and smiled towards the small boy who brought some much light into her life. "Goodbye, Lucas."

"No, Isabelle! Wait!"

She stifled a sob as she heard his desperate cries from behind her as she ran towards the western field. There she would be in the open, and spotting her was as easy as looking in her direction.

She only had the vaguest of plans in her mind.

As she ran past the open gate into the western field, feeling raw and exposed, she thought back to when she first met Emmett. She remembered the men at the gas station, and how they had wrestled him to the ground. Until that man moved towards her, until she screamed, then Emmett moved like a wild beast to get to her. He did whatever he could to protect her. That's what she was doing now. That's what her plan was.

Protect the people she cared about, no matter what.

She would protect them the only way she could think of, by not being around them. By leading her black cloud away from them and running as far away from her sanctuary as she could. Even if it meant she never returned. That would be fine with her, because that would mean the people she so dearly cared about would be spared the suffering and mayhem her black cloud brought with it. A small part of her prayed that Lucas safely made it home, and the call to the police got made, but a larger part of her knew she couldn't rely on that.

"*MA BELLE!*" his wicked smooth voice called out with joy behind her.

She risked a quick look back only to see two men running towards the entrance into the field. One had a long, black coat that flapped in the wind like Dracula's cape. *That's him,* a voice inside told her and commanded her little legs to run faster as the two men gave pursuit.

Belle forgot all about her tears, and her sobs, as her feet pounded down onto the loose snow covering the ground, kicking it up as she ran along the fence. She knew they were gaining on her. Even though, she had an impressive head-start and was running with every ounce of her being, it wasn't enough. She didn't have to look back to confirm it, she just knew it in her heart.

To her left, shrouded in amongst the bare trees in a small clearing before the highway, was the large vehicle shed where Emmett stored the summer equipment over the winter months. Belle had explored the shed thoroughly in her walking adventures with Max. Without a second thought, she veered towards the barbed wire fence. Belle quickly slipped between the lower lengths of wire and didn't even look back as she sprinted towards the shed.

She knew the large vehicle doors would be locked up tight, just like she knew the small man-door to the side of it was unlocked. Belle practically collided with the door as she fumbled madly with the knob to open it. Once inside, a strangely familiar mixture of scents assaulted her nose as the neatly parked farm equipment loomed in front of her like steel behemoths. She moved into the darkness of the large storage shed and walked between the equipment on her way to the back of the building.

She knew he would follow. Her tracks in the snow made it easy. He would expect her to hide in here somewhere. As she approached the small patch of sunlight at the rear of the shed, she tried to imagine how much time he might spend searching this place before he realized she wasn't here.

Belle saw the small metal hatch built into the steel wall of the building. It had a simple sliding door with a handle on it so you could pull it up, except for reasons she couldn't explain, the door was jammed into the up position. Beside it, a small length of a two-by-four leaned up against the wall. Before this day, she fondly thought of it as her secret entrance, but now, it was her secret escape route.

Belle hurried towards the small hatch, hunkered down onto her knees and slowly leaned out the hatch to look towards the fence line. Her heart jumped dangerously in her chest when she saw a black flowing shape running along the fence. She quickly moved herself back.

He's coming, a voice told her remorsefully, confirming what she already suspected. She told herself she would count to ten inside her head, exit out through the small hatch and make her way to the south. She was sure it would be harder to follow her through the trees. If she was able, maybe she could make it to the highway.

When she got to five, Belle's eyes drifted to the wooden board off to the side of the hatch.

Suddenly, a different plan popped into her mind.

She smiled.

CHAPTER 28

Lucas

Everything happened so fast. One moment he was watching his second favorite Avengers movie in Isabelle's living room; the next, he was being ushered into Mr. Brooks's room and madly putting on his boots and parka before he was roughly lowered out a window. It seemed like he and Isabelle were escaping something, but he didn't know what it was. When he asked Isabelle the first time, a horrible crash from inside the house was the only response he received, but it was enough.

They ran.

A creeping sense of mortal danger pricked him at the edge of his consciousness, making him direly wish his father was here to guide him through whatever this was. Lucas clumsily ran down the path in the trees with Isabelle, feeling like one unsuspecting misstep on his part would be the end of him. Inside him, a cruel little whisper reminded him of all the things in his life he loved that he wouldn't have anymore after today. He very much wished not to be here in this moment. Lucas wanted to be back home, safe in his bed with his dog, Roscoe, snuggled in by his legs. He looked down at Isabelle.

She was crying.

He couldn't blame her, he started crying the second his boots touched the snow at the back of the house, and the tight knot of panic in his stomach had forced the tears from his eyes ever since. However, Lucas didn't notice his tears as much as hers. He reached out and put his hand on her shoulder to comfort her, but it was his growing unease that made his questions slip from his lips again.

"His name is *Zeke,"* she angrily said the name like this person was her archnemesis, but it soon cracked with despair. "He's here because of me."

He remembered that clearly. It was how she said it that stuck out to him the most, like she was confessing something she had done to cause these events. Lucas didn't know about any of that. *I was born*, she had said a moment later in response to a question he asked. He didn't understand her meaning, and before he could ask, a man's voice called out. Lucas didn't understand what he said, he wasn't speaking English. Isabelle seemed to understand though. On the ground, he felt her entire body tense up at the sound of it. She looked back at him with a fearful expression that stole his breath away, before it inexplicably softened.

"I love you, Lucas." She didn't say it like his parents did. Isabelle said the words like she was apologizing for something.

Before he could say anything, she jumped up from the ground and hugged him. She squeezed his sides to the point that he found it hard to breathe.

"I'm not going to let him hurt you," she whispered into his ear with a conviction that turned his veins to ice, because as good a friend as Isabelle was, she was just a kid. A little older, maybe, but that didn't mean much when it came to adults.

In his experience, adults always win.

He knew he should say something back to her, and he would have. Before he got the chance though, Isabelle pulled herself away and she yanked him forward to follow her along the little path. After that, there was little opportunity to say much as they ran through the trees. At the clearing, Isabelle rushed towards two rows of rounded bales that were tightly wrapped and placed next to each other. She pushed him towards the crawlspace's small opening between the two rows. Lucas didn't resist it, it seemed like a good idea, but he cried out in frustration when it became clear that she wasn't planning on joining him in the hiding spot. He pleaded with her to stay with him, and tried to pull her into the crawlspace.

Then she said something that pulled the tears from his eyes again.

"Goodbye, Lucas." She briefly smiled at him with her sweet smile. In the next breath the warm expression evaporated from her face, she turned away from him, and ran towards the western field.

Lucas had an unobstructed view of the entire field, and her escape.

He watched his best friend sprint through the field, along the fence, with an increasing sense of dread. It was then that his brain decided to remind him about a very important item that was currently poking him on top of his thigh.

His smartphone.

"Ah, *stupid!*" he quietly hissed to himself, and his stupid, forgetful brain, as he quickly rolled onto his back and fished his phone out of the front pocket of his pants. When it was safely in his hands, he rolled back onto his stomach and looked back to Isabelle. "*Call Dad,*" he whimpered quietly into the phone, like he was pleading with it.

"There she is!" a voice called out excitedly back from where he and Isabelle had emerged from the trees.

A small sob escaped Lucas's lips as he quickly stowed his phone into his jacket pocket before he scooted himself deeper into the crawlspace with a racing heartbeat. A second later, a loud joyous roar shook Lucas to his core.

"*MA BELLE!*"

Lucas trembled like lightning was coursing through him at the sound of it. A second later the rapid sound of footfalls came rushing towards him and Lucas held his breath. His terror-stricken body refused to move an inch as the *something* rapidly approached him.

A moment later, an impossibly black shadow flashed across his vision.

He jumped and clamped his hand over his mouth to trap the tiny yelp inside his mouth. He didn't allow himself a single breath until he was sure it was gone. When his brain settled from the sudden fright, it quickly informed him there was one more approaching him. This one wasn't moving as fast as the other one had, but another pair of legs soon scooted by him.

Lucas waited, and watched the two men pursue his friend from the agonizing safety of his hiding spot. He waited until the second man was at the entrance to the field before he moved. It felt like a dire mistake to leave the crawlspace, and he couldn't help the little sobs and sniffles that escaped his lips as he scrambled out into the open.

He ran for the pasture's fence the instant he had his legs under him again. However, just when he built up a good amount of steam, his foot caught on one of the numerous tire tracks, and his arms flailed out hopelessly as he tumbled to the ground. The impact knocked the wind from him but a sound ripped through his ears that caused an explosion of adrenalin within him.

"Hey kid!" a voice called to him, and Lucas's eyes shot to the source. The second man running into the western field had looked back. He was waving his hands at him as he turned back and began jogging towards him. "Stop!"

"Leave me alone!" Lucas shouted to the man before he shot up from the ground and ran for the pasture with a renewed energy.

Lucas caught the fabric of his jacket on one of the barbs of the fence. He yelped at the unexpected restriction, tugged heatedly on his jacket and completely ignored the ripping sound until his jacket freed up from the fence. He risked a glance back and was disheartened to see the man was dangerously close to him now. He could see the dark skin of the man's face, and his slicked-back black hair. That was all his mind could register before he looked away from him and ran into the pasture.

"Leave me alone!" Lucas cried out again to the dark-skinned man when he looked back and saw that he was awkwardly scrambling over the fence in pursuit.

Lucas ran toward a small group of cows blocking the gap in the fence he needed to cross. He madly waved his arms and weakly shouted at them.

"Move! Get out of the way! Stupid cows!" He awkwardly maneuvered through the rapidly exiting livestock that towered over him. He knew they could easily trample his small body underneath those mighty hooves, but cows weren't mean like that. They just lazily scattered and mooed their annoyance at the approach of the small, noisy child, like they didn't need the hassle he would bring them.

Lucas ran past the entrance to the newly built animal shelter as he madly made his way towards the last fence in his path. Behind him, the menacing dark-skin stranger shouted angrily at the livestock as well. Lucas didn't listen to his words as he smoothly moved between the wires. Ahead of him, to his left and besides a collection of feed-silos, he saw the dirt track that led into the field that separated the Brooks's land from the Adler's. Lucas didn't spare a second thought as he sprinted for the opening as quickly as he could.

In gym class, they did hundred-meter sprints, and all sorts of running to prepare for the track and field games his school put on in the spring. He never *really* tried during those times. Lucas liked to have fun, to run, jump, and play with the other kids on the playground. That's what he liked. He didn't see the point in trying to run fast, or for long distances.

Until now.

Lucas madly pumped his arms and desperately willed his legs to move faster across the snow-covered ground. He *had* to move faster. He knew in his heart that not only his life depended on it, but Isabelle's as well. Maybe Miss Talbot's too, he didn't know. It was a reasonable assumption. He *had* to get home. Never before in his life had he been responsible for so much, and he couldn't fail. Lucas couldn't help the ugly sobs that came, nor did he try to fight them. He just tried to focus on his breathing and his foot placement. He couldn't afford a misstep now.

"Kid!" the man called out hoarsely to him. To Lucas's ear, it was terrifyingly close. "Stop! I won't hurt you!" Lucas didn't listen to his lies, or even look back at him.

He ran.

He ran as hard and as fast as he could, and then he pushed past that. Tears and snot streamed down his face, cooled by the November breeze and the speed at which he was running towards his home. Everything seemed to hurt, but strangely enough, at the same time he didn't really feel anything. It was like he was controlling his body from a distance. The man shouted behind him, but Lucas didn't hear him. He only heard the ragged breaths that hotly exited his mouth in desperate little yelps, and the sound of his own heartbeat as it pounded away inside his chest. The edges of his vision pulsed in time with it as he looked towards the wooded area of his family's ranch across the road ahead.

"Fucking stop!" He was startled by the proximity of the voice, and screamed a second later when he felt the man grab the back of his parka.

Lucas didn't hear his own scream, he knew he was doing it, but he couldn't focus on it. He planted his legs into the ground, pushed himself away from the horrible man with all his might, and madly shook his upper body away from the man's grasp. He was rewarded with blessed freedom, and he didn't waste it. He unexpectedly shot forward onto his hands and knees. The tiny rocks of the gravel dug painfully into his palms and knees for a short breath before Lucas launched himself forward again in a mad dash towards the other side of the road.

He told himself he just had to make it to his family's property; he would be safe if he could only make it there. It was a cruel lie he told himself, though. He passed into the wooded section before the houses and other buildings of his family's property, and he didn't feel one lick safer.

Find daddy! His brain commanded him as he-.

Lucas's foot caught on a root that was buried beneath the snow. He reached out for anything that might slow his descent to the ground, but nothing was within reach. He tumbled painfully to the ground. He couldn't help himself at that point. Lucas looked back.

"No!" he shouted when he saw the dark-skinned, slicked-haired man standing over him, well within arm's reach. Lucas breathed in a shuttering whimper, as his failure became apparent. "No," he said it again, quieter this time. Lucas inched himself back, as the man breathlessly reached behind his back.

"Sorry kid," the man said with some regret as he then produced a rather large knife from behind his back. Lucas's heart wanted to escape his chest at the sight of the long, shiny curved blade. "You were just in the *wrong place*, at the *wrong time*." The man looked down at him with sad eyes.

"You can't," Lucas whined through his sobs as his eyes locked onto the gleaming blade in front of him. He wanted to turn and run, but his body wouldn't answer his call to escape. Lucas looked to the man's remorseful dark eyes, and then back to the blade in his hand. "You can't."

"I'll make it quick," he said softly and took another step towards him. "Close your eyes, kid."

Lucas sobbed horribly, but he did as the man said. Maybe it would be better this way.

BAM!

Lucas's body practically jumped off the ground at the sudden, and all-encompassing noise that filled the entire world around him in the space of a heartbeat. Then it was gone.

Wait?! He didn't have a gun, he had a knife.

Lucas fought against his better instincts, and forced his eyes open, just in time to see the dark-skinned man land roughly onto the ground a few feet back. Once there, he angrily contorted his body before a series of coughs and weak groans escaped him.

"Lucas!" his grandfather's voice suddenly came like a bestial roar that cut through all other sounds.

"Grandpa!" he shouted in disbelief and looked towards the source.

He saw something he had never seen before today. His grandfather was running, *without* his cane. He wasn't doing a great job of it. His large, round frame teetered dangerously with each angry little hop he took. In his hands, was the old shotgun he kept in his truck, for coyotes. *Old faithful*, he called it, because it had never let him down.

"Grandpa!" Lucas shouted again and ran towards him, away from the writhing man on the ground.

They collided with a force that threatened to send them both to the ground, but his grandfather held fast and lowered one hand from the shotgun to pull Lucas's body in close to him.

"Are you alright, boy?" he asked quickly as he dropped down to one knee with a pained grimace and an angry groan. "Did he hurt you? Where did he get you?" He didn't pay any attention to his questions. Lucas just held onto him fiercely and sobbed into his denim coat.

"LUCAS!" his father's frantic voice came a second later. "LUCAS!" He turned to look towards the yelling and saw his father sprinting through the trees towards them. Unlike his grandfather, his father only had his cell phone in his hand.

"Go to yer daddy, boy." His grandfather gently eased Lucas away and pointed him towards his father.

Lucas didn't need to be told twice.

"Daddy!" he cried out through his sobs, and ran towards him.

His father didn't stop running until Lucas was in his arms. Once there, safely away from the horrible calamity that started the moment he was eased from the window at the Brooks's farm, Lucas opened the floodgates and wept wildly into his father's chest. To his surprise, he felt his father sobbing right along with him.

"Jesus Christ, Lucas!" he wept. "I heard everything. I was so scared. Are you okay?" His father peeled him away and looked at him with a red, puffy, tear-stained expression that still somehow managed to look stern before he repeated his question. "Did he hurt you?"

"No," he answered quickly. "I'm okay, but you gotta listen to me, daddy!" Lucas looked at his father with wild eyes as his story leapt from his mouth.

Lucas left nothing out.

From the moment the sound of crashing plates came from the Brooks's kitchen, right up to the moment he saw his grandfather. Lucas told the entire story, with a strange clarity, in record time.

"You *fucking* asshole!" his father spat towards the dark-skinned man on the ground. The man's fancy suit jacket and shirt was peppered with tiny holes, and his shirt was caked with blood. The man had his hands up in surrender, and looked at them from the ground. "What the hell are you planning to do with Isabelle?!"

His father stepped forward and kicked the man in the meat of his leg. The man winced in pain, and groaned a bit, but just stared at his father with a cold, reptilian look.

"Hey, man!" he countered indignantly. "You want me to talk? No problem. I'll start spilling my guts to the first cop I see, *after* the ambulance arrives." Lucas could feel his father tense up beside him, but it was his grandfather who spoke up first.

"Oh yeah?" he growled hotly. "Maybe you can answer just two questions for me, smart guy. Why were you chasing my grandson?" his grandfather asked in that tone he used when he was *really* mad. Lucas watched as he used *Old Faithful's* barrel to point towards the knife on the ground beside the man, just outside his reach. "And what *exactly* were you planning to do with that knife?"

The man only looked at him smugly.

"Like I said, old man, as soon as that ambulance arrives. I'll tell you everything I know," the man said easily before he let out a weak cough, and his next breath came in a loud wheeze.

His grandfather just snorted angrily.

"Yeah, there's a bit of a problem with that plan, son."

He sharply racked the shotgun to load another shell into the bore. The spent shell was shot into the air, and everyone who saw it, knew the dire implication of what it meant.

"I didn't bring any rope," his grandfather said slowly. He then tilted his head towards Lucas's father. "Take Lucas, and get everyone settled into the main house. Tell them to lock the doors, call the RC's, and send them over to Emmett's." His father didn't say a word, he simply nodded. "Then get Robbie, and meet me out front. We're going over to Emmett's." His grandfather reached out and grabbed is father's arm, and looked at him sternly. "And Owen? Bring your rifles."

The air between the men seemed to get thicker, but again, his father said nothing. He just nodded towards Lucas's grandfather. He dropped down and scooped up Lucas into his arms, and held him close to his body. Lucas didn't have to ask what his grandfather was going to do, he was young, but he wasn't stupid. Part of him felt sorry for the injured man on the ground, but a larger part remembered the knife in the man's hands as he stood over him with a dispassionate look.

He deserves it, Lucas told himself as his father carried him away.

None-the-less, Lucas still closed his eyes and nestled himself into his father's neck and breathed in his scent. He didn't have to worry about the man anymore, he was safe in his father's arms.

BAM!

CHAPTER 29

Emmett

Calvin's truck took the corner onto his farm's approach like an angry bull charging on ice. Emmett, just like he had for almost the entire journey, held onto the handle above the door with a white-knuckle grip, and tried to steady himself in his seat.

The highways were packed with sedans, farm trucks, and tractor-trailers, but Calvin sped past them all. He kept the hazards on and flashed his high beams to clear the way. A few drivers honked their annoyance at the truck screaming dangerously down the road. Emmett admitted there were close calls that made him clench his jaw.

Calvin was unwavering.

Russell was a bit of a nail-biter as they flew by vehicles doing well over a hundred kilometers in a seventy zone. The east bound lane through town had two lanes with nice paved shoulders on each side. Calvin didn't confine himself to one lane as they burned through the town, he used the whole road.

"Who the fuck are these guys?" Calvin growled with surprise as they sped towards the yard. He eased off the gas when he saw two people step onto the road like they were some authority figures in charge of a scene.

Emmett leaned forward to see if he recognized the shapes. At this distance, all he could make out was that one was medium height and kind of skinny, while the other one was tall with a broad form. He watched as the pair curiously raise their hands.

Then the popping sounds came.

"Jesus!" Calvin yelped when the windshield was hit and the crack spider-webbed out from the impact point. Emmett heard other *plinking* sounds coming from in front of them. "They're shooting at us! Get down!"

Calvin reached over to pull Emmett down and jumped awkwardly in time with another strike to the windshield. He didn't see the bullet hit, but Emmett saw the way his friend reacted to it, and he saw the blood. Calvin tensed up. His foot unintentionally pressed on the gas, but he still struggled to keep the truck on the road. Bullets continued to pepper the truck as they raced straight towards the gunmen who were inexplicably on his land. It was only a matter of time.

For Isabelle.

Emmett reached over, grabbed the steering wheel and savagely pulled it down.

The truck flew off the approach and careened into the ditch, bouncing the occupants in the truck against their seatbelts. There was a hard bounce then a sharp crack came from the front of the truck as it smashed through one of the wooden posts of his fence. More bullets plinked off Calvin's side of the truck, and the driver's side window blew apart as they raced headlong towards the treeline that encircled the northern edge of his yard.

Emmett steered the truck as far from the road as he could, despite the chaos inside the cab. He desperately wanted to tell Calvin to take his foot off the gas, but saw only his friend's pained expression and the crimson patch spreading across his chest. Ahead of them, the treeline raced towards them with surprising speed.

This isn't going to feel good, Emmett thought a second before releasing the wheel and bracing for impact.

They had been lucky. Before the line of older, larger trees was a zone of saplings that helped to slow them down, so when they finally did crash into one tree that would not bend to the truck's momentum, it was a fairly gentle stop. The airbags didn't even deploy.

"Go!" Calvin growled painfully beside him, and he felt his friend's bloodied hand on his shoulder gently pushing him towards the door. "Get out of here!"

He unclicked his seatbelt, fumbled with the handle, and fell out of the truck. Emmett scrambled back up to his feet before he spared another quick glance to his injured friend.

"*Go*!" Calvin hissed loudly and waved him away with a bloody palm.

Emmett ran into the trees at full speed.

He ran towards the house and thought madly about what firearms he still had on the property. Before Isabelle came into his life, he had sold off his family's impressive collection of guns. He kept some for himself. There was a shotgun hidden away in his bedroom, and a .22 lever-action rifle in the cab on the tractor in the Quonset. That was mostly for gophers, coyotes, and magpies, but it would put a hole in a man just as easy.

He decided to head towards the Quonset.

What the fuck are you doing?! He asked himself as he raced through the trees. *You don't even know what's going on. Just stop and think for a minute before you run straight into a bullet.* He couldn't stop, he knew that. Part of him worried that if he did actually stop and try to figure out this madness, it would be too late. Isabelle was involved in this. He couldn't afford to sit back and try to figure out the safest way for him to proceed. Everything that mattered in his life was in that house ahead of him, and they were in danger.

He would figure it out when he came to it, or he would die trying. There wasn't a third option.

He entered into the small, secluded clearing just before the house that has always been lovingly referred to as the Brooks's family junk yard. This is where his father had put things he no longer had a use for. He had accumulated an impressive collection of rusted-out cars, broken-down farm equipment, and various other pieces of junk. Emmett sold most of it off to a scrap dealer from Brandon, but there were still a few choice pieces. Of course, with this being his family's farm, there were also numerous oversized rock piles from the stones Emmett picked off the fields every year.

He reached the clearing at almost the same time as the larger man he saw from the road. Emmett came in from the north, and the man from the road burst through on the east side. He was maybe twenty feet away from him, and he had a gun in his left hand.

He was pointing it at Emmett.

"Stop!" the large man with the sandy-blonde hair commanded loudly. "Don't move!"

There was no place for him to go. He couldn't outrun a bullet. Emmett slowed to a disappointed stop, and slumped his shoulders as he turned towards the man. He didn't raise his hands though, because he wasn't surrendering. Not yet, anyway.

"Get on your knees," the man said.

Emmett just looked at him. The sandy-blonde gunman was about the same size as he was, which was saying something. He had the smooth features and doe-eyed looks of someone much younger, though. Honestly, this man looked like he should be on a beach somewhere with a surfboard under his arm, not in the frozen prairies of Manitoba, holding a gun.

"Get on your knees, goddammit!" he said, louder this time.

Emmett slowly shook his head.

I'll stand, thanks. Emmett signed quickly towards the man, knowing the response he would get.

"Oh, shit!" the man exclaimed with a bit of embarrassment. "You're deaf. Fuck, no wonder you're just standing there like a dummy. Get. On. Your. Knees."

He used the barrel of the automatic pistol in his hands to motion towards the ground. Again, Emmett slowly shook his head. He was hoping the man would approach him, he desperately needed the man to cross the distance between them. Once he was within reach, Emmett felt he'd have options. Until then, at this distance, the gunman had him dead to rights.

"Ah! Fuck it!" the man said angrily and lowered the gun. He then inexplicably pulled back the slide and showed Emmett the empty chamber.

The gun's empty!? Emmett realized with a bit of wild excitement.

"They told me to bring a gun, they *didn't* say I should pack enough bullets for a goddamn shootout," the man grumbled sourly, to himself, as he tossed the useless pistol to the ground beside him. "Can't shoot for shit with my left anyways."

Emmett couldn't believe what he was seeing, or what he was hearing. *Did this guy seriously just say that?* He hid his astonishment well, and his heart sank a bit when the man then smiled warmly at him.

"I've seen your fights," he said slowly, needlessly over-enunciating his words for Emmett's benefit. "You're really good." Emmett stiffened when the man then reached behind his back. "This isn't *personal.*" The man said and produced a small curved blade.

Emmett recognized it by its unmistakable profile. It was a Tanto. A nice one, too.

"I want you to know that," the man said stupidly.

Emmett snorted dismissively.

It kind of feels personal, Emmett thought to himself as he watched the man awkwardly hold the knife in his left. Emmett smirked at him as he clearly had never used his left as his dominant hand before. *Is his arm broken?* Emmett wondered when he looked down at his right hand and spied a solid-looking cast poking out from the sleeve of the man's jacket. It definitely didn't look new. He could see the worn, frayed edges of it, like he had been wearing it for some time. The sandy-haired goon certainly didn't look hampered by it in any way. Emmett was sure he would use it as a weapon. He guessed that cast underneath the man's sleeve probably weighed in excess of two pounds, and was probably as solid as concrete. Why wouldn't he use it as a weapon?

"I'll try to make this quick," the kid said confidently and flashed a smug smile at him.

Me too, Emmett signed quickly before he brought his fists up in a guard.

As Emmett faced off against the large surfer-dude in the form-fitting parka and the knife in his hand, he figured he had three things going for him.

First, he actually had a lot of experience fighting with knives. Sort of. When he was younger, Tommy and him developed a game of sorts. They each had a stick that was little over a foot long, those were the *knives.* The game was simplicity in itself. They simply tried to "*kill*" each other with honest, brutal intent, and the first one to kill the other three times won. Years later, when Calvin was up to it, he would play the same game with him using high-impact plastic knives he bought off the internet.

Second, and this was more of a technical advantage he had over the surfer dude. With the cast on his right, he's forced to put his best weapon into his left hand. So, when they squared off across from each other, the knife would be on his right side. That was good for Emmett because he was better with his right.

Third, the surfer kid revealed his hand a bit when he admitted to watching Chester's little videos of him. He said he was impressed. Emmett grinned a bit at the idea that this guy thought those videos neatly summed up his fighting technique, and he might have some sort of edge on Emmett because he watched them.

If this guy was smart, he would have kept that to himself. If he was really smart, he would have seen how Emmett played with those guys. Those fights weren't about winning, not really. At Chester's little road show, it was more about mitigating the damage he took, and trading blows with his opponent until he found a clean way to finish the fight without seriously injuring his opponent. There are rules you have to adhere to in the ring, it wasn't a *real* fight. In the ring, the person across from you was your opponent, he wasn't your enemy. That was a very important distinction Emmett learned a long time ago.

This man was his enemy.

Emmett took a deep breath as the large man with a plaster cast on one arm and a knife in the other closed the distance, grim determination etched on his face.

Fighting is like chess. Instead of moving pieces on a board, fighters use attacks to wear down their opponents' defenses. By the smug look on his face, Emmett could tell he thought the cast and knife gave him the advantage. Against a normal person that might have been true, but the *real* truth of it was more complicated. Emmett knew a capable unarmed man could attack in a hundred ways and strike a dozen areas. That was a lot to compensate for, and adjust to. A weapon, however, such as a knife, in a less-than-capable attacker's hands, had far fewer viable attacks, making it more predictable. This guy in front of him, as far as Emmett was concerned, would put himself at a large disadvantage if he relied on those weapons too much.

He knew what he wanted. He wanted a back-handed slash at shoulder height. That attack could let him finish the fight in under ten moves, if he was luck. Emmett knew he could finish the fight in less than ten moves, if he was lucky, if that attack came his way. As the two of them inched towards each other's range, Emmett had a list of half a dozen attacks he thought he should be ready for, and more importantly he had responses for each.

Let him attack first. Just let him come, he told himself, trying to calm his nerves.

They moved until they were both just outside their striking range, and then the two of them slowly circled each other with their weapons in front of them. The beefy surfer-kid was grinning wickedly like this was some sort of game that he was determined to win. Emmett just narrowed his eyes at him and concentrated on the spot between the man's shoulders. The trick was not to focus on the weapons. Instead, he tried to focus on the man.

The surfer made sharp feints to test if Emmett would flinch or drop his guard. Emmett held firm and didn't even appear to register the movements, but the truth was he was waiting. When the real attack came, Emmett didn't hesitate.

There!

The surfer dropped the knife low and came in fast on his right side, attempting to plunge the knife deep into his ribs. Emmett chopped out with his right forearm and easily blocked the attack low on the forearm. With his left, he sent a sharp jab to the man's mouth that painfully whipped his head back and staggered him back a bit. It was a minor hit. It was a minor hit that opened a cut on the man's lip and it also pissed off his attacker. That was just fine with Emmett. Angry people made mistakes.

This guy was no different.

He faked with a straight punch from his plastered hand before he stepped in with the knife for a hard low stab. The young brute growled angrily as he thrust the knife towards Emmett's gut. It wasn't the back-handed slash he was hoping for. It wasn't even at the top of his list of attacks he was looking for.

But it *was* on the list.

Emmett reached out with his right and caught the blonde kid's wrist and stopped the knife dead, then he waited for a fraction of a second. He knew the stone gauntlet was coming, it was only a matter of time. If he attacked too soon, he risked being struck with it, and that wasn't a chance he could take. As predicted, the man dropped the cast towards him in a fierce hammer-fist, like he was trying to drive a nail in with it. Emmett easily swatted it away. It didn't feel great, though. It felt like Emmett had just struck a concrete post with his forearm. There was a good possibility he had just fractured his arm, but he couldn't worry about that now.

He had a fight to win.

Emmett balled up his left hand tightly and used his legs to push his fist up underneath the man's chin in a brutal upper cut that weakened the surfer's knee's. While keeping the knife in a vice-grip with his right, he kept the weapon at a safe distance. Emmett then hooked his left hand behind the man's neck and pulled him forward, straight into the knee Emmett thrusted towards his gut. His blonde attacker barked painfully as the knee sunk deeply into his abdomen, and Emmett quickly released his grip on the blonde kid's neck and reared his left hand back. When his attacker looked back to him with his glazed-over eyes, Emmett continued to follow his attack plan. He shot his arm forward and elbowed the dazed brute in the face before he moved in and swept the man's front leg out from under him. At the same time, Emmett used his left arm to clothesline the dazed, and bloodied surfer to the ground.

Then he waited a short breath.

When the dazed blonde immediately rose up and tried to bring his heavy cast around to strike, Emmett punched him in the face and sent him back to the ground.

Now comes the ugly bit, Emmett told himself to steel his resolve.

He shot his right leg forward, while pulling the knife arm he still held by the wrist towards him, and used his knee to strike the man's arm, just above the elbow. Emmett grimaced sourly when he heard the wet sound of twigs breaking that came from his arm a half-second before the man bellowed out in pain.

He didn't scream long though.

Emmett folded his left hand around the man's hand on the knife. He grunted angrily as he twisted the man's freshly broken arm until the blade was pointing the other way, and used both hands to plunge the knife down into the surfer-dude's chest.

The man's cries ended as abruptly as they started, and the man beneath him looked up at him wide-eyed with an expression of utter shock.

You did what you had to, Emmett told himself as he looked down remorsefully at the man as he struggled to breathe.

He only managed to suck in short, pained little gasps. The blonde-haired kid dying on the ground looked to him with a pleading expression, like he was begging for Emmett to save him. They both knew it was too late for that. By the way the color was rapidly draining from the man's face, it wouldn't be long for him now.

I'm sorry, Emmett slowly signed to the dying man with the watering eyes before he rose up and left the man to his end. They had played a mortal game together. They both knew only one of them would walk away from that encounter.

It could have been you down there, he told himself as he stepped away from the man and left him to his last moments on earth.

Emmett dumbly walked towards the spot on the ground where the dying man tossed his gun. He picked up the 9mm pistol and stuffed it into his waistband. *This might come in handy, if I find some bullets for it.* It felt like a long-shot, but he could still use it to bludgeon someone, if need be. Emmett didn't want to retrieve the knife from the man's chest, he didn't want to touch it.

He turned back towards the house and started to run. He only got one step though before a thought occurred to him that made him feel a horrible sense of guilt. *Calvin!*

Shit!

Emmett turned back to the spot in the trees his attacker had first emerged from, and ran for it. He swerved to the side, towards one of the rock piles, and only slowed his stride enough to bend down and scoop up a good-sized stone off the top.

As much as he direly wished to sprint towards the house, towards Brooke and Isabelle, Emmett knew he wouldn't be able to live with himself if he left his friend behind to the mercies of the skinny man who was also on the road. *He has a wife, and kids for fuck sakes, you asshole!* He was closer to Calvin.

He couldn't put Isabelle's and Brooke's lives over and above that of his friend's. No matter how much Calvin might want him to.

He just had to get to him before that skinny bastard did.

CHAPTER 30

Brooke

The serious man marched her in front of Emmett's door. He sternly grabbed her hands and zip-tied them behind her back with foot-long black zip-ties. Brooke recognized them, the hardware store sold those exact ties in a pack of a hundred for four-ninety-nine. Once her hands were secured, the stern-looking man with the cold expression roughly grabbed her chin and shoved a dish cloth into her gaping mouth. She gagged at the sudden intrusion but the man wasn't bothered by it one bit. He pulled out the roll of duct tape they brought with them, and tore off a length to put over her mouth.

"Put your feet together," he coldly commanded. After she complied, the man then secured another zip-tie around her ankles. "Stay quiet," he said and gave her a gentle shove in the center of her back that sent her tumbling into the room.

All Brooke could do at that point was twist onto her side to fall on her shoulder instead of flat on her face. She landed with a pained grunt that was muffled by the gag in her mouth. Behind her, the serious man closed the bedroom door, and she heard his footsteps as he walked back to the kitchen. She was helpless.

Brooke wept loudly.

This was the end for her, something inside her told her that. It was like some long forgotten primitive instinct had suddenly kicked in to help her prepare for her own end. Inside her head, she was saying good-bye to all the people in her life she was going to leave behind. Her parents, her sister, her nieces and nephews. She wept for Emmett. Of all the people she wished to see one last time, she wanted to see him the most. She needed his strength, right now. Then her fearful mind conjured up another name for her to say good-bye to, *Isabelle.*

Then Brooke's sobs turned into an angry growl.

She and Lucas were out there, just the two of them, alone and afraid. Desperately trying to escape that *fucking* psychopath, and she was tied up in here like a hog waiting for slaughter.

Isabelle needs me!

Brooke screamed in frustration into the gag in her mouth, as she tensed and painfully squirmed her body against her bonds. Everything hurt, but Brooke took that red-hot agony and pushed it down to fuel the fire in her belly as she pulled on her bonds until they dug painfully into her flesh. Then she pulled some more.

Nothing happened.

When it became clear that all she was doing was wasting energy and time, she slumped back to the ground and let a weak sob escape her throat.

Beside her, a tiny whine came from under the bed.

Brooke turned her head. She was already on the floor and had a perfect line of sight to the noise. There, laying flat on his belly with his little furry head buried between his front paws, was Max. When their eyes met, he made a small yelping noise before he excitedly shook his head.

That's when Brooke noticed it.

In front of Max and off to the side a bit, was a small folding knife.

Brooke looked at it wide-eyed for a moment, concerned it might be a horrible, cruel trick. Like a mirage. It didn't last, though. She quickly scooted herself over to it. She knew she couldn't reach for it with her hands tied behind her back. Once she was perpendicular to the bed's frame, Brooke rolled onto her back. *Here comes the fun part,* Brooke told herself and she used her core to lift her upper body into a seated position. Normally, this would be relatively easy, but that was before she got kicked in the ribs. White-hot pain flared up on her left side and quickly spread to her whole chest. Her muted howls filled her ears as the edges of her vision pulsed dangerously with the effort. When she was finished, she wildly sucked air in through her nose and felt sweat start to form on her brow, but she did it.

She was upright.

Brooke used her hands to support her weight as she inched herself forward and slipped her legs under the bed. When she was sure she was in position, she desperately felt around the area with her socked feet while feeling a growing anxiety that the serious man could walk through that door again at any moment.

Hurry, dammit!

She scooted herself to the side in hopes her feet would stumble across the knife. Brooke sucked in a breath to steel herself against the coming agony before she leaned herself back to peer under the bed for the knife. She saw it, it was just a few more inches to the right. She growled loudly as she once again lifted her upper body back into a seated position and scooted herself a smidge to the right.

There it is!

She cheered inside her head when she felt the hard, flat exterior of the knife against her foot. Brooke quickly hooked her foot around it, and slowly eased her legs back. Again, pain flared in her side that caused her to growl angrily, but her focus was on her feet as she slowly brought the knife out from underneath the bed.

Just a little more, she told herself as she fought to ignore the pain in her ribs and focus on the job at hand.

When she moved the knife out from underneath the bed, Brooke grunted and groaned as she used her hands to slowly turn herself around on her butt before she blindly inched her way back towards the knife. Behind her, her fingers madly probed and searched the floor until they finally brushed up against the cold steel of the small knife. She quickly scooped it up into her hands, and they worked feverishly to unfold the knife until it clicked into position.

Come on, goddammit! Brooke cursed inside her head as her bloodied fingers clumsily maneuvered the knife into position. Each step of the way she risked dropping the damned thing because her hands were slick with her own blood. It was like she was learning how to use her hands again. She quietly growled out her curses as she struggled to work the blade against her restraint. When she finally did, she could only move the blade a paltry inch or two, and she hardly had any leverage on the knife at all.

It will have to do, she told herself and started sawing the knife against the hard plastic of the zip-tie.

Her shoulders and wrist cramped up painfully from the weird angle she was forced to hold the knife. It was so bad that tears were forming in her eyes, but she didn't stop. She couldn't. In her mind, she pictured Isabelle desperately running from *that man*. Brooke wouldn't stop as long as she still had breath in her lungs.

She needs me, she needs me, she needs me, Brooke said over and over again in her head. She bit down on the dish towel in her mouth to keep the fiery cramps at bay and kept sawing the knife against the restraint.

Her hair stuck to her sweaty face. She breathed in hoarse, ragged breaths, and breathed out heated growls while her fingers continued to awkwardly work the knife. Images of a terror-stricken Isabelle with a crying face burned inside her. Brooke knew exactly what she was going to do once she got out of these damned zip-ties. She would go out the same window Isabelle and Lucas did. Sure, it doesn't open wide enough to fit her frame through, but she was being polite when she slipped Isabelle and Lucas through it.

She wouldn't be so nice this time.

Brooke was confident she could get that window open enough for her to fit. It might never close properly again after that point, but that didn't concern her at the moment. She knew she could follow Isabelle's tracks in the snow outside as easily as that psychopath. If she found Isabelle first, she would hold her close and run her straight to the highway. This time of day, they could surely flag someone down within a short amount of time. If she ran into *that man* again, Brooke promised herself she would take that knife, stab it straight into his eye and push it with all her might, straight into his demented brain.

You can't do any of that, a familiar voice taunted her. *You can't even get out of these zip-ties with a goddamn knife. What use would you be to her? Do you really think you can stop someone like* that? *You? You couldn't even keep your marriage together. You're just this sad, broken thing that had to run back home to mommy and daddy, and you've been hiding there ever since.* Brooke growled angrily, and kept working the knife. There was little else she could do. *You're not built for this. You're not a mother, you never were. You've just been pretending this whole time, but you and I both know you don't have it in you.* Brooke hated that voice with a wild passion. Graeme gave it to her. It was the last thing he gave her, or more honestly, it's what he took from her that caused the voice. *After all, if you did, God wouldn't have taken away your womb.*

Brooke had heard enough

"SHUT UP!" she screamed hoarsely into the gag and painfully tensed her whole body, forcing the words out in an effort to silence that fucking voice.

The zip-tie around her wrists suddenly broke free.

Brooke's arms flew out from behind her back, and the knife flew from her grasp, tumbling to the floor beside her. She was free. She brought her newly freed hands into her lap. They were a shocking color of red and slightly trembled on her thighs. Her blood was everywhere she looked. Her arms were caked with it. She looked down to her cute little half-sleeve sweater and her blood stained the entire front of the garment. Brooke gave herself a single breath to allow the blood to rush back to her hands, and for her cramped muscles to loosen before she swept her bloodied hair away from her eyes and reached for the knife again.

The second zip-tie around her ankles came off almost instantly compared to the effort she put into removing the first one. Brooke reached up and pulled the tape from her mouth. It felt like the first couple layers of her skin went with it. Plus, for an added bonus, the serious man who gagged her had placed the tape over the edge of the cut on her cheek. When she pulled it off, she yelped at the fiery sting that came from it, and she was sure she could feel blood start to seep from the wound again. She pulled out the wet, blood-stained rag from her mouth and coughed painfully when she took in her first deep breath.

Underneath the bed, Max yelped weakly.

"Stay!" Brooke whispered harshly after she dropped down to look the puppy in the eye.

She didn't need the dog causing a fuss and possibly attracting one of the men from the kitchen. Brooke had a tiny advantage in the fact that they didn't know she was free. That counted for little, though, if they just walked right in and tied her up again. Brooke doubted she would be able to escape a second time.

Brooke took a step towards the window, fully intent on enacting her master escape plan by forcing herself through the window, when a thought occurred to her. She was in Emmett's bedroom, *and* he was a farmer.

She then moved towards the dresser and started quietly opening the drawers, and roughly searching through them.

She had grown up with rural farmers, and she would be the first to admit they were all unique in their own way, but they also shared a lot of similarities. She could probably write a whole essay highlighting the commonalities of all the farmers she had known. Right now, a couple stuck out to her. They all believed staunchly that it was both their right *and* responsibility to protect their property as well as their livestock. Every farmer she knew had a story about how they were woken up in the dead of the night, and had to run out to shoot a coyote that was harassing a calf or something. So, out of habit, Brooke had found that most farmers keep at least one firearm in their bedroom.

Emmett was a rural farmer.

"Come on!" Brooke softly hissed as she gently closed another drawer after she had rifled through it. When the dresser was done, she moved to the night stand. There, she found a rather large fixed-blade knife in a sheath. It looked like it could cut through plastic zip-ties like butter. Brooke took the knife and stowed it in her back pocket, but she didn't find a gun.

She quickly moved into the walk-in closet and madly pushed clothes out of the way, searching the space.

"Shit!" she hissed when she found nothing.

A part of her refused to believe that Emmett didn't have at least one gun. *Maybe not in the bedroom,* she thought with a certain amount of dread. If that was the case, she might have to abandon this whole idea and head back to the window. *Think,* she told herself with a deep breath. *Where would Emmett hide a gun?* Her mind frantically considered the question. When nothing came, a sly part of herself considered the question a different way. *Where would a tall person hide a gun?*

Brooke looked up to the top shelf.

The shelf was packed with a bunch of boxes, so she reached up and pulled a number of them down before she went up onto the tips of her toes to check the back of the shelf. There her fingers quickly came across a heavy nylon bag. When she gave it a tug, she found that it had some weight to it. *Bingo,* she thought hopefully and clamped her hand down on the bag to pull it free.

The rounded gun-bag slipped easily from the shelf and fell heavily into her arms. Brooke immediately dropped to the floor of the closet and unzipped the bag. Inside, was a large black shotgun. Brooke knew, just by looking at it, this weapon wasn't meant for hunting. It looked new. Hell, it looked like it had never been used before. Around the stock, was a nylon sleeve that held two red shells. At the trigger, Brooke was disappointed to find a trigger lock with a three-digit combination.

"Shit," Brooke whined broken-heartedly when she saw it and beat her bloody hands softly against her thighs. *No! We're so close. You can do this. Think!*

Brooke scooped up the shotgun and laid it across her lap as she furiously picked numbers to try. She didn't know Emmett's birthday, or Isabelle's; the fact came with a tinge of guilt. It's not that he didn't tell her, but she was just horrible with dates. *Think!* She tried all the number combinations she could think of from Emmett's phone number. Both the landline to the house, and his cell. She tried double-o seven, because she knew Emmett liked action movies. She even tried double-o six because of that one Bond movie that featured a rogue agent. That wasn't it. She tried his PO box number. *How do I know his post office box number, but not his birthday?!* She tried six-six-six, because why not? When she exhausted every other option, one combination occurred to her that she hadn't thought of before, for obvious reasons.

Brooke tried one-two-three.

The lock on the trigger turned free.

"Jesus Christ, Emmett!" She was both a little disappointed, and utterly elated when the trigger lock separated and fell away from the gun.

Then she heard a rapid succession of pops coming from the front of the house, and Brooke just knew they were gunshots. The men in the kitchen confirmed her fears.

"What the fuck was that?!" one of them asked loudly and with obvious concern, when the popping sounds ended. Brooke suspected it was the nervous one who stood in the corner. The one who stopped *that man* from shooting her.

"They're shooting at someone," the serious man spoke up. He seemed concerned as well.

No! She cried inside her head, and looked down to the shotgun on her lap. *They're shooting at someone,* the words flashed by in her mind. Isabelle and Lucas fled to the west, or at least, they should have. Honestly, she didn't know, but she knew bitterly that a good mother *should* know. Then she remembered the text she sent Calvin.

Oh no! What have I done!? A cruel wave washed over her, stealing all the warmth from her as well as sucking all the air from the room when she considered the possibility she had led Emmett and Calvin to their own deaths. Her eyes stung when she thought of Emmett laying dead out there in his own yard, his life's blood leaking out and mixing with the snow. She stifled a sob with her bloody hand. She pulled in a deep silent breath and pulled the two shells free from their holder and slowly loaded them into the shotgun. Then her ears picked up the men talking loudly in the kitchen. She didn't hear everything, but she heard enough.

"I'm getting the girl…I don't know who was shooting…Just get in the fucking SUV and get ready to go."

I'm not going anywhere, Brooke promised as she picked herself up off the floor.

As slowly as she could, she racked the shotgun and moved back into the bedroom. There she positioned herself in front of the bedroom door. She wasn't a gunfighter. This wasn't a Hail Mary move that would win her the game. Brooke knew this was her last stand. She had two shells and there were two men between her and the people she cared about. She couldn't help but think this was fated to happen somehow. It was like all the horrible pieces came together to make this nightmare happen. She didn't know, but she knew she wasn't going anywhere with those men. She would die first.

Brooke raised the shotgun, tucked the butt tightly against her shoulder, like her father had shown all those years ago, and aimed down the barrel towards the center of the door. She quickly double-checked to ensure the safety was off; it wasn't. So, she used her thumb to press the small button by the trigger. Her weapon was now live, and ready to go.

She heard footsteps moving from the kitchen.

Please, Brooke pleaded with the universe as she heard the footfalls move into the dining room. *Please, don't open that door.*

She didn't want to kill someone. She knew, in her heart, she would blast the unfortunate soul that opened that door, but she didn't want to. Mostly because she didn't want to cross that particular line in her life. She, under no circumstances, wished to be a killer. She was pretty sure she recognized the sounds of those steps.

Stop! Just turn around and leave!

He wasn't though.

He was stepping down into the living room. Brooke moved her finger and touched it to the cold steel of the trigger. She focused on the spot on the door where she thought the man's chest would be, and reminded herself to wait until she saw the whites of his eyes. She couldn't shoot through the door. She didn't know how solid that door was, and she was past thinking about the safe way out of this situation.

As the man stopped in front of the door. Brooke spied the knob slowly turning, and one thought seeped into her brain.

Don't!

CHAPTER 31

Calvin

Calvin stiffened painfully in his seat when he saw the skinny man from the road walk toward him. The bullet had struck his right shoulder. He probably would've been fine if he didn't reach towards Emmett. Calvin figured it had to be a pretty heavy caliber to smash through the windshield like that and still remain intact enough to blow through his phone before tearing into his shoulder. He was more than sure his collarbone was broken, and the blood leaking down his chest wasn't ideal either. He was alive, though. He was also in a lot of pain. So, that was a good sign.

As the skinny gunman approached awkwardly, and with some cheer, Calvin wondered if this was one of the men who visited Henry's store. He certainly looked *city*. He wore black dress shoes, that were entirely inappropriate for a snow-covered field, dark colored slacks and a colorful silk shirt with a tight leather jacket.

This is the guy who's going to kill me? Fuck off! Calvin smirked disappointedly at the man through the open driver's window. He sighed.

He didn't look like a killer. Hell, he didn't even look threatening. He just looked cold. Honestly, the scariest thing about this guy was the large revolver in his hand.

"Howdy!" The man waved with his free hand. Internally, Calvin was memorizing his description. "Do you have any last words?" he asked in a poor cowboy imitation that Calvin assumed was meant to be insulting.

"You don't want to do this," Calvin said calmly shaking his head at the goofball.

"Yeah," he quickly admitted. "You got me there, *but* I also don't want to go to prison. Zeke said no witnesses," he said remorsefully, like his hands were tied. Calvin mentally jotted down the name, hopefully for later.

"Listen to me," Calvin said sternly, attacking the problem at all angles. "I'm a cop. A Mountie. You kill me, there is no place on this earth they won't find you," Calvin softly explained to him. "When they do find you, they'll throw the book at you. There won't be any plea deals for you, my friend. Straight to jail, and you'll stay there for the best part of your life. Think about it. *Or*, you drop that gun, call in the cops yourself, and start thinking about what's best for *you*. You're a smart guy," Calvin said nodding towards the goof. "You know this is going to end badly. Kidnapping a girl?" Calvin said it like a statement, he was fishing at this point. He sucked loudly on his teeth to emphasize his point. "That's big-league shit." The fancy-dressed goof looked at him quietly and slowly nodded his head.

"Wow!" The man looked genuinely impressed. "Okay, I'm convinced, you're a cop. Like, you don't *look* like a cop. You *look* like a farmer," he said proudly, like he had figured out Calvin's bluff. The man used the barrel of his revolver to gesture at Calvin's shot-up truck, which currently had white smoke gently drifting up from the hood. "And this *looks* like a farm truck, but only a cop could spew out some convincing shit like you just did." The man pulled back the hammer on the gun and raised it up to Calvin's head. "Look on the bright side," the man offered with a smile. "If you *are* an actual cop, your family is going to get a big payday after your dead, right? Like, way more than normal people would get. So, there's that."

Calvin didn't look away from the gun, he studied it. He could see the bullet that was going to kill him was the last live round in the cylinder. It had a grotesquely large barrel, so it wasn't a stretch to imagine it was a-.

CLICK!

"*Jesus Christ!*" Calvin exclaimed painfully as his heart dropped from his chest, and then, just as quick, leapt up into his throat. *He just killed me!* The thought roared through his head as the man outside his window laughed wildly and looked at the revolver in his hand with amazement.

"Holy shit!" he cried out with a laugh. "*Holy-fucking-shit!*"

Calvin could only look at the man who pulled the trigger on his life with heated disgust. The chuckling dimwit in the leather jacket only laughed harder when he saw his sour expression.

"I get it, dude. That's a serious *dick-move*." His laughter slowly subsided. "I *swear* to you, though. That was an honest mistake. I was sure I only fired *five* bullets, but shit! Heat of the moment, I guess." He popped the cylinder open and drained the spent cartridges onto the snow. Calvin's heart sank a bit when the man fished his hand into the pocket of his jacket and pulled out a handful of bullets that were slightly. smaller than his little finger.

Yep, those are .44 bullets.

Calvin thought of the damage those little terrors would do to his skull at close range. This silly, little idiot will definitely regret standing so close when he finally does manage to pull the trigger because the back-spray won't be pretty. They'll need to have a closed casket service at his funeral.

Joni won't like that one bit, he thought as he took in as deep a breath as his injuries would allow. Calvin savored the crisp air as he quietly said goodbye to the life he loved so much.

"I got a wife, kids too." Calvin owed it to them to at least try, but to him it felt like a moot point. This guy had made his decision, he had pulled the trigger once already. Doing it again shouldn't be a problem. As far as Calvin was concerned, he was just giving the man more of himself to take.

"Yeah," the man said, sounding a little bored as he loaded the first cartridge into the cylinder. "I bet you do. You're a pretty old guy, I'd be more surprised if you didn't. You know, if I'm being honest." Another cartridge fell into the cylinder. "I feel for you, pal. I do, but I got a boss that doesn't really take kindly to half-measures. I could easily walk away from this," the man bragged as he loaded another bullet. "But you'll die anyway. It'll just be one of the others who does it, and then *I'm* in shit. Plus, you don't know how Zeke is about this girl he's after. I swear to fucking God," he said lightly complaining, like the two of them were old friends having a coffee. "He's obsess-."

Before the man could finish his sentence, and without any warning, he was struck in the side of the head. From the way his head and body recoiled, the blow must have come from a large, heavy object. Calvin flinched away from the small drops of blood that splattered against his cheek.

"Guh!" the man complained drunkenly as he teetered dangerously on his feet a bit before he turned back to Calvin.

Oh fuck!

He could see the corner of the man's forehead, right by the hairline, and it was severely dented. The flesh split down the middle of the injury, and blood flowed down his face with surprising force. One eye was fixed and horribly bloodshot, while the other lazily searched the space in front of him. On the dent's side, the eye was fixed in place, and horribly bloodshot. The other eye lazily searched the area in front of him. Calvin stared at him with wide-eyed horror as the man regarded him absently.

"*Do you smell that*?"

He asked with great interest, slurring his words as a small spurt of blood suddenly launched into the air. The man convulsed and Calvin saw blood draining from the man's ear, nose, and the corner of his eye. It was a grisly sight.

"*It smells like-*," the man started to say, but before he could finish the life drained from his body and he slumped to the ground.

Calvin's focus shot to the front of the truck when he noticed movement from that direction. Fear and confusion spiked his heart rate until his frantic brain finally recognized Emmett running toward him.

Then Calvin barked out a crazed, painful, laugh.

It quickly turned into weak little sobs, and stinging tears when something inside him accepted the possibility that he might live to see Joni and the boys again.

"*You son of a bitch*!" Calvin cried out joyfully through his tears as Emmett stopped in front of the truck. "I thought I was a goner there," he wept before he chuckled again. "I've never been so happy to see your ugly face as I am right now!" Emmett smiled and reached inside the cab and squeezed Calvin's uninjured shoulder with the slightest pressure. Emmett then peered deeper into the cab and studied Calvin's gunshot wound with grave concern.

Are you okay? That looks bad.

"No, fuck it, it's fine." Calvin quickly waved it off. It hurt like hell, and he was more than sure he couldn't get out of the truck without screaming bloody murder, but he was awake and alert. That was a good sign. "Look, Emmett! They're here for Isabelle. There's more of them," he said to Emmett's quizzical face. Calvin answered the question before he could even ask it. "I don't know how many."

Just then, a loud booming gunshot came from the direction of the house. Calvin shared a grim look with Emmett for a breath before he spoke again.

"Okay, give me your phone, grab that guy's gun, and then you'd better high-tail it to the house."'

Calvin was pleased Emmett didn't hesitate. He quickly removed his phone, unlocked it, and handed it to Calvin before he dropped down to retrieve the dead man's gun. Calvin opened the phone app and started to dial dispatch as Emmett rose up and dumped the large revolver on his lap with a splatter of loose bullets. Before

Calvin could object, Emmett shot towards the trees in the direction of the house.

"Wait! Emmett!" he cried out weakly, but it was too late. "*You* were supposed to take the gun *with* you," Calvin complained weakly before he returned to the phone.

He just prayed Emmett wouldn't need it.

CHAPTER 32

Emmett

Emmett sprinted towards the corner of his and Isabelle's home and hugged the exterior wall as he moved towards the front door. He immediately heard shouting from inside the house. When he moved under the kitchen window, he recognized Brooke's voice.

"YOU STAY RIGHT THERE!" she screamed at the top of her lungs. "YOU DON'T *FUCKING* MOVE!" Emmett didn't like her tone. She was shouting commands, which he didn't expect, but she also sounded terrified.

"I'm not moving!" a male voice yelped in response.

The shouting continued as Emmett moved to the newly ruined front door. He reached towards the door, and then stopped. As much as it pained him, something in Brooke's tone caused him to pause.

It suddenly occurred to him that maybe the gunshot he and Calvin heard was because of Brooke. He ran here with visions of her and Isabelle lying on his floor, bleeding out and breathing their last breaths. Now that he was here, he wondered if maybe he misunderstood the situation.

Though, he still felt some trepidation at the prospect of opening the door and simply walking in.

She's liable to shoot me by accident, Emmett thought suddenly and pulled his hand back from the knob. Instead, he knocked softly three times on the door's frame.

"I have a gun!" Brooke yelled from inside the house. "I will *fucking* blow you away if you come in!" By the way she said it, Emmett didn't doubt her.

Again, he knocked softly three times, he slowly reached for the door and cracked it open.

Then, he whistled.

He let out a high tone for a full second, before he dropped it down a few octaves and held the low tone for a short breath.

"Emmett?!" Brooke cried out weakly.

He took that as his cue to slowly push the heavy wooden door open before he peered around the corner.

The sight made his breath catch in his throat.

First thing he saw was the blood. Brooke was covered in it, almost head to toe. She had a nasty gash on her right cheek, and a dark red stain covering almost everything below it. There were several spots on her sweater where it had soaked up blood, and there were smudges and smears of blood all over it, her jeans, as well as her face. Her arms were also stained a deep red, all the way up to the elbows.

The next thing that he noticed, was the shotgun in her hand. It was the Mossberg his brother had bought him as a graduation gift. Brooke's bloody hands were holding it tightly against her shoulder, and its large, menacing barrel was firmly pointed to the trembling man kneeling with his head down in front of his sink.

"Emmett!" Brooke said breathlessly as she looked to him, then she started to sob.

Then the man kneeling by the sink made the mistake of turning his head slightly towards the door. Brooke caught the slight movement immediately.

"DON'T MOVE!" she shrieked loudly and took a small step towards the man to threaten him further.

"I'm not moving!" the little man squeaked and hid behind his upraised hands.

It's okay, Emmett signed slowly as he stepped up into the kitchen. *You can put the gun down.* Emmett didn't like the red-hot look of anger on her face towards the sniveling man on the floor. *You're safe.*

"He's one of *them*!" she angrily informed him

Emmett looked to the man cowering in front of him, and took a step towards him. He turned his head and looked into the living room. He saw someone's legs poking out from in front of his recliner, and on the north wall was a large splatter of blood that was leaking down it.

For the first time since he arrived, Emmett allowed himself to feel *real* anger.

Who the fuck ARE these guys?! He wondered angrily as he saw the horrible taint they had brought into the home he was trying to make for Isabelle. Like a goddamn act of God, these pricks descended upon their quiet lives, fully intent on ripping everything they had built into pieces. He looked to Brooke, and the state she was in, and Emmett finally understood why Tommy did what he had done all those years ago.

Emmett reached out and cradled the side of the man's head in his large hand. Then he hissed drily as he slammed the man's skull into the side of the kitchen counter. He didn't plan it, but he savagely rammed the man's head into the counter for every life these people were trying to ruin. Calvin's, Brooke's, Isabelle's, and finally his. Beside him, Brooke yelped at the suddenness of the violence, but she made no attempt to stop it. On the fourth hit, Emmett felt the man's skull shift sickeningly underneath his grasp. He let the man's limp body fall to his kitchen floor, before he rushed towards Brooke.

She let the shotgun clatter loudly to the floor as she rushed forward to meet his embrace head-on.

It didn't last though.

"You can't stay!" Brooke said frantically as he pushed him away. "Isabelle and Lucas are out there, with *the man in the black coat*."

Brooke's expression scrunched up in anger when she hissed out the vague description. Part of Emmett suspected that *the man in the black coat* was the one who had done this to Brooke, and probably the one hunting Isabelle as well. The thought of such a person made his blood boil.

"There's another one too,' she added quickly. "They're both after them!" Brooke then turned and madly pointed towards the west side of the house. "I dropped them out the window in your bedroom, and told them to run. They're still out there!" She looked at him with wide, pleading eyes. "We have to help them!"

You're staying here, he signed quickly and shook his head.

Thankfully, Brooke didn't argue with him. Her eyes had a fire to them, and he was sure she would insist on going.

I'll go. Emmett bent down to retrieve his shotgun and checked the loading port before he eased back the forestock to inspect the chamber. It was loaded with only one shell.

On the table, inexplicably standing on its end, was a single 9mm cartridge. *What the hell?* Emmett furrowed his brow towards the single round, like it had appeared on that table, next to his mother's meat cleaver that was stuck into the table's surface, as if by magic. He didn't have the luxury of pondering how that bullet got there. It was there, and he needed it. Two enemies, two bullets, in two different guns.

It was like it was meant to be.

Emmett hooked his arm around the shotgun before he awkwardly withdrew the pistol from his waistband. He pulled back the slide, scooped the single round off the table, and loaded it into the pistol's chamber. He didn't miss the way Brooke was keenly watching as the cartridge travelled from the table into the gun. Nor did he miss the frightful way she jumped at the loud metallic noise the gun made after he hit the slide release button. He used two hands to ease the hammer on the pistol back down, and left it as is when he stowed it into the front of his waistband.

He then turned back to Brooke. She trembled where she stood as her tears weakly drained from her eyes, mixing with the blood on her face. Her expression showed the deep inner turmoil that was going on inside of her shaking body. To Emmett, she looked like a soldier on the battlefield who had experienced too much. He looked at her with a saddened expression because it tore him apart inside to leave her like this. Bloodied, broken, and alone.

Call the police, and then find Calvin. He's in his truck in the north field by the approach. He lowered his eyes to her. *He's been shot. There's a first-aid kit in the bathroom. Stay with him until the police show-up.* He told himself that this was the best course of action. It was the only way he could leave her. This way, she and Calvin could take care of each other until reinforcements arrived. Emmett just prayed they got here in time.

"Okay," she said with a weak sense of determination, like she just found out there was one more kilometer to the marathon she was running. "Emmett!" she called to him after he turned to the front door. He looked back to her bloodied, crying, beautiful face, and saw her lower lip quiver as she struggled to say her next words. "I...I...I..." Each failed attempt to speak just sank her deeper into her despair.

I'll bring her back, Emmett signed and nodded to her reassuringly, even though he had no right to. *I promise.*

Emmett then exited the front door, leaving the woman of his dreams in the kitchen in pursuit of the girl who gave him those dreams.

He found Isabelle's and Lucas's tracks in the snow easy enough. They were right where Brooke said they would be, and they weren't alone. There, mixed in with the kids' tracks, where two sets of larger tracks. All four tracks disappeared into the trees. Emmett followed them until they came out into the clearing before the western hay field.

From there, they broke up. The kids made a beeline for the hay bales at the edge of the grove, but the adults headed off towards the entrance into the western fields. He followed the kids' tracks towards the bales, and grew frustrated as the tiny feet made poor impressions amongst the tire tracks all around the area. Best he could tell, one of them ran towards the hay field, while the other ran straight ahead into the main livestock pen.

They're after Isabelle, he reminded himself and ran towards the western fields. He followed the tracks along the fence for a short distance, but decided to keep going after one of the adult's tracks inexplicably turned back towards the house.

A heart beat later Emmett's ears heard something moving in the snow behind him, and it was approaching fast.

He turned sharply to see what was making the tiny scraping noises, and Max's furry little body came running through the snow towards him. His black fur sharply contrasted by the snow around him. *He must have gotten out when Brooke left*, Emmett decided and then something caught his interest. Instead of running towards him, Max veered off at the entrance into the heavily wooded western pasture and sprinted towards the trees.

What does he know that I don't? Emmett wondered.

He quickly raced back to the entrance and followed Isabelle's dog, hopefully towards her, because if there was one creature that loved Isabelle more than him, it was Max.

CHAPTER 33

Zeke

Zeke didn't let the sounds of gunshots coming from behind bother him as he trudged clumsily through the snow in his Italian shoes towards the large steel building. He couldn't be distracted, not now. Not when he was so close to his *little beautiful*. He could practically smell her scent on the chilled November breeze. His *little beautiful's* tracks led him directly to the door of the building she was hiding in.

She probably doesn't know it's me, Zeke smiled to himself.

He reached for the knob. The silly bitch back at the house probably told her some bullshit to run off someplace and hide. It's been five years out in the cruel world without him, and Belle's first instinct had always been to run away from things. It was a nasty habit she learned from her junkie mother.

"*Ma Belle!*" he called out into the dark, and dusty building.

Strange looking pieces of farm equipment stood like frozen steel monsters in front of him. He sneered a bit because there were *literally* a hundred places she could hide from him.

"It's me! *Papa Zeke!* You remember me, don't you *mon cher? Papa Zeke!"* he said joyously. His voice echoed wonderfully throughout the building. "I told you all dose years ago dat I would find you, *mon cheri*. No matter where they ide you."

He remembered the solemn promise he quietly gave to the small trembling child, like the thought of being without him terrified her.

"We *belong* togeter. Come out, *mon cheri!*" He froze and simply stood in front of the machinery, listening intently for the sounds of...anything. "Why do you ide from me?" he asked with some concern and his own echo was his only reply. "Are you afraid, *mon cheri?* You don't need to be, you know I would never urt you. You and I are da same. Dat's why you're special. I've always known dat," he said lovingly and slowly walked deeper into the building. "Nobody else saw dat, not even your moter, but *I* did. Come out, *mon cher*, it's time for us to go ome."

He listened intently as he strolled between the machinery, careful not to actually touch anything because every surface in here was horribly dusty.

When nothing stirred, he switched gears.

"You tink dose people back dere will take care of you? Eh? No, no, no. Dat woman back in da house? She doesn't care about you, *mon cheri*. Who do you tink it was dat led me ere? She gave you up in a heartbeat, all I ad to do was ask. Dey don't care about you, not *really*, not like I do. None of dem can love you like I do, *Ma Belle*." Zeke turned in an angry circle within the stillness of the building. *"Ma Belle!"* he growled loudly and it resonated in the metal structure until it sounded like a deep throated roar.

He sternly walked forward, feeling like she had tricked him somehow, and she wasn't here at all. Further into the building, instead of becoming darker, a small source of natural light was coming in through the wall. It was like there was a window up ahead, except the light was lower to the ground. Zeke soon saw the small square hatch that was built into the back wall for a reason he couldn't even fathom.

Goddammit! She must have gotten out that way. Zeke sighed with some frustration when it became clear that he had been talking to himself this whole time.

He approached the hatch and sneered at it when he thought of how dirty his coat was going to get crawling through that fucking thing. *It's the quickest way,* he told himself and growled softly. *It will all be worth it in the end.* He thought of the elation he would feel when Belle was once again in his arms, hiked up his pant legs and like some sort of animal, bent down to crawl through the opening.

As soon as the cold air from the outside hit his face, so did a large object.

The first blow hit him squarely on the back of his head, and sent him into the snow as his vision flashed weirdly in front of him. Zeke cried out in surprise a half second before another blow struck him solidly in the back. Thankfully the bulletproof vest he wore underneath his button-up shirt eased the majority of the blow. In the chaos, Zeke recognized the tiny yelp that came with the second attack.

"*Ma Belle*! *Ma Belle*!" he cried out quickly. "It's me!" Another blow rained down, this one on the back of his leg. "It's *Papa Zeke*! It's *Papa Zeke!*"

His flight instinct forced him to scramble his way forward out of the hatch; only then could he deal with the blows coming down on him.

"It's *Papa Zeke!*" he cried out again, but Belle was too far gone in her fury to hear his words. Zeke reached forward, and watched as the pale two-by-four crashed down onto his outstretched right arm. A sharp pain exploded from his arm as his forearm bent at a shocking angle.

Zeke screamed, but Belle screamed louder,

"I FUCKING *KNOW* WHO YOU ARE!" she screamed down at him with a surprising ferocity.

On sheer animal instinct, Zeke somehow turned onto his back in a blink of an eye, just in time to see Belle raised the piece of lumber in her hands over her head. She looked down at him with a red face of utter rage, and growled loudly before she pulled the board down.

Zeke's good arm flashed out and roughly swept Belle's legs out from under her. The board in her arms flew to the side as her small body tumbled roughly to the ground.

"Belle!" He clawed at her with his good hand, but she was already on her feet and sprinting away. "Wait!"

Zeke held his broken right arm in close to his chest, as he quickly struggled to his feet and started to chase after her. *This isn't going to work,* he quickly told himself after a couple painful steps. There was no way he was going to keep up to her.

Zeke quickly pulled the pistol free from his waistband and shot towards Belle.

BAM!

The shot went wide, like it was supposed to, and kicked up a tuft of snow when it struck the ground in front of Belle. He watched with some satisfaction as her little body stiffened up and stopped moving entirely.

"Stop!" Zeke commanded roughly as he limped hurriedly towards her. "Just-*fucking*-stop!" he hissed when he approached her. "I ave come *too* far, and ave done *too* much to get to dis point, *for you*, to just ave you run away from me like dis. Turn around," he growled with frustration.

Belle stiffly shifted on her feet to turn and face him. Her face was a strange mixture of fear and resentment that Zeke found exhilarating. He looked at her, standing there awkwardly favoring his right leg, with his right arm held close to his belly, and with blood seeping down from his scalp, but he wasn't bothered by any of it. *There she is!*

"Maintenant je t'ai, ma belle."

Now I have you, My Beautiful.

CHAPTER 34

Isabelle

"Maintenant je t'ai, ma belle."

He stood there weakly, the man from her nightmares. He was holding his injured arm close to his stomach, while his other hand hung loosely by his side, clenching menacingly onto the black pistol. His hair was wet with his own blood and clung tightly to his scalp while small trails of crimson rolled down his neck and soaked into his dark shirt.

In her dreams, the ones where she wakes screaming in her bed with tears and sweat running down her face, the man in front of her is kicking her mother on the ground. Isabelle frantically tried to run towards her to stop him, except her muscles move like cold molasses. Isabelle had to grunt with extreme effort to push herself forward. She felt helpless watching her mother get savagely beaten, while all she could do was scream, "I'm sorry" over and over again, because deep down she knew this was all because of her.

She usually woke when he looked at her with those black, unfeeling eyes of his.

Now here he was, standing in front of her, smiling that devilish grin that was devoid of any warmth.

"Come on, *ma petite.*" He waved her towards him with the barrel of his gun, and kept that same grin on his face, like he expected her to obey.

No more.

"No." It came out like a weak sob. Isabelle growled a bit, sweeping the pain and sorrow aside for now so the steely resolve she learned from her time with Emmett could shine through. "No," she said again, this time it came out more like a snarl. "I'm not going anywhere with you."

"Yes," he replied coldly. "You are. Let's go, *Ma Belle.* We are on a timeline." The little grin slipped from his face, and he once again waved her forward using the gun in his hand.

Like it was a threat.

"Don't call me that," she snapped at him. "That's not my name. That was *never* my name. That's just what *you* called me," she hissed at him.

She couldn't help it. She hated that name because he had *branded* her with it, like she was his property to do with as he pleased.

"My name is Isabelle! ISABELLE LAMOINE!" she screamed the name her mother had given her with all the fury she felt inside, as if she could hurt him with it.

No more!

Zeke was unimpressed.

"Yes, yes," he said with a bored nod of his head. "Dat is all very dramatic, *ma belle,*" he said spitefully. "But we ave places to go." He hurriedly limped towards her. Isabelle matched his steps with retreating ones of her own. The way he was limping, he couldn't catch her, they both knew that. "Wat do you tink you're doing?! We *ave* to go!"

"I'm not going anywhere with you, *ever!*" Isabelle leveled him with a hard look, paying no attention to the tears in her eyes.

No more!

Isabelle held herself together with every ounce of her being. It felt like she was being torn apart by the competing elements inside of her. One part of her wanted to desperately run away from this man, this stalking nightmare, as fast and as far as she could go. To selfishly leave everyone and everything in her wake as she frantically escaped him. The other part knew there wasn't anywhere she could go. It advised her, that all she would accomplish is getting the people she cared about, like Brooke, hurt in this monster's pursuit of her.

No, she told herself, *this needs to end now*. However, there was only one way she could think of for this cycle to end.

One of them had to die, and *he* was the one holding the gun.

Again, Zeke rushed forward, and again, she easily skipped out of his reach.

"Don't!" he warned loudly, and raised the gun up to her, only to drop it again. She could see he was clenching his jaw.

"Or what?" she challenged him loudly. "You'll shoot me? Do it!" She looked at him wide-eyed and stuck out her chest to him, like she was offering it to him. Zeke didn't raise the gun like she wanted, instead he just looked sad.

"I would never urt you," he said unconvincingly before he added, "like dat. You and me, we're in dis togeter. We're da same. I'm ere to keep you safe. Dis world just wants to step on people like us. *I know*," he said angrily before his tone suddenly changed like someone had flipped a switch inside his head. "I've been trough it already. You don't need to dough, don't you see dat? Only I can keep you safe. You're mad, I get dat. It must have felt like I left you alone all tose years ago. Your moter poisoned you against me, I can see dat now. I'm sorry, *ma petite.* I am, but I can't change any of dat now." Isabelle looked at him with a furrowed brow. "*Please,* just come wit me now, and I'll make everyting better. We are running out of *TIME!"* he howled angrily and pressed the butt of his gun against his head.

It was then that Isabelle heard the last sound on this earth she wanted to hear.

Max's barking came from the trees off to her side, and a second later, his furry little body came bouncing through the tall grass and in between the trees towards her. When she looked back to Zeke's teetering form, he just smiled wickedly at her.

"If you come wit me now, *right now*, you can bring da dog." Max ran straight towards her and hopped excitedly by her side, yelping for her attention. Isabelle didn't take her eyes off Zeke, or the pistol in his hand. "Or else..."

"You leave him alone," she said weakly with a crack in her voice.

"Decide!" Zeke said sharply. "If he dies, it will be because of you. Just like everybody else."

NO MORE!

Isabelle knew exactly what she was going to do, and when she was going to do it. She was strangely at peace with it. It was like a natural conclusion. She didn't know what would be on the other side, but she was thankful for the time she got to spend at this quiet piece of perfection. Isabelle breathed in the cool air and let it fill her lungs up completely, before she responded.

"Go fuck yourself," she said sourly. "I'll die before I go anywhere with you."

"Fine," Zeke said lightly. "Makes no difference to me."

This is it.

She keenly watched as his arm raised the pistol towards Max, and she was already in motion. She dropped down towards Max, to wrap herself around him. One way or another, this would be the end of *Ma Belle*.

Before she could reach Max, though, a shrill sounding whistle erupted from the trees.

"What da hell?" Zeke said and turned the gun towards the source of the noise.

Emmett.

He charged through the trees, close to where Max had emerged from. Isabelle could see he had something raised up to his shoulder, but before she could recognize what it was, she saw fire leap from it.

BOOM!

Her heart jumped inside her chest, and she flinched away from the horrible noise. In the corner of her eye, she saw Zeke's dark form launch backward until his feet left the ground. When he landed roughly, the force of the shot skidded him back on the earth. The pistol in his hand flew off to the side and out of sight. Before she could even get a breath out, Emmett was storming towards Zeke's downed body with the shotgun held over his head like a club.

When he stopped over his body, posed to strike, Zeke suddenly turned over.

With a knife in his hands.

"DAD!" she screamed as the knife plunged deeply into Emmett's stomach.

The word just slipped out.

CHAPTER 35

Emmett

He wasn't expecting the man in the dark coat to turn over like that, nor did he expect the knife, and he certainly didn't expect the man to be able to thrust the knife as forcibly as he did into his gut.

It felt like lightning as it pierced his waistline just above the rim of his jeans, like it was meant to be there. It surprised him how easily the blade slid into his belly. His flesh just parted and welcomed the foreign object in. The slimy-haired man beneath him flashed his teeth in a wild grin, like he knew he had already won.

Then Isabelle screamed.

He didn't hear her words. The sickening feeling of the foreign object in his gut stole his attention away, but whatever she said, it lit a fire inside him. If he had vocal cords, he probably would have released a deep, heated roar, but he couldn't.

So, instead, he hit the man with the shotgun.

Emmett clenched his teeth. His hands clamped down onto the useless weapon until his fingers ached and he swung his shoulders to the side. He slammed the metal barrel of the shotgun into the side of the man's face with such force that blood and teeth flew from his mouth and splattered against the snow. The man recoiled from the blow.

Taking the knife in Emmett's gut with him.

It felt a thousand times worse leaving his stomach than it did going in. When the knife sharply exited his gut, it felt like the man was pulling a white-hot rod from his stomach. Pain exploded from the wound and sent icy spikes up his spine, causing the shotgun to slip from his grasp. His hands shot down to the fresh wound on his body. Emmett staggered back a step, feeling like his legs might fail him at any moment.

Below him, the greasy man stirred.

With a low groan, followed by a weak cough and choking noise, the man clumsily raised himself up with his good hand while still loosely clutching the knife. His shattered jaw hung loosely from his face, like it wasn't attached to anything solid anymore. Emmett could see that most of his front teeth were either missing completely, or reduced to tiny jagged stumps. Blood freely drained from his gaping mouth, and his dark eyes swam within their sockets. Soon enough, though, those eyes focused back in on him.

"*Geeee...beeeylloongs...too mmmaaayyyy!*" a weak guttural voice gurgled up from his ruined mouth. Emmett didn't listen to his words; he was locked in on the man's eyes as they sneered wickedly at him.

Emmett knew that look.

He quickly staggered back another step as his hand reached towards the gun tucked into his waistband. A weird growl suddenly erupted from the man with the ruined face on the ground, as he inexplicably shot up with surprising speed. Emmett watched in horror as the man's lower jaw grotesquely waggled to the side as he lunged towards Emmett.

Steel flashed between them.

BAM!

The bullet struck him in the forehead, slightly above the corner of his right eyebrow. Emmett watched brain matter and gore fly out the back of the man's head. For the briefest of moments, a shocked expression flashed across the dead man's face. It was only a moment, though. The next instant the man's bloodied, ruined face slackened and his limp body fell back to the snow-covered ground. Where it didn't move again.

The slide locked back on the pistol, and Emmett tossed the useless weapon down onto the man's belly with a look of distain on his face, like the pistol suddenly disgusted him. He took a deep breath, and felt warm fluid leaking down his pant leg.

A second later, the most beautiful sound in the world came.

"Emmett!" Isabelle yelled, her voice practically dripping with concern.

He couldn't blame her; he was concerned too. She ran to him and threw her arms around his waist. If he had vocal cords he probably would have cried out from the pain, but thankfully only a slight hiss escaped his lips. It wasn't enough to stop Isabelle's embrace. He weakly welcomed the small hug with his one bloody hand, while his other pressed deeply on the wound to staunch the bleeding.

"Are you okay?" Isabelle asked with tears in her eyes after she pulled back. She looked to him for an answer and when he didn't give her one right away, she looked to the wound. "You're bleeding a lot, Emmett." She informed him with a cracked voice.

I'm okay, he lied and forced a smile as he looked down at her. *Let's go.*

He offered his hand to Isabelle. It was sticky with his own blood, and Isabelle quickly put her small hand inside his. Emmett walked them slowly out of the trees, feeling the bitter winter winds biting at his exposed flesh. To the west, the sun was slowly sinking into the horizon, casting a fiery light on the clouds ahead of them. In the distance, sounds of sirens could be heard all around them.

That's good, he thought drunkenly as he staggered forward, leaking crimson onto the ivory-white snow with each step.

"Emmett? What's wrong?" Isabelle nervously called out to him. When he looked down to her, he discovered that he wasn't walking forward anymore. His body felt numb.

He wearily looked ahead. They were almost to the gate exiting the field. Beyond that, he could see the corner of their house poking out from the grove of trees.

So close, he thought and took in another deep breath to steady himself only to drop down to his knees. *I'm sorry, Tommy.*

"Emmett!" Isabelle cried out beside him. "No!"

He pitched forward, but he was able to catch himself before he fell flat on his face. It only cost him pain. The hole in his abdomen sent nails up his spine. There was nothing he could do to resist it. He was too far gone to fight anything else. Emmett managed to fall onto his side, and let gravity pull him the rest of the way down onto his back.

Above, Isabelle looked down at him in horror before she turned back to their house and screamed.

"SOMEBODY HELP US!" she hoarsely bellowed towards the house, like his poor girl had been screaming all day. He was sorry for that, because he knew he should have been here.

She's safe now, he lied to himself, because if she wasn't then that meant he would have to get up again, and he didn't want to do that just yet.

"Emmett!" Isabelle looked at him with fresh tears, her bottom lip quivering. "You can't die," she pleaded with him, like he had some control over it. "You *can't.*"

She sank down and wrapped her arms around his wide shoulders. He felt like he was a million miles away, but he still felt the warmth of her embrace. When she spoke next, her words stung his eyes.

"I love you, Emmett." She whispered weakly into his ear, like it was a secret between them. "I love you *so* much," she said it like it pained her to admit such a thing to the open air. Emmett felt his tears drift down the sides of his face, and he reached up and gave her a slight squeeze.

It was all he could manage.

"You can't leave me now. I won't forgive you if you do," she weakly threatened between sobs.

Emmett slowly clicked his tongue three times.

When Isabelle pulled away, he looked at her with his wet eyes and smiled before he signed *their* word.

Forever.

Isabelle broke down into fresh sobs before she turned back in the direction of the house.

"HURRY!" The sound hurt his ears. Emmett figured that was a promising sign.

With what seemed like a herculean effort, Emmett raised his head up to see who Isabelle was screaming at. In the distance, a slim figure was running madly towards them. *I know that figure,* he thought to himself as he watched Brooke sprint towards the gate into the field.

Behind her, a loud roar of an engine and a bright pair of headlights burst onto the scene. Emmett's heart spiked in his chest with fear until he saw that Brooke wasn't running away from it. She turned and waved her arms at the approaching truck before she madly directed them to him and Isabelle.

"He's hurt," Isabelle cried out to Brooke when she was close enough. "He's hurt *bad*. Help him," she whimpered beside him.

With a spray of snow, Brooke dropped down beside him and frantically looked him over. She was looking for something she could fix, but she wasn't finding it.

"Jesus Christ!"

She looked like she was afraid to touch any part of him. He direly wished he could just hold her hand one more time. Brooke soon gave up trying to solve the problem of his injuries. She instead grabbed the side of his head and looked deeply into his eyes.

"You're fine," she said sternly. "You *hear* me? *You're fine*!" Even with the tears in her eyes, she sounded fierce.

Behind her, he caught the sound of a truck pulling up, and a second later he heard some people loudly exiting it. Emmett tried to focus on Brooke's face as the edges of his vision shrank.

"Holy shit," a voice he recognized said with shock. "He needs an ambulance." A heartbeat later gruff voice boomed.

"Yeah, well, we ain't going to wait for any goddamn ambulance! Load him into the truck!"

Hands descended upon him from seemingly all directions, and then agony ripped through him as those hands lifted him off the ground. He hissed, winced and grimaced, but there was little else he could do as they stuffed him into the back seat of the truck.

When it was done, he was pleased to find his head resting comfortably on Brooke's lap, and Isabelle crouched beside the seat, holding his hand. *This is a good way to go,* he told himself because as far as he was concerned *this* was heaven.

"Calvin! We're in the truck! Emmett's hurt bad, where's the ambulance?! What?! No, that's not *good* enough. Okay! Yes! We'll meet them in Binscarth." He heard Brooke say into a phone above him. "The ambulance will meet us at the gas station."

"You heard the lady, boy! Step on it!"

A deep rumble filled his ears, drowning out the other voices in the truck. The truck jounced and rebounded down the road, and Emmett felt the gravity shift inside the truck with each turn. He breathed as deeply as he dared and looked over to the tiny miracle holding his hand, weeping quietly onto his chest.

Emmett let his weighty eyelids descend slowly over his vision, and he felt a warm calm spread over his body.

"Emmett?!" a voice called from impossibly far away.

I wonder what they're so excited about, he wondered and let the darkness slip in a little more. "EMMETT!"

****

He first became aware he was awake when he heard the muted sounds of the outside world start to invade his dark sanctuary. Against his better instincts, Emmett strained to open his eyes. The dim light surged in and he hissed painfully as his eyes struggled to keep up with the new light level. His eyes didn't work right. It felt like he couldn't open his eyelids all the way, nor could he focus on any one thing. His vision swam precariously in front of him and he had to lull his head to the side to look around his surroundings.

He immediately saw the fresh cast on his left arm, and that his right had two IVs going into it. Besides him, was a medical monitor of some kind. Emmett couldn't even begin to decode its complicated display, so he didn't even try. His throat was horribly dry and scratchy. He weakly cleared his throat in an attempt to wet it, but there wasn't any moisture left to use.

"Emmett?" A low growling voice came from across the room. Emmett numbly lulled his head to the side to focus on its owner. "Are you awake, son?"

It was John Adler.

Out of habit, Emmett weakly reached to where his breast pocket and his notepad should have been. John Adler slightly groaned as he rose off his seat and hobbled forward to the edge of the bed. Emmett felt his warm, callused hand clasped onto his own and gently lower it back to the bed.

"None of that now. You need to rest." Emmett noticed he briefly turned away before he returned with a small white cup in his hands. It had a little straw sticking out of the top of it. "Here. Drink this. Wet yer whistle a bit." He moved the cup slowly towards him until the straw brushed against Emmett's lips.

He cautiously sipped on the tiny straw until his mouth filled with gloriously cool water, then he drank deeply from the cup. After three big gulps, Emmett came up for some air. He sighed contently and fell back against the pillows in his bed.

"Feel better?" he asked when he pulled the cup back.

Emmett nodded slowly

"You alert enough to talk? I can wait, if you want. I just thought you'd want to know what's been going on since you blacked out," he said with some amusement. When Emmett looked to the gruff, old farmer, he had a sly knowing grin on his weathered face.

Emmett nodded.

"We got you to the ambulance in time, but from what I'm told, it was *real* touch-and-go there for a while. Once they got you stable at the hospital, they took you into surgery to repair a *proliferated bowel,*" John Adler said the words like he was reciting them without the benefit of knowing what they meant. "You've been out for a couple hours now. Doctors say you're going to be laid up for a week."

With his right hand, Emmett made a gentle swirling motion. *Get on with it.*

"Okay, okay. Just relax. There's a lot of shit to get to," John Adler chuckled softly before he returned to his spiel. "Calvin's a couple doors down. He's recovering from a minor gunshot wound, and a broken collarbone. He's going to be wearing one of those funny casts for about a month, but after that he'll be fine. Your girl, Brooke got a shit-ton of stitches on her arm, and a prescription for painkillers to help with her broken rib. She was released that same night. She and Isabelle spent the night at her parents' place. They'd be here now, but I kicked them out so they could get some breakfast. I just texted them. So, I imagine they'll be along shortly."

Emmett nodded and let out a heavy breath.

"Listen," John Adler's voice dropped a bit. Emmett's interest kicked up. "I'm actually glad we have this moment to talk. There's a few things I'd like to get off my chest, if you don't mind. I know this isn't the best time, but from my point of view, this is something I should have said to you a long time ago." Emmett lulled his head towards the heavy-set man, he looked distressed.

Emmett nodded for him to continue.

"I'm sorry. I'm sorry for everything my family has done to yours. Truly. I know your brother died in prison, but he would never have been in that place if it wasn't for *my* boy." John paused for a moment before he continued. "I think about it sometimes, you know, about all the terrible things that came from that one horrible act, and it boggles my mind. It's like we're all being punished for what Clive did. I see the way people look at me and my boys, like we're all diseased or some shit. That's fine, I told myself. Hell, maybe we even deserve it, but then I see it happening to little Lucas." Old man Adler's voice cracked when he mentioned his grandson's name and he forced himself to stop. John sucked loudly on his teeth and angrily shook his head, like he was pushing the emotions down so he could continue. "I'm getting older, Emmett. I'm starting to feel time's icy fingers on my bones. I don't give a lick what other people think about me, but I don't want this *thing* between our families to be my legacy." John paused for a moment. "Did you want some more water?"

Emmett nodded.

This time, he drained the whole cup before he came up for a satisfying gasp. Adler Sr slowly limped towards the bathroom and soon returned with the cup full again. Emmett sipped some more from it, feeling the water rinse away the fog inside his head with each swallow. Soon enough though, John returned to what he was saying.

"Lucas told us all about what Isabelle did for him," John said as a matter of fact. Emmett struggled to look at him with a questioning expression. "She basically tried to save his life in the bravest way possible. It didn't quite work out the way she wanted, but she *tried*. That's what gets me. Everything our families have been through, and she puts Lucas's life above her own. Shit! I still can't believe it." John looked at him warmly. "You've got an amazing little girl on your hands, son."

Emmett nodded.

"I want to help, Emmett." John's expression deepened, like they were approaching the important part of John's speech. "I want to try to atone for some of the blackness my son has put into the world. I *need* to," he said before he gave Emmett a sad look. "I can't do it alone, though. I would, if I could, but I can't force you to let me help you. Nor would I disrespect you like that," he said reassuringly. "So, I'm asking you *man-to-man*...no...I'm *begging* you. Please. Please, let me help you. Not like *charity* or anything," he said it like it was a bad word. "But if you need help, *for anything*, I just want you to feel like you can ask, because you can. Clive ripped our families apart, as quickly as he ripped a piece of paper in two, but I feel like Isabelle might be able to bring us back together. With a little help from the adults in the room, mind you."

For Isabelle.

Emmett nodded slowly before he weakly raised his hand up to the man, offering it to him. John Adler Sr quickly clasped his hand firmly and gave it two gentle pumps. It didn't feel great as the motion kicked up about a dozen different aches in his body, but he smiled anyway.

"Thank you, Emmett. I appreciate the gesture, and the willingness to hear an old fool out." John looked at him with watery eyes and a warm smile. "We'll talk some more later, I'm sure. For now, just rest up. Owen already volunteered to look after your herd until you're back on your feet, but there's no hurry. You take as much time as you need." John Adler reached out and solidly patted Emmett on the shoulder, it was one of the few places that didn't ache.

Then the sounds of sneakers squeaking on linoleum came from outside the room and down the hall. It was quickly followed by a woman's stern voice.

"You can't run in here!"

Beside him, John Adler chuckled softly.

"I think you'd better brace yourself, son."

"Emmmmmmmeeeeettttttttt!"

Isabelle wept his name over the space of two full seconds as she loudly ran into the room and straight towards him. Her tiny face was scrunched up in joyous agony as she dropped herself onto his chest and spread her little arms across him and wept uncontrollably onto his bare chest.

Emmett, mindful of the IV tubes running from his right arm, reached up to place his hand on her back and rubbed it gently.

A few seconds later Brooke jogged into the room, slightly out of breath. When the occupants turned to look at her, she stopped and regarded them with a mildly embarrassed, tearful expression.

"I can't run as fast as *her*." She gestured to Isabelle, as she stepped closer. "Sue me."

When she reached his side, Brooke cupped his cheek in her hands, bent down and kissed him softly on the lips. "I told you that you were fine, didn't I? Everyone else was worried, but I knew." She pointed to her head and smiled, like she was bragging about how smart she was.

"I knew you wouldn't leave us."

By the look on her face and the way her lower lip slightly quivered, she was close to breaking down into a full-on sob. Instead, she kissed him on the lips again. She eased herself in over Isabelle, and fanned her arm over her before she lowered herself down and gently hugged them both.

"Don't you *fucking* ever scare me like that again," she whispered sternly into his ear.

Emmett promised he wouldn't.

EPILOGUE

Emmett

"Are you guys ready?" Brooke asked with a hint of restrained annoyance as she walked through the dining room, her fancy heels clacking loudly against the hardwood floor.

They were going to Birtle to have dinner at the local Chinese restaurant with Brooke's entire family. As long as Emmett had lived in the area, he'd never actually eaten at that particular establishment. Brooke swore to him it would be the best Chinese food he'd ever have. Apparently, it was a Talbot holiday tradition to have Christmas Eve dinner there. Over the years, the Talbots had to phone ahead to reserve tables because their family kept growing.

Emmett was proud to be a part of it.

Out of the corner of his eye, he saw Isabelle race out of her room wearing her purple dress with dark stockings. He quickly spied a brightly-colored package in her hands. Emmett soon returned his focus to the mirror, and his third attempt at getting his tie right. He didn't like the knot to be too large. He, once again, wore his one set of dress clothes. The black dress pants, white shirt with a black tie, and a black vest over top. Brooke scowled when she saw it because she instantly recognized it, and knew that he hadn't washed it since their date night. Emmett promised her in the spring she could take him to buy a new suit. Or two.

"Oh, sweetie, we're not exchanging gifts tonight," Brooke said softly in the kitchen. "It's just a dinner."

"I know," Isabelle replied quickly. "This one is special."

Emmett hissed sharply as he quickly unfurled the dark tie and began the process all over again. Honestly, he didn't even know why they needed to dress up. The restaurant in Birtle was hardly a five-star restaurant, it was barely a three, but he wasn't about to mention that to Brooke. Instead, he just kept working on it while the girls talked quietly in the other room.

"Okay, but are you sure you don't want to wait until Christmas?"

"I can't," Isabelle replied quickly. "I'm too excited." By her tone, Emmett imagined Isabelle was hopping up and down when she said it.

The fourth try was a success. He snugged the knot up into his buttoned collar, and gave himself a quick look in the mirror. *Not bad, you clean up pretty good.*

When he came out, Isabelle was standing in the middle of the kitchen, with her package held tightly to her chest. Brooke, however, was absently looking at the top of the kitchen table. She was laser-focused on one spot near the center, and he didn't like the look on her face one bit.

He clicked his tongue to get her attention.

Everything okay?

He knew she was still having a hard time of it, being in the house. There were a lot of bad memories here for her. Things nobody else were privy to, because everyone else who had been in the house that day was dead.

Only she survived it.

Emmett knew she killed one man with his shotgun, at close range too. Calvin told him that much. Everything else was locked tight inside Brooke's mind, and she never spoke of how she got the nasty cut on her arm.

Her *Tiger Stripe.*

That's what she called it, like the linear scar on her arm was some kind of badge of honor. Like she was proud of it.

As she was looking down at that spot on the table where his mother's cleaver had been, it didn't escape his notice that she was lightly rubbing her partially healed wound.

"Yeah. Fine," she said quickly as he drew her attention away from the table. Brooke smiled reassuringly before she gestured to Isabelle. "Someone has a *very special* gift for you."

Isabelle was grinning ear-to-ear, and practically vibrating with excitement.

Emmett couldn't help but smile down at his niece. She was amazing, after all. She had been hit the hardest after *The Attack,* but also the one to move on from it the quickest. For the first few nights, at Brooke's place, she slept in the bed with Brooke while Emmett slept on the floor nearby. He was too big for the couch, and his injured gut required him to lay relatively flat in order to sleep. After Owen and Robbie had replaced the carpets in the bedroom and living room, repaired the kitchen counter where Emmett crushed that man's skull against it, and repainted all the walls, it was like Zeke Simard and his band of shitheads had never happened to this place. When they moved back, Emmett slept in Isabelle's room for a bit.

Then Brooke moved in. Kind of.

Isabelle wasn't the only one plagued with bad dreams. Brooke never said it, and Emmett never asked, but he suspected Brooke found being next to Isabelle as comforting as Isabelle felt next to her. So, for a week, they all shared a room. Then Emmett moved back into his own bedroom, and enjoyed a bed that was large enough for his frame, while the girls cuddled up next to each other in Isabelle's room. There was barely enough room for Max in the bed.

What?! Very special?! Well, I can't wait to see what you got me.

Emmett winced and hissed as he eased himself down onto one knee. He still gets a sharp stab of pain in his gut if he moves the wrong way. Isabelle patiently waited for him to get settled before she thrusted her gift into his hands.

"I hope you like it," she said quickly. "I bought it with the money I made, *at my job*."

What?! He flashed a look of surprise towards Isabelle. *When did you get a job?* Isabelle giggled. He showed Brooke his concern. She just waved it off. Isabelle looked at him with pride, before she nodded excitedly towards the package.

"Open it!"

Emmett mimicked her excitement as he tore the wrapping paper off the gift with gusto. It was a framed picture. He turned it over in his hands to see the photo inside.

And something inside him broke.

A tidal wave of emotion just swept over him. There was no other way to explain it. In an instant, the sight of his and Isabelle's first picture together in Henry's store called up a massive tide of feelings inside him that just obliterated all his defences.

There was no hope in stopping the tears.

"What's wrong?" Isabelle asked as his face tightened up as the first few tears leaked from his eyes. "Don't you like it?" she asked.

He wished he could respond but his hissing sobs paralyzed him. All he could manage was to use one of his hands to wave off the very idea that he might not like it.

"Oh, he likes it, sweetie."

Emmett could only point towards Brooke and nod his head. He looked to Isabelle, who had her own tears streaking down her face, and reached out and pulled her forward into a crushing hug. Emmett's body painfully shook as he sobbed uncontrollably, his knife wound sent heated barbs up his spine with each convulsion, but he couldn't care less.

It occurred to him, when he looked upon that silly, awkward photo, of the little girl in the oversized hoodie, who shyly hid behind her hair, that he had *everything* he'd ever wanted in life. Right here, right now. That picture reminded him of how much his life had changed in such a short amount of time. All because of Isabelle Lamoine. It reminded him of the sad, lonely, hateful person he used to be and the path he was sure he was travelling down. It taunted him with the knowledge that the old version of himself would have been fine with the ruin he would find at the end of that road.

I love you so much, Emmett struggled to sign gracefully as he continued to sob.

"I love you too." Isabelle wept happily, in the midst of her own ugly cry.

He pulled her in again, and held her close against his body. Eight months ago, he would have never even considered the possibility of loving someone, let alone *being* loved by someone. Now, he had two people he could share his life with.

That picture was taken the day everything started to change for him.

The day he received Tommy's last gift.

The End?

Also By Keith McIntosh

Visit McIntoshBooks.com

OBERON'S CALLING

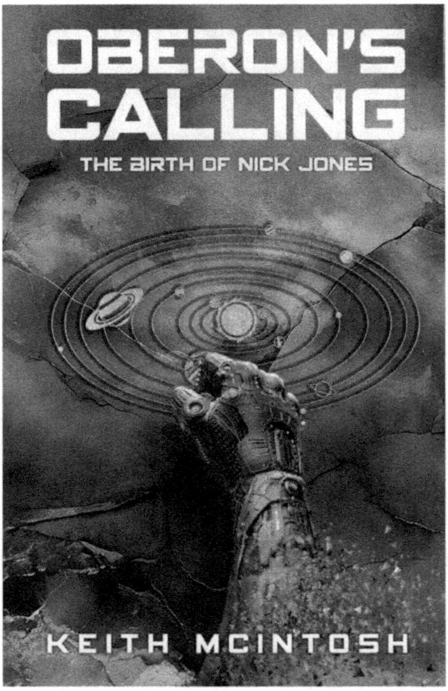

RONIN OF THE DEAD
BOOK ONE

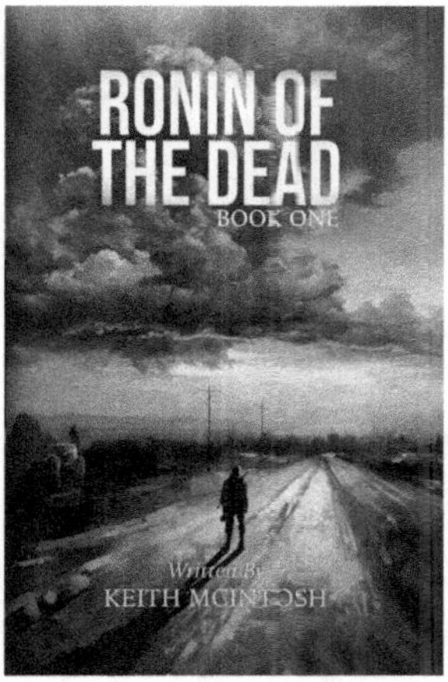

RONIN OF THE DEAD
BOOK TWO

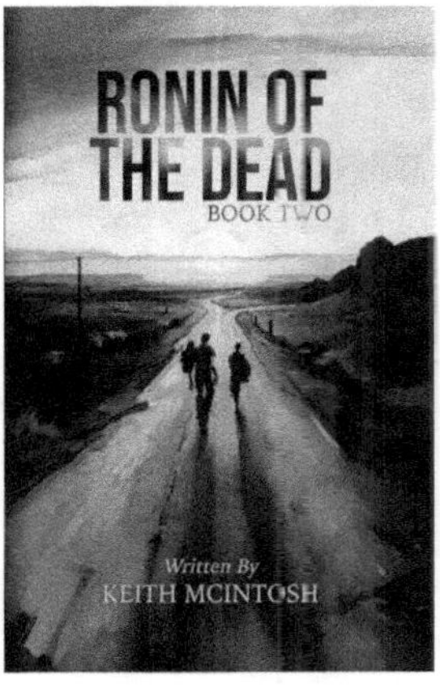

RONIN OF THE DEAD
BOOK THREE

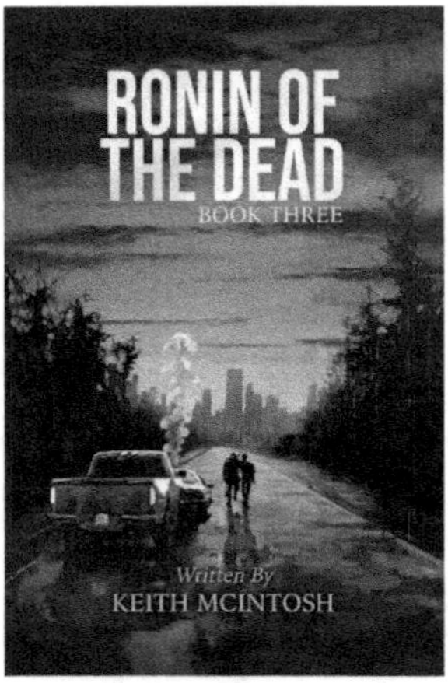

RONIN OF THE DEAD
BOOK FOUR

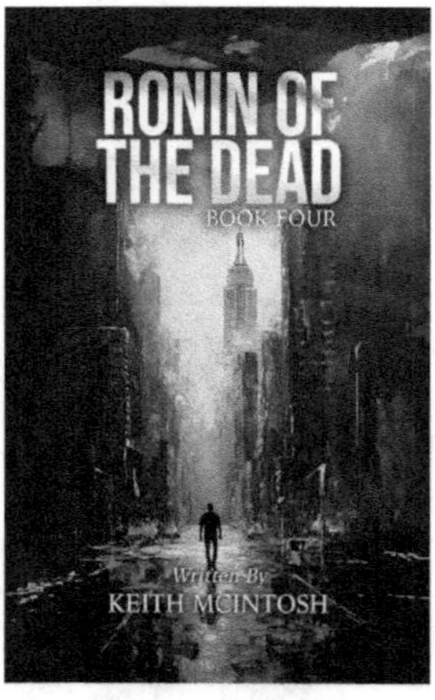

www.ingramcontent.com/pod-product-compliance
Lightning Source LLC
Chambersburg PA
CBHW072014020726
47501CB00006B/1802
* 9 7 8 1 7 3 8 1 2 7 3 1 3 *